A Shelter in the Storm

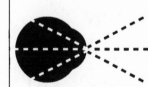 This Large Print Book carries the
Seal of Approval of N.A.V.H.

A Shelter in the Storm

Debra White Smith

Thorndike Press • Waterville, Maine

Published in 2004 by arrangement with
Harvest House Publishers.

Thorndike Press® Large Print Christian Fiction.

The tree indicium is a trademark of Thorndike Press.

The text of this Large Print edition is unabridged.
Other aspects of the book may vary from the original edition.

Set in 16 pt. Plantin by Elena Picard.

Printed in the United States on permanent paper.

Library of Congress Cataloging-in-Publication Data

Smith, Debra White.
  A shelter in the storm / Debra White Smith.
    p. cm.
  ISBN 0-7862-5750-4 (lg. print : hc : alk. paper)
  1. Southern States — Fiction. 2. Large type books. I. Title.
PS3569.M5178S54 2004
  813´.54—dc21   2003054746

To my best friend, favorite person, and the most wonderful man in the world — my husband, Daniel W. Smith.
I love you, Daniel!

As the Founder/CEO of NAVH, the only national health agency solely devoted to those who, although not totally blind, have an eye disease which could lead to serious visual impairment, I am pleased to recognize Thorndike Press★ as one of the leading publishers in the large print field.

Founded in 1954 in San Francisco to prepare large print textbooks for partially seeing children, NAVH became the pioneer and standard setting agency in the preparation of large type.

Today, those publishers who meet our standards carry the prestigious "Seal of Approval" indicating high quality large print. We are delighted that Thorndike Press is one of the publishers whose titles meet these standards. We are also pleased to recognize the significant contribution Thorndike Press is making in this important and growing field.

Lorraine H. Marchi, L.H.D.
Founder/CEO
NAVH

★ Thorndike Press encompasses the following imprints: Thorndike, Wheeler, Walker and Large Print Press.

The Seven Sisters

Jacquelyn Lightfoot: An expert in martial arts, private detective Jac is "married" to her career and lives in Denver.

Kim Lan Lowery: Tall, lithe, and half Vietnamese/half American, Kim is a much-sought-after supermodel who lives in New York City.

Marilyn Douglas Langham: Newly married, Joshua and Marilyn, along with Marilyn's daughter, Brooke, live in Arkansas. Marilyn works as an office manager for a veterinarian.

Melissa Moore: A serious nature lover, Dr. Melissa Moore recently established a medical practice in Oklahoma City.

Sonsee LeBlanc: A passionate veterinarian known for her wit, Sonsee grew up in a southern mansion outside of New Orleans. Although she lives in Baton Rouge, she visits her father at LeBlanc manor often.

Sammie Jones: The star reporter for *Romantic Living* magazine, Sammie is an expert on Victorian houses, art, and finding the perfect romantic getaway. She and her husband live in Dallas.

Victoria Roberts: A charming, soft-spoken domestic "genius" who loves to cook, work on crafts, and sew, Victoria is married and lives in Destin, Florida.

A Shelter in the Storm Cast

Alana Prescott: Sonsee's half-sister, Alana is plagued by doubt and bitterness.

Carla Jenson: A long-time servant at the Manor, Carla has served the LeBlanc's faithfully.

Cerberus: A person of mystery. Cerberus seeks to cover sins of greed by jeopardizing others.

Damian Aster: The LeBlanc family lawyer.

Hermann LeBlanc: Sonsee's half-brother who never leaves a stone unturned.

Natalie Houk: Sonsee's half-sister who covets LeBlanc Manor and harbors a grudge against Sonsee.

Rafael Houk: Natalie's latest husband, Rafael is extremely handsome and ten years younger than his wife.

Taylor Delaney: A successful Texas rancher, Taylor is Sonsee's childhood friend. As a child, his heart was deeply wounded when his father deserted the family, so he is unable to return Sonsee's love.

Prologue

Jacques LeBlanc pulled out the drawer and set it beside the package tape atop his teak dresser. Despite the solitude, his shoulders cringed as if he felt someone peering through the window. Methodically, Jacques reminded himself that he was in the privacy of his own room, and the curtains shielded the windows, no one would witness his secretive deed. Carefully, he retrieved the note to Sonsee from his bathrobe pocket, folded it, and applied a lengthy piece of package tape across the back. He set the note aside and pulled an ancient iron key from his pocket. His fingers quivered when he considered the antique key lying against his palm. After an illogical glimpse over his shoulder, Jacques placed a piece of tape on the key. He secured it in the back of the drawer cavity, then strategically taped the note to cover the notched piece of iron.

With the sound of wood sliding against wood, Jacques replaced the drawer and glanced at the rare crystal clock claiming his nightstand. *Sonsee needs to know about the key as soon as possible,* he thought. Yet the clock, as if arguing against him, declared eleven o'clock was too late to call his hardworking daughter. *I'll wait until morning,* he acquiesced. Of his four children, only Sonsee would appreciate what the key represented. He could trust her with the secret. If any tragedy were to befall him, Sonsee would adhere to his wishes.

Jacques removed his bathrobe and climbed between the cool sheets. A sinister atmosphere filled the room like a dense cloud. The cloud darkened and penetrated his soul, sending a chill down his spine. Tightening his hold on the sheet, he relived the recent odd turn of events . . . and his emotions churned like the roiling wall of a hurricane. Trying to shake the uncanny feelings, Jacques picked up the mug of decaf steaming by the lamp and took a hearty swallow. He replaced the mug and picked up the novel lying nearby.

"Enjoying your book?" The intruder's sarcastic voice hit Jacques like a fist in his midsection. The invader hovered near the door, a .38 in hand, a cloak of greed on determined features. The rumble of doom rushed from the distance.

"You!" Jacques gasped. His chest tightening, Jacques shrank against the bed's satin sheets.

"Yes, me." With a slight shove, the bedroom door snapped shut. The ancient grandfather clock in the hallway tolled ominously. Each strike heightened the aura of danger. The book slid from Jacques' shaking hands and onto the bed. The last time they had spoken, the visitor had been agitated. Even then, a precognition of doom had descended upon Jacques — he'd erroneously swept aside.

"Why?" he rasped.

"Why?" The aggressor's malicious chuckle held no mirth. "I can think of ten million reasons why."

Fingers trembling, Jacques pushed his hair away from his forehead. "Look," he pleaded. "I'll-I'll honor our original agreement." He licked his lips. "I'll give even more . . . seventy percent . . . and I'll send you out of the country. I promise I'll never mention this to anyone."

In three easy strides the transgressor hovered above Jacques, and the familiar scent of expensive cologne swirled with the smell of coffee.

"No, you scum! I want it all! You tried to kill me —"

"But I didn't! The accident was a terrible mistake. I'd have never —"

"Save your breath. We're settling this now. If you want to live, give me the key."

Jacques stared into hateful eyes that reminded him of the beady orbs of a murderous rattler. After a lengthy silence, the intruder's hand snaked out to slam against Jacques' face. Hot tingles erupted from his cheek and coursed down his neck. Spears of panic pierced his soul.

"Hand over the key," the visitor growled.

"It belongs to Sonsee, too!"

The attacker raised a threatening hand to deliver another slap. A voice within Jacques demanded he fight. He lunged upward only to be met with the muffled sound of a bullet leaving its chamber. A sharp pain shot through his chest like a spike driven deeply. A gasp, garbled and desperate, escaped as he stared in fixed horror at his assailant. Yet the seemingly cold-hearted killer abandoned his brutal mask for dismay. His ice-blue eyes, once flaming with barbaric determination, now widened, as if shocked by the sequence of events.

This can't be happening. . . . It can't be. I haven't told Sonsee about the key yet. There's so much she doesn't know . . . Sonsee . . . Sonsee . . .

12

Memories of her childhood flooded Jacques. He recalled a redheaded toddler . . . a little girl with eyes of emeralds . . . a teenager, intent upon being the school's star golfer . . . an independent adult, her freckles making her look younger than her thirty-four years. Jacques had hoped he would live to enjoy Sonsee's children. He had prayed she and Taylor Delaney would eventually marry. But all of those dreams now blurred into despair.

Sonsee . . . Sonsee . . . I love you . . . Please, God, help her find the key. . . .

One

The next morning, Sonsee LeBlanc fumbled with inserting the key into the lock of her Baton Rouge townhouse off Highland Road. Her hands quivered. Her mind whirled. Her swollen eyes produced a new film of tears that blurred her vision. The reality of her father's murder choked her with a fresh onslaught of sobs.

Last night, upon learning of her father's death, Sonsee had immediately driven to the LeBlanc Manor in New Orleans. Early this morning, she'd stood in the doorway of her father's room, staring emptily past the teak furniture and fine linens into the gloom of death. Stunned, tearless, numb, she'd felt as if she were in the midst of a nightmare. Whoever murdered her dad had also ransacked the room in search of something. Something obviously important. After several agonizing minutes, Sonsee had raced from the room and down the massive stairway, intent upon hurrying outside for some desperately needed fresh air. But the conversation filtering from her father's downstairs study stopped her on the last stair. After breathless minutes of intense listening, she'd rushed back to Baton Rouge.

Now she stood outside her own home, wondering if she would be able to perform the simple task of unlocking the door. At last her fingers maneuvered the lock. The key did its job, and her door swung inward. Sonsee stepped into the neat home. The southwest decor that had previously cheered now left her flat. Her life, once blooming with color, had become a blasé blend of black and white. The stale aroma of last night's vanilla coffee still hung in the air. Sonsee dashed aside the tears dampening her cheeks. Her father loved gourmet coffee. Vanilla was his favorite.

Unceremoniously she dropped her purse on the table by the doorway, locked the door, and dashed to the cordless phone. Yet as her fingers touched the cream-colored receiver, she halted and blindly observed the knots in the pine table. Wave upon wave of paranoia overwhelmed her. But given the events of the last twelve hours, myriad fears might develop in the sanest of individuals.

15

Sonsee had chosen not to place the important call from LeBlanc Manor because she didn't want to take any chance of being overheard. At first, she'd planned to use the first pay phone she found but feared someone might be following, suspect her intent, and call the police. She hadn't used her cell phone because she worried that a police scanner might accidentally pick up the conversation. Her cordless might be detected in the same manner. The chances were almost nonexistent, but Sonsee couldn't take risks.

As if she were being chased by the hounds of Hades, Sonsee fled up the hardwood stairs that led to her spacious bedroom. She sat on the edge of her bed and grabbed for the phone on the nightstand, only to have the receiver topple from her sweating hands and land at her feet. Clumsily, she grabbed the long cord and pulled up the phone. She paused as another thought bombarded her agitated mind. *The phone company will have a record of any calls I make.* Sonsee hung up the phone and ran back downstairs. From her purse she retrieved the prepaid phone card that her father had insisted on supplying every month. After hurrying back upstairs, she picked up the receiver and momentarily hovered over the keypad, furiously blinking in an attempt to end the ever-flowing wash of tears. Her fingers violently shaking, Sonsee pressed in the calling card's number, then Taylor Delaney's number. When the ringing began, her stomach clenched against a flood of nausea. Desperately she glanced at the bedside clock and prayed Taylor was inside his ranch house.

Her shoulders sagged as a brisk greeting floated across the line.

"Hello?" Taylor said again, as if he had precious little time to waste.

"T-Taylor?" Sonsee rasped.

"Red? Are you okay?" Her childhood cloud of red hair had earned her the nickname. Eventually, Sonsee's locks had darkened to a deep shade of auburn, but Taylor refused to release the rankling name.

"Yes," she said, collapsing against the stack of overstuffed pillows. "It's Father . . ." she said, jerking the pillowcase's garnet-colored fringe.

"Uncle Jacques?"

"He's been murdered," Sonsee squeezed out the words that seemed a surreal chant from a horror-filled dream.

"What?" Taylor gasped. "But I was just there last night —"

"Yes, I-I know," Sonsee said, closing her eyes tight. "That's why I'm calling. Over an hour ago, I overheard Carla Jenson telling the police that she saw you leave F-Father's room j-just before she found him dead . . . around eleven last night." Sonsee's free hand curled upon itself until her short nails ate into her palm. "She also said she saw you sneak behind the-the house, into that grove of-of oaks out back and that you were carrying a department store bag." Sonsee paused in an attempt to control her wavering voice. She stared upward at the brass-trimmed ceiling fan until it blurred. "Carla said she hadn't wanted to implicate you last night, but that her conscience had gotten the best of her. When I left LeBlanc Manor, a p-policeman was heading out the door to see if he could find the m-murder weapon in the trees."

The silence on the other end wrenched Sonsee's heart almost as violently as did the news of her father's death. At last, Taylor exploded. "But I left at ten! I wasn't even there at eleven! *I did not kill him, Sonsee!* With God as my witness, I didn't even know he was dead until you called!"

"I know you didn't kill him, Taylor." Sonsee's voice oozed with the love she didn't attempt to hide despite Taylor's inability to reciprocate. "You loved Father. I know you loved him. You could *never* kill him."

Sonsee and Taylor had grown up together. His mother, Joy, was the sister of Jacques' first wife, Vickie. When Vickie died of a rare liver disease, Jacques remarried and fathered Sonsee. Later, when Taylor's father deserted his family, Sonsee's mother and Jacques agreed to take Taylor under their wings and assist Joy all they could. Through the years, Sonsee and Taylor spent so much time together, they were like brother and sister — or they had been until Sonsee suffered the unfortunate fate of falling in love with him.

Despite the difficulty of their present relationship, Sonsee was convinced beyond any doubt that Taylor had not murdered her father. She would come closer to suspecting one of her half-siblings — Hermann, Alana, or Natalie. But even the thought of one of them killing their father left Sonsee nauseous.

"That's the reason I'm calling, Taylor. I knew Carla was lying from the minute I heard her. I wanted to warn you as soon as I could." The idea that the trusted family employee would lie hurled Sonsee's mind in to the confusion of the emotional cyclone swirling through her life.

Sonsee imagined Taylor's dark-blue eyes rounded in shock; his curly, dark hair disheveled from work; his square jaw ever in need of a shave. And she wished, oh how she wished, she had the right to wrap her arms around him and hold him tight . . . that the two of them could somehow be transported to a deserted island and flee this nightmare that was thrusting itself upon them.

"Someone must be trying to frame me," Taylor said, a stunned note to his voice.

"Yes, I know."

"Are they saying what weapon was used to kill Uncle Jacques?"

"A .38 pistol," Sonsee said. Sitting up, she crossed her legs and propped her elbow on her thigh. Wearily, she rested her forehead in her hand.

"Oh, Lord, help me," Taylor muttered.

"You own one?" Sonsee said, more as a statement of fact than a question.

"Yes. Just a minute. Let me see if it's even here. I'll go get the cordless phone, and —"

"No! Don't do that!" Sonsee said, sitting erect. "Sometimes conversations on cordless phones can be picked up by police scanners. That's why I drove back home before calling you. I didn't want anyone to know we had talked. I —"

"Okay, okay," Taylor said. "I'm laying down this receiver. I'll be back."

As the seconds slowly ticked by, Sonsee's mind raced with the reasons for her desperate need of privacy. Taylor was in a fix. Somebody needed to help him. Because of his detective father's underhanded dealings with the Mafia, Taylor never completely trusted law enforcement officials.

T. C. Delaney, Taylor's father, had been one of New Orleans' most respected detectives until his dealings with the Mafia were unearthed. Then he had fled the country, leaving behind a family, an overdue mortgage, and enough heartache for a lifetime. No one in the United States had seen T.C. since. At the time, Sonsee had been eight and Taylor twelve. From that day forward, Taylor had been suspicious of anyone who wore a badge.

As if that weren't enough, when Taylor was seventeen, he was at the wrong place, with the wrong crowd, at the wrong time. The result implicated him during a major drug bust. Without the skill of the LeBlanc family's attorney, Damian Aster, Taylor would have been sent to prison, despite the fact that he had been blissfully ignorant that he was in the middle of a significant drug deal. Once all facts were known, the police chief's son turned out to be at the center of the drug operation. The police chief had planned to let Taylor go to prison to save his son.

Taylor would never calmly allow himself to be arrested now. He had been the victim of dishonesty mixed with law enforcement one too many times.

The muffled fumbling on the other end of the receiver attested to Taylor's return. Sonsee's hand instinctively tightened on the phone.

"My .38 is missing," he ground out.

"Oh, no," Sonsee groaned, pressing her fingers against her eyes. Her oversized yellow cat, Tripod, clumsily hopped onto the bed. The cat had arrived at the back door of her veterinary clinic last year. The poor thing's front leg had been so chewed up, it had to be amputated. Now Sonsee shamelessly spoiled the three-legged cat.

She listlessly looked at the feline as he rubbed his head against her arm and purred. Sonsee felt like Tripod looked when she first met him — chewed up, destitute, desperate. She scratched behind his ears and wished life were as simple for her as it was for him. Even though he'd lost a leg, Tripod still lived an innocent life of peace. Right now, Sonsee would give up one of her legs to have her father back . . . and to know that Taylor was safe from the blame of murder.

"I need your help, Sonsee," Taylor said grimly.

"Yes, I know. That's why I called. And that's the reason I didn't want to use any other phone than mine. I also used a pre-paid calling card. I didn't want anyone to link us. I knew from the minute I heard Carla that you'd dodge the police."

"You know me too well."

Those simple words spoke a truth that left Sonsee aching with unrequited love. No one in the world was any dearer to her than this man accused of her father's murder. She would do everything in her power to help exonerate him.

"Look," Taylor clipped out, "I have Mom's car here at the ranch. Before her trip to Egypt, she left it with me so I could take care of some repairs. I figure I've still got a few hours before the police try to catch up with me here. I'll leave as soon as possible and drive Mom's car to her house. Tonight I'll walk to LeBlanc Manor."

"What? Are you crazy?" Sonsee asked. "Your mom's house is ten miles from

LeBlanc Manor, and — and how in the world are you going to get in? Are you just going to knock on the door and ask Carla to let you in?"

"No. I still have the key to the back door. Your father gave it to me when Mom was there after her mastectomy, remember? I forgot to give it back to him. I'll just let myself in the back and sneak up to the third floor."

"But the whole family will eventually be there — probably starting tomorrow and certainly after the funeral on Wednesday."

"Exactly. You'll be there and we can meet. No one will suspect that I'm there. Plan to meet me on the third floor. It's the perfect spot. Let's meet after the funeral," he rapped off the commands with staccato speed.

"I don't even know what time the funeral is going to *be* yet."

"Plan it for the afternoon. Can you do that?"

"I can try."

"Good. I'll be waiting."

"But . . . but what if . . . if you just-just got a lawyer and defended yourself?" Sonsee said, hoping he might at least consider this option. "Surely you have an alibi and can prove Carla's lying."

"I don't have an alibi," he bluntly stated. "I left LeBlanc Manor last night at ten. The truth is, Carla might have seen me leave his bedroom then. We sat in there and played chess together until I absolutely had to leave. I told my ranch manager I'd start home last night so I would be at work this morning." A frustrated growl erupted over the line. "I should have left at eight last night, but neither of us wanted to stop playing. I finally left, then drove for a couple of hours until I caught myself going to sleep. I pulled over at a rest stop and slept awhile, then drove on home. I got here around seven this morning." He paused and expelled a distraught sigh. "Man! I can't believe this is happening."

"Why couldn't you have just checked into a hotel like a normal person?" Sonsee snapped, her sorrow giving way to temper — a temper that had gotten her into trouble more than once. "I've told you over and over again that your infernal roadside camping is going to get you into trouble. Now look!" Her fist curled tightly before she slammed it against the bed's paisley comforter. Last fall she'd warned Taylor against his penchant for snoozing in roadside parks. Sonsee was truly con-cerned somebody would break into his

25

truck, slit his throat, and take his wallet. As usual, Taylor had ignored her concern. At the time, his lack of respect for her opinion had been infuriating. Now all the old exasperation surfaced to fuel full-blown ire.

"Listen to me, Red, the last thing I need right now is you bossing me around!" Taylor challenged.

"Don't call me Red!" Sonsee growled. She was in no mood to be badgered with the childhood nickname that still irritated.

"Look, are you going to meet me on the third floor or not?"

"Yes!"

"Okay then, 'bye!" The phone's click in her ear left Sonsee blinking. Closing her eyes, she took a deep, steadying breath and purposed not to become any angrier than her clammy palms already attested. In all the years she had known him, Sonsee never remembered Taylor hanging up on her. Furthermore, she usually didn't blow up at him as she had today. But to say they were both reeling under the burden of excessive stress was certainly an understatement.

Tripod, purring incessantly, pressed his head against Sonsee's hand, and she automatically stroked his thick coat. With every stroke, several strands of fur attached itself to her damp, quivering palms. "Tripod," she breathed, looking into half-closed, green eyes, "we've got a mess."

"Oh, Lord . . ." Sonsee prayed as she placed the receiver in its cradle. Closing her eyes, she swallowed against an ever-increasing lump in her throat. "Father, please tell me Taylor will be okay. I couldn't bear the thought of losing my dad *and* him."

Never had Sonsee needed the prayers of her six closest friends any more than now. When her mother had died, she'd certainly required her friends' prayers and support, but this was worse than death from natural causes. This was murder. Murder and lying. Lying and conspiracy.

Without further hesitation, Sonsee picked up her receiver and punched in Melissa Moore's office number. Including Sonsee, there were seven friends who had graduated together from the University of Texas, where they fondly dubbed themselves the "Seven Sisters." Over the last decade, they'd maintained their friendship and even came together for a semiannual "sister" reunion. All seven — Sonsee, Melissa Moore, Kim Lan Lowery, Marilyn Langham, Victoria Roberts, Jacquelyn Lightfoot, and Sammie Jones — represented a wide variety of careers and personalities. Nonetheless, they shared a strong bond that competed in many cases with their biological siblings. Certainly Sonsee felt closer to her friends than she had ever felt to her brother and two sisters.

Sonsee, Kim Lan, and Melissa had recently participated in a mission trip to Vietnam. During the trip, Melissa and Sonsee had grown closer than they had been since college. Melissa spent many hours praying and talking with Sonsee over her hopeless love for Taylor. At last Sonsee grew spiritually stable, which created a peace that assuaged her aching heart. Today she would give anything to taste that blissful peace once more.

As the phone continued its ringing, Sonsee hoped she'd dialed the right number. Usually she kept all her needed phone numbers filed safely in her head. Occasionally, she would accidentally switch the numbers, but for the most part the memory that served her splendidly through the rigors of vet school worked just as well on a social level.

At last, the receptionist cheerfully answered, "Oklahoma City Children's Clinic. How may I help you?"

"I need to speak with Dr. Moore,

28

please," Sonsee said, wondering how to get through to her friend.

"I'm sorry but Dr. Moore is currently with patients. Might her nurse be of service to you?"

Sonsee rubbed her eyes as her shoulders sagged. "No. Just tell Dr. Moore that Sonsee is in trouble. This is an emergency." In a matter of minutes, Sonsee was talking with one of her closest friends.

"What's going on?" Melissa asked, her alto voice laced with concern. "Jenny says this is an emergency. Are you okay?"

"No. I'm about to fall apart," Sonsee said, biting her lip. "It's Father. He's been murdered. And-and it looks like Taylor is accused of-of-"

For once the usually unflappable member of the seven sisters remained silent. At last she whispered, "I don't know what to say, Sonsee."

"I-I know. Me, neither," Sonsee choked out, rubbing her tear-dampened fingers against her khaki shorts.

"It seems like just yesterday you lost your mother, and now . . ."

"Yes." Sonsee swallowed hard, determined to keep her composure. "I just called to ask you to pray for me and to please contact the other sisters. I don't think I've got what it takes to call all of them or even the presence of mind to compose a sensible e-mail."

"Yes, of course — of course. I'll do anything I can to help. *Anything!*" Melissa insisted.

"Right now, the main thing is that you guys lift me and Taylor up to the Lord. I don't believe for one minute that he killed my father."

"No, of course not." Melissa's assuring voice bolstered Sonsee's courage. "I don't know Taylor that well, but I know you have the ultimate faith in him. I can't imagine anybody you think so highly of being a murderer."

"P-please just seek God for him. He's refusing to turn himself in to the police, and I don't know what's going to happen. I'm so confused I don't even know what *needs* to happen right now."

"You know I'll pray, and I'll make sure all the other sisters know what has happened. When is the funeral? Do you know . . . oh, just a minute Sonsee . . ."

While the sound of muffled voices carried over the telephone line, Sonsee imagined Melissa being pulled in numerous directions — just as she often was in her own veterinary practice.

30

"Listen, I really hate to go, but it seems like we've got a rather serious emergency on this end," Melissa said.

"Yes, I understand. Believe me, I've been there."

"So, do you think the funeral will be in a couple of days?"

"Yes, probably Wednesday. When I know for sure, I'll contact all of you."

"Okay, good." Melissa paused. "I can't speak for everyone else, but I'll be there. And Sonsee?"

"Yes."

"You know I love you dearly," she said in her no-nonsense manner.

"Yes, I know."

With a brief adieu, the friends ended their phone call. Sonsee dashed aside yet another tear. As if he sensed his owner's distress, Tripod rubbed his face against her chin. She lovingly stroked his ears and made mental plans to take him to the clinic during her return trip to New Orleans. The cat attempted to rub his face against hers again, and Sonsee turned her head. Her attempts to evade her pet led to looking toward the family photo hanging on her wall. The whole family stood in the front yard of LeBlanc Manor, that pillared mansion surrounded by lush trees and a yard full of summer flowers. Sonsee's father, her mother, Sonsee, Hermann, Alana, and Natalie all smiled as if life were near perfect. Despite her half-siblings' silent disapproval, Jacques had insisted upon Taylor's presence in the picture as well. The photo, only six years old, seemed to have been transported from another world. A world where all was bliss. A world to which Sonsee could never return.

Two

Two days later Sonsee's stomach knotted in spasms. The hair on the back of her neck prickled with every step she took. Shadows along the narrow, musty corridor shifted in sequence with the wind-blown cypresses outside the dome-shaped windows at the end of the hallway. Biting her bottom lip, Sonsee eyed the boiling clouds, their blue-black hue blotting out the sunshine. They blew in off the Gulf of Mexico shortly after her father's funeral. Those ominous clouds seemed as wicked as the storm hurling into her life and threatening to snatch her very soul into its swirling vortex. A distant rumble of thunder seemed to mumble the earth-shattering facts that left Sonsee numb with disbelief. *My father is dead . . . dead . . . dead. The evidence says Taylor Delaney killed him . . . killed him . . . killed him.*

For the second time in five years, Sonsee had sat through a parent's funeral. Grief over her mother's death arose again during her father's service and almost choked her with a fresh onslaught of sorrow. The anguish increased in the face of the unjust accusations against Taylor.

Her mind whirling, Sonsee forced herself to walk farther into the corridor's dusky depths. The third floor of LeBlanc Manor consisted of five rooms and a short hallway. Sonsee never remembered a time when the floor was in use, other than for storage. Now she was on the verge of a third-floor tryst with Taylor. She hadn't seen or heard from him since that rushed phone call two days before. As suspected, the police had found the murder weapon buried in the midst of those trees behind LeBlanc Manor. They traced the .38 to Taylor Delaney and obtained a warrant for his arrest. The hallway seemed to gradually narrow until Sonsee felt as if it were squeezing her mind in a steel vise. Her soul wrenched with fresh agony. The agony of losing her father. The agony of discovering he had been murdered. The agony of knowing her lifetime friend was the accused killer. Even her six "sisters" could not supply enough support at the funeral to ease her torment. As close as she was to her friends, Sonsee was equally close to Taylor — and she desperately missed his presence during these days of woe.

Reaching out to steady herself against the cool wall, Sonsee took a cleansing breath and peered into the ghostlike shadows, searching for any sign of Taylor. Logic insisted he would be hiding in one of the rooms. The humid New Orleans air wrapped its dank arms around her and nagged her spirit into an even deeper state of despair. Resolutely she trudged onward and pushed against the first door she neared. The hinges squeaked as the door swung inward. Squinting, she peered into the dusty room stacked with boxes.

A flash of lightning momentarily illuminated the room, revealing an ancient fireplace with a brass lion's face below the mantel. In the burst of electricity, the lion's eyes seemed to glow with a light of their own. The windows rattled with the impact of the storm, and Sonsee jumped and rubbed her upper arms. A new thought, as perilous as the lightning, assaulted her: *What if Taylor didn't make it here? What if he was captured?*

Sonsee closed the door and hurried up the hallway toward a storage closet. A creaking on the stairway behind her sent a rush of panic through her mind. Rigid with fear, she paused outside the closet door as the sound of footsteps on the stairway echoed along the hallway. The last thing she wanted was to be caught up here. There was no logical reason for her to be prowling around the third floor. Sonsee's heart raced, causing her senses to reel. The dizzy streaks of light split the dismal July sky. As the person neared, she gripped the closet's doorknob and debated her dilemma.

"Sonsee? Are you up there?" Hermann, her older half-brother, called from the stairway. "We're ready to read the will now."

Without a sound, Sonsee opened the closet door, stepped inside, and closed it behind her. A firm hand snaked out from nowhere and pressed her lips against her teeth. Sonsee's eyes widened. She grunted then struggled against the arm that clamped her limbs to her sides. One thought repeatedly stomped through her mind: *The murderer! He's going to kill me!*

"It's just me," a familiar voice whispered into her ear.

The sound of Taylor's Texas drawl swept aside Sonsee's terror. She wilted against her lifelong friend. As he removed his hand from her mouth, she felt as if her blood were draining to her feet.

"Sonsee?" Hermann's call now sounded from the top of the stairs.

Taylor's rapid breathing mingled with Sonsee's as Hermann entered the hall and neared the closet. "Back up with me and keep quiet," Taylor whispered. Stealthily, they moved toward the rear of the closet and, much to Sonsee's surprise, eased through an opening into a dark room. Taylor released her and silently placed a panel over the opening. Sonsee, barely breathing, cringed as Hermann's slow footfalls neared the closet.

"Sonsee?" he called again. His impatient voice was only feet away. The faint sound of squeaking hinges witnessed his opening the closet. Sonsee gripped Taylor's arm, praying that Hermann would not detect the mobile panel. After breathless minutes, the closet door slammed. Hermann's repeated calls testified to his investigating every room. Finally his footfalls faded down the stairway, and Sonsee released her vise grip on Taylor.

"Good grief, woman," he complained while flipping a light switch near the panel. "You almost dug your fingernails into the bone."

"Sorry," Sonsee said, eyeing the indentations in his skin as he rubbed his forearm.

"Tell that to the plastic surgeon," he grumbled.

"Oh, get real." Sonsee rolled her eyes. "It's not *that* bad."

Taylor chuckled then bent at the waist. "Welcome to my castle," he said in the lofty voice of a British lord.

Sonsee, glancing around the unkempt room, recalled all the years Taylor's comic voices had brightened her life. An unexpected rush of love filled her, and she savored the heightened moment. The resulting silence spanned poignant seconds, and her passion beckoned to be requited. The yearning had started over the Christmas holiday only seven months ago when her father had invited her and Taylor on a Hawaiian vacation. Jacques LeBlanc retired early every night, which left Sonsee and Taylor alone to enjoy the evenings. They walked along the beach in companionable silence, took in a few movies, and enjoyed Hawaiian dining experiences. In the midst of it all, Sonsee began to look forward to Taylor's presence with more warmth than she had ever experienced. At last she acknowledged that she'd been in love with Taylor far longer than she allowed herself to realize. Even now Sonsee wondered if her father orchestrated the whole setup in hopes that she and Taylor would fall in love. Ironically, she *had* fallen in love. Taylor had not.

Much to Sonsee's embarrassment, he had painfully explained his lack of love last spring at LeBlanc Manor's kitchen table. . . .

"Don't waste your love on me. I'm not worth it, you know," he said, his words barely audible.

Sonsee, sitting across from him, swallowed hard. "What?" she gasped, desperately hoping she had misunderstood him.

For his answer, Taylor solemnly stared at her, his dark-blue eyes communicating a message that left Sonsee's eyes stinging.

"You — you know?" she asked, her voice trembling.

Once more he didn't answer, but he observed her with a pathetic, lonely glint in his eyes that revealed his soul.

"But — but h-how did you find out?"

"You told me." Restlessly Taylor scooted back his chair. The legs produced a scraping noise against the white Italian tile. He stood and walked to the nearby floor-to-ceiling window. His back turned, Taylor scrubbed his fingers through his dark curly hair, ever in need of a trim, then crammed his hands into his jeans pockets.

Her head spinning with the implications, Sonsee prayed for the strength to calmly walk out of the kitchen. Unlike her friend, Kim Lan, who had her moments of spontaneity, Sonsee was known for her cool composure. True, she usually released her self-restraint when she was in the company of friends. She enjoyed incessantly teasing her six long-time friends. She also freely participated in the never-ending banter with Taylor, but overall she exercised a strong hand of control over her emotions. Or so she thought. Sitting at the kitchen table watching Taylor as he labored for words, Sonsee wondered if she had deceived herself.

"You might be able to come across as Miz Practical with everyone else," he said at last. "But you've never been that great at hiding your feelings from me." Taylor turned to her, his features tightened in anguish.

"So — so what are you saying?" she whispered. Her lips stiff, Sonsee gripped the hot coffee cup until the heat burned into her palms.

"I'm saying . . ."

"Why did you even tell me you knew?" The question erupted from her very soul.

40

"If — if you don't-don't — aren't —"

"Sonsee, you know I can't! That's the whole point! I can't!" He closed the distance between them and gripped the top of a green wrought-iron chair. "And I didn't think it was fair to you to let you think and — and hope."

"What do you mean, you *can't?*" Sonsee asked, her temper, the only defense left to her, flared in response to Taylor's stating exactly what she feared the most.

"I'm telling you that my heart is as hard as a rock," he said in a tortured voice. "I can't fall in love."

"You can't or you're just so stubborn you won't?" Sonsee stood, and the hot coffee spilled onto her hand.

"I've tried, Sonsee. I've tried ever since Hawaii. With God as my witness, I have tried."

The sincerity of his words dampened the flames of her fury.

"You've known since Hawaii?" she whispered.

"I suspected then." Once again, he turned from her. "But by the time Mom had her surgery, I was certain."

Sonsee stared at his back, at the tall, lean lines of his physique. She had envisioned Taylor one day discovering her love, wrap-

41

ping his arms around her, and declaring he had felt the same for years. All Sonsee's prayers for a commitment from Taylor mocked her.

"I even toyed around with the idea of proposing, Sonsee." He propped his arm against the windowframe and rested his forehead against his arm. "But that wouldn't be fair to you. I'm just like any other man alive, I guess. I would enjoy the physical intimacy of marriage. But —"

"That's all it would be."

Slowly, he turned to face her. "I have always cared for you — as if you were my sister. But the kind of love a marriage requires . . ."

"It all goes back to your father leaving you and your mom, doesn't it?"

He didn't break her gaze.

"It's not that you can't love; you're afraid to love." Sonsee stared at the puddle of coffee on the table and felt as if she hadn't slept in weeks. The inner turmoil from her newfound love had drained her of all energy — emotional, mental, and physical. Recalling the last few weeks, Sonsee couldn't remember one night when she had been blessed with a full night's rest.

Love . . . Sonsee always thought that when she fell in love it would be like a storybook. Boy meets girl. He proposes. She accepts. And they live happily ever after. Instead, love ushered in misery.

Three

As the memory of that early morning conversation wove its way between them, Sonsee instinctively inched away from Taylor. An aching tension settled around her shoulders, and the musty room's faint light added to the strain.

Sonsee had never seen this room before. The bare, dim bulb hanging from the low ceiling did nothing to camouflage the dilapidated state of the tattered green couch and matching chair. Only the backpack in the corner and the clutter of paper plates and plastic cups suggested Taylor's recent habitation.

"Since when have you known about *this* room?"

"Since I was thirteen. Uncle Jacques showed it to me and told me the place was my secret hideout. According to him, every boy needs a fort. This was mine." His tug on her arm prompted Sonsee's stepping farther into the room.

"Since you were thirteen, huh? Just about the time you started telling me there was a one-legged ghost up here!" Narrowing her eyes, Sonsee propped hands on hips and recalled those nights she had lain awake imagining all sorts of horrors about Taylor's "ghost."

"You got it. I couldn't let you come up here and find my hideout. That would have been a breach of a sacred trust." Sonsee, glad for the lighthearted diversion, joined him in a chuckle.

Yet the laughter soon scurried away, and gloom reclaimed the premises. Head bent, Taylor took three steps toward the dingy green sofa, collapsed onto the cushions, and propped his head against the back. Never did Sonsee remember his face so pinched and pale.

Her mind spun with the options that posed themselves. Sonsee didn't know whether to join Taylor on the couch and lovingly offer her support or bolt from the room and hide from him. She was slipping into the bottomless abyss of eternal mortification. Taylor knew she loved him, yet he could never return her love. Sonsee would rather never face him again.

He produced a tired smile, revealing dimples that suggested boyish charm. That smile represented the years of camaraderie they had shared. Yet today it was uncertain . . . questioning . . . vulnerable.

With determination, Sonsee crammed her hands into the pockets of her black suit jacket and decided the best means of saving face was acting as if nothing had changed between her and Taylor. Right now there was no room for messy emotions.

As she returned Taylor's appraisal, his dark-blue gaze seemed to bore into her mind. The smile vanished. A pall of apprehension settled upon his features. A jolt of panic flashed through his eyes. "I'm in big trouble," he gasped. A boom of thunder attested to the evil storm's continuing assault upon the countryside.

Sonsee, suppressing a jump, curled her fists into tight knots and asked, "Does your mother know what's going on?"

"No. Not yet. She's still on that tour of Egypt. She's not due back until next week."

Sonsee closed her eyes and recalled the perilous weeks last spring when Joy Delaney underwent a mastectomy. The near brush with death changed Joy's perspective on numerous things. She decided to enjoy life more by traveling to some countries she had long desired to see. She also revealed some things to several people she wanted to say for years — including that she prayed Sonsee would be her daughter-in-law. Sonsee forced her thoughts to the present. Dwelling on anything related to her hopeless love for Taylor left her wanting to hide her face.

"It's a good thing your mom isn't here. Your name's in every paper and on every TV station in southern Louisiana."

"That's what I figured," Taylor said.

"The police are out in full force. I can't believe you made it here without getting caught."

"Well, I think I had plenty of help." He glanced toward the ceiling and pointed upward. "Somebody up there seems to be on my side." Wearily Taylor rubbed his eyes. Sonsee recalled the years Taylor had been so intent upon making everyone laugh. Recently she wondered if his bent toward humor was a cover for the wounds of his heart. But now all traces of the "class clown" had vanished. The man who was so intent upon making everyone laugh had no laughs to give.

"I can't believe this is happening," he said. "I'm wondering more and more if your brother or sisters might be involved.

All three of them probably stand to inherit a fortune now." His fingers, white with the intensity of his grip, clenched the couch's arm as if it were his anchor to reality.

"Well, so do I, for that matter. And you, too," Sonsee added. "Father loved you as much as he loved them." Her spirit heavy with dread, Sonsee crossed the room and plopped onto the arm of the moss-green chair. Nervously she fidgeted with a brass button on her jacket. "I-I've already been considering the possibility of one of them being involved, but-but the thought of one of my sisters or my brother being a murderer makes me sick." Sonsee swallowed against the rush of tears burning her eyes. The sound of wind-blown rain, driven against the aging mansion, reflected the buckets full of stormy emotions she had already released.

"Why does it make you sick? Because you don't believe one of them would do it or because the idea of someone murdering their own father is disgusting?" Taylor asked, as if he had no problem believing Hermann, Alana, or Natalie could be involved.

None of Sonsee's half-siblings had ever really cared for Taylor. Their esteem for Sonsee wasn't much greater. Looking back on her childhood, Sonsee suspected that her father wasn't blameless in creating their negative feelings. He had clearly favored Sonsee over his older children, and Jacques had likewise bestowed ample preference for Taylor. Even though Sonsee recognized the root of the problem, she still struggled with her attitude toward her brother and sisters.

"Well, if one of them *is* involved . . ." Sonsee's stomach tightened. If Hermann, Alana, or Natalie were involved, Sonsee would be hard pressed to withhold retaliation. Hard pressed, indeed.

Taylor leaned his head against the couch again and shut his eyes. The shallow lines from his nose to mouth claimed deeper grooves than they had the last time she saw him. Besides the deeper lines, he didn't look much different than he had the morning he told her to not waste her love on him. Taylor was bronzed from the hours he spent outdoors on the Houston ranch her father helped finance. As usual, Taylor's curly hair was in need of a trim, his face in need of a shave. His standard faded blue jeans and western shirt looked a part of him. Sonsee reflected upon his smile only moments before. His boyish dimples had made their usual charming show; dimples that increased Taylor's appeal with their every appearance. *A grown man has no right to be so endearing!*

Trying to smother the betraying flutter of her heart, Sonsee recalled her recent mission trip to Vietnam. On that trip the Lord showed her that she had put her dreams of marrying Taylor above her desire for God's perfect will. With a heavy heart, Sonsee had acknowledged that her relationship with Jesus Christ must come before her romantic dreams. Furthermore, if the Lord wanted her to remain single for life, then she realized she must be content with His plans. After all, God knew what was best for her far more than she ever would.

The peace Sonsee gained stayed with her, even during the wedding of one of her "six sisters," Marilyn Langham. Before the wedding, Sonsee had cringed, wondering how well her tranquility over Taylor would remain in the presence of an ecstatic bride and glowing groom. However, God had been faithful. Sonsee's serenity never wavered.

Until her father was murdered.

Her heart swelling, Sonsee observed the object of her love. Seeing Taylor so vulnerable . . . realizing his precarious circumstances . . . sensing his growing need for her . . . all swirled together to annihilate the peace she had prayed so hard to gain. Her vulnerability after the death of her father, her need to step into the embrace of comforting, masculine arms, her heart's renewed cry for fulfillment in marriage left Sonsee reeling with unrequited love and desires. *Oh Lord!* The helpless wail silently erupted from deep within. *I feel as if I'm drowning!* But her heavenward plea did nothing to decrease her panic.

After seconds of floundering for equilibrium, Sonsee gritted her teeth and purposed to control her thoughts. Deliberately, she closed the door on the torment, pressed her lips together, and forced herself to mentally address Taylor's immediate problem.

Sonsee peered around the windowless room and contemplated the numerous hours Taylor must have spent here. Ironically, the person Taylor was accused of murdering had unknowingly provided a place of refuge from the law; a place Jacques had shown Taylor during a hard era of the young man's life. Only Taylor's praying mother and the incessant influence and prayers of Sonsee's parents had steered him from his flirtation with the wild life. Looking back, Sonsee saw that Taylor's adolescent courtship with rebellion had been a direct result of the anger caused by his father's desertion. Furthermore, Taylor's loyalty to his father had been replaced by loyalty to Jacques LeBlanc. The grief now shadowing Taylor's eyes suggested that Jacques' death was as devastating to him as to Sonsee.

"Taylor . . ." she said, not certain how to suggest what she wished Taylor would do. "Um . . . I've been thinking. Look, I know you've had a couple of negative experiences with the law. But maybe if you would just go ahead and hire a lawyer and —"

"Come on, Sonsee!" he barked. "You know how I feel about the police. Sure! They say I'll have a fair trial, but how do I know they're not in with the murderer! Blast it, Sonsee! If my own father could rub elbows with the Mafia and keep up the front of an honest detective, then anybody could. And you know I almost landed in the slammer because some police chief would rather an innocent kid go to prison than have his guilty son sent there. I can't take the chance! I have no choice but to find who killed Uncle Jacques on my own." He raised his hands. "All I can think about is the sound of that prison door closing on me. I've almost been there once, and I don't want to go there for real!"

"And if you get caught anyway?" Sonsee asked, her palms clammy.

"I won't get caught."

She swallowed, hoping he was right. But the rumbling thunder and gusting wind seemed to prophesy Taylor's doom. "If they catch you now, it will make you look even more guilty. After all, at this point you are a fugitive."

"I know that."

Sonsee, weighted with stress, slid from the chair's arm onto its cushion.

"I need some help, Sonsee." Taylor's eyes took on the frenzy of a hunted animal and dared her to look away. "I think we can get to the bottom of this quickly. I already have a few clues. I know I can prove who did it. With your help, I'll just do it sooner. Don't renege on me, Red."

Sonsee closed her eyes. Two nights with precious little sleep were taking their toll. She had lain awake both nights wondering if there were any way Taylor could disentangle himself from this mess. No options posed themselves.

If this were anybody but Taylor . . . But she and Taylor had been a pair during childhood. They had pulled together when

Alana, Hermann, and Natalie had often expressed their disdain. As adults, they were the greatest of friends. For Sonsee, that friendship had blossomed into love.

But harboring a fugitive was dangerously against the law. Sonsee would be risking a lot, including her freedom. On the other hand, Taylor deserved her loyalty. He had been a stronghold to her for more than half her life. He also held her heart.

Sonsee opened her eyes. Despite attempts to control her voice, she could not stop love from oozing out with every word. "You know I won't renege," she whispered. "I'll help you. Was there ever a question?"

The crease in his forehead relaxed. "I knew I could count on you," he said in a tired, rough rumble.

"Father would have expected me to help you," she said, desperately attempting a practical tone. Sonsee's attempt failed, and she sounded pathetic. As their gaze lengthened, the truth of her love marched out between them, and Taylor's eyes darkened with something akin to sympathy. A hot rush flashed through Sonsee, and she stopped herself from blurting, "The last thing I need is your sympathy!"

Abruptly, Sonsee stood, walked across the room, and kept her back to him.

"Okay, then, we need to decide how we're going to get you out of here."

"Yes," Taylor agreed. The sounds of his rising and approaching caused Sonsee's spine to tighten. "But there's one more thing you need to know," he said from close behind.

"What's that?" Sonsee asked, determined not to face him.

"Your helping me will be even more dangerous than you might believe." A new roll of retreating thunder filled the ominous pause. "Someone shot at me when I was leaving my mother's house two nights ago."

Sonsee spun to face Taylor, her expressive green eyes wide, her freckled face pale, her cheeks stained with the tears that spoke of Taylor's own heartache. Never had he felt so out of sorts with Sonsee. *Never.* In one second he suppressed the urge to shout, "Why did you let yourself fall in love with me?" The next second he wanted to share a grief-filled hug with her, a hug that would reflect the platonic friendship they had known since childhood.

"So you think the killer is after you now?" she exclaimed.

"Yes," Taylor said as he recalled those bullets whizzing past his head while hurrying from his mother's yard. When the gunfire started, he had been thanking God that he'd escaped police detection. In the shadows of midnight, Taylor had ducked inside a grove of trees in the neighbor's spacious yard, then eventually crawled into a culvert and waited while the assailant's footsteps crunched all around him. Finally, a car came to life and sped away. Taylor wasted no time in his escape. "It would make perfect sense for the murderer to be after me. The police think I'm the murderer. If I come up dead, then the case is closed." He slammed his palms together as if shutting a book.

Sonsee nodded as a thoughtful silence settled between them. Part of Taylor despised himself for involving Sonsee, yet another part of him reasoned that he had little choice. She was the only person he could fully trust. The only person who could help him. Nonetheless, he hoped she didn't think he was using the knowledge of her love as a tool to manipulate her for his own gain. Taylor would never do that. He thought many times after the trip to Hawaii that, if at all possible, he would have cheerfully willed Sonsee out of loving him.

Taylor had even consulted Sonsee's father about the complications of this relationship. The two-day visit with Jacques included valued time deep-sea fishing. During one excursion Jacques had hinted there might be a romance brewing between Taylor and his daughter. Taylor was speechless. Then he honestly shared the detestable truth of his stony heart. A truth that left a strained silence hanging between him and his surrogate father. A silence that spoke of disappointment, of sadness, of embarrassment. And Taylor at once glimpsed a reality he never suspected — Jacques LeBlanc had tried to play matchmaker in Hawaii.

Thoughts of Jacques sent a tidal wave of grief crashing against Taylor's spirit. The older man had embraced Taylor in a powerful hug before their visit ended. Taylor loved that man. He hadn't realized exactly how deep his love ran until he learned of Jacques' death. His eyes stinging, Taylor averted his gaze from Sonsee's understated beauty. When she produced a telltale sniffle, he sensed their thoughts were traveling the same path. A path lined with the inky shadows of pain and the sinister threats of danger.

When Sonsee produced a broken sob and covered her face, Taylor compressed his lips. Silent tears dampened his cheeks.

Instinctively he wrapped his arms around Sonsee and cradled her head against his shoulder. All the messy emotions of the last months became a vague memory, and the two of them were carried back to an era when their relationship was simple.

Gently, Taylor stroked her hair and muttered thickly, "I'm so sorry, Sonsee. I'm so, so sorry. And I'm as sorry for me as for you." His voice cracked. "I-I'm going to miss him, too. He was a better dad to me than my own father ever was."

Sonsee responded with a round of sniffles, and she clung to him all the tighter. The smell of her sporty perfume reinforced the image of her no-nonsense personality. Sonsee was a woman of few frills. Her trace makeup and straight auburn hair, forever pulled back in a ponytail, reflected her desire to keep life uncomplicated. One of her favorite sayings was, "I want to keep my life simple so I have more time for golf." The two of them had spent many companionable hours on the golf course with her father and mother. Right now, Taylor wished this whole ordeal were a dreadful nightmare, that they could go back to the carefree days of childhood.

But Taylor's childhood had never been carefree. Not really. His father's disappearance had, in some ways, been an anticlimactic event upon the heels of a stormy home life. As a child, Taylor lay awake numerous nights listening to his mother's sobs — before and after her husband left. At last Taylor decided he could live without the pain his parents' marriage represented, so he systematically hardened his heart against falling in love . . . *ever.*

With a jolt, Taylor realized that the hug that began in friendship had turned into the clinging of two desperate people. Taylor was holding on as tightly as Sonsee. She stiffened. His arms tensed. And Taylor wondered why he'd wrapped them around her. He didn't want to encourage her in any way. There was no future between them.

At last Sonsee awkwardly pulled back, and Taylor looked down into eyes that were red-rimmed and vulnerable. Vulnerable and searching. Searching and hopeful. Feeling as if he were being tugged down by a powerful current, Taylor's gaze was drawn to her lips — lips that beckoned him to taste their sweetness. His gut churned. Abruptly he removed his arms, stepped away from Sonsee, and made a monumental job of stuffing the used paper plates and napkins into a trash bag.

He waved toward a cache of nuts, fruit, and canned meat. "I sneaked down to the kitchen last night and took some things from the back of the pantry," he said, desperate for any diversion.

"Well, I guess I'll go on down, um, down to the will reading. Hermann is looking for me."

"Fine," Taylor replied, keeping his back to her. "Can we meet in your room after dark?" As images of her inviting lips teased his masculine instincts, Taylor wadded a paper towel into a tight ball and slammed it into the garbage bag. *I refuse to become attracted to her just because of the way she feels,* he stormed inwardly. *I will not use her! I will not! Sonsee deserves more!*

"Yes . . . I-I guess. I hadn't planned on staying here that long, but —"

"Good. I think I can crawl down the trellis on the other side of the house and land on your balcony," he said, searching the room for something else to cram into the plastic bag. "From there, we can decide how I'm going to get out of here."

"Okay," she said in a bland voice seconds before the panel gave a faint click.

Taylor glanced over his shoulder. Sonsee was gone. Once again, he was alone in this miserable little room. *Alone.* For a man who had spent his life emotionally isolating himself from almost everyone, being alone had never been so forlorn.

With a tired sigh, Taylor collapsed onto the worn sofa. He allowed the trash bag to fall to the floor, then firmly rubbed his face with both hands. Resting his elbows on his knees, he considered the last fifteen years of his life. Years in which he served the Lord. Years in which he did all for Christ that he knew to do.

But where is God now? The disillusioning thought barged in, hardening his heart all the more. Taylor had adopted a Christian belief system. He had turned from the paths of sin that had led him down more dark alleys than he ever wanted to re-member.

As a twenty-two-year-old college drop-out, Taylor had given mental assent to Jesus Christ as the Son of God. From that point a new door was opened in his life, a doorway that brought in sunshine and goodness and laid a fresh journey before him. Despite the years he had goofed off in college, Taylor had been able to apply him-self to academics, salvage what he could from the past, and graduate with a Bachelor's degree in agriculture. From there, Jacques LeBlanc had helped him establish his Houston ranch — a horse and cattle operation that prospered.

Taylor assumed he and God had a deal. The rancher studied and learned biblical doctrine. He lived by the precepts set before him in Scripture. He attended church regularly and bargained with God: *Lord, I'll do anything You want me to do. You just make sure nothing bad happens.*

Taylor slammed his fist against his knee and restlessly paced the disheveled room. Despite his service to God something had happened. Something that could swallow his life. Something that could slam him behind bars.

"Where are You, God?" Taylor pleaded, raising his hands upward. "Where are You?" His cry, laced with confusion and disenchantment, sailed around the silent room like the tailwinds of a heinous cyclone.

His stomach tightened . . . his teeth clenched . . . his head pounded with renewed protest to the stress of recent days. And for the first time since he had acknowledged Jesus Christ, Taylor wondered if he truly understood what a walk with the Lord was all about. At the moment Taylor needed Him most, the Lord seemed miles away.

Four

Fingers trembling, heart softly palpitating, Carla Jenson hovered in the hallway and dialed the telephone number. She knew even before the phone rang that she would get an answering machine. The person she was calling sat in LeBlanc Manor's den. That person daily checked the machine from the same cordless phone Carla was using. The next time the machine was checked, Carla's threat would be the latest message.

As the phone began its monotonous peal, Carla ducked from the long, narrow hallway into a small room. Silently, she closed the door and stumbled past an upright vacuum cleaner. Carla didn't want to risk anyone seeing her on the phone. Getting caught using the family phone for personal business could threaten her job. Getting caught in the act of blackmail would involve the police.

Finally, the machine answered and a voice requested that she leave a message.

"Cerberus, I want you to listen to me and listen closely," the black receiver shook like an extension of her hand. "If you don't pay me double what I asked, I swear to you, I'll go to the police. Leave the money in —"

Footsteps. Someone was rushing down the nearby stairs. Carla was well out of the way, and the person probably wouldn't hear her. Nevertheless, she would take no chances. Swallowing against a throat tight and dry, Carla rushed on, her voice piercing the closet's darkness. "After dinner tonight leave the money in a white envelope between Jacques' mattresses. Right side. At the foot." She pushed the button that ended the call, slipped from the closet, and hastily replaced the phone on its wall jack.

Carla wished she could remove the guilt from her soul and, like the phone, hang it up on a wall and walk away. But that possibility was nonexistent. With every hour that passed, the guilt embedded itself deeper into her mind, sinking its iron talons into the very essence of her being. The weight of carrying that burden of blame was much greater than she had originally presumed — a weight worth at least twice the money to which she had agreed . . . maybe even three times the original agreement.

Sonsee raced down both flights of stairs, covered in red oriental runners. She couldn't remove herself from Taylor soon enough. Those moments in his arms had thrown her into an ocean of torment. His incredulous expression when his gaze lingered on her lips left Sonsee momentarily hoping for the impossible. His abrupt turning away spoke exactly what Sonsee already knew. Taylor would never offer more than friendship. The aftermath of his taking her in his arms engulfed Sonsee in longing. Longing and bitterness. Bitterness and exasperation. Before stepping from that hidden room, Sonsee had wanted to shout, "Don't ever touch me again, Taylor Delaney." Instead, she fled.

As she stepped off the last stair, the foyer's rich milieu and the faint odor of raspberry potpourri enveloped Sonsee. Little had changed in the old mansion since childhood. The scarlet Persian rug still claimed its usual spot on the anteroom's dark hardwood floor. The curving stairway with its teak banister still invited Sonsee to race upstairs to her room, to her haven. The family portraits, hanging along the wall above the stairway, still spoke of a long line of Frenchmen who never flinched in the face of adventure.

A movement from the narrow hallway snared Sonsee's attention. Carla edged into the anteroom and eyed Sonsee as if she didn't know whether to run or dissolve from existence. In childhood, the maid had sneaked Sonsee more cookies than she could remember, and the two of them had shared a pleasant friendship — at least until she lied about Taylor.

"Hi, Carla," Sonsee said, desperately trying to keep the disdain and disappointment from her voice. Instead of a pleasant greeting, she wanted to demand an explanation.

Carla glanced down and tugged at the hem of her white apron. The head maid always wore the traditional black-and-white uniform, even though Jacques had repeatedly admonished her to dress more casually. She muttered an unintelligible answer and raced past Sonsee toward the kitchen. As usual, the smell of her heavy perfume floated across the distance and mixed with the faint potpourri odor, causing Sonsee to fight a sneeze.

Fervently Sonsee watched the plump maid's hasty retreat. Since she could remember, Carla had been a trusted employee. She had picked up Sonsee's toys, fed her sandwiches, and supplied all the snacks a kid could want. Carla knew every inch of LeBlanc Manor. She was the hidden but all-seeing eye of its habitants' every move.

What does she know about Father's murder that she isn't telling? The haunting question echoed as Sonsee fought the urge to chase down the maid and challenge her . . . to defend Taylor's innocence . . . to expend the fury brewing since Carla's betrayal to the police.

Sonsee stepped toward the kitchen then stopped herself. Already, she was thirty minutes late for the will reading. The task should have been completed by now, and her tardiness was thwarting the family lawyer's schedule. Deciding to pry into Carla's claims later, Sonsee hurried across the old hallway and stopped in front of the massive teak doors. With her hand on the brass doorknob, Sonsee waited and willed her heart to slow its pace.

She must force thoughts of Carla from her mind and concentrate on surviving the looming encounter with her half-siblings. She didn't want to face them, didn't want to listen to the will while danger hovered over LeBlanc Manor like a sinister dragon, ready to blister the innocent with its fiery breath. Despite Sonsee's wishes, Natalie had insisted on the family attorney reading the will today, thus saving her a return trip to New Orleans.

Sonsee imagined Hermann, Alana, and Natalie crouched on the other side of these doors like three hungry vultures awaiting their share of the kill. As an adolescent, Sonsee had exposed her siblings to the same sarcastic attitude to which they had presented her. As an adult, she tried to avoid them if possible and be polite when forced into their presence. But recently, even before her father's death, the Lord had been dealing with Sonsee about trying to repair what she was responsible for in the bad relations in her family. The days of always faulting her siblings stopped when God showed her she did not love her brother and sisters the way He loved them. Only God, through His miraculous power, could turn her dislike to love, especially if one of them had murdered her father.

Each of them could easily possess the same motive: greed. Not one of her siblings was free of the taint of avarice. Jacques' will would probably leave all of them wealthy. As she had wondered since the news of her father's death, Sonsee once more pondered whether their appetites outweighed their love for their father.

With dread and resolve, Sonsee opened the door and walked through. *God is my helper,* she reminded herself. *I will survive this encounter.* Sonsee strove to block out thoughts of squabbling siblings and her father's presence, but the smell of Jacques' favorite vanilla candles, the white marble fireplace, the classic decorations, all came together to recreate a picture of Jacques in his haven of relaxation, the place where he enjoyed indulging in "off limits" snacks. For years Sonsee had feared her dad's carelessness about his high cholesterol would be the end of him. But somebody killed him before his diet could take its toll — someone who could be in this very room.

Sonsee glanced at her brother and two sisters. Natalie, blonde and petite, stood in front of the antique grandfather clock and snuggled against her latest husband, the muscular Rafael Houk, ten years her junior. Rafael, who looked like a blond, west-coast surfer, treated Natalie like a fragile doll who might break with the slightest injury. Sonsee wondered if he knew he was really husband number five — or if he even cared, considering Natalie's existing trust fund.

Sonsee felt Hermann watching her. She glanced toward him. Wearing worn jeans, Hermann, tall, slender, and fair, leaned against the fireplace, his arms crossed, his lips tilted a fraction. Over the years, Hermann had displayed an unrelenting loyalty to his father. His resentment of Sonsee had been far less than that of her sisters. However, a faint rancor still created tension between them. Today, Hermann looked as if he were wondering more about what Sonsee was up to than contemplating whether he had received equal love from his father.

Alana's fidgeting diverted Sonsee's attention. Plump and redhaired, Alana sat on the edge of the navy Victorian settee. Nervously, she gnawed one of her coral-tinted fingernails then snapped shut the magazine in her lap and plopped it on the Chippendale coffee table. Alana, who was only three years Sonsee's senior, had never been without a heaving dose of bitterness directed toward her younger sibling. Jacques LeBlanc had left precious little doubt that he favored Sonsee over Alana. The effect was nothing short of devastating. Their father's misplaced devotions had served as a malignancy, spreading its fingers of decay, dividing what should have been a unit of love.

"So, you've decided to grace us with your presence," Hermann said, his shrewd eyes narrowing.

Grappling for an appropriate response, Sonsee glanced toward her sisters. While Alana and Natalie eyed her speculatively, Hermann uncrossed his arms and continued focusing on Sonsee. As always, his steel-gray eyes gave her chills — perhaps because Hermann's sharp intellect missed little. During her adolescence, Sonsee was convinced he could read her mind. The time or two she had tried to test her father's boundaries, Hermann, a full eleven years her senior, had been there to point out her mild adolescent rebellion. And even though he had never shown Sonsee much affection, he had bestowed love and devotion on their father. *But was it fake?* Sonsee had never doubted Hermann's genuine regard for his dad until now.

"I was upstairs and didn't keep track of time," she said at last. The grandfather clock chimed five o'clock, as if to underscore Sonsee's claim.

"Exactly where were you?" Hermann asked. "You weren't in your room, weren't in the kitchen, weren't on the third floor . . ." He trailed off as if he suspected she had been involved in something underhanded.

Sonsee swallowed. "I-I wanted a few moments alone. So —"

So what? The words seemed to hang between them.

Fluttering her false eyelashes, Natalie stared at Sonsee in blue-eyed scrutiny. Natalie was the only one who had not wept at the funeral, and Sonsee was hard pressed not to resent her all the more.

"Well now, darlin', we wouldn't want you to go changin' your plans for us," Natalie crooned. Rafael had moved forty-one-year-old Natalie to his home in Georgia three years ago, and now Natalie was a self-appointed Georgia princess. At the very least, her feigned accent grated on Sonsee's nerves.

Sonsee ground her teeth in an attempt to stay a retort. Natalie had just saved Sonsee from having to explain her tardiness, but that didn't make the sarcasm any easier to swallow.

With a glass of tonic water in hand, Natalie's reticent husband silently observed Sonsee. The first time they met, Sonsee had sensed a heavy dose of disdain flowing from Rafael, as if Natalie had already informed him of Sonsee's every flaw.

"She never has changed her plans for us," Alana scorned. "She and Taylor always changed our plans to suit them." Her cool, though swollen, hazel eyes did nothing to hide her contempt. Not now. Not in Sonsee's childhood. At least as long as Jacques was alive, Alana had attempted to hide her dislike. With Jacques' death, her reason for feigning friendship had likewise died. Alana no longer needed to please her father.

Clearing his throat, the elderly family attorney, Damian Aster, rose from the massive wing back chair behind Jacques' desk. "Since you're all here, I think it's time we started." Reaching into his gray suit pocket, he pulled out a white handkerchief, dabbed at his forehead, then picked up his leather briefcase.

The thunder, faintly rumbling in the distance, suggested the storm was ebbing. Sonsee knew another storm was about to begin.

"All our dear relatives aren't here," Alana said with undercurrents of hidden meaning.

"Where's Nick?" Sonsee asked.

Alana raised her finely penciled auburn brows. "Not here."

"She kicked him out again," Natalie said, walking toward the love seat with Rafael close behind.

"I wasn't talking about Nick," Alana said, staring coldly at Natalie. "I was talking about our cousin — *Taylor*." She shifted her scrutiny toward Sonsee.

Feeling as if she were being dropped into a script everyone else had rehearsed, Sonsee cautiously glanced toward Hermann. His brows furrowed in query, and he stepped toward Sonsee. "You wouldn't happen to know where he is now, would you? Seems there are some nice police officers looking for him. From what I understand he killed our father and trashed his room. I wonder what he was looking for?"

"Why would I know where Taylor is?" Sonsee asked, moving away from Hermann. *Are you the murderer?* The possibility seemed increasingly plausible. Hermann seemed too eager to see Taylor indicted. But could a murderer fake the grief Hermann had exhibited at the funeral?

Mr. Aster cleared his throat and put on a pair of silver-rimmed glasses that matched his hair. The lawyer, a close friend of the LeBlanc family, was well acquainted with the familial undercurrents. He had been solely responsible for proving Taylor's innocence twenty years ago. Sonsee wondered if, given the opportunity, he might be able to exonerate Taylor again. "We need to get down to the reason we're all here," Mr. Aster said, his lined face firm with intent.

Hermann resumed his position by the fireplace. Sonsee seated herself in her father's favorite black leather recliner and stared out the window toward the rich green lawn stretching beyond sight. Somehow Jacques' recliner made Sonsee feel as if she were a little girl again, sitting on his knee.

Mr. Aster started reading the document. He droned on and on about this charity, that organization, and even plots in the private cemetery where Sonsee's mother and Jacques' first wife were buried.

At last the lawyer paused, glanced around the room, and hovered above the will for a moment of pregnant silence, looking as if he were about to jump into a frigid pool. Sonsee followed his gaze. Alana sat on the edge of the navy settee. Her rust-tinted lips, the same hue as her hair, pursed as she tugged on the hem of her navy-blue suit. Natalie hung onto Rafael's coat sleeve as if he were reading the will. Hermann stared at Sonsee, then stepped away from the fireplace and leaned against the bisque-colored wall. His arms crossed, Hermann boldly observed her as if he knew she were hiding something . . . or someone.

Sonsee, her stomach knotting with dread, jerked her gaze back to Mr. Aster, who smiled kindly. "And the residual of the property that I own on the date of my death goes to my heirs, Sonsee LeBlanc, Hermann LeBlanc, Alana Prescott, Natalie Houk, and Taylor Delaney. LeBlanc Manor and four million dollars goes to my daughter, Sonsee LeBlanc."

Alana gasped.

Natalie jumped up. "But that's not fair! I wanted LeBlanc Manor. I-I-" The tears, so absent at the funeral, now made a timely appearance.

"It's okay. It's okay," Rafael crooned, standing to wrap a consoling arm around his wife.

Natalie opened her red, trembling lips as if to continue but closed them in pathetic silence. Sonsee suppressed the overwhelming desire to groan and roll her eyes upward. Deep down inside, she wondered how on earth she was going to maintain LeBlanc Manor while living in Baton Rouge. And while she was thankful for her monetary inheritance, the enjoyment of the money would be laced with sorrow. Sonsee would have far preferred having her father alive to having his money.

"If I may resume," Mr. Aster said. Before anyone could disagree he continued. "To my son, Hermann LeBlanc, I leave LeBlanc Oil Exports and one million dollars. To my daughter, Alana Prescott, I leave all my real estate holdings and interests except for the California ranch. To my daughter Natalie Houk, I leave the LeBlanc family jewels, art collection, and one million dollars. To my nephew, Taylor Delaney, I leave four million dollars and the California ranch."

Sonsee glanced around the room, waiting for a reaction to Taylor's inheritance. She didn't have to wait long.

"Well, well, well," Hermann drawled. "I guess Taylor had plenty of motive to kill Father. Strange, isn't it? He's not even Father's blood relative, and he gets a hefty piece of the pie."

"You know Taylor was like a son to Father — and to Mom, too!" Sonsee twisted her mother's plain gold wedding band now on her right ring finger and wished more than ever her mother were still alive. Had five long years elapsed since her mother's death? It seemed like yesterday that her mom had filled her life with the support and encouragement only a mother can give.

Gripping the recliner's arms, Sonsee braced herself against the acidic swell of emotional heat filling the room, a heat intent on swallowing her like a tidal wave from the past. However, she had specifically begun to pray — even before her father's death — that God would somehow begin a healing in her family. The Lord, in His grace, had begun to ask Sonsee to reverse some of her opinions. The process of removing her fleshly attitudes and allowing God to replace them with His love had been painful and almost impossible even before her father was murdered. Now, she suspected that God would have to perform a miracle in order to mend the relationship between her and her siblings. A miracle that she needed as much as they did. *Lord,* Sonsee began, *I don't know how I could have ever made it through this day without You. Please, please, get me out of here without my verbally punching one of them.*

Sonsee had done little more than munch on a few potato chips since lunch yesterday, and her stomach churned with the tension of the day. Not only was she mourning her loss, but now she must fight a spiritual battle as well.

Before the Lord began to deal with her about her lack of love for her siblings,

78

Sonsee's pattern of behavior had sometimes mirrored theirs. She had simply returned negativity for negativity. But now God was asking her to grow up in Him and return good for evil. She saw today, more than ever, that she would be able to do that only through the strength of the Lord. Right now Sonsee would have preferred resorting to her own barrage of cutting remarks. Slipping into the old pattern of returning insult for insult beckoned. The only way Sonsee would get out of this confrontation without the usual sarcasm was through the power of God's presence.

As if by divine guidance, her thoughts roved back over the years that her father spoiled her, the years she had basked in his favoritism without ever considering the feelings of her brother and sisters. As if she were pushed forward into a new beam of light, into a fresh flood of wisdom, for the first time Sonsee couldn't say she blamed them for their antagonism. *Perhaps I would feel exactly the way they feel if Father had treated them as favorites and me as the second best.* Although the truth seemed disloyal upon the aftermath of her father's death, Sonsee fully realized on a deeper level that her father's actions had heftily contributed to the present state of familial discord. Although he was a man who loved the Lord, Jacques LeBlanc had used little wisdom in dealing with his own children.

Sonsee stared so intently at the floor that the pattern of the oriental rug blurred into a mélange of vibrant colors. *Oh, Father,* she pleaded again, *give me compassion for Natalie and Hermann, and especially Alana.*

Finally, Mr. Aster cleared his throat, removed his glasses, and peered around the room. He laid the document he had been reading into his open briefcase as if to signify the completion of his job.

"That's not all, is it?" Rafael asked, a consoling arm still around Natalie.

"Of course it's not all," Alana claimed. "It can't be."

Mr. Aster cleared his throat again, put on his glasses, and stared at the will. "I'm afraid that is the extent of it."

"What?" Natalie cried. "That's it?" Her bottom lip trembled again.

And all of Sonsee's prayers for compassion vanished in the face of fresh disgust. Natalie didn't shed one tear during the funeral but she certainly could muster an abundance of grief over money.

"Good grief, he left each of us a fortune!" Sonsee said, her tongue finally getting the best of her. "Exactly what did you expect?"

Natalie, ignoring Sonsee, squirmed in her seat. "There's more, I know there is!" she whined in the voice of a spoiled seven-year-old.

"Oh shut up, Natalie," Alana snapped, twisting her fingers into a tight ball. "I told you he wasn't as loaded as you thought."

Sonsee, overwhelmed by her sisters' badgering, could stand no more. "Stop it! Just — just stop it!" she sputtered, standing on shaking legs. "Someone killed our father, and all you can do is gripe because you didn't like the will." She stared around the silent room. "Don't you want to know who killed him?"

"We know who killed him," Hermann drawled, his steely eyes like the points of two cold spikes. "The question is, how long can he hide?" His chilled gaze seemed to pierce into Sonsee's mind as if he could read her every thought.

Resisting the urge to look away, Sonsee held his gaze in daring defiance. "Taylor couldn't have killed him, and if you'd just think you'd realize," she said evenly, "that he loved our father as much as I — as we did."

"Well the next time you see him, tell him the police — and I — don't believe that," Hermann said, as if there were no question that Sonsee was communicating with Taylor. "Carla witnessed him leaving the room just before she found Father." He raised his index finger. "Then she noticed him walking into the trees." He lifted his middle finger. "And if that's not enough, a gun that has been traced to Taylor was found buried out there." Hermann pointed toward the back of the house. "He was almost sent to prison twenty years ago because of drugs. Frankly . . ." Hermann glanced at the family lawyer as if he were weighing his next words. With resolve flitting across his features, he boldly continued. "Frankly, I was never convinced of his innocence then. It could very well be that he's just like his father. He hasn't changed colors in the least. He's just learned to keep his dirty work hidden — until now."

Sonsee, stunned to silence, felt as if she'd been slapped.

"And if he *did* kill my father, I will make sure he pays," Hermann continued, stabbing his index finger in the middle of his chest. "I loved that man, and —" He broke off and turned his back on Sonsee. Resolutely, Hermann propped his elbow against the white mantel and pressed his fingers against his eyes. The family's brass-framed photos above the fireplace were a hollow portrayal of harmony.

Taylor's being framed and his claims of someone shooting at him suggested only discord. The vengeance burning in Hermann's eyes underscored his threat. If he were bent on making Taylor pay, Sonsee wondered if he were the one who tried to shoot Taylor. Or maybe Hermann was trying to kill Taylor so he wouldn't be indicted himself. Perhaps the grief was all one huge act. The possible scenarios swam together in a perplexing whirlpool that filled Sonsee's mind and left her reeling with the implications.

As the tension continued to mount, Sonsee could conjure nothing to say, nothing that wouldn't add to the volatile situation. Her head held high, she marched toward the teak doors, opened them, and escaped.

Five

Sonsee strode across the foyer, trotted up the stairs, marched down the hallway, and stopped outside her bedroom. A new barrage of decisions assaulted her mind. Taylor said he would meet her here after dark. Hopefully the rest of the family would be gone by then, and she could smuggle him out under the cover of night.

Melissa Moore had said she would do anything to help, but did her "anything" include giving Taylor a spot to sleep for a few nights? As Sonsee stepped into her bedroom, she debated whether or not she should call Melissa in Oklahoma City or just show up with Taylor. Knowing Melissa, she meant what she said and would allow Taylor access to her home. But the methodical and organized doctor would be unnerved if Sonsee unexpectedly showed up with a houseguest.

"I'll call her later," Sonsee said under her breath as she closed the bedroom door.

Melissa had mentioned that she should be back home by six that evening. The six "sisters" had come to New Orleans to be with Sonsee during the funeral. They all silently stood around her at the graveside, each offering support, love, and sympathy. As in the past, Sonsee wondered what she would do without them. Certainly they had made her life richer, sweeter, and, during tragedy, easier to bear.

She leaned against the door and observed the room where she had grown up. The brass bed sat in a spacious room filled with memorabilia from her life. Carla removed numerous items from storage and redecorated the room after Sonsee graduated from college. Sonsee's doll house claimed the corner beside the windows that were covered with lace sheers. Her high school bulletin board, filled with class pictures, hung on the wall beside the cherry dresser. On the wall near the fireplace hung her first bicycle. The highboy, which matched the cherry dresser, held an abundance of Sonsee's framed photos from infancy to college graduation.

Sonsee padded toward her dresser and carefully picked up the ornate silver hand mirror that once had been her mother's. She looked into the mirror at her own freckled face, straight hair pulled back into a low ponytail, upturned nose, and close-set eyes. Then she glanced toward the nearby photo of her lovely mom, framed in silver. Sonsee favored her father more than her mother, although she did possess her mom's green eyes. She never had considered herself beautiful in the classic sense, but she had been so secure in her father's love she had been long satisfied with her physical appearance.

Not so with Alana. The thought barged in upon Sonsee and left her with new insight into the older sister. Sonsee relived the previous moments when she had wanted to lambaste Alana and Natalie for their bickering. They had behaved like two insecure children disputing over an insignificant game of marbles. When compared to the value of his life, Jacques' money meant about as much as marbles to Sonsee, and she couldn't stomach her sisters' pettiness. Then she began to wonder if Alana had ever felt emotionally secure — really secure. Most of their childhood arguments usually ended with Alana storming away, crying uncontrollably, and screaming that she hated Sonsee because she was "Daddy's favorite." The caring ministrations of Sonsee's mother did precious little to ease the wounds of Jacques' favoritism. For the first time, Sonsee wondered if Alana were still crying on the inside.

Fresh tears sprang into Sonsee's eyes. Tears of compassion. Tears of regret. Tears of repentance. As if God Himself were tugging her toward her older sister, Sonsee stepped toward her bedroom door, intent upon approaching Alana with a word of peace.

But as Sonsee's fingers closed over the cool doorknob, an icy knife of doubt pierced her soul. *What if Alana was involved in Father's murder?* All desires to extend grace vanished. Knitting her brows, she curled her fist against her tense lips and pressed until her teeth dug into tender flesh. Wave after wave of heat flooded her soul. Black, destructive heat that in no way reflected her steadfast walk with the Lord that began when she was sixteen — the year she made her parents' faith her own. Sonsee recalled that hallowed week that forever changed her life. The week when Sonsee moved from mentally accepting Jesus as the Son of God to the beginnings of deep intimacy with Him.

During a church camp, the Christian foundation her parents had laid began to surface. Sonsee felt as if a supernatural force were drawing her toward the cross of Christ. Soon she began to recognize God's handiwork in all she saw. She spent several nights staring at the star-encrusted sky and marveling at creation. She spent days entranced by the variation of God's animal kingdom. She spent hours in her dreams running toward loving, nail-pierced hands.

Finally, on the last day of church camp, Sonsee, out for a stroll in the woods, had stumbled upon an abandoned chapel. The supernatural force that had been drawing her all week urged her to open the church door. Sonsee soon found herself weeping at a dusty altar. Now those days of encounter faded in the past's distant fog.

As she turned toward her brass bed and sat on its edge, she longed for those years, for the time when life had been simple and straightforward. When Sonsee had laid everything on the altar as a sixteen year old, she never imagined life would take such a nasty turn. "Oh, God," she breathed, desperately wanting to confess her need for vengeance upon her father's murderer. Sonsee knew she should ask God to forgive her, but His complete forgiveness would require her repentance. Today, her spirit floated far from the banks of repentance, forever drifting toward the turbulent waters of revenge.

⟋

Louis Tyra restlessly paced his hotel room and awaited the important phone call from Cerberus. The New Orleans traffic just outside his window seemed a distant echo compared to the raging inferno filling his mind — an inferno feeding upon the torment of one thought, one fact: *Jacques is dead, and I still don't have the key!* Despite his and Cerberus' thorough search, they had been wrong in assuming they would find the key in Jacques' room.

Louis pinched his bottom lip and repeatedly castigated himself for his haste in killing Jacques. He should have made the old man produce the key. Instead, Jacques' surprising attempt to fight back had startled Louis and he had pulled the trigger. Even now the sword of guilt carved his soul into bloody shreds. When he started on this journey, he had never intended to kill anyone. But then Jacques had tried to kill him. Despite the old man's insistence to the contrary, Louis would never believe that the boating incident was really an accident.

But that doesn't justify murdering him. The thought that heaped distress on top of guilt

89

was spawned by the years his mother had dragged him to church. A nauseous bile rose in his throat. *What if Mom finds out?* And then there was his wife, Brenda. She believed Louis was just visiting relatives. In the past, he had lied to Brenda to cover indiscretions. Never had those improprieties included murder.

With a groan, he crammed stiff fingers into thick hair and paused by the telephone, gazing at it as if he could will the device to ring. But the phone remained mute. Any minute now his partner would call to report the results of the will reading. Louis would at last discover whether or not Jacques mentioned the treasure in the will. A part of Louis wished the treasure were openly willed to a relative. He would then leave New Orleans, go back home, declare bankruptcy, and move to Alaska . . . or Mexico . . . or Europe . . . any place to get away from this cloud of crime that seemed destined to gobble him up.

Yet a contradictory vein of thought barged in upon his regret. Louis knew exactly where the treasure rested. If only one person had to die in order for him to gain financial independence, then perhaps the crime would be worth the money. Once he settled his debts and was enjoying luxury, his conscience would undoubtedly ease and he would eventually forget that destructive moment. But the problem now rested with getting to the treasure — something that was impossible without the key.

Louis flopped back onto the bed's comforter and pulled the stale-smelling spread across him to ease the incessant chill. He grabbed the TV remote and furiously punched the buttons. His mind, still spinning with the events of the last few months, took in little of what the television offered. Instead, he thought of that day nine months ago when he found that ancient bundle of letters, yellowed with time, stuffed beneath a closet floorboard in his aging, over-mortgaged mansion. The letters, a distraught correspondence between a mother in North Carolina and her daughter in New Orleans, indicated that Louis had relatives in New Orleans — relatives who possessed a French family treasure worth millions.

According to the letters, the treasure should have belonged to Louis' great-grandfather and great-uncle. But after their father's death, the brothers feuded over the fortune, and the great-uncle proved the victor. Louis' widowed great-grandmother, Idella Marie, and her son had been forced to flee New Orleans for the East Coast where Idella's family provided a safe haven. She and her son dropped the LeBlanc name from that day forward.

The final letter reflected correspondence between the young widow and a former servant. The servant reported that Jacques' murderous great-grandfather soon lost his mind. The loyal servant had hidden the treasure in the lion's secret vault, and instructed Idella Marie to turn the brass nose in order to access the safe. Vowing loyalty to her mistress, the servant resigned her post at LeBlanc Manor then mailed the vault key to Idella Marie. Due to age, the brittle letters each suffered some form of decay. At the end of the final letter, the servant scrawled a note stating she had hidden an extra key, but the piece of paper on which the location had once been written remained no more. Despite the servant's steadfastness, Idella never claimed the treasure. Even now Louis recalled her tragic words written on a scrap of paper in which the key was wrapped, *I shall never touch the pelf that has bred such sorrow.*

When he first read the letters, Louis assumed there was no way the mansion, let alone the treasure, could still exist. But after several weeks of searching court records, he decided to see if he could locate the New Orleans mansion named LeBlanc Manor. He soon discovered from general query that many of the old mansions in the area were either erased from existence or reserved as historical sites. His hopes initially plummeted, but he chose to forge forward.

Louis' accounting firm had been on the verge of bankruptcy and the chance of finding LeBlanc Manor was well worth the time. If the treasure was still hidden, Louis hoped to take it all himself. If that didn't work, he might be able to convince the owner to split the cache with him. Even half of such a treasure would rescue Louis from the jaws of bankruptcy and gain him financial stability.

Upon inception, the plan seemed far-fetched. Louis was delighted when he discovered LeBlanc Manor still inhabited by the original family heirs, and he convinced Jacques to search for the secret vault. "The lion's secret safe," their only hint, proved all they needed. After a thorough search of the entire house, they discovered the head of a brass lion hanging over a fireplace on the deserted third floor. An inspection of the fireplace revealed the air shaft had been sealed. Strangely, a wooden panel served as the back wall. Louis recalled the moment of suspense when Jacques gripped the lion's snout and turned. After several minutes of manipulation, the aging brass responded. The nose twisted and the wooden panel struggled upward with the grate of wood against stone. The door to the steel safe awaited the key Louis had found with the letters. Even now the memory of the brief minutes Louis fondled the antique diamond necklaces, ruby-studded knives, and solid gold goblets sent a rush of anticipation down his spine, warming his gut with renewed greed. Jacques had suggested they leave the treasure in the vault and discuss their strategy.

Later that day, the day of the boating incident, Jacques and Louis agreed upon their approach. They would have the treasure appraised then decide how to divide it. But Jacques had tried to kill Louis in order to hoard the wealth. Soon Cerberus offered Louis the support needed to secure the cache. The fortune that had bred one murder more than 100 years before had now borne another.

The phone's ringing ended Louis' anticipation. His stomach tight, he sat straight up, clicked off the television, swung his feet around, and reached for the receiver. "Hello," he snapped.

"I was just checking my answering machine," Cerberus said. "Carla Jenson left a message stating she wants twice the money we paid her."

"What?" Louis barked. "But we've already given her $10,000!"

"I know. I'm beginning to wonder if we're going to have to deal with her a little more forcefully."

Louis expelled a pent-up breath, and the air hissed through his teeth like steam escaping from a pressured chamber. "I don't want to kill her, too."

"Look, don't go soft on me."

"You're a fine one to talk," Louis snapped. "*I'm* the one who killed Jacques. *You're* the one who let Carla sneak up on us!"

"Yes! And *I'm* the one who helped pull you out of the Gulf of Mexico before you drowned!"

"How could I ever forget that?" Louis asked, with a trace of resentment. Cerberus made certain Louis would never overlook the debt he owed after that near-fateful day when Jacques clobbered him on the head and pushed him into the cold ocean. Continually the good deed was held over Louis' head like an account that could never be paid.

"So what do you want me to do about Carla?" Cerberus asked, as if oblivious to Louis' criticism. "If we don't pay her, she says she's going to the police."

"Do you have another 10,000 you can get your hands on?" Louis asked, his fist curling against his knee.

The partner produced a short laugh. "I just sat through a will reading that left me rich."

"Good. Go ahead and pay her what she wants. Maybe it will keep her quiet long enough to give us time to get the treasure and leave the country." Louis, wondering how he would explain all this to his wife, stood and paced in small semicircles. "Did the will mention the treasure?"

"No. My guess is the old man was planning to give the whole thing to Sonsee behind our backs." Louis was beginning to expect the twist of hatred laced with every reference of Sonsee LeBlanc and Taylor Delaney. Thoughts of Taylor sent Louis' into another onslaught of censure. *How could I have allowed myself to be part of framing an innocent man?* Accusing Taylor of the crime had been Cerberus' idea. At the time, Louis had been so shocked by the murder that he'd readily gone along with the plan. His cohort had convinced Carla that she could either cooperate and receive 10,000 dollars for her trouble or she would find herself joining Jacques. The next morning the two coached Carla with her story, which she dutifully reported to the police. And only then did Louis understand that the .38 Cerberus supplied actually belonged to Taylor.

"Did Sonsee show any indication of knowing about the treasure?" Louis asked.

"No," Cerberus said. "But she's sneaky —"

"Well, is there any sign of activity at the vault?"

"There's no sign of disturbance that I can see. You know that every time that old panel moves, a new layer of dust falls down. Right now everything looks as it did the last time we checked it."

"Then there's the chance that Sonsee doesn't know about it." Louis' grip on the phone relaxed a fraction.

"That means nothing. She's a crafty one. She may be planning to wait until we're all gone to sneak the treasure out."

"Have you tried to open the door again without the key?"

"The only thing I haven't tried is dynamite."

Louis nodded. "And Taylor Delaney? No word from the police on him?"

"None. Our best bet is to kill him, too," Cerberus said, as if talking about crushing an annoying insect.

"Look, I never planned to kill *anybody* over this. I just came down to hopefully divide a treasure — *that's all!*" he said as images from childhood raced through his mind . . . his mother praying into the night . . . his father as church choir director . . . Louis kneeling before an altar at the tender age of ten. But somehow his spiritual life went askew during adulthood. Now, at age fifty-seven Louis couldn't remember the last time he had been in church or even considered God. Only after pulling that trigger had he been catapulted into an ocean of torment.

Following a lengthy pause, Cerberus spoke without emotion. "We have no choice. Don't you understand? If Taylor goes to trial, he might be able to convince them of his innocence. Then the investigation will start all over again and perhaps point to us. But if Taylor comes up dead, the police will stop their search for the killer."

"Yes, and they'll *start* looking for Taylor's killer," Louis snapped.

A long pause witnessed that Louis had given his companion in crime a plight to ponder. At last Cerberus spoke slowly, "We'll have to make it look like suicide."

Louis pinched his upper lip until darts of pain shot toward his nose. "Well, I say we just focus on finding the key, split the treasure, sell it to our contact, and leave the country. If we play our cards right, we might have this whole thing settled within a week."

"Okay, so where do we go from here?" Cerberus asked with a sarcastic twist to stilted words. "Since you're so smart, you tell me."

"Well, we didn't find the key in Jacques' room, and you think there's a possibility that Sonsee might be covering her knowledge of the treasure. . . ."

"Maybe we should start by searching her apartment like we planned. He might have given her the key. I made Carla take her keys from her purse, and I duplicated them. One of them will fit her home."

"Works for me," Louis said, glad to change the subject.

"Okay. I'm supposed to stay here at LeBlanc Manor for awhile to keep up appearances. I'll stay until after Sonsee leaves. That lets me keep an eye on her and see if she slips up to the vault. When she leaves, I'll pick you up at the hotel and we can watch her from there. The first chance we get, we'll search her apartment."

"Good." Louis replaced the receiver and gazed at the hand resting on the phone, a hand that had taken the life of another. A thin film of sweat formed along his palms and Louis rubbed them along the front of his shirt. The sweat thickened, feeling more like oil than perspiration. Compulsively, Louis stepped to the spotless lavatory and grabbed the small bar of hand soap. He ran the water as hot as he could endure then plunged his hands into the stream, lathering furiously. The pleasant floral scent and the feel of foam did precious little to ease the band around his heart. After three thorough scrubbings, his hands proved externally clean, but he couldn't shake the notion that some evil residue remained under his fingernails. Louis grabbed one of the complimentary toothbrushes and scoured his fingernails until one cuticle burned then produced a thin trickle of blood that mixed with the water.

After Louis rinsed his hands a final time, he turned off the water. Pressing his lips together, he forced himself not to scrub his hands anew, then he grabbed one of the numerous towels stacked on the counter. As he dried his fingers, Louis observed his countenance in the mirror. *Is this, then, the face of a murderer?* He leaned forward and peered into pale-blue eyes that seemed void of anything but turmoil. His disheveled auburn hair, streaked with gray, looked as if it were gale-tossed. Yet no wind had touched his hair that day. No winds — only torment. Torment and worry. Worry and avarice.

Six

Taylor Delaney opened the closet door and peered into the dark hallway illuminated by shafts of moonlight spilling onto the hardwood floor. The third floor remained just as uneventful, musty, and shadowed as Taylor had always remembered. Silently, he stepped into the hallway and closed the closet door. Only the faint squeak of hinges and the click of the doorknob attested to his exiting the hidden room. Stealthily, he walked across the hallway, the wooden floor creaking as he progressed.

Soon he entered a room graced with a stone fireplace. A tarnished brass lion's head was embedded below the mantel, and Taylor experienced the uncanny sensation that the lion's sunken eyes were following him. Shoving aside the irrational impression, he tread toward the window. The trellis outside the balcony was the path to Sonsee's bedroom balcony below.

He'd promised to meet her in her room

after dark and had full faith that she was dutifully awaiting him. Sonsee was forever loyal and brave, which made what Taylor was doing seem ever the more detestable. He hated involving her in this mess, but he saw no other choice.

Carefully, he picked his way through the numerous boxes and leftover furniture heaped around the room. As he reached the balcony door, Taylor debated his best mode of interaction with Sonsee. Considering the aftermath of that hug, he was hard pressed to determine what to say or how to behave. The rancher had never considered himself skilled in the knowledge of the ways of women. He had been too bent upon keeping the opposite gender at arm's length, upon insulating himself against heartache. The few romantic attachments of his adult years had been short-lived and shallow. However, the one woman he thought he understood and allowed closer than any other had managed to take him completely off guard by having the audacity to fall in love with him.

"Beats me," he muttered as his desire to kiss her haunted him.

Years had passed since Taylor had kissed a woman — not that he didn't think about the prospect on numerous occasions. However, as he matured, Taylor decided that romance only complicated his life. He had no intentions of marrying. Given that fact, any romantic relationship was highly unfair to the lady involved.

The prospect of a lasting relationship made Taylor want to run. His heart had been ripped out when his father abandoned him. Then, the first romantic attachment of his early twenties ended with a brokenhearted Taylor keeping a rejected engagement ring. At the time, he was numb with Eva's rebuff, despite the fact that Sonsee hadn't liked her from the start. Looking back, he thanked God Eva had turned down his proposal. Now Taylor had grown too circumspect to take the chance on marriage. Any attraction he might develop for Sonsee simply because he was aware of her love must never — absolutely never — be expressed.

At last his question of how to behave with Sonsee required only one answer. With renewed determination, Taylor vowed to treat Sonsee exactly the way he had always treated her. In the past, their relationship had been one big round of teasing and humor accompanied by the camaraderie of a brother and sister. The moment Taylor landed upon her balcony, he would revert to the old pattern. Furthermore, he purposed to forget that electric moment when he wanted to feel her lips on his.

As he prepared to unlock the door, the room's abundance of dust penetrated his nostrils and produced an annoying tingle. Taylor pinched his nose, yet the pinch did little to ease his need. With unsteady hands he clamped his mouth and nose in an attempt to stifle the imminent sneeze. Then he waited — waited to see if someone on the second floor might have heard even the slightest trace of sound. His spine stiff, Taylor cringed with thoughts of getting caught. Yet all remained silent, still.

Relaxing but a fraction, he firmly pushed against the aging, metal lock and opened the balcony door. The squawks of disuse mingled with chirping crickets, and Taylor stepped into the night. Sonsee's room was directly under this one. The ivy-laden trellis hung only inches away.

Accompanied by the smell of rain and the cool, summer breeze, Taylor reached out to dubiously shake the trellis. Surprisingly, the crisscrossed wood didn't budge. Apparently whoever built the thing had planned for it to stay awhile. *But it was made to hold ivy, not a 190-pound man.* Taylor considered taking his chances by sneaking down the stairway and walking the few feet to Sonsee's room. *But if anyone saw me . . .*

With renewed determination, he subjected the trellis to yet another severe shake then straddled the balcony banister as if it were a horse. Carefully he hung onto the wide banister and leaned out far enough to catch a brief glimpse of Sonsee's balcony, about ten feet below him. Taylor decided to use the trellis only as a support until his feet could reach the top of Sonsee's banister and he could slip onto the balcony.

His heart pounding, he peered to the ground three stories below, lighted with decorative landscaping lamps. The attractive, oval swimming pool featured a wide, concrete walkway. A walkway that Taylor might easily land upon. A thin film of sweat popped out on his brow.

Shooting a prayer heavenward, Taylor tightened his jaw and reached for the trellis. *Nothing ventured, nothing gained.* Yet the chirping crickets chanted like a Greek chorus cautioning their tragic hero. Taylor swung out, found footholds, and took three tremulous steps downward. The trellis creaked under his weight. The sound of splintering wood twisted Taylor's stomach into a tight coil and perspiration trickled down his temple. The trellis, accompanied by the swish and tear of ivy, swayed from the house. His legs trembling, Taylor stifled a yell as gravity threatened to tug him toward the pool walkway. He glanced downward to Sonsee's balcony then up to the third floor balcony. At the level of his descent, the third floor balcony rails were now out of reach, yet Sonsee's balcony was not quite close enough for a sure jump. As the trellis continued its wavering, Taylor chose to take his chances on Sonsee's balcony.

Gasping, he released the trellis and flung himself forward. The banister slammed against his midsection. With an explosive swoosh, most of the air left his lungs. Accompanied by a resounding series of bumps and rumbles, he toppled head first onto Sonsee's balcony. Biting his lip to stop the moans, Taylor clutched his gut and rolled onto his side, his head pounding from the force of his skull striking wood. He squinted as a pair of tennis shoes neared his face.

"Taylor?" Sonsee whispered, kneeling at his side. "Are you okay?"

"Yeah, sure, Red," he said through a few gasps. "I just fell off the trellis and onto my h-head. I-I've never been better."

"Ha, ha," she said without mirth. "Think you can crawl into my room?"

"Sure. I'll just slither right — right in there," Taylor said. At least he had the presence of mind to adhere to his plan to revert back to their old behavioral pattern.

Taylor managed to gain his footing and hobble past the brass bed. He collapsed in the corner chair. His aching gut would undoubtedly sport a few bruises by the morning. "Just for the record," he said as Sonsee hovered over him. "I don't recommend your ever climbing on that trellis. *It ain't made for people!*"

"Don't worry. That's not on my list of things to do." Her gaze diverted, Sonsee supplied a footrest and helped Taylor prop his feet atop it.

"Didn't think it was, but I never know about you, Red. Sometimes you surprise me." As the words left his mouth, Taylor wished he had never said them. Those words were too close to the truth. Never had he been so shocked as the night he had, quite by chance, caught Sonsee staring at him across that Hawaiian restaurant. Left alone by Jacques, they had ducked into a local restaurant to get out of the rain. Deciding they were hungry anyway, the two had placed their order for Hawaiian cuisine. Soon, Taylor excused himself to the men's room and just happened to glance back and see the adoration spilling from Sonsee's face. He had spent extra minutes in the men's room trying to convince himself he had imagined the whole thing. When he stepped back to the table, she seemed the same ol' Sonsee he had known his whole life. Yet that moment began the growth of Taylor's suspicion about her true feelings.

Sonsee's practical voice jolted him back to the present dilemma. "Well, where do we go from here?"

Taylor glanced up to see her observing him, her green eyes intense when contrasted with the pink cotton shirt she wore. *Whoever said redheads don't look good in pink must have missed meeting Sonsee,* he thought. Never had he seen her look so appealing. Once again his masculine instincts took precedence over his former vows and he wondered . . .

"We can't just sit here all night, you know," she said, sounding more like an army sergeant than a friend.

"Well excuse me while I try to recuperate from having my guts slammed into my spine," Taylor drawled, a tad bit exasperated with her tactics. *Okay, I'm a lot exasperated,* he admitted. And he was just as aggravated with his own reaction to Sonsee's slender figure in jeans as he was with her brusque treatment.

"Does it hurt too terribly?" she asked, her brows knitting.

"Well, what do you think?" he groused. "I jumped off the trellis and landed smack in the middle of the balcony banister." Taylor, his stomach still aching, purposed to address his worn boots rather than be exposed to tender eyes filled with care.

"I'd better take a look." Carefully she examined his head and checked his ribs. "You'll live, but you're sure going to be sore. Want me to get you some aspirin? I've got some in my suitcase." The soft concern in her voice belied her previously firm tone.

Taylor, despite his determination to avoid eye contact, found himself gazing into her eyes — searching eyes filled with compassion. Compassion and fear. Fear and love. Feeling as if he were losing his grip on logic, Taylor wondered if Sonsee would feel as good in his arms now as she had that afternoon. Once again he pondered what her lips would taste like against his.

Silently Sonsee strolled toward the bathroom. In seconds she was back with a glass of water and two tablets. "Here. Take these. As soon as you're better, we'll talk about how to get you out of here," she said, the practical edge back to her voice.

Glad for the diversion, Taylor swallowed the pills and downed the glass of water. "I didn't get a chance this afternoon to tell you about the visits," he said, resolved to stop his musings about Sonsee. *I will not use her just because I'm getting older and . . . and lonely,* he thought. *Yes, lonely.* Lately, Taylor had found himself working until dark because he didn't want to spend the evening by himself in that massive ranch house Jacques had helped him build. Now he wondered what he had been thinking when he built such a home. All he needed was a cabin — a cabin big enough for one.

"The visits?" Settling on the edge of her bed, she picked at the appliquéd flowers on the sea-green comforter.

For the first time, Taylor noticed that her almond-shaped, emerald eyes appeared sunken in her freckled, ivory face. Undoubtedly she had been crying. Taylor wished he could somehow ease her pain, but that was impossible. Only time would heal her pain. Time and God. But then, God hadn't done much to heal Taylor's pain. Thoughts of his father's desertion still tore at him. Over the years, the pain had diminished somewhat, but healing remained a fantasy.

The Lord will heal you, Taylor, if you will be still long enough to let Him. His mother's words increased his tension. Words she'd spoken before the trip to Egypt. Words she'd said she wanted to speak for years. As Taylor dashed aside her claim then, he shoved it aside now.

"What visits?" Sonsee asked again. "Are you going to tell me or sit there and stare at your boots all night?"

"That's the thing I like about you, Red," Taylor drawled. "All charm and discretion."

She rolled her eyes. "Like you ever won Mr. Congeniality."

"Hey! I'm the personification of congeniality," he said with a smirk.

"Yeah, right, and I'm Little Red Riding Hood."

"You could be. All you need is the cape, a basket full of goodies, one grandma, and one big bad wolf," he said, then added a long, "Grrrr . . ."

"And all you need is a gentle reminder that we don't have all night. We need to get you out of here." Sonsee glanced around as if someone might be hiding in her room.

"Bummer." Taylor snapped his fingers. "Totally slipped my mind."

"Oh? What's *really* going on inside that head of yours, Taylor Delaney?" she asked. Her searching gaze seemed to penetrate his soul.

Taylor glanced away. He had already been vulnerable with Sonsee once today, and that was enough vulnerability for months. He purposed to reinforce his emotional wall and resorted to stating the facts about the recent visits to his ranch by two of Sonsee's siblings.

"Within the last few weeks, Natalie and Alana have both visited my ranch," he said.

"What? I didn't think either of them ever came near you!" Sonsee scooted back on the bed, crossed her legs, propped her elbow on her knee, and placed her chin in hand as if she were intent upon absorbing Taylor's every word.

"They don't. But it appears Alana was in the red."

"She asked for money?"

"Yep. Seems Alana's latest interest payment from her trust fund was playing out, and she needed some extra cash," Taylor said, recalling Alana's well-placed hints.

"Probably *Nick* needed the extra cash."

"My thoughts exactly. And she wouldn't go to Uncle Jacques because, as we all know, he was against her marrying Nick in the first place."

"I think that's the only reason she married him. Seemed she was always trying to do something to either get Father's attention or make him miserable." Sonsee paused and observed the lampstand near Taylor's chair. "You know, for the first time today, I saw Alana in a different light. I . . . um . . . you know, Father always favored me over her and Natalie. I guess over Hermann, too, but it was the most obvious with Alana and Natalie. I don't know . . ." Sonsee sighed. "I guess for the first time today, I put myself in Alana's shoes and figured I might feel and act exactly the same way she does if I were her."

"Dealing with a father's rejection is not a fun experience," Taylor said, his thoughts turning to the day he realized his dad was not coming home. He had been twelve — only twelve — standing in the front yard, waiting on his dad to arrive from work. Looking back, Taylor wasn't even sure why he was waiting for his father. T. C. Delaney never did much with his son anyway. But he was still "Dad." He was still around — until that horrid day Taylor's teary-eyed mother had related the cold facts of her husband's desertion.

"So do you think Alana could be in on the murder?" Sonsee queried.

"She could be." Taylor glanced at the cherry dresser laden with photos of Sonsee's mother.

"Did you give her the money?"

"No way. She's crazy if she thinks I'm going to dish out what I've worked hard to get in order to support Nick's habits. If she really needed money for food or a real emergency, then that would be different. But the way I see it, if she and Nick want more money to blow, they can get extra jobs."

Sonsee nodded. "I think Nick is like Hermann. He enjoys gambling too much. I honestly don't think Father ever found out about Hermann's gambling."

"I know," Taylor said. "And if he had, it probably would have killed him. He really loved Hermann."

"Yes," Sonsee said. "I just wish . . ." She paused as a variety of conflicting thoughts played across her features. "On one hand, I'm wishing that he had shown as much love for Natalie and Alana. On the other hand, I'm really fighting some negative feelings for them. If they were involved in

Father's murder . . ." Her voice, full of menace, trailed off into thoughtful silence.

Taylor, leaning forward, placed his feet on the floor, and started to prop his elbows on his knees. He groaned, then roughly rubbed his face. In reality, he was tempted to tug his hair out by the roots. Whether he wanted to admit it or not, he had experienced the exact emotions Sonsee was manifesting — emotions that suggested he should repay the murderer with the same punishment he or she had dealt Jacques. Never had Taylor experienced such a ricochet of grief and panic and revenge, all reverberating within him like a gunshot echoing down a canyon.

"Anyway, that was Alana's visit," he said, his voice dull. "And Natalie and Rafael showed up about five days before her."

"What did they want?"

"A horse. They wanted to buy one of my stallions for breeding."

"Did you sell it to them?"

"Sure. They were willing to pay my price. Besides," he said, "the Lord has helped me see that I need to try as much as possible to repair my relationship with them — all of them. Anyway, I wound up inviting them to dinner. I also invited Alana to dinner. I wasn't rude to her about the money; I just suggested that she should consult with Uncle Jacques." Taylor paused, reflecting upon the irony of his invitations. If one of them had killed Jacques and blamed Taylor, then his invitation meant he was now a laughingstock.

"Do you think Alana knew you knew she wouldn't go to Father?"

"Well, yes." His lips twisted. "That's probably the reason she didn't hang around for dinner. Rafael and Natalie did stay. And I really tried to enjoy their company and do whatever I could to make peace. I'm so tired of all the undercurrents in this family —"

"I understand what you're saying. I feel the exact same way. After the will reading, I almost approached Alana in an attempt to make peace, but —" Sonsee stopped and stared at the floor, her features shadowed with uncertainty. Uncertainty and fear. Fear and foreboding. "So I guess Natalie and Rafael had access to the gun?" she asked, abruptly changing the subject.

"Well, they were in my house, so I guess they did."

"Just like Alana. Don't you think it's strange that they showed up so closely to each other?"

"Yep."

"Do you think they might be in on it together?"

"I don't know. I know Alana needed money, so she'd have a motive. But what would Natalie's be? And why trash his room? Whoever tore everything up was looking for something more than just what was in the will."

"Yeah, and I'm wondering if the will covered everything." Sonsee stared at Taylor and bit her thumbnail.

"So what happened at the will reading?"

"Oh, I guess I should tell you — I now own LeBlanc Manor and four million. You now own the California ranch and four million," she said as if she were stating the contents of a grocery list.

Taylor whistled. "You're kidding! He gave me the same as you?"

"Yes." Sonsee didn't blink.

Another thought struck Taylor. A thought that swept aside all astonishment. "Oh, great!" He slammed his hand against his knee and stood. "That's just great! Now it probably looks like I had all sorts of motives to kill your father — about four million of them!"

"That basically sums up what Hermann said." Sonsee wearily pulled away the band holding back her hair. The auburn locks

118

fell around her shoulders, gleaming like the final rays of sun on an autumn horizon.

Taylor crammed his hands into his jeans pockets and paced toward the balcony doors. The ache in his abdomen and head reminded him to keep movement to a minimum.

Sonsee whisked by him and snapped the drapes shut. "You shouldn't stand near the window," she said, her lips tight. "Anyone could be out on the lawn."

Taylor rubbed his eyes. "You're right. I wasn't thinking. I'm addled, to say the least."

"Listen." She laid a hand on his arm. "Why don't we talk about how we're going to get you out of here. We can discuss our problems in the car."

"Where are you planning to take me, anyway?" Taylor asked, stepping away from her touch. With every passing minute, his vulnerability seemed to increase tenfold. Any contact with Sonsee drastically increased his chances of throwing himself at her mercy, hauling her to him, and begging her to ease his mental torment.

"My friend Melissa offered to help me in any way she could. She lives in Oklahoma City. I thought I'd drive you there tonight."

"She's one of your six sisters, right?"

Taylor drew imaginary quotes in the air.

Sonsee nodded. "She's the doctor. You met her at Mom's funeral."

"Does she know we're coming?" Taylor asked, vaguely recalling a dark-headed woman with penetrating eyes.

"No, not yet. I'm planning to drive to my apartment and call her from there."

"Does she know I'm running from the law?"

"More or less."

"And she doesn't mind my staying with her?"

"She said she'd do anything to help." Sonsee lifted her chin a fraction. "I would say this falls into the category of anything."

Taylor, filled with renewed appreciation, held Sonsee's gaze until he felt as if their spirits were melting together. In the midst of all this mess, one person stood faithful. One person. His Sonsee. "You have no idea how much I appreciate all this, Sonsee. Already, I owe you my life. I . . ."

Erecting a shield between them, Sonsee stiffened. Her expression hardened. She glanced down and stepped away. "Of course, it's the least I can do," she said in a strained whisper as she bent to close her suitcase sitting near the dresser.

Taylor groped for something else to say.

Something light and funny. Something that would reflect their former relationship. But he was beginning to wonder if all bets were off regarding the Sonsee he thought he knew so well. That Sonsee seemed to have been replaced by a stranger — a stranger who loved him. He thought about her earlier challenge, *And what's really going on inside that head of yours, Taylor Delaney?* The truth was, he didn't quite understand everything that was going on inside his head . . . or his heart.

"I've been thinking," she continued practically as she zipped the suitcase and stood it on end, "how would you feel about sneaking into Father's room before we leave. Maybe we could find something that would give us a lead."

"But how? I can't exactly go traipsing down the hall."

"My room and Father's share the same sitting room, remember? We can just go through there." She pointed toward the doorway.

"Okay," Taylor said hesitantly, "but I'm nervous about this. I want to get out of here as soon as possible."

"And I want you out of here as soon as possible. But whoever killed Father was looking for something. If we find it —"

"That's one more step toward finding the murderer," Taylor said. "You're smart, Red."

"Don't call me Red!" she snapped, whirling to face him. "You know th-that has always bugged me."

"Sorry," Taylor raised his hands. "I had no idea it was such a sensitive issue."

"And while you're at it you can stop looking at me like . . . like . . . like . . ." She sputtered to a standstill, her cheeks flushing.

"Like what?"

"Like there could ever be anything between us," she forced out, her voice thick with tears. "I'm not some — some plaything you can flirt with just because you're feeling grateful or because — because —" Her outburst came to a halt, and Sonsee spun to grip the edge of the dresser, her head bent.

Taylor floundered for words, only to find annoyance. He grabbed the nape of his neck. "Look, Sonsee," he said, his voice tight. "The last few days have been some of the worst of my life. Give me a break, will ya?"

Without so much as a glance his way, Sonsee stepped from the bedroom and into the sitting room. The faint click of a door attested to her entering her father's room.

Stifling a pent-up growl, Taylor rubbed his face then looked upward, as if the heavens could somehow deliver him from the precarious situations that had been thrust upon him. But, as with the last few days, the heavens seemed silent.

My God, my God, why have You forsaken me? The words spun around his numb mind until he ached with their significance. Never had Taylor felt so spiritually, emotionally, and physically isolated. For the first time in his adult life, he was dependent — completely dependent — upon another human being. And perhaps upon the mercies of God . . . a God that seemed to have removed Himself to another universe.

Seven

Taylor stepped through the spacious sitting room and gently pushed on the door that led to Jacques' room, filled with the finest in teak furnishings. The faint smell of hair tonic still hung in the air, engulfing Taylor in an onslaught of fresh grief. Only a few nights ago he had sat across from his beloved uncle and interacted in a challenging game of chess. Now the chessmen lay scattered against the far wall — scattered like the pieces of Taylor's life.

Warily, Taylor glanced toward the hallway door to see it securely locked. The heavy drapes were drawn. And Sonsee, her back to him, sat on the floor, sorting through the contents of Jacques' disheveled nightstand. Her telltale sniffles attested to her tears.

He grasped both sides of the doorframe and debated what to say. His previous decision to mimic the banter they had once shared now mocked him. Finally, Taylor saw that Sonsee and he could never go back to the way things were before he knew of her love. Never. A fog of guilt, heavy and dense, settled upon him. A guilt that seemed an appropriate addition to the night. *Why not add a dash of guilt to the whole mess?* he thought sarcastically. *I've felt every other negative emotion known to mankind in the last three days anyway.*

"I'm sorry," Taylor muttered, groping to understand this woman he thought he knew better than any other. But all chances of understanding her now escaped him. Her hair, like copper satin, glistened on her shoulders, and Taylor rubbed his thumb against his fingers imagining how the tresses would feel beneath his touch. His stomach clenched, and he pressed his fingers and thumb against his eyes.

Only the Lord knew how empty his life would be without Sonsee. Despite her quirks, she was his dearest friend. For years they had virtually read each other's mind. Now Taylor had no idea what was going on within her.

Abruptly Sonsee scrubbed at her cheeks then turned to face him. "Are you going to get busy or just stand there?" she snapped.

"I said I was sorry," Taylor repeated, not

really sure why he was apologizing.

"Me, too," she said evenly. "Now see what you can find, and let's get out of here before we get caught."

The pressure of the last few days plus the gut-wrenching effect of entering Jacques' room swirled together with fresh frustration and irritation. A thin film of sweat burst out along his upper lip, and Taylor took a step toward Sonsee. Pressing his lips together, he pivoted to face the polished dresser. But in his attempt to steel himself against verbally confronting Sonsee, he instead faced a full view of himself in the mirror. The eyes that peered back at him were those of an angry, distrustful stranger. The face, darkened with three days of stubble, appeared haggard and drawn. The dark circles under his eyes added to his exhausted demeanor.

In an attempt to avoid his own bleak reflection, Taylor dropped to his knees and began furiously fumbling through the clothes in the dresser drawers.

"All I've found over here is a bunch of old prescription receipts." Sonsee's cool voice reflected little of their strained interaction.

"Nothing but a bunch of old boxer shorts with holes in 'em over here. Good grief. I bought him six pairs for Christmas. Where are they?"

"Voila."

Taylor glanced over his shoulder.

Sonsee held up two packages of unopened boxer shorts. "He must've liked the old ones better." She ducked her head as a tear streamed down her cheek.

Earlier, Taylor had told Sonsee to give him a break. She probably needed a break or two herself. Neither of them was exactly stable at the moment. With determination he decided to pretend she never accused him of using her as a plaything. Taylor closed the top drawer and went to the next one — a jumble of undershirts, socks, and a few personal letters.

"All this stuff's an infernal mess," Sonsee muttered.

"Yeah. I guess Carla must've tried to straighten up after the investigation and just crammed everything back into the drawers."

"That must have been a big job. This room was a disaster area."

"I keep wondering what the person was after." Taylor tried to shove the second drawer back into place but something obstructed it. Pulling the drawer completely out, he bent over and peered into the dresser's dark, vacant cavity. Nothing.

"What's the matter?" Sonsee asked, scooting behind him.

"I don't know. The drawer won't close." Taylor set the drawer on the floor and reached into the dresser to skim the wood's smooth surface. "Probably something caught in here."

His fingers encountered a metal object lodged at the back, right where the drawer would rest. "Aha! Found the culprit." Straightening, he produced an antique key, large and unpolished, with a piece of clear tape dangling from it.

Sonsee squinted. "True. He was a pack rat. But an old key? What did he want with a key? This looks like something somebody would have carried across the frontier in 1803. It can't possibly fit anything in LeBlanc Manor."

Taylor dropped to his knees and studied the dresser's cavity. "He must've taped it in here somehow." A hint of white claimed his attention.

"But why?"

"Look at this." Taylor removed a piece of paper from the drawer, and the hair on the back of his neck prickled as if they were approaching unknown danger. A small piece of folded paper. That's all. But as he pulled away the broken strip of tape and began unfolding it, his hands shook.

"What's it say?" Sonsee knelt beside him.

"Sonsee," Taylor began reading his uncle's almost illegible scrawl, "this is the key I told you about. Be careful."

Sonsee grabbed the paper. "He never told me about a key. This doesn't make sense," she said as all vestiges of their former tension dissolved.

Taylor rubbed the rusting key between his forefinger and thumb. A heavy key. A simple key. A key that looked as if it should have hung from the chain of a dungeon master in an old black-and-white thriller.

"And what's the deal with this map? Look." Sonsee, shoving the paper in front of him, pointed to the center. "This is apparently the third floor. And it looks like there's some kind of hidden vault in this room. There." Her finger trailed the series of arrows Jacques had drawn.

Taylor followed Sonsee's unpolished fingernail as it traced a crude drawing of the hallway and the room directly above Sonsee's. An "X" marked the fireplace.

"You know," Taylor said, "when I was a kid, I went into that room off and on all the time. Other than tonight, I haven't been in the room for years. I never thought much about that fireplace, but there's this really strange brass lion right in the middle below the mantel."

"Yeah, I know. That thing always gave me the creeps. Look." Sonsee bent over the map. "There's a scribbled message in the margin. 'Turn the lion's nose,' " she read.

"Weird," he mumbled. "The third floor seems to be full of all sorts of secrets."

"You got that right." Sonsee nibbled one of her fingernails. "Should we check out this room tonight or wait?" she asked, her brow wrinkling.

A faint knock next door startled them back to the dangers of the moment. Sonsee grabbed Taylor's arm. His every muscle tensed. They shared a hunted gaze then scrambled to their feet.

The knock came again, this time accompanied by Hermann's calling out a soft, "Sonsee. Are you in there?"

"It's Hermann," she whispered, as if Taylor needed an explanation. "He's at my bedroom door."

Within seconds, the doorknob on Jacques' room rattled. Taylor's heart raced.

"Sonsee?" Hermann's voice was accompanied by an impatient rap on the door.

"Yes, coming," she squeaked out.

"I'll be on the balcony," Taylor muttered next to her ear.

"No," she mouthed back, her eyes wide. "Get in my closet — at the very back," her whisper was barely discernible. "There-there's a stack of boxes you can hide behind."

With a slight nod, Taylor swiveled, but a hand on his arm stopped him. Sonsee thrust Jacques' note into his grip. Grasping the paper and key, he silently rushed back toward her room.

Sonsee swallowed against her quivering throat and forced her face into an impassive mask. She unlocked the bedroom door and opened it to face Hermann's impatient demeanor. Except for his light-brown hair and keen gray eyes, Hermann favored Jacques as much as Sonsee did. His long, square jaw line, prominent nose, and eyes topped with heavy brows spoke of a man of determination. Perhaps that was part of the reason Jacques loved Hermann so much. Not only was Hermann his only son, but he also represented Jacques in resemblance and disposition.

"What are you doing in here?" Hermann blurted.

"I was just going through some of-of Father's things," Sonsee said, turning to glance over her shoulder. *I do own this house now, remember?* She suppressed the caustic remark as it poised itself on her tongue. A pointed question followed: *Did you kill Father?* Sonsee's hand tightened on the doorknob.

The hard edge in Hermann's eyes softened a bit as he looked past Sonsee and into the room. "I just came to say goodbye. Are you leaving soon or will you be staying to settle up your portion of the estate?" he asked, his voice kinder than at the will reading.

"I'm leaving tonight." A slight tremor raced down her spine as she contemplated the wisdom of telling Hermann when she was leaving. She was more ready to believe Hermann was trying to keep tabs on her than really wanting to bid farewell. Sonsee recalled his earlier hints about her knowing Taylor's location, and she wondered if he planned to watch her. She shuddered. While awaiting Taylor's arrival in her room, Sonsee had avoided contact with her siblings. Other than grabbing a quick snack in the kitchen, she'd spent the evening in her room. She didn't even know whether Alana and Natalie had left.

"I'll be back in a few days," she added, trying to sound as natural as possible. "I left instructions with Carla to keep the house running as smoothly as possible until I come back." That brief, strained conversation took place in the kitchen when Sonsee retrieved her evening snack. Carla, keeping her eyes diverted, had readily agreed to Sonsee's every request. Sonsee didn't mention that Carla would no longer have a job when all this mess was cleared up. "Right now I just need to get out of here and do some thinking."

"Yes, I understand," Hermann said.

"What about Alana and Natalie and Rafael? Are they still here?" Sonsee stifled the inner turmoil that surfaced with every contemplation of her closest relatives.

"Yes. Alana is leaving in the morning." Hermann eyed her. "Natalie and Rafael are planning to leave within the hour. They've been with Mr. Aster most of the evening, trying to settle everything they can."

"I see," she said. A pause, awkward and heavy, ensued. Sonsee refused to look Hermann in the eyes another second. She sensed the intensity of his scrutiny as if he were marching though the corridors of her mind, thrusting a penetrating light into every crevice, probing for a clue that would reveal Taylor's location. Inside she squirmed as if she were once again an adolescent testing boundaries while her big brother looked over her shoulder.

"You know, Sonsee," he began, his voice subdued and cunning, "if you *are* helping to hide Taylor, it's against the law. You could even land in prison."

Forcing herself to maintain composure, Sonsee masked her expression and dared to take on the full force of her brother's appraisal. Refusing to look away, she mustered every scrap of bravado and exposed him to the same hardened evaluation he dealt her. Taylor called it the "pit bulldog look." Sonsee's mother had ominously dubbed it the "LeBlanc glare." However, neither Alana nor Natalie possessed the strength to produce what came with little effort from Jacques, Hermann, and Sonsee.

At last the corner of Hermann's mouth lifted in something close to a grimace. "If he did kill Father, I'll never forgive him." Hermann's voice never fluctuated. "Perhaps you can pass along that message for me." A trace of hatred played upon his features like an imp dancing before the lake of fire.

Once again, Sonsee's suspicions wavered. *Would Hermann be so passionate about avenging Father's death if he is the murderer?* The question that seemed to point to her brother's innocence was soon followed by another vein of thought. *But what if the whole thing is an act? This is the person who hid a gambling addiction from his own father for a decade. If he could do that, couldn't he pretend grief and the need for revenge?*

"Keep in touch!" Hermann shot back as he walked toward the stairway.

Sonsee maintained her composure until she closed and relocked the door. Then, she collapsed against it, quivering as if she were a spent race horse. Only one thought bore through her mind: *I've got to get Taylor out of here!*

She dashed through the sitting room, into her bedroom. Sonsee threw open the closet door, snapped on the light, and stepped into the spacious storage area. She moved toward the stack of boxes at the back of the cluttered closet, initially expecting Taylor to step from behind them. Instead, she remained alone. Sonsee glanced behind the boxes to confirm her suspicions. Her mind raced with all sorts of scenarios. Perhaps Hermann had diverted her while someone else sneaked into her room and nabbed Taylor. Panting, Sonsee stumbled out of the closet and frantically looked at the bedroom door. It remained locked. Her frazzled nerves relaxed but a fraction, and she hissed a strained, "Taylor?"

Wondering if perhaps he had crawled under her bed, she stepped toward it, only to notice the drapes had been pulled open about six inches. Sonsee remembered closing them only minutes before she and Taylor entered her father's room. Assuming Taylor must have stepped onto the balcony, as he originally mentioned, Sonsee twisted the French door's cold knob and entered the night, heavy with the scent of earth and the aftermath of rain.

"Taylor?" she hissed again, straining to find even a trace of his form in the shadows. No sign of him appeared. Her heart pounding, Sonsee walked the few feet to the banister and examined the ground below, expecting to find Taylor's still form plastered against the concrete surrounding the pool. Yet nothing unusual posed a clue. The customary outline of the manicured grounds remained the same. She hastened back into her room, grabbed her purse and reached for the car keys she had placed on the dresser. The keys were gone.

Carla Jenson was finishing with kitchen duty in the pristine, white kitchen when she heard the thud just outside the dining room window. Cautiously she stepped into the dining room, clicked off the light, and moved toward the window. She inched aside the lace sheers and hand-painted blind just enough to glimpse the form of a man, recovering his balance, in the glow of the pool's decorative lights. At last, Taylor Delaney straightened, scrutinized the shadowed lawn, then sprinted from the house toward the collection of cars parked in the back driveway.

Her limbs trembling, Carla released the blind and darted back into the kitchen. Glancing over her shoulder, she closed the swinging door and collapsed at the wrought-iron table near the window, a table where she had served Taylor and Sonsee coffee on numerous occasions. The tormenting guilt that increased with every hour descended upon her. She silently weeped into her work-worn hands. She had thought the second bundle of money that had been placed under Jacques' mattress would prove a balm for her conscience. Instead, the money had done nothing to ease her mind. Indeed, it had increased her anxiety tenfold. For with the money came a note. A note that threatened her life.

Carla debated her options, only to realize she had no choices. She had incriminated an innocent man — a man she respected. She lied to the authorities in order to save her own life. With horror she recalled the moment she stepped into Jacques' room, holding the usual tray, laden with his nightly tumbler of ice water, cholesterol medication, and vitamins. She had happened upon a scene that was far from routine. And the perpetrators had demanded that she either assist them or die on the spot. Carla had also been forced to agree to stay and carry on her normal activities. Cerberus and the accomplice insisted any deviation from routine would increase suspicion. Once her story was released to the police, the felons also forced her to agree to report any sign of Taylor to them.

Her tongue thick from weeping, Carla sponged her face with the end of her spotless white apron. She recalled the seconds in which she had encountered Sonsee as she stepped from the stairs and into the anteroom, then later, when they had briefly spoken in the kitchen. Both times, the young woman exposed her to a gaze that yelled, "How could you?" And those breathless seconds had confirmed Carla's every suspicion. She might be able to fool the police and the rest of the LeBlanc family with her story about Taylor Delaney, but she would never fool Sonsee.

With a groan, Carla wrung her hands until her fingers felt as if she were twisting them off. She had promised those heathens she would tell them if she saw Taylor, but . . . but . . . The vision of Sonsee's heartbreak as she stood at the base of the stairs once more danced through Carla's mind.

The kitchen door swung inward and the one person Carla wanted to avoid stepped over the threshold, observing her with calculating eyes. The door closed behind Cerberus with a nerve-rending sigh, and Carla stiffened under an evil gaze. The criminal had chosen the code name Cerberus as a means of communication without incrimination. The name had intrigued Carla so she researched its roots. According to Greek mythology, Cerberus was the three-headed dog who guarded the gates of Hades. The image had only intensified her horror, and Carla wished she had never learned the meaning.

"Are you alone?" the dog hissed.

"Yes." Carla gulped.

"Did you find your money?"

She nodded.

"Do you understand the terms?"

Carla produced a barely discernible nod.

"I just want to make sure you know there will be no more money. Got it?"

"Yes."

"And if by chance you happen to see Taylor Delaney and don't report it to us . . ." Cerberus left the rest menacingly clear.

A vision of Taylor running across the back lawn only minutes before flitted through Carla's mind. However, a new resolve settled upon her. From somewhere within, she tapped into a courage she had never before experience. "I understand."

Eight

Sonsee raced through the damp grass toward her Honda parked beside Rafael and Natalie's gold Mercedes. She pulled up on the door handle to find the vehicle locked. Frantically, Sonsee tapped on the window, hoping her suspicions were confirmed and Taylor was inside. The front door popped open as if it had a mind of its own. Sonsee whipped open the door, plopped into the driver's seat, and dropped her purse in the passenger seat.

"Hi. What took you so long?" Taylor's mocking whisper floated from behind.

She glanced over her shoulder. He awkwardly lay in the backseat, his lips twisted in a wry grin. She slammed the door. "What did you do?" she whispered. "Jump over the balcony?"

"If only I were so accomplished," he drawled. "Actually, I hung onto the balcony and dangled over the side, then I dropped down. Not exactly the stuff that

Superman is made of, but I made it to the car."

Sonsee rolled her eyes. "Well, you scared me to death," she said over her shoulder. "When I looked for you in the closet and you weren't there, I thought for a minute somebody had nabbed you."

"Not yet, anyway."

The silent pause that followed ominously underscored Taylor's precarious circumstances.

"Give me my keys." Sonsee twisted around and extended her hand, steeling herself against even the slightest contact with Taylor. She was more than a little embarrassed to interact with him after her unexpected outburst in her bedroom.

"Here's the key we found as well," he said.

As their fingers brushed, Sonsee's face heated, and her hasty words replayed in her mind: *I'm not some plaything you can flirt with just because you're feeling grateful or because* . . . She had been going to say *because you found out I'm in love with you,* but had stopped herself before the words tumbled out. Then, when in her father's room, she had been so uptight she'd cried. Her tears had only increased her anger. Sonsee prided herself on being in control of her emotions and spontaneous tears did not fit her self image. Neither did being eternally embarrassed. She had no idea where her relationship with Taylor might be heading, but she certainly did not want him to feel as if she were manipulating him into an admission he was far from feeling. She was not so blind that she didn't recognize the spark of attraction in Taylor's eyes. However, she was also not so gullible that she thought for one minute Taylor Delaney was ready to give his heart to anyone — including her.

Silently she tucked the antique key into her purse, then inserted the car key into the ignition and started the vehicle. Right now she needed to get Taylor to Melissa's. The rest of this mess could be analyzed later.

"Aren't you going to put your suitcase in?" Taylor asked.

"Oh, no," Sonsee groaned, resting her head against the seat. "I left it sitting in my room." She rubbed her eyes and shook her head. "I can't believe . . ." she muttered, turning off the engine.

"Want me to go get it for you?" Taylor asked.

"Ha, ha, very funny," Sonsee shot back. "I'll be back."

"I'll be waiting." The note of humor in Taylor's voice belied the grimness of their situation.

Without a response, Sonsee retrieved her keys from the ignition, got out, locked the door, and slammed it behind her. Within a matter of minutes, she was once again poised at the front door of LeBlanc Manor ready to exit. This time with her suitcase in tow. Yet the faint sound of feminine weeping flowing from her father's den made her hesitate. Something in the deepest recesses of her soul tugged her toward the crying woman. Yet logic insisted she must hurry back to Taylor. Besides, the one crying most likely was either Natalie, Carla, or Alana. Sonsee didn't want to chat with any of them. Still, a gentle pressure in her spirit suggested she investigate.

Leaving her suitcase by the door, Sonsee walked across the Persian rug and hovered but a second outside the carved teak doors. Silently, she grasped the knob, turned it, and opened the door but an inch or two. The weeping now struck her with clearer intensity as she peered across the classically decorated room to see Alana, slumped on the settee near the imposing grandfather clock. On the end table numerous photos formed a mirage of familial

144

harmony. The plump Alana, dressed in slinky house pajamas, clutched one particular photo to her breast. Through her tears, she pleaded, "Oh, Daddy, Daddy, if-if only I had ev-ever known you. I can't even remember my real — real m-mother and you — you — all I ever wanted was your love and approval."

Sonsee recognized the frame. It held a snapshot of her and her father, taken in the rose garden. To Sonsee's knowledge, there were no photos of Alana and Jacques together. None. The reality struck Sonsee like a knife in the heart and brought back her former reflections. The same man that doted on Sonsee left Alana feeling as if she didn't even know him. *Father, how could you?* the mental accusation came from nowhere. In its wake, a fresh bath of tears stung Sonsee's eyes. Shortly after the will reading, she'd almost approached Alana in an attempt to begin to reconcile their rift. Yet her own fears had stopped her. Fears of Alana being involved in the murder. Fears that she could not maintain a forgiving spirit, if indeed Alana were the killer.

But would a killer grieve as Alana was grieving?

As if she sensed someone were watching,

Alana's tears abated. Then gradually she turned and looked toward the door. Sonsee's hand tightened on the brass knob. Every muscle tensed. She returned Alana's appraisal for a microsecond before fully opening the door.

Her elder sister's reddened eyes narrowed a fraction. "Was there something you needed?"

"N-no. I — I was just leaving and — and heard you crying . . ."

Alana awkwardly set the photo back on the end table and pressed at her eyes with the tissue. "If you don't mind," she grumbled, "I need some time alone."

Wave upon wave of memories washed over Sonsee. As if the years were peeled away, she looked past all of Alana's negative behavior and saw before her a child deeply wounded. A child who just wanted to be loved by her daddy. A child who resented the recipient of her father's adoration. And something deep within Sonsee whispered that Alana would have never killed Jacques LeBlanc because she revered him.

Sonsee took a step toward Alana then halted when her sister hunched her shoulders as if to close Sonsee out. "I'm sorry," Sonsee said, and the scent of a burning candle seemed to sweeten the words as they left her lips.

Alana's head snapped up and she eyed her sister with keen suspicion. Sonsee returned her appraisal, not certain exactly what else to say. The two of them had managed to avoid one another the last few days. At the time, Sonsee had been grateful that Alana kept her distance. Now she marveled at her own selfishness. *I've been so wrapped up in my pain I've been blind to hers.*

Yet a deeper, more haunting, truth barged in upon Sonsee: *My whole life I've been so concerned with my own plans that I've never taken the time to look past Alana's actions and see her need.*

The sound of someone at the door distracted Sonsee. She swiveled to see Hermann, standing nearby, curiously taking in the scene before him. Like a wary, watching wolf, Hermann's suspicious gaze reminded Sonsee that Taylor was in the car, still awaiting her.

"I was just leaving," Sonsee muttered, brushing past him. Only the sound of her sneakers across the scarlet rug, then on the polished marble floor accompanied her to the front door. Without a backward glance, she deftly grabbed the suitcase's extended handle and rolled the piece of luggage onto the massive front porch. The imposing pillars surrounding the porch seemed to close in upon her like the legs of giants who were intent upon snatching her up.

Sonsee wasted no time rolling her suitcase through the moonlit night, into the shadows, toward her car. Accompanied by the distant sounds of traffic and a balmy, coastal breeze, she unlocked the trunk and deposited the luggage inside. Within seconds, she opened the car door and cast a brief glance at her passenger.

Despite his cramped position in the backseat, Taylor was dozing. Sonsee's heart twisted with aching love as she took in the features of the man, so familiar, yet so far away. She longed to reach out and smooth the lock of wavy, wayward hair from his forehead. Sonsee imagined bestowing a gentle kiss upon the lips that were often tilted in humor. She yearned to stroke those eyelids, closed in slumber. By her very touch Sonsee wished to remove the heartache that had been below the surface of his deep-blue eyes for as long as her memory served her. Eyes that were the color of sapphires . . . sapphires marred by life's unforgiving chisel.

Steeling herself against making more

noise than necessary, Sonsee settled into her seat, closed the door, and started the engine. The car had rolled forward a few feet when a taunting voice spun its way around the car's dark interior. "So, Red, what's for dinner?"

Sonsee jumped. Her grip tightening on the steering wheel. She wondered if he had been awake when she stole those few minutes to lovingly cherish him. "My name is Sonsee!" she growled, glad for any diversion from the reality of her hopeless love.

"Okay, okay. Give me a break, will ya? Seriously, I'm starved," he said through a yawn.

"Could have fooled me. You were sleeping like a baby when I got into the car."

"I'm exhausted, to say the least. I haven't slept much since you called me two days ago. When you started the engine, I guess that woke me up. My stomach woke up with me."

Her fingers relaxed. "I'll stop at a fast-food place soon and get us something. I'm hungry myself." Her no-nonsense voice contradicted the memories that were quickly becoming her tormentor — memories of his gaze roaming to her lips.

"Okay. I could eat a roasted porcupine

right now — quills and all."

"Yeah, right," Sonsee quipped.

"Listen, pilgrim," he said in a drowsy drawl, "a cowboy'll eat just about anything that don't eat him when he's been on the trail all day." His voice, deepened for effect, reminded Sonsee of all the years Taylor had used his "John Wayne" tone to procure a smile from her and anyone else in the vicinity. But tonight she didn't feel like smiling. She was tired, really tired, of the Taylor who reverted to his jocular strategies to avoid the real issues. Once again, Sonsee wanted to say *and what's really going on inside that head of yours, Taylor Delaney?* but she didn't. Instead, she concentrated on driving and stared ahead at River Road, stretching out of New Orleans. Silently, she endured the strained silence that spun its way between them. A silence laden with the undercurrents of the last few days. Undercurrents, filled with attraction. Attraction and fear. Fear and panic.

Sonsee's mind began the traitorous journey that had so characterized her thoughts before that humanitarian aid trip to Vietnam. A journey that led her back to Hawaii . . . to those romantic evenings when she had realized her love. She recalled the pining, the hoping, the praying that Taylor would somehow return her love. Never had she needed his love like she needed it now. The fact that she had come to a point of peace with facing life without Taylor at her side now mocked her. Her stomach tightening, Sonsee's fingers once more curled around the steering wheel until they protested in pain.

Finally, Sonsee decided to push the boundaries a bit and play the part of the daredevil. The issues that lay between them were the products of Taylor's past. He told her in the spring that he couldn't love. Sonsee responded by suggesting he was too stubborn to love. Well, he wasn't the only one who was stubborn. "Tell me about your father, Taylor," she said in an even voice. "You've never once discussed him with me."

This time the resulting hush took on an ominous aura. "And I don't plan to start discussing him now," he snapped. "We've got more than enough to keep our thoughts occupied without talking about me." The words came out like the rapid fire of an army sergeant's command and were followed by an under the breath comment she didn't think he wanted her to hear: "Women!"

Tightening her lips, Sonsee slammed on

the brakes and pulled the car to the shoulder of the road. She threw the vehicle into park and faced him. The nearby Mississippi River's lazy meandering belied the current rushing through Sonsee. "Listen you!" she said, not certain she understood the source of the anger boiling through her veins.

Taylor sat up, his widened eyes evident in the illumination of an oncoming car.

"I am risking a lot for you!" Her voice quivered with the force of her emotions. "The least I deserve is your civility! Understand?" She pointed an unsteady finger at his nose.

"What is it you want from me, Sonsee?" he barked, his heavy words falling like bricks in the darkness. "If I'm too nice you accuse me of — of flirting with you, for Pete's sake. And if I'm not nice enough you go into orbit! Would you stop this?" Another approaching car illuminated his distraught features before it whizzed past them. "I can't take all this strange behavior from you right now. The last thing I need is — is — your going ballistic."

"Well, I *am* going ballistic," she said, her voice growing louder with every word. "And I'm really sick and tired of all these tactics you use to keep me and everybody else in the universe at arm's length." All the disappointment, rage, and sorrow from the last few days surged through Sonsee, shaking her to her core. A rational side of her brain suggested she was overreacting in the severest manner, but Sonsee had been rational for about as long as humanly possible for that day. The tragic events of the week all surged together to produce an internal gale. Taylor's rude response had incensed her all the more. In her youth, Sonsee had been known to explode a few times. As she matured, she had beseeched the Lord for self control, which He had graciously granted. But at that moment, she felt as if she were twenty again — twenty, and losing her temper in the most obnoxious fashion.

"So, you're tired of my keeping you at arm's length?" he snapped. "Okay, then, how's this for arm's length?"

Before Sonsee realized Taylor's intent, he reached through the bucket seats, leaned forward, cradled her head in his hands, and crushed his lips against hers. Sonsee, her eyes bugging, gulped for breath and tried to adhere to the sensible notion that she should break free. As the kiss deepened and her eyes involuntarily closed, Sonsee found herself reaching for

Taylor rather than trying to push him away. While the kiss lengthened, she felt as if she were drowning in the fiery passion purling from her love. Love and ecstasy. Ecstasy and sweet torment.

Sonsee remembered that conversation she had endured in the kitchen at LeBlanc Manor. Taylor admitted that he had thought of proposing and that he would enjoy the physical side of marriage as much as any other man. Perhaps this kiss meant much more to her than it did to him. To Taylor, the contact was probably nothing more than a masculine need for release. For Sonsee, the kiss represented her untainted love expressed without reserve.

Taylor raised his face only inches from hers and his breath brushed her lips. "Sonsee? I'm — I'm s-sorry. I didn't intend to . . . I never planned to . . . the last thing I wanted to do was take advantage of you." He gulped.

Sonsee ground her teeth, faced the road, placed her shaking hand on the steering wheel, and pulled the floor gear shift into drive. The hours in the car with Taylor stretched before her like an endless chasm. The tension, the attraction, the confusion swirled around her like the hot waters of an acrid sea.

Nine

The next morning, Melissa Moore paced her living room and glanced at her sporty wristwatch for the sixth time in ten minutes. Eleven o'clock swiftly approached, and Sonsee and Taylor had yet to arrive. Sonsee had called last night at ten to ask if Melissa would allow Taylor a brief stay at her house. With mixed emotions, Melissa agreed to Sonsee's request. However, she had expected the two by now and had arranged for an associate to see her patients until one o'clock — something the pediatrician did only in emergencies.

She stopped the pacing and collapsed onto the mauve sofa. Melissa stared around the room that smelled of new carpet and cranberry candles. The purchase of the renovated home on Mantle Drive had been the result of her mother's urging. Melissa had balked a bit at the price and the size of the homes in Green Hills, where her mother had originally suggested. So Darla had begrudgingly suggested this street, insisting that the young doctor would be more deeply respected as a member of the community if she owned a home. At last Melissa had grown accustomed to the idea and decided to just look at houses.

Something within Melissa was reawakened when she inspected this classic home . . . something that had died when Kinkaide Franklin never bothered to show up for their wedding six years before . . . something that insisted she needed a "nest." A haven. A home with a mailbox at the street, flowerbeds, and a garage. Melissa fell in love with this house — and fell hard. Her mother relinquished and stopped pushing about the bigger homes.

This house was the smallest of the ones lining the street. The outside was understated; but the inside had been transformed into a designer's paradise. Owning her own place created a new sense of accomplishment within Mel, a fresh awareness of roots. She admired the balance wrought by the decorator's hands: the muted shades of mauve and green mixed with touches of burgundy; the elegant lines of Queen Anne furnishings; the classic paintings hanging here and there.

Once again she checked her watch and restlessly stirred. Mel brushed aside a piece of lint from her linen shorts and decided to change clothes in preparation for work. Standing, she debated what to do should Sonsee and Taylor not arrive before she had to make afternoon hospital rounds. Those rounds could not be postponed and should not be left to the care of another. The doorbell's cheerful chime sent her racing forward. As agreed, she had left the garage door open so Sonsee could drive her rental car into the garage. Mel planned to lower the door and let Taylor slip into the house through the utility room. Why Sonsee was ringing the front doorbell was perplexing.

Without reserve, Melissa unlocked the oak door, decorated with etched, beveled glass, and swung it inward. The person standing on the other side was not Sonsee or Taylor. This was a well-tanned man Melissa had not seen in six years. The man whose velvet-brown eyes once snared her heart, then broke it by cowardly being a no-show at the church.

Theirs was going to be a quiet, simple affair — just Melissa, Kinkaide, and the minister. She hadn't even invited the six sisters. Melissa and Kinkaide had planned to surprise them with the news of their marriage. Then Kinkaide had not arrived at the all-important moment. Even to this date, none of the six sisters knew that Kinkaide had left Melissa standing at the altar. The betrayal had been too painful for Melissa to discuss with even her closest friends. To date, all six of them just thought the engagement had been broken, which actually represented the truth.

"Hello, Mel," Kinkaide said, an unsure twist lifting the corners of his mouth. "You haven't changed a bit." The nuance of every word stroked Melissa's spine, sending tingles of memories dancing into her soul. Memories of love. Memories of bliss. Memories of heartache, dimmed by time but never forgotten.

Louis Tyra pivoted, eyeing every corner of a living room that had once been spotless. Now, not one cushion was slit free. Not one drawer remained in place. Not one video or CD was in its holder. He glanced toward the adjoining kitchen and dining room. Cerberus shook out a drawer full of dish towels. They landed on the floor in a disheveled heap. Unceremoniously, the partner dropped the drawer atop the dish towels and glowered at the countertop laden with the food and dishes once in the cabinets. Muttering, he kicked the silverware, already scattered across the tile, then paced toward Louis.

"I didn't find anything," Cerberus declared.

"Me neither," Louis said. The two of them had watched Sonsee LeBlanc's townhouse all morning, certain she would eventually exit. After all, the blue Honda she had driven to LeBlanc Manor was sitting in the townhouse parking lot. But after patiently waiting all morning, the two decided to see if she was home. When no one answered, Cerberus inserted the duplicate key that Carla had provided and eased open the door. Cautiously, Louis called out a greeting. Soon the two of them knew they were alone and began searching for the ancient key.

Now the rooms upstairs resembled the downstairs rooms. The two had left nothing unsearched. Sonsee would be devastated when she returned. Louis thought of his wife's penchant for keeping a spotless house, of her reaction to someone virtually turning her home upside down and shaking the contents into a heap. An unexpected tendril of guilt sprouted in his heart and wormed its way into every vein.

Yet a fresh wave of rage washed over him. Rage and impatience. Impatience and logic. *Who cares about Sonsee LeBlanc and her stinking little townhouse? I've got more at stake than a few pieces of shredded furniture and some emptied cabinets and drawers.* Thoughts of what might happen should the authorities discover the truth hardened Louis' heart. As much as he despised adding to his list of crimes, he detested thoughts of spending time in prison even more.

"Where are Sonsee's keys?" Cerberus asked. "Didn't you pick them up when I dropped them?"

"Yes. They're in my pocket." Louis speculatively observed the shorter person whose hard, beady eyes reminded him of the unrelenting gaze of a predator. Cerberus extended an impatient hand and stubbornly waited for Louis to produce the keys. For a second, Louis contemplated the possibility of not handing them over. Frankly, he was sick to death of being bullied by someone both younger and smaller than he. In his accounting firm, *he* was the boss. In his relationship with his wife, *he* had the upper hand. As a father, *he* had been the dictator. Louis loathed being out of control, and he had long ago stopped feeling in command of the present state of affairs.

"Give me the keys now!" Cerberus demanded.

Twisting his lips in distaste, Louis reached into his pocket and plopped the ring of keys onto the outstretched palm. "There," he groused.

"I'll drive Sonsee's car. You follow," Cerberus said.

"Wait a minute!" A trickle of sweat slipped down Louis' spine, despite the air conditioner's efforts. "What's the sense in stealing her car?"

"We need to search it, too, and I don't want to do it in broad daylight right in front of her apartment," Cerberus said condescendingly.

Louis' tightened his fist and pressed his lips together.

"Just do what I say and follow me. We'll take the car to a secluded spot and tear it apart. Hopefully we'll find the key. If we don't . . ."

Raising his brows, Louis waited. He thought of Brenda. Of her trusting nature. Of her shock if she learned he had actually killed another human being. In all the years Louis firmly controlled Brenda, he suffered only trace regret, usually on the occasions he listened to her cry herself to sleep. But now, standing in the center of a neat home turned to chaos, he felt as if he were in the grips of a giant octopus pulling him into the caverns of an unrelenting abyss of guilt. Guilt that choked him and made him wish he had indeed lost his life in that boating accident. Anything would be better than the echo from his past . . . an echo of "thou shalt not kill." The essence of evil seemed to ooze from his palms, and Louis rubbed his hands along the front of his slacks.

"If we don't find the key," Cerberus continued, "we'll be forced to make Sonsee give it to us."

"What if she doesn't have it?"

"She's got to have it."

"Look," Louis said, coercing his voice into consoling tones. "Why don't we just go back to the mansion and see if we can't force open the vault door."

"I've tried that! How many times do I have to tell you I tried that?" A crazed glimmer flickered in the depths of eyes like granite. For the first time, Louis' irritation with his demanding partner gave way to a pall of apprehension that settled upon his spirit like a dense, forbidding fog. He glanced away and followed Cerberus toward the front door, all the while wondering if his partner might one day turn on him.

～

Melissa took in Kinkaide's Italian eyes, his dark hair, the fine lines around his eyes, and the short beard that wasn't there the last time she saw him. The beard added an air of mystery to his demeanor. The pleated slacks and polo shirt, the color of cream, contrasted with his dark complexion and fitted his carefree personality — a personality that had complemented Melissa's more practical bent. Despite attempts to deny any reaction to her former fiancé, her heart fluttered.

"Hello." Kinkaide's eyes, although cautious, danced as if he weren't sure whether he should smile or run.

"H-hello," Melissa stuttered, thankful to be able to verbalize a response while wondering how he knew where she lived.

"Is this a bad time?"

"Uh . . . I-I was just expecting someone else. You surprised me."

Kinkaide's brows shot up in that familiar gesture that suggested she expound. But as if the very mention of her expected guests made them materialize, a nondescript sedan pulled into Melissa's driveway and into her garage. "Oh, I think that's them now. Uh . . ."

Melissa debated her options. She was certain Sonsee would not approve her allowing Kinkaide to witness the smuggling of a fugitive into her home. Furthermore, Melissa wasn't exactly enamored with the idea of anyone learning that she was going to house an accused criminal, despite the fact that she was convinced he was innocent. She could only imagine how news of her hiding Taylor would affect her reputation as a trusted pediatrician. On the other hand, Melissa didn't suppose for a second that Kinkaide would immediately recognize Taylor. There was a huge possibility that he didn't even know what the media was broadcasting in southern Louisiana. However, the fewer people who actually saw Taylor at Melissa's house, the better.

"Would you excuse me for a minute? I'll be right back." Without giving Kinkaide a chance to respond, Melissa slammed the door against his nonplused expression and rushed through her kitchen, into the utility room. In a matter of seconds, the garage door was closing and Melissa was ushering Sonsee and Taylor into her home. The two of them had the "I've-been-in-a-car-all-night" look, replete with creased clothing, unkempt hair, and dark circles under their eyes.

Taylor inhaled deeply. "Something smells good," he said.

"That's lunch. Nothing fancy. Just vegetable soup," Melissa said. As Taylor silently walked toward the kitchen, Mel grabbed Sonsee's upper arm, halting her beside the clothes drier. "That was Kinkaide Franklin outside my front door when you drove up," she whispered as calmly as possible.

Sonsee's weary eyes widened and her drooping shoulders rose. "As in *your* Kinkaide?" she asked, wrinkling her brow.

"Yes," Melissa said, not even attempting to correct Sonsee's implying that Kinkaide in any way belonged to her. Now or ever. "I'm going to let him in the front door," she said under her breath. "He's already seen you driving up in the car, and there's nothing we can do about that. But that's no sign he could identify you. Just keep a low profile. You know where the guest rooms are. Stay hidden until I come get you."

"We're starving," Sonsee said.

"I'll get rid of him quick."

With a silent nod, Sonsee whisked past Melissa. Nervously adjusting her wire-rimmed glasses, Mel moved toward the door and opened it. However, the porch was empty. Melissa blinked, wondering if she had imagined him. Then she noticed the piece of white paper lying near her feet. She bent to retrieve the folded missive, opened it, and read the words, penned in a distinctive scrawl that was once as dear to her as her own breath.

Mel,
Looks like I've caught you at a bad time.
I'll call later.

Kinkaide

Melissa sighed as the words reverberated through her mind in Kinkaide's melodic voice. A voice that had haunted Melissa's dreams for three years after their broken relationship. A voice that had once pledged love and devotion for a lifetime.

The note grew bleary, the years blurred into nonexistence, and Melissa was once more parking her car outside the economy apartment complex that housed numerous University of Texas med students . . .

As she gathered her ankle-length dress and stepped out of her Ford, Kinkaide neared from across the parking lot. Numb from his rejection, Melissa watched his approach. A tense silence arrived seconds before Kinkaide stopped, only inches from her.

"I'm sorry," Kinkaide said, his liquid-brown eyes regretful, vulnerable, yet determined. He slipped his hands into the pants pockets of the charcoal suit he'd bought for their simple wedding.

"The least you could have done is called before I left. That way I wouldn't have stayed at the church like an idiot for almost an hour!" The words, full of venom, exploded from Melissa. "I feel like a complete fool!"

"Well, if it's any consolation, so do I," Kinkaide said, his carefree manner replaced by that of a serious stranger.

"So what's the deal?" Melissa snapped. "Do you just not love me any more or is there someone else?" The mention of a potential rival sent a knifelike pain shooting through Melissa's spirit. Her hands clenched into tight balls. Her eyes filled with burning tears. Her legs trembled.

"No, Mel, no one else," he whispered. "I just . . . I . . ." He glanced past her and Melissa cast a gaze over her shoulder to see a couple of college women who were a tad too interested in their conversation. "Can we go into your apartment and finish this?"

"No," Melissa said bluntly, and Kinkaide winced. She wrenched the simple solitaire from her finger and held the ring between them.

"I hate for it to end like this," he said, his eyes narrowing as if he, too, were in pain. "It's not that I don't care for you. I just . . . I . . . I couldn't go to the wedding. I . . . I . . . the more I tried to make myself go, the more I panicked." Exhaling heavily, he gripped the back of his neck and hung his head as if weighted by bewilderment.

The irony of this moment filled Melissa's stomach with bitter gall. The two of them had met in church. They prayed together. They beseeched the Lord about their marriage. Melissa had been filled with nothing but peace, all the way to the church. Then Kinkaide didn't bother to show up!

"I'm just not ready for all this, Mel," he said, taking the extended ring. He shook his head and looked deeply into her eyes. "I couldn't get peace about our marriage," he continued. His voice's melodious nuance that usually charmed now rankled. "It all started last night after I dropped you off." Wearily he rubbed his eyes marred by dark circles. "I didn't hardly sleep last night. This morning I got up determined to marry you — despite it all. I even got

168

dressed." He motioned toward the immaculate suit. "But I just couldn't . . ."

"You don't love me," Melissa accused, full of tormenting disillusionment.

"I don't know." His dark eyes rounded, he slowly shook his head. "I just don't know. That's the whole point. I'm just not certain this is God's perfect will for me." He held up the small solitaire, which produced a merry wink that belied the grim moment.

Melissa swallowed hard. Her world had just been tilted. Her heart had just been bludgeoned. Her hope had just been crushed. But she determined she would not make a nasty scene. Instead, she adjusted her glasses, gripped her handbag, and marched toward her apartment like a soldier retreating from battle.

The next time Melissa saw Kinkaide Franklin was in the Bible bookstore on the cover of his newest Christian CD. Kinkaide's dream had come true. A dream Melissa had longed to share. He gained recognition as an acclaimed concert pianist. Driven by an undefined need, Mel purchased his first CD — and every one after that. The discs remained in neat stacks near the front of her office player, the cellophane wrappers still intact. Owning them kept her connected to Kinkaide, but the thought of his music reverberating through her sphere brought the anticipation of unbearable pain. Mel wasn't sure if she had ever seen her heart again. Some recurring reality demanded that Kinkaide had taken it with him when he walked away on their wedding day.

The telephone's shrill ring snapped Melissa out of her reverie. Gripping the note, she retreated into her living room. After her third step toward the phone, she stopped. *What if the caller is Kinkaide?* The imposing thought sprouted renewed dread, and Mel allowed the machine to take the call. At the moment, some sick children awaited her at the hospital, and some weary houseguests needed a quick meal.

Ten

Taylor had never seen Sonsee looking so haggard. The dark circles under her eyes and pale skin spoke of a desperate need of sleep. She sat across from him in Melissa's breakfast nook and devoured her simple lunch of a ham sandwich and vegetable soup. Taylor, having inhaled two sandwiches, now awaited Melissa's offer of another helping of soup.

Sonsee had barely spoken to Taylor since he kissed her last night. The realization that he had actually given in to the masculine impulse left him increasingly uncomfortable. He would have been far better off if she had not kissed him back . . . if it had not been ages since he'd kissed a woman . . . if he had not felt as if he were flung into the front seat of a roller coaster shooting straight down a thrilling hill.

"I'm sorry about last night," he mumbled, not certain of his sincerity. On one hand, he was sorry he made her uncomfortable. Taylor abhorred the very thought of taking advantage of any woman — especially Sonsee. Despite all of those truths, he had thoroughly enjoyed those moments when her lips were against his.

She paused, holding her soup-laden spoon just above the crockery bowl, and Taylor's chest tightened as he awaited her response. For the first time since the kiss, she looked him in the eyes. The anguish churning in her soul reminded Taylor of the clouds that had boiled through southern Texas last summer, producing several deadly twisters and enough suffering for a lifetime.

"The next time you kiss me, Mister, you better make sure it means something to you. Or . . . or . . ."

"Or what, Red?" Taylor couldn't define the perverse urge that overtook him. An urge to needle her a bit. An urge to see the sparks shooting through her eyes, the color of emeralds. As an adolescent, he had caused her endless irritation. Somehow that immature bent to aggravate Sonsee resurfaced despite the inappropriate timing.

She leaned over, her face flushing. "Or I'll call the police and tell them exactly where you are!" she growled. "And don't — I repeat, *do not* — call me Red ever again as long as you live. Got it?" she finished through gritted teeth.

A bland smile pushed itself against Taylor's mouth, regardless of the shaft of fear that her threat sent through him. He paused but a second to consider her words then dismissed them. He wouldn't believe for one second that Sonsee would turn him over to the authorities, no matter how angry she grew. At last he calmly said, "So, what do you want me to call you? Blue?"

"Aaaahhh," she exclaimed as if her limits had been thoroughly violated. Sonsee slammed her spoon down on the table and stood. "I am going to bed now. Then I am going to drive that rental car back to Baton Rouge. Please just stay out of my sight until I leave!"

"Ah, come on, Sonsee, give me a break," Taylor said, standing.

"I *have* given you a break. Now it's your turn to give *me* a break!" Her voice rose with every word, and she pointed at his nose.

"Okay, okay." Taylor raised his hands. "I give up. Apparently you aren't in the mood to communicate. I'll just give you some space, and —"

"A mood! You think this is a mood?" she shrieked. With another huff, Sonsee turned on her heel and marched toward the hallway. Before she had taken six steps, she swiveled back around, stalked to the table, grabbed her diet cola, directed another glare toward Taylor, then stomped out of the room.

"Good grief. I was just trying to apologize," Taylor muttered as wave upon wave of confusion washed over him. Certainly this was not the Sonsee he had known his whole life. That sure, steady, predictable woman had vanished to be replaced by a capricious stranger.

"Is it safe to come out now?" Melissa asked from behind him.

Taylor looked over his shoulder. Sonsee's friend, hovering by the doorway, held a bowl of steaming soup.

"Yes, I guess," he said, rubbing his gritty eyes. Taylor lowered himself onto the padded brass chair and eyed the steaming soup that Melissa placed before him. The churning inside dulled the food's appeal. He dawdled with the bits of potatoes and carrots in a rich tomato base, trying to show the doctor some respect for her thoughtfulness. After Melissa cleared Sonsee's dishes, she settled beside Taylor and began munching half a sandwich.

He had only briefly met Melissa on a few occasions. From what Taylor remembered, coupled with Sonsee's remarks, Melissa was considered the brainiest of the seven sisters. Even though Taylor had often admired Sonsee for her sharp mental capacities, she had referred to Melissa as "the genius among us." As they sat across from each other, Melissa's keen eyes made Taylor more than uncomfortable. He supposed she'd clearly overheard his and Sonsee's spat, and he wasn't in the mood to expound on the details.

"You know, she's risking a lot for you," Melissa said as she stirred her soup with the tip of her spoon.

Oh, great, Taylor thought. *Here we go with the sisterly lecture.* "Yes, I know," he said, his hackles rising a bit.

"She's a wonderful woman. You'd be hard pressed to find a match for her."

"I know," Taylor repeated.

Melissa adjusted her glasses and observed him. Taylor met her gaze with a direct one of his own. Her full, brunette hair was cut in shoulder-length layers. She wore a trace of makeup and put forth the aura of a woman in charge of every thought. Briefly Taylor wondered if she had ever considered being a lawyer. Melissa's eyes held the hint of an interrogator. Nonetheless, her self-assured demeanor coupled with girl-next-door looks combined to create an attractive woman.

"It's nice to finally get to know you a little better," Taylor said dryly.

She glanced downward and spied the kosher spear on the edge of her plate. "I'm sorry." Melissa discreetly cleared her throat. "I'm probably being too protective. It's just that I heard the two of you arguing, and —"

"You automatically took Sonsee's side?" Taylor asked, stifling a yawn.

"I guess." She shrugged. "You look like you're beat, and here I am splitting hairs over an argument that wasn't any of my business," she rushed, as if trying to cover her shortcomings. "I have a tendency to ask too many questions at times. But so does my mother, and my mother's mother, too."

Nodding, Taylor smiled. "It's okay. Really. I guess we're all stressed to the max at this point. If it's any consolation, I was trying to apologize to Sonsee for an — an . . . uh . . . indiscretion on my part, and I don't think she's rested enough to consider forgiveness."

He directed a thankful smile her way. "On another note, I really appreciate your allowing me to stay here." Taylor glanced out the bay window that allowed an excellent view of a rose garden snuggled against a lawn of lush grass. "I don't know what all is going to happen, but it means a lot to have a safe place to come and get some rest. I shouldn't be in your hair too long. I've got to find out who killed Uncle Jacques. I can't do it cooling my heels in Oklahoma City."

"I understand," Melissa said. "Have you and Sonsee discussed possibly calling our friend Jac Lightfoot? She's a private detective out of Denver. She could probably help you a lot."

Taylor placed his elbows on the table and rubbed his face. He directed a fatigued gaze back outside. This time he noticed a sleeping Great Dane sprawled on the back patio. "No. Sonsee and I haven't discussed Jac. But now that you mention her, I remember Sonsee talking about her not long ago. You seven gals are certainly a close-knit group — that's all I've got to say."

"Well, we try," Melissa said. "And you look like you're about to go into a coma, right in your leftover soup."

Taylor chuckled. "And here in this ring we have the world famous Melissa-the-Mind-Reader," he said like an exhausted circus announcer.

Melissa joined in his lighthearted snicker and pointed down the hall. "Take a left. Third door on the right. There's a bathroom across the hall."

"Yeah. I already discovered the bathroom. Left my backpack in there. If you don't mind, I think I'll shower before I hit the hay."

"Make yourself at home."

After a sound sleep, Sonsee arose at nine, showered, then grabbed a light meal. She avoided Taylor's room and planned to be gone before he awoke. The last thing she needed was to look into those sapphire-blue eyes, so familiar, yet so distant. Her heart cried for Taylor to wrap his arms around her and whisk her away to some remote island where no one would ever find them. But that could never be.

With Melissa waiting in the living room, she made a final trip into the guest room to retrieve her overnight bag. Just as she stepped into the hallway, Sonsee encountered Taylor staggering toward the restroom. Dressed in an oversized T-shirt and well-worn gym shorts, he stopped when he saw her. His hair rumpled, his eyes sleepy, Taylor slowly lowered his gaze to her overnight bag. A shock of guilt started at

Sonsee's feet and rushed straight up to the roots of her hair.

"Where ya goin', Re—" He cleared his throat. "Uh, Sonsee?"

"I'm going home for right now," she said, her voice much firmer than the tremor up her spine suggested it should be.

"So you're leaving me to the mercy of that interrogator?" He produced a lazy yawn and a drowsy smile.

"Melissa will take good care of you. You're just lucky she agreed to take you in."

"Yes. She seems to have the same opinion of you." He arched one brow. "I will say the two of you shouldn't feel unloved. Seems I've stepped into a hot bed of the mutual admiration society."

Sonsee, shifting the overnight bag to the other hand, exposed him to a bland expression that belied the churning of her stomach. Despite his typical flippant remarks, Sonsee wanted to step into Taylor's arms and have him tell her everything was going to be fine.

"So what's up?" he asked, pointing toward the suitcase. "Are you going to take your key and see what you find at LeBlanc Manor, or are you going to wait so I can go with you?"

She glanced down. "I don't know right now. Really, I dread going back there. But I am curious about what's in that hidden room and, now that I own LeBlanc Manor, I'm going to have to make some decisions." Thoughts of the maid's dishonesty sent a bitter twist through Sonsee. "I think I'm going to fire Carla. I don't have much choice. And frankly, I'm not certain I want to keep that old mansion. Even though I grew up there, it's the place where . . ." *my father was killed.* A tide of silent communication flowed between Sonsee and Taylor. She held his gaze only a second, but his sleepy eyes, full of compassion, spoke of their years of friendship and Taylor's unyielding support.

Immediately Sonsee recalled their heated words before she'd dropped into bed after lunch. If her memory was correct, the poor man had tried to apologize and she had exploded on him. The volatile scene seemed to dance between them, leaving a trail of regret in its wake. "I'm sorry about . . . about . . . uh . . ." Sonsee observed the carpet, the color of cranberries. "I'm sorry about what happened after lunch. I think I was —"

"It's okay —"

"I was just —"

"You don't have to explain," he rushed. "I should have never —"

"I should have been more —"

"The whole thing was my fault in the first —"

"I shouldn't have been so pigheaded on the side of the road," Sonsee insisted. First, she told him at LeBlanc Manor that he was too nice; then in the car, he wasn't nice enough. No wonder the man detonated like a grenade.

"But none of that excuses what I did, Sonsee." The gentle undercurrent of Taylor's deep voice wove its way between them, creating the essence of respect and remorse. "You know when I was younger, before I found the Lord, I was less sensitive about whether or not I took advantage of a woman. But now the last thing I ever want to do is take advantage of anyone — especially you. I never intended —"

"So that's all it meant to you?" she rasped, not realizing she had verbalized the strong thought until a hint of dismay nibbled at the corners of Taylor's mouth. "I'm sorry," Sonsee whispered as she rushed for the dining-room doorway. "I should have never . . ."

Taylor caught up and laid a hand on her arm. "Sonsee, wait," he urged.

181

She stopped. Refusing to look up, she instead scrutinized his callused hand, lightly gripping her forearm. Through the years, Sonsee had taken his brotherly touches as nothing more than the interaction of two friends. But that could never be again. For now, his every touch, his every glance, the nuance of his every word shot darts of yearning through her heart — darts that were the source of almost unbearable agony.

"I . . . I . . ."

Unexpected tears sprang upon her. Tears of humiliation. Tears of longing. Tears of unrequited love. Sonsee blinked hard and forbade herself to release the messy emotions.

"I really don't know what to say, Sonsee," Taylor finished. "I . . ."

"You've said it already." His claim of never being able to love laced her words with sorrow. "There's nothing left to say." Sonsee stepped away from his touch. "And you don't have to worry, Taylor." From somewhere deep within a root of courage gave full blossom to a boost of bravado that allowed Sonsee to dare encounter his appraisal without a flinch. "After all this is over and we find out who really killed my father, you don't have to worry about ever seeing me again. I will fully understand if you —"

"Oh, good grief, Red!" he said, exasperated. "Let's just get melodramatic, why don't we?"

"Don't call me Red!" she snapped then stomped her foot. "I hate that! How many times do I have to tell you that it drives me nuts — absolutely nuts? It drove me nuts when I was eight. It drove me nuts when I was nineteen. And it still drives me nuts now!"

"Okay . . . okay." He raised his hands, palms outward. "I give up!" Taylor turned toward the restroom. "Just go on back home and do whatever it is you think you've got to do — and let me know *when in the name of common sense* you plan to come get me." He pivoted to face her, his eyes rounded. "Or have you just decided to leave me here forever?" The telephone's ringing punctuated his question.

"Oh, yeah, right." Sonsee rolled her eyes and adjusted her shoulder bag. "Like Melissa would let me do that. She's worried sick somebody is going to find out you're staying here even for a few days."

"Well, I'm glad you at least see the problem," he said, a sarcastic twist to his lips. "I have this gut feeling she'll feed me to that overgrown Great Dane of hers for breakfast if I overstay my welcome. That thing is the size of a horse!"

"I beg your pardon," Melissa said from the end of the hallway. "I would never feed you to Bernie." She adjusted her glasses and eyed Taylor as if he had just spoken the most outlandish of insults.

"Oh, great," he said under his breath.

"Don't take the man seriously, Mel," Sonsee said, walking toward her friend. "He doesn't mean a thing he says. Before his stay is out, he'll have you charmed senseless and you won't have a clue who he really is." The hardened edge to Sonsee's voice surprised even her. She cut a glance over her shoulder. Taylor squinted as if he were thoroughly vexed, and a perverse thrill zipped through Sonsee's midsection. *Serves him right.*

"So, *Miz Psychologist,* are you planning on our going over a plan of any sort before you waltz off into the shadows or are you just going to leave me in suspense until you deem to reappear?" Sonsee paused and eyed Taylor as he tucked his fingers under his upper arms with the thumbs resting on his chest.

She narrowed her eyes and dismissed half a dozen retorts that flashed through her mind.

"Sonsee," Melissa interrupted, "the

reason I came looking for you is because we've got a conference call on now with the sisters. Want to join us?"

Sonsee, taken off guard, gazed wide-eyed at Melissa. "Of course. I didn't know. Or did you tell me and I forgot?"

"No, I didn't tell you." Melissa shook her head. "I set it up over e-mail while you were asleep. Everyone wants to talk with you."

Sonsee fell into step beside her friend and followed her to the living room. "Did you tell them we're hiding Taylor?"

"No." Melissa shook her head. "I didn't know how you felt about telling them. I thought I'd leave that decision to you." She pointed toward the answering system sitting on a Queen Anne end table near the sofa. "You get that phone. I'll grab the one in the kitchen."

"Will do," Sonsee said, depositing her overnight bag and purse near the floral sofa where she took her seat.

Eleven

Sonsee lifted her receiver only seconds before Melissa and was met with a chorus of friendly greetings from her dearest friends. Kim Lan Lowery, Marilyn Langham, Victoria Roberts, Jacquelyn Lightfoot, Sammie Jones, and Melissa — all of them had been at the funeral and stood by Sonsee as if they were self-appointed sentinels awaiting a false move from any of her family members. Over the years, the six of them had gained full understanding of the negative undercurrents that plagued the LeBlanc Manor household. And they were intent upon guarding Sonsee against even a moment's unnecessary discomfort during that difficult day.

"Hi, guys!" Sonsee said in response to their greetings. "What's up tonight?" She and Melissa waited as the other five sisters each gave a brief explanation of their evening. The recounting ended with Marilyn talking about her five-year-old daughter. "I just got through putting Brooke down for the night, so I'm enjoying a little R and R."

"Now it's time for marital bliss," Kim Lan teased. The other sisters joined in a round of wolf whistles and well-meant banter.

Marilyn, the newlywed among them, had been wed to Joshua Langham all of one month. The Lord at long last turned the dirge of her past heartache into a chorus of joy. When Marilyn's first pastor husband divorced her for another woman, all the sisters had wondered if she would ever recover. With God's help, she recovered and married again — this time to a pastor who would stay true to his Lord, his wife, and his adored stepdaughter.

"Kim Lan, you're just jealous that you and Mick aren't married yet," Marilyn shot back.

Despite her gloomy spirits, Sonsee joined in the fresh round of laughter. No one had ever suspected that Kim Lan Lowery, a sought-after supermodel, would break up with her movie star fiancé and agree to marry a mission coordinator. But the Lord had worked in miraculous ways during that mission trip to Vietnam. Kim had come back a changed woman — a woman with a deeper commitment to Christ, a woman in love with Mick O'Donnel.

"Just allow me to say that I'm not jealous of anybody," Jac Lightfoot injected. "I'm perfectly content with my man-free existence. So don't any of you get any ideas about —"

"Hey, there's a really neat new guy at my church," Victoria Roberts said. "Want me to introduce you the next time you're visiting?"

"No, no, no!" Jac said emphatically.

As the group continued in another round of laughter, Sonsee toyed with the hem of her pleated walking shorts.

"You guys will never guess who showed up on *my* doorstep today," Melissa ground out. An expectant pause followed. "Kinkaide Franklin."

"You mean *your* Kinkaide?" Sammie Jones asked.

"You sound like Sonsee," Melissa said.

"How romantic," Victoria crooned. She always enjoyed the very hint of lovers intrigue, whether it be past, present, or future.

"Oh, Victoria," Sonsee said with feigned censure. "You just want everybody to get married so you can cater our weddings."

"You finally figured me out!" Victoria said with a soft laugh.

"Don't knock her talents," Marilyn responded. "She did a great job at my wedding."

"And I'm placing dibs on you right now for Mick's and my wedding," Kim said. "We're going to keep it simple and small, by the way, just friends and family."

"That's much larger than my wedding plans were," Melissa said with a hint of sorrow in her voice. "We planned for just me, him, and the preacher. The problem . . ." She stopped talking and Sonsee thought she heard Mel gulp. "Kinkaide never showed up."

"What?" Sonsee sat straight up and leaned forward so abruptly that Melissa's sophisticated answering machine almost toppled from the end table. As Sonsee reached to steady the phone, the other five sisters repeated her shock in one form or another.

"I didn't know anything about this," Jac said.

"I didn't tell any of you. It was supposed to be a surprise," Melissa responded, her voice wobbly. "Frankly, it was all too painful to discuss at the time. My mom knew, of course. I could never hide anything from her. But for everyone else, the engagement was just off. And I was telling the truth. It was off."

"So he just showed up on your front porch today?" Sammie asked.

"What did he want?" Kim Lan questioned.

"I don't have the foggiest idea," Melissa said. "I left him on the porch while I let Sonsee and T— and, um . . ." She cleared her throat. "While I let Sonsee in the garage door. And when I went back, he was gone. He left a note saying he would call."

"So he gave no hints in the note?" Marilyn asked.

"None," Melissa said. "But if he thinks he's going to just waltz right back into my life and . . . oh, never mind. That's the craziest idea I've had in years."

"You never know. Stranger things have happened," Sonsee said. *Much stranger things,* she thought, recalling all the upheaval of the past few days.

An awkward pause settled upon the group; a pause that suggested the sisters had detected that Sonsee had not arrived at Melissa's house alone. Restlessly shifting, Sonsee picked up the framed, eight-by-ten snapshot sitting near the phone. The photo of the seven sisters was identical to the one Sonsee had hung in her bedroom among her collage of photos. The six close friends were surrounding the new bride, Marilyn

Langham. Marilyn, blonde and fair, was dressed in a tea-length, ivory wedding dress. Kim Lan had been Marilyn's maid of honor and the other five had been delighted to serve as bridesmaids on Marilyn's special day. They were dressed in navy-blue dresses that complemented the Victorian style of the whole wedding.

Kim Lan Lowery, the drop-dead gorgeous model of Vietnamese descent, stood behind Marilyn. She held up her left hand to flout the jade engagement ring that Mick O'Donnel placed on her hand that very day. Kim Lan's smile clearly said, "I'm next."

On the other side of Kim stood Melissa, grinning as if she were thrilled with Marilyn's happiness. Then, Victoria, the most petite of the seven, stood in front of Marilyn. She wore her naturally curly hair in a droopy bun that made her look as elegant as her composed nature suggested. Private detective Jac crowded in on Marilyn's left side, next to Sonsee. Jac's dark hair and eyes contrasted with Sonsee's fair skin and auburn hair. Jac boasted of a mixed heritage with ancestors that were Native American, African American, and Caucasian.

Near them Sammie Jones, magazine reporter and romance author, raised her hand for a flirtatious wave at the camera. Sammie's fiery-red locks made Sonsee's auburn tresses pale in comparison. *She wouldn't have a chance with Taylor,* Sonsee mused. *Not even Sammie's imagination could conjure up a love-struck Taylor.*

Thoughts of the rancher jarred Sonsee back into the present. Considering the amount of banter bouncing back and forth between the women, the conversation was still alive and flowing, yet she had no idea concerning the subject at hand.

At last Jac Lightfoot said, "You're really quiet, Sonsee. Is everything okay?"

Sonsee shot a prayer heavenward, begging for divine guidance on whether she should tell her closest friends the real reason she was at Melissa's. She firmly believed that the fewer people who knew she was helping Taylor, the better. However, she also understood the power of prayer and the force of intercession her friends represented. At last she made her decision.

"Actually, gang, I — that is, um — Taylor and I really need your prayers." Once she spoke Taylor's name, Sonsee recognized that he had been an avoided subject throughout the whole conversation. Apparently nobody really knew how to broach the subject of his being an accused murderer. In a succinct manner, Sonsee briefed her best friends on the facts of her and Taylor's present circumstances.

While the rest of the sisters maintained a stunned silence, Jac exclaimed, "Good grief, Sonsee. Harboring a fugitive is a serious misdemeanor. You could be fined up to $4,000 or spend a year in prison or both! Melissa, you're staking your whole medical practice —"

"We know," Sonsee and Melissa said in unison.

"But he's so stubborn he won't even think about allowing the police to catch up with him!" Sonsee explained as she examined a sunset painting hanging on the far wall. She wondered if Taylor, like his father, would eventually walk off into the sunset, never to be heard from again. "He's had some really negative experiences in the past with dishonest law enforcement officers. And — and I can't just let him go through all this alone. I —" A movement at the door snared Sonsee's attention, and she stared into the stormy face of the very subject of her conversation.

Taylor stepped into the living room, a look on his rigid face that shouted, *How could you have been dense enough to tell them where I am!*

"Uh, Mel," Sonsee said. "I — I guess I need to go now." Her hand shaking, she hung up the phone and struggled to stand. Within seconds, Melissa stepped into the living room. Her eyes widened and just as swiftly as she entered, she exited.

Taylor neared like an eagle swooping down on a helpless rabbit. "I didn't believe you after lunch when you said you would turn me in to the police, but now I wonder if I've been a fool!"

Sonsee, having never seen Taylor so angry, stumbled backward until she bumped into the console television. Taylor didn't stop his approach until he was inches from her. At this close range, the faint scent of his aftershave teased her senses.

As the silent seconds ticked off, Taylor's tightened lips softened. Like a deluge approaching a flaming forest, the flood of attraction drenched the blazing sparks of anger in his eyes. In the place of ire, an electric current of memories flashed between them. And Sonsee recalled that kiss, that potent moment when the world halted and no one existed but her and this man. As she stiffened against her legs' telltale trembling, Taylor's blue eyes darkened with a new wave of emotions. At last the remaining flames of fury were annihilated, to be replaced by a flicker of confusion.

Her mouth dry, Sonsee finally stuttered to produce an explanation, "I-I just — just th-thought that — that my — my friends would b-be prayer support. We — we need all the prayer we can get right now."

"But are you sure they can be trusted?" he asked, the fine lines around his eyes crinkled.

"Yes." She nodded her head. "I'm sure. Taylor, believe me, I — I wouldn't have ev-ever told them otherwise." Without a thought, Sonsee gripped his forearm. "About what I said after lunch. I would *never* turn you over to the police. I was just angry about — about —" *that kiss.* The unspoken words resonated between them like a taunting chant bent upon teasing its victims into another embrace.

As if Taylor were mesmerized by his own reactions, his gaze wandered across Sonsee's face, her mouth, and back to her eyes. For once, Sonsee got a glimpse of Taylor's soul, of the real man beneath the flippant humor. And what she saw suggested he was reliving that moment their lips touched, reliving it and enjoying every second — not just because he was male and Sonsee was female, but for deeper reasons as well. A zip of glee tingled her midsection, and a tiny bell of hope jingled in her heart. Perhaps, just perhaps, there was a chance that Taylor might one day love her.

"I . . . I guess I owe you another apology," he said.

"It's okay. I'd probably have been angry if I were in your shoes." Sonsee glanced downward, not certain exactly what she should say or do. If Taylor tried to take her into his arms, she would certainly melt into a heap. But if he had no intentions of that nature, Sonsee refused to push herself on him.

After another weighty pause, Taylor rubbed the back of his neck and stepped away. He stared toward the sunset painting over the floral love seat, and Sonsee reached behind herself to grip the edge of the television.

"I never did answer your question last night, did I?" Taylor asked.

"M-my question?" Sonsee nervously cleared her throat.

"Yes, about my father. You asked me about my father." Other than crossing his arms, Taylor didn't change his stance. Sonsee stared at the side of his face, wondering exactly where this new vein of conversation would lead.

"I remember," Sonsee said, afraid to speak even that much.

"Well, I don't guess this is the time or place, but I would like to talk with you about all that one day." He turned to face her. "That is, if you're still willing to listen?" Taylor tilted his head to one side, arched one brow, and the faintest dimple attested to his slight smile.

"Of course," Sonsee agreed, repressing the desire to spin around the room. "I'll be glad to listen any time."

The sound of footsteps preceded Melissa by only seconds. "Hi," she said, entering the room. "I hate to interrupt, but Jac wants you to call her — now, Taylor, if possible. She wants to fly to Louisiana and see if she can't get to the bottom of who really killed Sonsee's father, but she won't come unless both of you agree. She doesn't want to horn her way in."

"What are her fees?" Taylor asked.

Sonsee snorted in disbelief. "We just inherited four mil apiece. I don't see a problem."

Melissa whistled.

"I know this is going to sound really stupid," Taylor said. "But I completely forgot about that detail. I've been so

197

caught up in running that everything else has been blocked from my mind."

"Well, if I know Jac, she won't charge you a penny, anyway." Melissa fidgeted with the button of her oxford shirt as if she were as nervous over Taylor's potential imprisonment as Sonsee and he were. "And Kim's offering to pay Jac's airfare here as her contribution to solving this problem."

"You know," Taylor said, laying a companionable hand on Melissa's shoulder, "Sonsee has great friends. You're all an excellent group of women."

"Nice try," Melissa said with a wry slant to her mouth. "But it still doesn't cancel out your caustic remark about my feeding you to my Great Dane. And might I add that your remark has certainly given me *food* for thought." Her face impassive, Mel pushed up her wire-rimmed glasses. "No pun intended."

Thirty minutes later, Taylor stood by the living room window, pulled aside the polished cotton drapes, and watched as Sonsee drove away. The rental car's headlights illuminated the road as Sonsee departed. She had rented the car in case someone were watching. This way her car sat in its usual spot near her townhouse and gave the illusion of her being home. Seeing Sonsee pull away in a vehicle not her own added to Taylor's disoriented thoughts. He felt as if all traces of light were vanishing from his spirit. The one person who had consistently brought joy into his life was driving back home, and Taylor was left in a strange town with a new friend.

Once Sonsee was out of view, he released the curtains and turned from the window. He called Jac Lightfoot, and she agreed to meet with him and Sonsee in Baton Rouge this weekend. Melissa planned to drive Taylor to Sonsee's townhouse. Right now he felt as if he were at the mercy of the fairer sex, and he didn't enjoy the sensation of helplessness his predicament brought him.

Taylor relished the independence of ranch life. He liked nothing better than mounting his horse and riding into the dawn to spend a day of labor in the great outdoors. Along with that, working with animals rather than people posed numerous benefits. Animals accepted a person at face value and didn't delve into the past or expect some sort of meaningful conversation.

With a heavy sigh, Taylor trudged through the living room, toward the dining area, only to encounter Melissa stepping from the kitchen.

"Hi," she said. "Looks like it's just you and me now, huh?"

"Yep." Taylor rubbed his neck. "And I'm wide awake."

Melissa stifled a yawn. "Wish I could say the same. I've got to start early in the morning."

"Do you mind if I stay up and watch some TV?"

"Not at all." Melissa slipped her hands into the pockets of her denim shorts, opened her mouth, closed it, then bit her bottom lip. Taylor, certain she was debating whether or not to make a statement, waited with a combination of dread and curiosity. Over lunch, he had been the recipient of Melissa's direct observations, and Taylor wasn't certain he was ready for more. A canine scratch at the patio door diverted her attention, and Melissa focused on letting Bernie-the-horse-dog into the dining room.

"You actually let him in the house?" Taylor asked as the Great Dane cautiously approached Taylor and sniffed his thigh.

"Yes. Every night. He sleeps on the floor beside my bed. Keeps me company and protects me." Melissa bent down. "Come on, boy," she coaxed, and the dog trotted toward her, wagging his tail and panting expectantly.

"So are you thinking you might need protection from *me?*" Taylor teased.

"Not in the least." Melissa gave him a serious stare, and Taylor wondered if she understood that he spoke in jest. "You don't scare me at all. I already have you figured out. You're nothing but a big pushover in disguise." The mild sparkle in Melissa's brown eyes spoke of her understanding far more than Taylor was comfortable with her knowing.

"Thanks a lot."

"You're welcome. Besides," Melissa added, "any man Sonsee LeBlanc admires as much as you is certainly a man of honor."

Her words introduced a second of uncomfortable silence. Not sure what to say, Taylor stepped toward the kitchen. "You know, I can't watch television without some popcorn. If you'll tell me where it is, I'll microwave my own."

"Nice sidestep," Melissa said with a quirk to her lips.

My relationship with Sonsee is none of your business. The thought marched through Taylor's mind and posed itself on his tongue, yet he squelched it.

"I'm just worried about Sonsee, I guess," Mel hurried, skillfully changing the subject.

Taylor followed her into the cheerful kitchen, decorated in taupe and blue, and wondered if his expression had spoken what his words had not. "Me, too," Taylor said. "I hope she makes it home okay. I made her promise to stop at a hotel if she gets sleepy."

"Good." Melissa opened one of the oak cabinets, retrieved a bag of microwave popcorn, and plopped it into Taylor's hands. "Sorry," she said with an apologetic smile. "I'm always getting myself into trouble by saying exactly what doesn't need to be said. I guess you could just say that I'm the mouth of the South." She marched toward the doorway, hesitated, and glanced over her shoulder. "Enjoy your popcorn."

"Thanks," Taylor returned, with a smile.

Twelve

Just before dawn the next morning, Louis Tyra drove Sonsee's car into the parking lot near the complex of townhouses. Purposefully he parked the sporty Honda behind the group of apartments, opposite Sonsee's home. In case she had arrived, Louis did not want her to witness his returning her vehicle. He turned off the engine, retrieved the set of duplicate keys, and observed the shredded interior. The blue vinyl seats, once pristine, now looked as if they had been passed through the jaws of a paper shredder. Cerberus insisted on exploring every possibility, despite Louis' belief that the key most likely was not hidden in Sonsee's car — especially not inside the seats. However, Cerberus had knifed into every inch of the interior, as if the act were as much a product of vengeance as a search for the key.

Furtively glancing around the parking lot, Louis slid dark sunglasses onto his nose and stepped from the vehicle. He flipped the lock, gently closed the door, and wasted little time walking out of the parking lot, around the building, and toward Sonsee's townhouse. Cerberus had no idea that Louis was returning Sonsee's vehicle or that he planned to search her apartment once again. A haunting voice deep within suggested that perhaps the key had been overlooked.

If Louis could find the key, he would drive straight to LeBlanc Manor, retrieve the treasure, sell it, and leave the country with his wife. Cerberus would never suspect Louis' intrigue until it was too late. Then, Louis simply would tell Brenda he took a chance on some high risk stocks that paid off. She would never have to know the whole story.

As Louis neared Sonsee's townhouse, a rush of adrenaline left his heart pounding with a combination of anticipation and apprehension. Apprehension and anguish. Anguish and aversion. Although he desperately wanted the key, he still detested the risk of getting caught — a risk that left him wanting to bolt.

Louis planned to ring Sonsee's doorbell and await her answer. If he heard no sign of her presence, he would use the townhouse key to let himself in. Of course, there was always the chance that Sonsee was asleep and would not hear the doorbell, but that was a chance he would have to take. The first room he would inspect was her bedroom. If she were in bed, he would quietly exit and plan another visit.

Accompanied by the sounds of sparse morning traffic and the bark of an occasional dog, Louis stepped onto Sonsee's small porch, pressed the round, lighted button, and waited. A balmy Louisiana breeze circled him like a frolicking imp intent on delivering a dose of dread. Gritting his teeth, Louis hunched his shoulders, steeled himself against running, and pressed the doorbell once more. After another brief wait, he unlocked the door, stepped over the threshold, closed the door, and turned the deadbolt.

Every nerve along his spine tingled. The hair on the back of his neck prickled. His toes curled inside canvass shoes. And Louis waited. He waited to hear any sign of movement. Only the refrigerator's purring and the faint hint of potpourri greeted him.

Louis removed his sunglasses and tucked them into the pocket of his dark T-shirt. As his eyes adjusted to the shadowed interior, he relaxed a fraction. The disheveled home looked as demolished as when he last saw it: lamps toppled, decorative pictures scattered across the floor, and the contents of drawers strewn atop the whole mess. If Sonsee had been home, she would have begun repairing the havoc by now.

Nevertheless, Louis picked his way through the chaos and approached the narrow stairway leading to Sonsee's room. Step by step, he inched up the stairs and paused at the top of the landing. The faint smell of feminine perfume attested that he was near her private quarters. Louis paused between two rooms and tried to remember which one was Sonsee's. At last he stepped to the right, swallowed against the lump in his throat, and gently pushed open the door.

Squinting, Louis peered across the shadowed room to an empty brass bed. His gut relaxed a fraction. He pulled a penlight from his hip pocket, clicked it on, and stepped toward Sonsee's dresser. Yesterday, he had dumped the contents of her jewelry box atop her dresser. Today he once more would sort through the gold, diamonds, rubies, and emeralds, some of which appeared to be family heirlooms.

A sinister voice suggested that perhaps he should take what jewelry he liked for

Brenda. Yet another voice from a childhood Sunday school class insisted on no more crime. Louis had listened to that voice when he returned Sonsee's vehicle. He hoped the insurance company would replace her mutilated interior. The exterior had not been harmed. Louis briefly pondered the incongruity of his concern for returning Sonsee's car after murdering her father. But facing that anomaly only added to his confusion. He forced his mind to focus on the task at hand. Inserting the penlight between his teeth, Louis directed the small beam at the dresser top, and began the task he had come to complete.

As he sifted through the jewelry, then the closet, nightstand, and roll-top desk, his gloved hands worked automatically. He scrutinized every inch that the penlight illuminated. All the while, Louis relived the day Jacques LeBlanc had attempted to take his life . . .

After the two of them discovered the treasure, Jacques suggested they present some pieces to a well-known buyer, Mr. Zavier Witherspoon, and ascertain their value. Mr. Witherspoon had planned a yacht outing that afternoon and invited Jacques and Louis along for the ride. But that day an unexpected guest arrived, and Jacques, the loyal patriarch, adhered to familial propriety and invited his relative along for the trip. That was the first time Louis met Cerberus.

The Gulf of Mexico was gentle that day. The cool spray rose above the deck as the sparsely staffed yacht sliced through the ocean. Louis recalled the smell of salt, the taste of expectation, the feel of the ruby-studded, golden goblet as he retrieved it from the velvet bag and placed it on the table between himself, Jacques, and the potential buyer. After the goblet, Louis pulled out a tarnished silver dagger, a golden brooch crusted in diamonds, and several strands of gold beads and pearls. They were snugly sitting in the captain's private quarters when Cerberus broke in upon their tryst.

"Oh, excuse me," Cerberus said, gaze flashing from Louis to Jacques to the cache in the center of the table. A flare of heightened interest glimmered in greedy eyes. "I didn't realize this was a private meeting." Before Jacques formed a reply, Cerberus snapped the door shut.

"As we were saying," Jacques said, shifting in the padded leather chair, "this is a joint venture. We are interested in obtaining quotes to see if selling the pieces would be worth the cost of losing the heirlooms."

Louis fidgeted with the drawstring on the velvet bag, feeling as if someone were tightening such a string around his neck. *No!* he wanted to yell. *We are not trying to decide if we want to sell. I don't give a flip about keeping this treasure. I need the money!* However, Louis remained silent and eyed Mr. Witherspoon as he nonchalantly stroked the row of rubies along the goblet's base. "And you say there's a small chest full of this type of stuff?" he asked, adjusting his bifocals to better examine the pieces.

"Yes," Louis said. "There is a set of eight of the goblets. There's also a wide array of jewels like these and numerous decorative daggers."

"How many pieces altogether?" Mr. Witherspoon leaned back in his chair and stroked his graying goatee. The yacht, buoying across the sea, creaked and yawned as lazily as Zavier's every movement.

"About seventy-five, give or take," Jacques said, his keen blue eyes honing in on the nuance of Witherspoon's every expression.

"Of course, I would need to see all the pieces together before making an official offer, but if we're talking about pieces of this caliber . . ." Witherspoon shrugged. "I'd say I could probably find buyers who would make a five million dollar bid worth my time."

Louis' mouth watered. *Five million! Yes! That means two-and-a-half million for me!* He suppressed the desire to cavort around the cramped cabin, cheering his luck. Finally, he would be able to gain some financial independence. Freedom . . . travel . . . peace of mind.

"I was thinking that ten million would be our absolute lowest price," Jacques derided.

Louis glanced at Jacques then Witherspoon. His fingers tightening around the drawstring, he held his breath.

Witherspoon's bland expression never changed. Only his eyes, creased at the corners, sparked with a surprised glimmer. "I could probably stretch to ten," he said, listlessly checking a gold pocket watch then slipping it back into his jacket's inside pocket. "But that would be my top dollar."

Jacques chuckled under his breath. "I don't think so."

"I would be happy with ten," Louis said,

determined not to lose the sale. He didn't have time to shop the treasure around to a dozen collectors. His financial needs demanded attention now. Within ten days he would be forced to either file bankruptcy or present the cash flow to prohibit his financial demise. Furthermore, keeping the pieces made no sense. Unsold, the heirlooms were worthless to him. "If Jacques isn't interested in selling his half, I'll gladly sell my half for five."

Mr. Witherspoon observed Louis and coolly nodded. Nonchalantly, he scooted his chair back and stood, the small cabin seeming to shrink in comparison to his bulky frame. "I need to buy all or nothing. I don't usually go in for halves. My customers almost always want complete collections." He exited the cabin, the narrow door's click adding a finality to the exchange.

"He's trying to snow us," Jacques said, shoving his hair away from his forehead in a way Louis was beginning to expect. "Frankly, that surprises me. I expected Witherspoon to be more honest. Otherwise I wouldn't have wasted our time. I'm bargaining that the pieces are worth closer to twenty." Jacques picked up the goblet and strained to read the inscription on the bottom. "While I've done my share of collecting rare furniture and paintings, I'm out of my league on these types of pieces. But I've got a hunch that these goblets might very well be unique. Witherspoon was obviously interested in the inscriptions. I was hoping he would play fair, and we could settle this little problem today. But now I say we get several appraisals before deciding whether or not we'll sell. Frankly, I would enjoy handing down some of these pieces to my daughter, Sonsee. She enjoys collecting things." Jacques placed the goblet on the notched table and gazed at Louis as if the final decision had been made.

The rocking of the boat, the smells of the sea increased the churning of Louis' stomach. "I really prefer to go ahead and sell," he insisted. "Five million each is a stack of money. Frankly, I need the money now. I really don't have the time to wait two or three months while we take our time finding the perfect buyer with the perfect offer." His final words, twisted with sarcasm, reflected his growing irritation.

Jacques' narrowing eyes suggested the gentleman had caught the full force of Louis' message. "But the treasure doesn't belong to you alone." Slowly he turned the goblet by its stem and watched as the rubies glistened in the light streaming in from a high window. "It's half mine." He replaced the goblet, propped his elbows on the table, and made a tent of his fingers. "You know, if I weren't the honest sort, I would have every legal right to claim the whole treasure as my own."

Louis resisted the urge to yank his hair out by the roots. From what he observed, the old man owned a house full of French provincial furniture, rare paintings, exquisite crystal, and a host of other priceless heirlooms.

"What are you saying?"

"I'm saying that it would profit you to cooperate. All I'm asking is a reasonable assessment from several buyers. After that, if I decide to keep my share of the treasure and you still want to sell, I'll pay you for your half."

"How much time are we looking at?"

"I can't promise. Might take a few weeks. Might take several months," Jacques said. "If Witherspoon's performance is anything to go by, it might be to our advantage to consult some international buyers as well."

"Would it matter in the least to you if I admitted that I was facing bankruptcy within a matter of ten days? I don't have that kind of time!" Louis' fists curled, and his blunt nails bit into his palms.

"I'm sorry," Jacques said, his blue eyes stirring with genuine concern. "I understand your predicament, but I can't jeopardize such a significant element in my children's inheritance by rashly accepting the first offer I receive." Jacques clamped his jaws together, and Louis was reminded of a bulldog determined not to budge.

Without another word, Louis shoved back his chair and rose. The cabin's low ceiling loomed overhead as if it were the threat of his financial doom.

He stormed onto the deck and into a fine spray of salt water. Louis stepped to the boat's rail, gripped it, and stifled the primeval roar arising within. Gazing into the water, purling with froth along the boat's side, Louis tried to calm himself through rationalization. *Even if I do have to file bankruptcy, it sounds like the old man will eventually give me my money.*

The reality began the gradual reduction of Louis' fury until he realized the old man had kept the key. In the excitement of their find, he'd never asked for the key's return after Jacques unlocked the vault. A cloud of distrust descended upon Louis, and he pictured Jacques saying, "You know, if I weren't the honest sort, I would have every legal right to claim the whole treasure as my own." *Perhaps the old man intends to sell the whole treasure behind my back. He has the key! He has the law on his side. What could stop him?* Louis' throat tightened, and he wondered if he had just been played for a fool. The sun, setting behind a bank of dark, brooding clouds, seemed a metaphor for the end of Louis' financial hopes. The shadows lengthened, the clouds increased. As a flash of lightning flickered along the horizon like a dragon's fiery breath, Louis' financial expectations grew bleaker.

A dull object colliding with his skull ended all speculations. The sickening thud seemed disconnected from the pain shooting across his head as he toppled into the cold ocean. Louis barely remembered the sensation of chilling waters sucking him into dark depths . . . depths that whispered of releasing his spirit into their care. The next thing he recalled was Cerberus, hovering over him on the deck. Louis coughed and gasped for air, despite the protest of his aching lungs. Jacques soon came into view, his eyes filled with concern. Shortly thereafter, they bustled Louis into a guest room at LeBlanc Manor.

That night Cerberus visited Louis' room. According to Cerberus, Jacques had been responsible for Louis' spill into the ocean. Louis shared his anxieties to ready ears, and Cerberus offered to escort him to a hotel. Certain that staying at LeBlanc Manor no longer proved safe, Louis agreed. Within two days, Cerberus proposed a plan that seemed foolproof. The two of them would scare Jacques into giving them the key. They would take the treasure and split it. Both planned to leave the country as soon as Mr. Witherspoon produced the agreed upon price. Cerberus suggested that Witherspoon would remain silent if he were given enough incentive.

Cerberus' plan to only scare Jacques failed. Memories of the moment Louis' greed had borne death left him stiffening, halting in his search of the jumbled possessions atop Sonsee's bathroom counter. He had managed to meticulously sift through all of her room and the other bedroom. Now he stood in front of the bathroom mirror, staring at the shadowed reflection of a killer. The penlight between his teeth highlighted his hardened features in an eery glow. He shuddered.

Louis grabbed the penlight from his mouth, dropped it onto the counter, and yanked his leather gloves from unsteady hands. He turned on the hot water and plunged his fingers beneath the flow. Louis grabbed a toothbrush lying on the cluttered counter and scraped it across a bar of soap that had fallen into the sink. Without mercy, Louis scrubbed his fingers until they burned. The scalding water, steaming amid the soap's fragrance, didn't seem half hot enough. Indeed, Louis wondered if oozing, red lava could scald away the essence of evil.

God, help me! Why did I let Cerberus talk me into carrying a gun into Jacques' room? So what if the old man tried to kill me? I should have just left and filed bankruptcy. Brenda would have understood. Brenda . . . oh, help me, Brenda!

Louis coughed against the tide of terror as rivulets of blood flowed from his cuticles. He dropped the toothbrush, turned off the blistering water, rotated his palms upward, and curled his fingers. As if his hands were decaying, he saw a grayish aura mingled with tinges of crimson oozing from his skin like fiery oil. "Hell waits," a wicked voice whispered.

Louis stiffened. The sudden sound of the front door's opening and closing froze him in place. He gazed wide-eyed in the shadowed mirror. Sonsee's scream floated from the living room. With a gasp, Louis grabbed his penlight and gloves then pivoted toward the shower. Remembering the telltale signs of his presence, he grabbed a towel, rubbed the sink area, then wrapped the soap and toothbrush in the cloth's soft folds. Within seconds, he stepped into the shower and gently tugged the curtain into place.

Before turning off the penlight, Louis checked his watch. The sparkle of tiny diamonds marking each hour mocked him, proclaiming the glitter of the bigger treasure. Their light gave no assurance that holding millions in rare artifacts would provide absolution from his haunting past.

Eight o'clock swiftly approached. Two hours had lapsed since he first entered Sonsee's townhouse. *Two hours.* The time had seemed nothing more than a few blurred moments of surreal recollections.

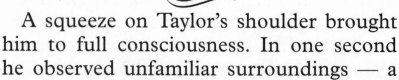

A squeeze on Taylor's shoulder brought him to full consciousness. In one second he observed unfamiliar surroundings — a new house with exquisite decor and deep red carpet. In the next instant, Taylor knew for certain he had been captured by whoever murdered Jacques and was now being held against his will. His need for survival superseded all logic, and he gripped the arm of the person touching him, sprang up, forced his captor onto the couch, and squared one of his knees into the perpetrator's stomach.

A feminine exclamation, ferocious growling, and the feel of teeth sinking into his left thigh brought Taylor to his senses, only to realize he was pinning Melissa to her own couch. And the grinding teeth in his thigh belonged to her Great Dane.

"Call him off, Melissa!" Taylor hollered as Bernie tugged from side to side and razor-sharp pain attested to tearing flesh.

"Call *him* off! Somebody needs to call *you* off. Get off me, you overgrown . . ." Melissa squirmed beneath him.

"I can't!" Taylor shrieked while Bernie's teeth felt as if they were sinking to the bone. "Your dog has my leg. If I move, he'll rip it in two." Bernie's growling grew deeper, more frantic.

"Down, Bernie, *down!*" Melissa commanded. "It's okay. I'm okay. Taylor's just playing. Playing, boy, playing." She glanced at Taylor. "He knows what that means."

A threatening growl and the heated breath dampening Taylor's leg, spoke of Bernie's doubtful response. Nonetheless, the dog relaxed his hold.

"He's letting up," Taylor said.

"That's a good boy," Mel approved. "Now, just back off."

With a confused whine, the dog removed his teeth. Yet the threatening, hot breath still brushed against Taylor's skin like a steady reminder of Bernie's disapproval. Taylor inched away from Melissa and lowered himself onto the couch. His first concern was for his throbbing leg. The smeared blood, puncture wounds, and lacerations declared Bernie's animosity. As if to punctuate his deed, the dog bared his teeth and produced a round of barks, and snarls.

"Come on, boy. We're going out back," Melissa said, tugging on the uncooperative canine.

"Sorry, Melissa," Taylor said, warily eyeing Bernie whose curling lip and hate-filled glares suggested he might repeat his performance at any given moment. "I was asleep. When you woke me up, I didn't know where on the planet I was. I thought I'd been nabbed."

"Bernie, come on, boy, I'll get you a treat," Mel coaxed while shoving the dog toward the door. Bernie's ears perked as if he understood and with a last, hesitant glare at Taylor, he consented to his owner's direction. "It's okay, Taylor," Melissa said with a relieved chuckle. "Just don't do it again. One word from me, and he really would have eaten you for breakfast."

"Why do I have a feeling this is not going to be a good day?" Taylor muttered as every heartbeat subjected his bleeding leg to a painful thump.

"I'll be back with my bag," Mel called over her shoulder. Twenty minutes later, the young doctor had cleaned Taylor's wounds and applied several butterfly bandages.

"Really, I think you could probably use some stitches," she said as she handed Taylor a glass of water and some over-the-counter pain medicine. "But this will have to do. Also, I don't recommend that you go into the backyard today." Mel produced a faint smile.

"Hadn't planned on it." Taylor downed the tablets with a generous swallow of water.

"All I was trying to do was wake you up to tell you I'm leaving for the day. There's bacon in the microwave. Help yourself to the coffee. And there are some blueberry muffins beside the microwave. You can't miss 'em."

"Sorry, my appetite seems to have vanished," Taylor said, eyeing the white bandage, snugly fitted around his thigh. The aromatic smells floating from the kitchen did little to stimulate his hunger.

"I'm sorry about Bernie," Melissa consoled.

Taylor glanced up. "Me, too. I guess my knee in your stomach wasn't the best expression of my appreciation for your hospitality, was it?"

"It's okay. I'll just call your name from across the room next time I need to wake you up." She inserted her hands into the pockets of her business jacket.

"I just hope Bernie can forgive and forget. This is going to be a long visit if he wants to attack me every time he sees me."

"Well, it's just a couple more days. If you can make it through today and tomorrow, we'll pull out for Baton Rouge tomorrow night."

The mention of Baton Rouge ushered in thoughts of Sonsee, and Taylor checked his watch. "It's eight," he said. "I wonder if Sonsee's made it back by now. We took every back road available on our way up here, so it took us longer. But she probably made better time, taking the direct route."

"I'm sure she'll call when she gets home.

Meanwhile . . ." Melissa glanced at the clock on the mantel, "I really need to get out of here."

Taylor, struggling to his feet, attempted to balance without applying unnecessary weight to his left leg. After several hobbles, he approached the entrance to the dining room and gripped the doorframe.

"During my lunch hour, I could bring you some crutches if you like." Melissa dubiously eyed his injury.

"No. I think I'll be okay." Taylor tried to smile but only managed a grimace.

"Okay, then I'm history. If the phone happens to ring, my machine will answer. I turned up the volume so you can hear who's on the other end. Feel free to answer if the call's for you."

"Will do," Taylor said. "If you don't mind, I might give Sonsee a call in an hour or so if she doesn't call me. I'm worried about her."

"That's fine." Mel paused to deliver a piercing gaze. "You know, you and Sonsee have a lot to pray about," she said without a blink.

The comment caught Taylor off guard, and he succumbed to the need to defend himself, his privacy, his heart. "What's that supposed to mean?"

"Never mind," Melissa muttered and turned to leave.

Scowling, Taylor watched as she walked through the dining room, into the kitchen, and out the utility room's door. This morning was certainly not at the top of his favorites, and the last thing he needed was a nosy friend of a friend — a.k.a. the mouth of the South — voicing well-placed hints about him and Sonsee.

He limped into the kitchen, approached the coffeepot, and reached into the cabinet to retrieve a mug. Frowning, Taylor filled the cup with the steaming liquid and suspiciously observed the substance. "This stuff looks like colored water." Tentatively, Taylor sniffed the liquid then took a swallow. "Just like I figured. As weak as a newborn calf." He gripped his mug, grabbed the carafe, and stepped toward the sink. Unceremoniously, Taylor dumped the contents of both into the sink then plopped them beside the coffeemaker.

"I don't know what in the name of common sense that woman is thinking," he grumbled. Taylor fumbled through three cabinets before he found the coffee. "She acts like she thinks that just because she's a doctor she's some sort of self-appointed advisor."

Continuing to mumble, he opened drawers until he found the silverware holder. Taylor fished out a tablespoon, yanked the coffee filter basket from its perch, and examined the leftover grounds. With a shrug, he removed the lid from the coffee can and heaped twelve tablespoons on top of the used grounds. "That oughta do it," he affirmed. Within seconds, the room smelled like decent coffee — the kind a man could sink his teeth into. Centering his weight on his right leg, Taylor waited for the coffeemaker to finish. He noticed the blueberry muffins next to the microwave and picked one up.

As if the act stimulated his masculine musings, images of Sonsee danced through his mind. Images of her standing within inches of him last night. Images of the emotions spilling from her deep-green eyes — the caution, the longing, the love, harnessed yet powerful. *Maybe Melissa's right. Maybe I* do *have a lot to pray about.*

Taylor bit into the blueberry muffin and grimaced. "Good grief! I don't even *like* blueberries." He plopped the offensive bread back onto the plate and forced the lone bite down his throat.

But you do like Sonsee. You like her too much. You especially enjoyed that kiss the night before last. "Okay, okay!" Taylor exploded, grabbing the coffeepot handle. "I like her. I admit it. I like her *a lot!*" He removed the carafe and filled his mug to the accompaniment of sizzling coffee as it poured directly onto the heating pad. He swiftly replaced the carafe and raised his hands as if he were defending himself in court. "All right. I'll admit it. I've liked her too much for a lot longer than she knows or I've wanted to admit. I even had a few romantic thoughts in Hawaii. So what! Somebody sue me! I'm a healthy male. I enjoy female companionship as much as the next guy, and Sonsee is — is a delightful woman. How do you expect me to react? I'm not dead, you know!" He pointed at his chest with both hands then stopped the outburst and wrinkled his brow.

"And now, on top of everything else, I've started talking to myself!" Taylor picked up the mug, gulped a mouthful of the hot, biting liquid, and shook his head in disbelief. "This is going to be a long day."

Taking his time, Taylor limped toward the doorway and paused for another large draught of coffee. No sooner had the hot liquid hit his stomach than the hair on the back of his neck prickled, as if he were being watched. He stiffened and glanced over his shoulder, expecting to see some brute coming through the utility room doorway. Yet the kitchen was empty. Nevertheless, his gut clenched with affirmation that he was not alone. He scanned the dining room until his gaze landed on the patio door, where a large canine eyed him with a look that said, "I'm planning to eat your other leg for lunch."

Relaxing a bit, Taylor walked toward the drape cord with all the nonchalance his injured leg allowed. He knew from dealing with horses and cattle that the less scared a person acted, the better. Taylor figured the same rule worked with horse-dogs as well. Refusing to break eye contact with Bernie until absolutely necessary, Taylor snapped shut the drapes and watched as the floral fabric came to a swirling halt.

"Next time you come after me, I'll be ready, you brute," he growled.

The dog released a cacophony of canine communication — the kind that fills the worst of nightmares. As if preserved for this precise moment, images from *The Hound of the Baskervilles* tromped through Taylor's mind and left him more determined than ever to be prepared should Bernie attack again. A firm thump followed by claws scraping against glass suggested that the dog would stop at nothing to demonstrate his displeasure.

Taylor scanned the room, noticing a pink bag of golf clubs propped near the dining room exit. He retrieved one of the woods, extended it toward the patio door, narrowed his eyes, and whispered, "You better think twice before coming after me, mutt." The hot abhorrence exploded with breathtaking velocity, and the fugitive soon sensed that Bernie represented those bent on framing him, destroying him, slamming him behind bars.

Melissa suggested that Taylor had much to pray about. She was right. Taylor observed his vengeful extension of the golf club: his knuckles, white with the intensity of his grip; the wrist, taut and ready to execute justice; the arm, lean and muscular, prepared to defend.

"Oh, God, help me!" Taylor breathed. Lessening his grip, he turned toward the doorway and used the club as a cane. With a last glance toward the drapes, he strained to hear signs of Bernie's flinging himself against the glass. The dog had reduced his communication to a few frustrated growls. Hobbling to his room, Taylor paused at the door to flip on the light. His khaki-colored backpack lay open near the nightstand and beside the backpack his untouched Bible. *Yes, I have much to pray about, Melissa. Much you don't even know about.*

As if the sight of the Word of God instigated his mother's advice, her words began to twine their way through his spirit, leaving him squirming with discomfort: *The Lord would heal you, Taylor, if only you would be still long enough to let Him. Be still . . . Be still . . . Be still . . .* Those haunting words ushered in a Bible verse that Taylor had recently read, "Be still, and know that I am God."

He peered at his cup of inky coffee, at the fragrant fingers of steam extending from the liquid until they disappeared. He tried to recall the last time he had been still — truly still — not only in his body, but also in his spirit and mind. Running a ranch certainly kept his life busier than most. Keeping his acquaintances at arm's length also took up energy. Taylor had a few church buddies he hunted with, but they didn't really know him.

He reflected over the years since his father's desertion. For the first time, Taylor saw himself the way he truly was after that tragic rejection. Even though he was just a kid, he had backed himself into a corner and, like an injured house cat, once docile and loving, lashed out at anyone who came near. Extending his "claws" protected him and prohibited others from deepening the gaping wound his father had left. As an adolescent some of his claw like endeavors had put him in the wrong place at the wrong time. That final episode when he was seventeen almost landed him in prison as a falsely convicted drug dealer.

From that point, Taylor reformed somewhat. Accepting Christ as his Savior softened his attempts at averting others from his wounds. Eventually, he turned solely to humor. As long as everyone was laughing, they couldn't see his tears. Only his mother knew. And he sensed that Sonsee understood — completely understood.

But can I trust her? A dark shroud descending across the threshold of Taylor's soul. Lately, every time he was with Sonsee, he felt as if he were being pulled closer to some sort of invisible precipice. Last night, before she left, he had been on the brink of toppling over that precipice. The realization left him cringing. If he slid over the edge, Sonsee would have the power to hurt him, hurt him deeply. He would extend to her the same power his father once held, a power he had chosen never to willingly give another human being. Of course, Taylor irrevocably loved his mother, but his mother would never purposefully harm him.

But what about Sonsee? The adoration in her eyes witnessed that all of her heart belonged to him — all of it.

Taylor gulped down half the hot coffee and looked around the silent room decorated with the same understated flare as the rest of the house. The only thing out of place was the poster bed's comforter, rumpled in a tangle of taupe sheets. While the room's silent serenity contrasted with the turmoil inside Taylor's soul, the convoluted bed clothes best illustrated his emotional and mental state.

He glanced above the poster bed to the lone print, framed in gold, hanging over the headboard, rounded and elegant. The painter had released upon canvas a symbol of Taylor's fate. The print, titled "A Shelter in the Storm," featured a sky, dark and ominous, cresting waves, violent and unrelenting, and a rocky cliff forced to absorb onslaught after onslaught of destructive power. Beside the cliff, standing on the sandy beach, a forlorn seaman stood near his sailboat, which was crumpled against the rocks like a child's flimsy toy. The sailor, wind-worn and gnarled, extended his arms toward the threatening sea, his face upward, his eyes closed, an expression of accepting forbearance leaving his travel-weary features assured and unharried. Beneath the painting's title, Taylor read the verse that had flitted through his mind only minutes before, "Be still, and know that I am God (Psalm 46:10)." He vaguely remembered having noticed the verse yesterday before lowering his exhausted body to the mattress.

While the acrimonious ocean, the shattered sailboat, the destructive wind all replicated Taylor's recent fate, the sea captain's stance proved foreign to his mind. Instead of exhibiting peace, Taylor personified hostility. Instead of closing his eyes and lifting his face heavenward, Taylor's eyes flashed with vehemence and volatile vengeance. Instead of extending his arms, Taylor gripped a golf club, ready to pulverize the enemy.

And that verse, as disturbing as the images of his stance, began a slow tattoo in his mind: *Be still and know that I am God. Be still and know that I am God. Be still . . . be still. Although the storm rages and your life is at stake, be still . . . be still . . . be still.* The thoughts drove Taylor to steer his soul toward a sorely neglected port — a haven that held the treasures the sea captain understood and embraced.

Without hesitation, Taylor stepped forward, scooped up his Bible, and lowered himself onto the side of the bed. He rubbed his thumb over the leather cover and pondered the time — or lack of it — that he had spent in the Word of God. He had never really considered himself a Bible scholar. Frankly, he did well to read the Bible and pray between church services. Even though he never wavered in his mental admission that Jesus Christ was the Son of God, even though he tried to live a life that would please the Lord, Taylor had never classified his Christian existence as victorious. Instead he often felt defeated, inadequate, and alone.

Perhaps you've been so busy building walls between you and everyone else that you've also built walls between yourself and God.

The thought barged in upon Taylor and left him pondering the validity of his mother's admonishment to allow the Lord to heal him. For the first time in his life, Taylor admitted he was tired of fending off people, of wall building, of staying on guard lest others see his pain. He deposited the coffee mug on a coaster atop the highly polished nightstand and reflected on his weak spiritual condition. If his mother was right, there was so much more available to him through the power of the Lord.

He fingered the bandage above his left knee and felt as if a similar bandage covered his heart. A bandage that he had placed there himself more than twenty years ago. A bandage of bondage so tattered, so soiled, he would never know freedom from the past until the confining folds fell away.

Thirteen

Sonsee gripped the doorknob for support and gazed in disbelief at the chaos in her townhouse. What had once been orderly now resembled the mounds of debris left in the wake of a tornado. With a groan, she covered her eyes. "Oh, no, tell me this isn't so," she breathed. But another look confirmed that her eyes were not failing.

She closed the door, leaned against it, and gazed toward the staircase, wondering if the upstairs quarters had endured the same treatment. Drawing her purse to her body, Sonsee stumbled forward. After faltering on the first stair, she raced upward, desperate to learn the fate of her bedroom. Her room contained most of her mother's jewelry. And the guest room held a curio that housed her mother's collection of rare Czechoslovakian perfume bottles. Sonsee treasured both the jewelry and the perfume bottles more for their emotional symbols than their material worth.

Panting, she lurched into her bedroom to see what she dreaded the most. Nothing, not even her mattress, had been left aright. Her hands shaking, she hastened to her dresser. Her large jewelry box's contents lay in a mangled heap, carelessly strewn across the doily her grandmother had embroidered. Sonsee's eyes stung. Her throat constricted. Coughing against a sob, she fingered the precious jewelry and mentally tallied off each item. At last she found a tiny token of peace when she realized every cherished article remained, including her mother's diamond-crusted bracelet — Sonsee's favorite since childhood.

"Thank you, Lord," she whispered, then immediately visualized the curio cabinet in the guest room. Whoever trashed her house was certainly not interested in preserving the likes of elegant, antique perfume bottles.

Sonsee whirled around, tripped her way through the mess, and entered the next room. As she feared, the contents of the glass-front cabinet had been tossed onto the floor. Some of the fifty-seven delicately carved bottles remained miraculously intact while others showed signs of cracks, chips, or irreparable damage. One of the rarest bottles — a dainty red affair with an ornate top — had been dashed into several pieces. Only the top, lying several feet away, remained unbroken.

Dropping to her knees, Sonsee released a broken cry. The shattered scarlet bottle represented everything her life had become. What once had been orderly beauty now lay smashed in discord. Nothing, nothing would ever be the same again. She covered her face with her hands and released the sobs that wracked her soul.

Louis, stiff and alert, remained in the shower while Sonsee's weeping vibrated against his spirit like the aftermath of a nightmare. A knot of regret, like a ball of steel, formed in his gut, but Louis repressed it. This was not the time or place for weakness. *You need to focus on getting out of here without getting caught,* he reminded himself. As Sonsee's lamentation continued, Louis decided now was as good a time as any to take his chances on exiting. Sonsee was presently distracted, and who knew what the next ten minutes would bring. Louis had precious little time to spare.

With only the faintest rustle of the plastic, he pushed aside the shower curtain and stepped out. Louis bundled the towel tightly under his arm and tiptoed toward the door. Beads of perspiration created a slick film along his upper lip, and he gritted his teeth. Holding his breath, he stepped from the bathroom.

A furtive glance into the guest room revealed Sonsee sitting near the perfume bottles, her head bent, her hands covering her face, her shoulder-length hair cascading across her cheeks. On his last trip through that room, Louis recalled stepping on a mound of the bottles. The rub of glass against glass had resulted in the destruction of one.

Sonsee's wailing seemed to represent all of Louis' evil deeds. As if his mind were bent on tormenting him, he relived the last few days in agonizing detail. Glancing at his reddened, stinging fingers, he reeled with the onslaught of conflicting urges: a primeval craving to brutally silence the one whose grief represented his darkness; a coward's need to run from her. The coward won.

Stealthily, Louis swiveled to face the staircase and crept downward. Only a few discernible creaks attested to his weight on the steps, yet he cringed with each noise. Once the door came into view, his every muscle tensed, ready to spring forward.

Then he tripped. He lunged forward, barely glimpsing the brass lamp before he landed on top of it. He vaguely recalled tossing aside the lamp yesterday. What an irony that yesterday's search led to today's collapse. The sound of his bulky body crashing into the mound of rubble seemed disconnected from the pain shooting up his shins. A swoosh of air erupted from Louis' lungs, and an involuntary exclamation followed. The door loomed only six feet in front of him. Behind him, Sonsee's muffled crying abruptly ceased. Where sorrow once tread, silence now reigned.

Sonsee sat straight up, her back stiff. As the seconds ticked by, she remained paralyzed — afraid to move, afraid not to. The hot tears that once warmed now created a damp chill along her cheeks.

The crash downstairs, the masculine protest, the scrambling of feet, the quick footfalls verified the sure presence of an invader. Sonsee, at last free of paralysis, clambered to her feet and lunged toward the stairway. On the landing, she gripped the railed banister and watched, wide-eyed, as her front door met its frame in the aftermath of the intruder's exit. The doorknob's faint click was the final punctuation to the person's departure.

Holding her breath, Sonsee coerced herself down the stairs. Once in the living room, she rushed to the door, flung it open, and stepped onto her small porch. After a fruitless glance both ways, yet another impulse overtook Sonsee — an impetus that demanded she hide from the scoundrel. As quickly as she had stepped outside, Sonsee dashed back inside and slammed the door. With quivering fingers, she turned the deadbolt lock, then collapsed against the door and gasped at the shambles of her life. Only her jagged breathing marred the eerie silence. One thought jolted through her brain, *The key, the key, the key. He must have been after the key.*

Gulping for air, Sonsee darted toward the stairs, up to her room, and stopped at her nightstand. The phone she reached for lay on the floor, partly covered by the miscellaneous contents of her nightstand drawer. Sonsee placed the phone in its rightful spot and dialed Melissa's number.

Her answering machine produced a cheerful greeting, and as soon as the beep sounded, Sonsee yelled, "Taylor! Are you there! Are you listening? Pick up the —"

"What happened? What's the matter?"

Taylor's urgent, yet mellow tones floated over the line and Sonsee suppressed the welling tears.

You've cried enough, she told herself. *Enough for a lifetime.* "Someone trashed my apartment, Taylor. The whole place looks just like Father's bedroom did."

"Is there anything missing?"

"Who knows!" Sonsee raised a hand.

"You think they were looking for the key?" Taylor asked, his voice solemn.

"There's no way to be certain, but . . . I think we need to see what's inside that fireplace as soon as we can."

"Where's the key right now?"

"It's still in my purse, where I put it two nights ago. At least I *think* it is!" Sonsee whirled around to spot her black leather purse still sitting on the dresser. "Just a minute!" She dropped the receiver on the nightstand, snatched her bag, then plunged her hand deep into the side pocket. The cool metal against her clammy fingers attested to the key's presence. Grasping it, Sonsee grabbed the receiver. "I've still got it."

"Good! Have you reported the break-in to the police?"

"N-no," Sonsee stammered, her exhausted mind as chaotic as her home. "B-but is that a good idea? I mean, I'm

241

helping you hide. The last thing I need is the police asking questions or having them patrolling this neighborhood more frequently or watching my home. And isn't that one of the routine things they do when you report something like this?" Sonsee rubbed her temple as a tired headache threatened to erupt.

"Yes, you're right. Good thinking, Red," he added and this time, the nickname held more the nuance of an approving endearment than a brotherly gibe.

Sonsee caught her lower lip between her teeth and relished the rush of pleasure his charming tone evoked. During the whole drive home, she had relived the kiss along with that potent moment in Mel's living room. Sonsee had almost felt as though he had kissed her again. If the flash of awe in his eyes was anything to go by, she believed that Taylor Delaney was on the road to being romantically involved, whether he would admit it or not.

"Sorry," he said after a long pause, "I guess I used the 'R' word again, didn't I? Are you going to hang me at high noon?"

"No. I don't have the time right now," Sonsee teased, a hollow ring to words that should have been flippant. "Maybe next week."

His chuckle, low and inviting, left a row of goose bumps down Sonsee's spine, goose bumps that bade her to fall at Taylor's feet and beg him to become her reason for living. A contradictory vein of musings barged into her mind. A few months ago during that journey to Vietnam, Sonsee had relinquished her dreams of marrying Taylor to the Lord. She had forged a deeper commitment to Jesus Christ and reaffirmed *Him* as her reason for living — not her career or herself or even Taylor. Now, contrary to her former resolve, she was falling into the old patterns of pining after Taylor with a fervor that supplanted her yearning for the Lord. The question that had plagued Sonsee during her homeward trek assaulted her anew: *Can you live without Taylor and still be at peace?* Sonsee's fingers tightened on the receiver.

Despite her vacillating thoughts, the expanding silence gradually developed into the unspoken communication of two hearts, confused and solitary. Solitary and searching. Searching and surrendering.

"I wish I were there with you." All traces of humor vanished from Taylor's voice.

Sonsee swallowed against her tightening throat. "Thanks," she rasped. "I really appreciate the offer, but —"

"But I'm stuck here, with a nosy doctor and a Great Dane who is using me as an appetizer."

"Sounds like Mel has asked a few too many questions," Sonsee returned, glad for the conversation's different direction. "She's famous for that. I guess I should have warned you." She leaned against the wall, and the surrounding shambles seemed to creep closer by the minute, as if bent on suffocating her.

"She told me she was the mouth of the South, whatever *that's* supposed to mean. And I'd say she owns a dog just like her. Dear little Bernie wrapped his *southerly mouth* around my thigh this morning."

"No!" Sonsee gasped. "But he's usually such a pet. He —"

"He didn't appreciate my body-slamming his owner on the couch."

"What?"

"Yeah, well, I wound up sleeping on the couch all night. When Melissa tried to wake me up this morning, I thought I'd been captured. And, well . . ."

"You attacked her?"

"I wouldn't exactly say I *attacked* her. I just pinned her to the couch."

"I'd say if Bernie is worth his salt, he had

every right to defend Mel — from a canine perspective, of course," Sonsee rushed.

"Whatever you say, Red." A hint of mockery laced Taylor's words, and this time the nickname sent a flush through Sonsee.

"Well, I guess I need to go. I just wanted to tell you about my apartment," she snapped.

"Ooo, sounds like I hit a nerve."

"I don't like to be called 'Red.' Remember?"

"You didn't seem to mind a few minutes ago."

"But that was different."

"Oh, yeah, how?"

"Never mind," Sonsee ground out, her shoulders stiffening with the very idea that the man would goad her about his previous endearing tone. His ability to nettle her, swiftly and thoroughly, had never wavered in their twenty-four year acquaintance. "I've got to go," she blurted. Purposefully, Sonsee removed the receiver from her ear and planned to drop it in the cradle. However, halfway to the destination, Taylor called her name, and she stopped, debating whether to hang up or give ear to his supplication.

"Sonsee, don't hang up!"

The faint cry twined a path straight into the center of her being. Her heart urged her to capitulate to Taylor's request, yet her mind suggested she adhere to the most logical road and disconnect the call.

"Sonsee LeBlanc, do not hang up on me!" This time Taylor's commanding tone demanded a response.

"What?" she barked into the receiver in the voice of a sister vexed beyond her limits.

"Have you discovered where they broke in? Was it a window or —"

"I don't know yet. I haven't had a chance to see."

"They most likely broke out a window. Don't waste any time trying to fix it. Get some plywood and nail it up from inside. That will work until later. Make sure your front door is locked, and —"

"I already did." She picked up the brass lamp, lying beside the nightstand, and plopped it in its rightful place with more effort than necessary.

"Good."

Another stretch of strained silence heightened Sonsee's awareness of her arms, aching to return Taylor's tender embrace.

"Sonsee," he choked out. "Don't go and

246

get yourself killed. I don't — don't know what I would do without you. You're one of the best friends I've got, and . . . and . . ."

The unfinished "and" spoke more than any words could have portrayed. Sonsee closed her eyes as every drop of annoyance drained away to be replaced by wave upon wave of ardent adoration — adoration that completely swallowed Sonsee in its warm, wondrous waters.

"With God as my witness, Sonsee, if we get through this alive, I'll . . . I'll . . ."

She barely breathed.

"We need to talk," he said at last. "We need to talk when we're both rational and rested. Right now, I'm so stressed . . ."

"So am I," she admitted, rubbing her temple in a tiny, circular motion. "And right now, I need some rest. I'm supposed to be at the clinic this afternoon. I'm going to lose all my patients if I don't start making at least some occasional appearances."

"Well, okay," Taylor agreed, his voice oozing with anxiety. "Might be best to stay at the clinic tonight. Don't you have a den set up there where you could sleep?"

"Yes. Yes, I do. That sounds like a good idea."

"Don't forget, somebody already shot at me. They might do the same to you." After only the briefest of pauses, he continued, "Blast it, Sonsee! I'm going to get Melissa to lend me her car. I'll be there —"

"No!" Sonsee demanded, deciding then and there not to mention the intruder's recent departure. "Stay where you are! The last thing we need is —"

"I can't stand this! I feel like I've taken you to the edge of a cliff and just shoved you off."

That's exactly what you've done, Taylor, Sonsee thought, *but it has nothing to do with my safety and everything to do with my heart.*

The doorbell's unexpected ring, shrill and jarring, held an uncanny note that left Sonsee's skin crawling. Her pulse increased, and she imagined a hulk of a man standing outside, ready to give her the same treatment her home had endured.

"Someone's at the door," she panted.

"Don't hang up."

"Should I even answer?" she asked as the bell rang again.

"You have a peephole, right?"

"Yes."

"At least go see if you know them. It might be important — something to do with this mess we're in. Just don't hang up," Taylor said, as if his being on the phone could somehow ensure her safety.

"Okay." Within seconds, Sonsee gripped the banister and descended the staircase with a beastly paranoia sinking its ugly claws into her shoulders. When she stepped into the living room, the doorbell chimed for the sixth time. She halted, debating the wisdom of even peeping out the door. Finally the doorbell stopped ringing. Sonsee tiptoed across the disheveled room, placed her eye close to the peephole, and caught a glimpse of a familiar profile as she moved away from Sonsee's porch.

Alana. Only two days had lapsed since Sonsee had seen her. Two days. Yet the time seemed an eternity. She recalled Alana's tear-stained eyes, her cries for a father she never really knew, her shock when Sonsee offered the ambiguous apology. A voice deep within Sonsee's soul urged her to allow Alana access to her home. She opened the door and called her sister's name.

Fourteen

"Dr. Moore, I'm so glad you're here," Bobbie Bailey, one of Mel's nurses, rushed down the long hallway as soon as the doctor stepped into her wing of the children's clinic. Bobbie's long blonde hair, caught in a ponytail, swayed with every step. The twenty-five-year-old registered nurse, fresh faced and vivacious, added plenty of drama to the office.

"Why? What's up?" Melissa asked, casually checking her watch. She automatically assumed that, as usual, Bobbie was probably overstressed about a minute matter.

Bobbie gripped her boss' arm and leaned forward. "There's *a man* in your office," she hissed, her thin blonde brows raised as if the two of them were conspiring the most outrageous of schemes. "He was here yesterday morning, but I told him you'd be in today. He just walked right in about ten minutes ago and refused to leave. I told him you have patients starting at 8:45, and he said he would wait."

Melissa glanced at her practical Timex to see she only had fifteen minutes to spare before her first patient. "Did he give you his name?" she asked, as she neared her office.

"No. I — I didn't ask, and he didn't volunteer. But he's really tall and has dark hair and dreamy eyes." A faint sigh accompanied the words.

Mel slowed her athletic gait in order to dart the nurse one of her no-nonsense expressions. The description perfectly fit Kinkaide Franklin — including the feminine sigh of appreciation and the fact that he had been trying to contact her yesterday morning. Yet the thought of Kinkaide in her office addled her as much as when she'd encountered him on her front porch yesterday. However, Mel didn't for one second reveal her discomfort to the young nurse. Instead, she continued to level a direct gaze at her that underscored their recent conversation.

Bobbie lowered her eyes, and the discourse from last week flashed between the two in a second of silent communication. Mel had addressed the issue of male callers during office hours. The nurse, cute and bubbly, never lacked for attention from the opposite sex, and Melissa had finally been forced to tell Bobbie to keep her personal life out of the office and off the phone.

"Sorry." Bobbie twisted her fingers into a knot. "I guess he's probably your brother or something. He did look vaguely familiar," she babbled.

"No. I don't have a brother, only three sisters." Melissa paused about six feet from the office door. "And whoever he is, I didn't invite him here. I will see that his departure is imminent and swift."

"Yes. I understand," Bobbie said, yet a glimmer of mischief twinkled in the depths of her guileless gray eyes.

The remaining staff of four busied themselves around the office as if they weren't the least bit interested in their boss' caller. Yet Mel felt as if they each had a set of extra ears straining to catch the faintest detail of the doctor's guest. Along the chest-high desk wall sat the usual kids' stuff that Mel insisted on for her patients: decorative stickers, sugar-free gum, a stuffed bear she would eventually give to a patient. Determined to maintain her aura of calm, Mel reached into the basket of gum and pulled out a piece. "Isn't Davy Sigmond due in this morning, Bobbie?"

"Yes." Bobbie glanced toward the dry erase board that listed the morning's appointments. "At ten."

"Great. Let's give him the bear today. I'm afraid we're going to have to take out his tonsils. I'll give him special permission to take the bear into pre-op. Hopefully that will help." Mel turned on her heel and stepped toward her office. On second thought, she swiveled to face Bobbie again, only to see that the four women had stopped their beehive activity to stare after their boss. Mel's meaningful cough instigated the staff's immediate action, yet Bobbie's twitching lips spoke for all of them.

"If you will, Bobbie," Mel continued, wishing she could dissolve into the carpet, "plan to leave for lunch a little early so we can replace the bear. Okay?"

"Right, Doctor," Bobbie said solemnly.

And Mel wondered if this were some kind of divine joke. Why did Kinkaide have to arrive only a week after she had lectured Bobbie about male callers?

Resolving to remain calm, Melissa stepped into the office, decorated with the same elegant flare as her home, not because Mel was a superb interior designer but because she hired one. Just as she had anticipated, Kinkaide awaited her. As she closed the office door, he turned from his perusal of the stereo system ensconced behind a walnut-and-glass entertainment center with book shelves beneath. He greeted her with the faintest hint of a smile — a smile that touched his searching eyes with a whisper of the joy they once shared. The only thing that had changed since she saw him six years ago was the dark, neatly trimmed beard and the few streaks of gray at his temples that added a certain distinguished maturity to his demeanor. The older Mel grew, the more ardently she admired distinguished maturity.

Schooling her features into a bland mask, she approached her conservative oak desk and deposited her purse-organizer on top of it. Mel's mind spun with the possible reasons for Kinkaide's visit — none of which posed a logical option. As the silence expanded, she absorbed his every feature: the prominent nose that spoke of strong character and Italian ancestors; the heavy brows that reflected a thoughtful, sensitive mind; the broad, lean shoulders that attested to his physical fitness. His carefree nature, expressed by the collar-length hair, appealed to Melissa as much now as when she first met him.

Without warning, she flashed back to the night before their supposed wedding when she had anxiously anticipated the consummation of their vows. They had planned a honeymoon as low-key as the wedding. Just Melissa and Kinkaide in an Arkansas bed and breakfast. Nothing fancy. But they didn't need anything fancy. They had each other. Or so she thought.

Kinkaide removed his hands from his pants pockets to reveal long, slender fingers that turned piano music into warm honey dripping into the soul with a sweet nuance of heavenward praise. He shoved his hands back into his pockets, and Melissa wondered if the visit unnerved him as much as her.

"I noticed you have all my CDs," he said, turning toward her stereo.

"Yes."

"And that they've never been opened."

"No."

"So?" He glanced back at her, his brows raised in query.

"So," Mel answered, not willing to give him the satisfaction of even suspecting the level of her intense embarrassment. She left the CDs in her office because she didn't want anyone — not her mother, sisters, or closest circle of six friends — to spot them and surmise the meaning of their existence. How ironic that the one place she thought they were hidden was the exact spot where they were discovered.

"I . . . guess you're wondering why I'm here," Kinkaide said with the same crooked smile that made her stammer through their first date.

"Yes, and make it fast," she said in a businesslike voice that denied the significance of those CDs. Mel flicked her wrist and checked her watch. "I have patients starting in eight minutes."

His eyes narrowed a fraction as he glanced at her watch. "Really, what I have to say is going to take more than eight minutes. Are you free for lunch?"

"No," Melissa bit out, not even sure if she would live to see lunch. At the rate her heart was hammering, she was more concerned about cardiac arrest than what was on the agenda for the noon meal. Yet despite what her schedule might or might not say, Mel was *not free* for Kinkaide. Today or ever.

"I don't believe you," he said, a daredevil light in his eyes.

"I don't care."

"Well, I guess my questions have been answered."

Melissa lowered her gaze to the top button of his classic gray polo shirt. When she spoke, her heart spoke for her. "Exactly what did you come to say?" The tremor in her voice contradicted her claims of not caring what he thought.

"Mel, I —" He hesitated then took a step forward. The tap on her office door resembled the decisive rap of a judge's gavel and spoke of Bobbie's impetuous nature. Kinkaide glanced toward the door and jerked at a tuft of his beard. Relieved by the interruption, Mel spanned the few feet and opened the door to encounter Bobbie, as expected.

"Dr. Moore, there's another *man* on the phone," she said, her eyes snapping with raging curiosity. "He says he's a close friend and that this is an emergency. I tried to tell him you were . . ." she cleared her throat "occupied, but he wouldn't —"

"Okay, just put him through." Mel figured the caller must be Taylor. Turning to her desk phone, she pondered what more the day might hold.

"Oh, and Doctor?" Bobbie anxiously called.

For an answer, Mel raised her brows in silent approval for her employee to continue.

"Your first two patients are here. We're ready and waiting." She cast another furtive peek at Kinkaide. "Both are just yearly checkups. We can go ahead and give them their immunizations and draw the blood and start labs if you like."

"Yes, yes, that's fine." Mel waved her hand, too rattled to worry about the results of a needle-affected child before her exam. Usually, Melissa preferred that her patients receive all blood work and shots after her visit so they were calmer during the exam. But this morning nothing was going as planned.

Shortly after Bobbie exited, Melissa's desk phone rang, and she picked up the receiver.

"Melissa, I'm worried about Sonsee," Taylor rushed before Mel had time to voice a greeting.

"Oh? What happened?" she asked, forcing her voice into a casual timbre. Tensing, Mel turned her back on Kinkaide and leaned against the desk. In the second that lapsed before Taylor spoke again, she imagined all sorts of horrors about Sonsee and her homeward journey.

"Someone ransacked her apartment. She called to tell me. While we were on the phone, someone came to the door. I told her not to hang up. She came back on the line to say that Alana was there. I don't trust her, Mel. I'm going back to Baton Rouge. I won't be here when you get home. I can't stand this — being here — being *stuck* here by myself in this house when Sonsee could be risking her life."

"Do you have reason to believe that . . ." Mel could only imagine how Kinkaide would interpret the phone call, ". . . that this individual in question is somehow connected —"

"Yes! I have reason to believe that any of Sonsee's *beloved* relatives could be up to their pretty little necks in it!" His voice crescendoed. "I told Sonsee not to let Alana in, but she said it was too late." Wincing, Mel tilted the phone away from her ear, then remembered Kinkaide. Instantly she clamped the receiver back to her ear. "When I tried to tell her to make Alana leave, she said she really didn't think Alana was involved!" Taylor shouted. "Somewhere between here and Baton Rouge, Sonsee LeBlanc has lost her mind! For all I know, Alana could be strangling her now!"

"Have you tried calling her back just to check —"

"Yes! She told me to chill out and that she'd call me when Alana leaves." He sarcastically mimicked Sonsee's inflections.

Mel checked her watch; 8:50 was history. "Look," she said in the voice of a perturbed sister, "you probably *do* need to chill out. Sounds to me like Sonsee is making logical choices and being as careful as possible. If she was okay when you called to check on her —"

"I'm going back to Baton Rouge today. I don't care how I get there, I'm going."

"I don't think that's a good idea. *I really don't.*" Her fingers curled all the tighter around the receiver, and she resumed her erect position. "I think you're asking for more trouble than you want. It will be better — much better — for you to wait until Jac gets here."

Out of the corner of her eye, Mel caught sight of Kinkaide moving toward the door. She fought the urge to fully face him, yet faced him anyway. With one brow cocked in a flirtatious manner, he said, "See ya later," and stepped out of the office before Mel had a chance to reply.

Watching Kinkaide leave the office without so much as a backward glance plunged her into the bitter remembrance of the day she had stood at her apartment window as he drove away, the engagement ring in his pocket, her heart in his hands. Standing at the window, all alone in that tiny apartment, Mel had vowed she would never — *absolutely never* — take Kinkaide back, even if he became the most celebrated pianist of the century and flung himself at her feet. As one year melted into another and Kinkaide chased his dreams, Melissa scoffed at herself for ever being naive enough to believe he would ask her back. Yet, today, Mel felt as if the layers of maturity she had gained were peeled away, inch by inch, and she was back to that naive med student, vulnerable and shattered. Shattered and vindictive. Vindictive and sure. Sure that Kinkaide Franklin had finally come crawling back.

Well, you can forget it, Mister! Mel stormed mentally as Taylor continued to voice his concerns about Sonsee. "Look, Taylor," she ground out, blasting him with the full intensity of her reaction to Kinkaide. "I have a practice to run here. There are patients waiting —"

The phone clicked in her ear. Mel pulled the receiver away and stared at it. With a tired sigh, she hung up the phone then covered her face for a moment of silent reflection. She had only been in the office twenty-five minutes, and already she was exhausted.

As if she were a robot moving to the

261

commands of a programmer's stimulus, Melissa pushed Taylor and Sonsee to the back of her mind and approached the entertainment center. She reached for the glass door behind which lay Kinkaide's CDs. Gently, Melissa tugged the door open and retrieved the top of a neat stack of six. On the front of the plastic case, Kinkaide stood near an ebony grand piano, his legs crossed at the ankles, his hand casually resting on the piano. Dressed in a black tuxedo with white shirt and red bow tie, his dark hair gleaming, he looked as if he were ready to sit at the keyboard and release his magical gift as a fragrant worship to the Lord.

Mel gently touched his face, then closed her eyes and hardened her features against the onslaught of threatening tears. Standing exactly where Kinkaide had stood, she inhaled deeply, as if she could somehow soak in his very essence and that, by acquiring his essence, she would find solace for a heart heaving with memories of what was, memories of what he had promised, memories of what should have been.

She had barely slept last night. For the first time in three years, Mel relived the nightmare that had plagued her until she begged God to deliver her. But last night the dream had returned, and Mel repeatedly awakened to her own mumbling, "Help! Help! I'm drowning! Kinkaide! Kinkaide, don't leave me! Save me!" Yet the man she thought loved her had stared straight into her eyes and rowed away in a ghostlike ship, leaving her to drown in a heaving ocean bent on swallowing her alive.

Poor Bernie had whined and fretted every time Mel awoke. Eventually the dog climbed into bed with his beloved owner and placed his head on her stomach. Bernie was so big that sleeping with him was usually an impossibility, but last night, Mel enjoyed his comfort. Once Bernie lay beside her, Melissa had been able to grab two untroubled hours of sleep before time to rise.

Those hideous dreams were far removed from the person Mel had become: a woman, self assured and independent; a woman who wasted precious little time on the illogical. However, those dreams fully reflected her heartache.

A familiar knock interrupted her musing. "Yes, Bobbie, come in," she called, certain of the visitor's identity. Mel replaced the CD and turned to face her employee.

Bobbie's inquisitive gaze went from Melissa to the stack of CDs and back to the doctor. Her eyes widened a fraction as if she were finally piecing together why Kinkaide looked so familiar. She probably snatched an occasional glance at the CDs when her duties required entry into Mel's office.

Deciding the best course of action was the direct, clear one, she chose to state the facts to her employee. Melissa pursed her lips and closed her heart's door, behind which still echoed the weeping of yesteryear. "His name is Kinkaide Franklin." Approaching the nurse, she took the proffered stethoscope and placed it around her neck. Mel stepped into the hallway and continued speaking loud enough for the staff behind the desk to hear. "Yes, he's the pianist Kinkaide Franklin," she said in a tone that broached no argument. "We were once engaged." Mel felt as if she were setting off one display of fireworks after another, and the eager staff anticipated the next round. "I had no idea he was going to be here this morning. Except for a brief visit yesterday, I have not seen him in six years." The determined doctor plodded toward the first room where a patient awaited. "In case you're wondering, I fully intend to live by the set of rules that I expect my staff to adhere to. If I have any say in the matter at all, Mr. Franklin will not visit me again during office hours." Melissa slowed her gait and leveled a meaningful glance toward Bobbie. "And as for the other person of male persuasion that telephoned — he doesn't belong to me. He belongs to a friend." Mel stopped outside the first examination room and retrieved the chart from the plastic holder attached to the door. She focused on the task at hand, thus freeing Bobbie to respectfully pursue her duties.

I'm glad Taylor doesn't belong to me. He and I would not get along. Despite her sarcastic musings, Mel realized she owed Taylor an apology. The poor man had been literally bitten by Bernie and then verbally bitten by her. Mel concluded that Taylor was undoubtedly overreacting, but who wouldn't in his position? Before she began her first exam, she marched back to her office, closed the door, and dialed her own number.

"Taylor, it's me, Mel," she said after the machine finished its greeting.

"What?" Taylor snapped into the receiver.

"I'm sorry," she confessed, rubbing the

frown lines between her brows. "If you'll just sit tight, as soon as I can I'll call and we can discuss this further. If you really think it's best for you to go to Sonsee's before tomorrow night, then I'll see what I can arrange. But please, *please* don't take off on your own while I'm not there. If anything happens to you, Sonsee will never forgive me. Besides, with your injured leg, you have no business out running around today anyway. Got it?" she added for emphasis.

"Yeah, I got it, Doc," he drawled, a smile lacing his caustic tone.

"Good." Mel replaced the receiver before he could produce another argument.

Fifteen

Sonsee checked the last window and glanced over her shoulder at Alana. "No evidence of breaking and entering," she said, shaking her head. After the shock of seeing Sonsee's domestic disaster, Alana had insisted upon helping her methodically inspect every window to pinpoint the location of the villain's entry. Only one option for entry remained. She and Alana simultaneously gazed at the front door.

"I didn't notice any signs of forced entry at the door," Alana mumbled as the two of them picked through the debris to inspect the doorknob and lock.

Sonsee opened the door and squatted to scrutinize the frame and knob. She looked up at Alana, whose plump, pale face and sorrowful hazel eyes mirrored Sonsee's own uneasiness.

"Do you think they had a key to your house?" Alana whispered, as if the intruder were listening.

"I can't imagine how, but . . ." Sonsee trailed off as her attention was snared by the row of vehicles, sitting in their normal spots near the townhouse. For the first time, she noticed her Honda was missing. Sonsee parked it right in front of her townhouse after she and Taylor arranged a late-night rental car from the Metropolitan airport. The two had decided that leaving her car in front of her townhouse, rather than parked at the airport, would be the wisest choice. That way she would appear to be home. Today, she had returned the rental car and taken a taxi home. She had been so intent on getting into her house after the long journey that she had failed to notice her car missing among the line of usual vehicles.

"My car's gone," she said, feeling as if her blood drained to her feet.

"No, it isn't," Alana said, tugging a strand of brassy red hair toward her temple. "I saw it when I drove in." She pointed to the west parking lot, blocked from view by the other section of townhouses. "I parked near it because I thought your apartment was nearby. Then I wound up having to walk across the grounds to get to you. I wondered why you parked so far from your house —"

"I didn't," Sonsee ground out. "I parked right there." She pointed toward a spot by an oak that a white Ford claimed. "I'm going to get my keys. Show me where you saw my car."

Soon the sisters approached the blue Honda. As Alana had said, her sporty Cadillac was parked only six parking spaces away from Sonsee's vehicle. Not certain what she would find, Sonsee peered into the Honda's window as she inserted her key. At the sight of the shredded interior, Sonsee gripped the key tighter and closed her eyes.

Alana, stepping to Sonsee's side, gasped. "Somebody is looking for something," she said, as if the obvious needed to be stated. "And whoever it is, is serious."

"Serious enough to kill Father." Sonsee shared a haunted gaze with her sister. The lifelong antagonism that dogged the two sisters had stopped them from the remotest possibility of a deep bond. Frankly, in just the short time Alana had been in her company today, Sonsee had wondered half a dozen times why she paid the visit — a first for the siblings. From Sonsee's standpoint, there was no logical reason for Alana to drive from New Orleans to see her despised younger sister. And so far, Alana hadn't divulged the reason for her visit. She had stepped into the demolished home and immediately helped Sonsee try to find the villain's point of entry. For once, all signs of discord had dissolved and the two sisters worked together as family should.

Sonsee opened the car door, placed a knee on the driver's seat, and scanned the tattered interior that had once been immaculate. The carpet, now ripped up, curled away from the floorboard, and the contents of her glove box cluttered the passenger seat. No possible hiding place went untouched.

After the horror over the house, discovering her vehicle in similar shape proved anticlimactic, numbing. However, the rage that was swiftly becoming her bedfellow erected itself from the ashes of her grief. Someone had killed her father and ransacked his room. Most likely, that same person was responsible for violating Sonsee's possessions. Once again, a breathtaking need for vengeance superseded all quests for righteousness. Sonsee vowed in her heart that, given the opportunity, she would annihilate the responsible party.

Shuddering, Sonsee stepped away from the vehicle, locked the door, and shut it. Her teeth clenched, she balled her fists, and slammed one against the top of her car. The pain erupting from fist to wrist only fueled her fury. Every spiritual truth Sonsee thought she had once absorbed now fled her soul. Only one compulsion motivated her: the need for revenge. A sinister voice suggested that Sonsee would not be at peace until the person who ended her father's life was punished with death.

"You look exactly how I feel," Alana whispered.

Sonsee turned to her sister — a sister she had never really known, a sister who, only a few days before, she had suspected of murder. But Sonsee's belief that Alana was innocent now flourished to full blossom. This grief-stricken woman was not a murderer. Her hazel eyes, reddened from crying, were too full of despair. Her plump cheeks, speckled with freckles, were too pale from sorrow. Her hunched shoulders, drooping with burden, were indicative of a soul overwrought with loss.

Impulsively, Sonsee reached for her sister. For the first time in their lives, they fell together in a hug that lacked the strain of antipathy. Alana's trembling added to Sonsee's growing understanding of the sister she'd thought she would avoid forever.

"I'm so sorry," Alana whispered against Sonsee's shoulders.

"It's only a car," Sonsee replied, her voice tight.

"No, not about the car." Alana pulled away and fished in her slack's pocket for a tissue. "About . . . about . . ." She shook her head and floundered for words.

As Sonsee awaited her sister's explanation, she noticed a slight bruise near her temple and wondered if her husband, Nick, had been the cause. Alana self-consciously pulled a strand of wispy hair closer to her eye and covered the dark mark. She peered downward at restless fingers tearing at the tissue. And the empathy from recent days resurfaced in Sonsee's heart. Alana desperately craved acceptance, love, appreciation. Ironically, that craving had been manifested in a lifetime of negative behavior that actually drove people away.

"Let's just go on back in the house," Sonsee said in a fatigued voice. "Maybe I can at least find us a soda."

"Okay."

Within minutes the two sisters sat amid the clutter in Sonsee's dining nook, sipping soda. Alana, visibly relaxing with every passing minute, at last looked Sonsee square in the eyes. "I've been doing a lot of thinking in the last couple of days. And I've decided that I don't believe Taylor killed Father. At first, I'll admit that I agreed with Hermann and really believed Taylor was the one. But the more I think about it, the more I'm convinced that Taylor Delaney might have an obnoxious streak here and there, but the man is *not* a killer. I never even believed he was involved in that drug deal twenty years ago. I really think he's just a kid who got hurt and still isn't over it."

Sonsee, in the middle of a sip, coughed against the misdirected soda. "Who do you think did it?" she squeaked out, half terrified to even discuss the issue with Alana.

"I don't know."

"Do you think it was one of the family?" Sonsee asked as images of Hermann, Natalie, and Rafael rushed through her mind: Hermann, with steely, calculating eyes; Natalie, with a voracious appetite for money; Rafael, blond and handsome, not concerned that his wife was ten years his senior and acted ten years his junior. After all, Natalie had a wealthy father.

Alana, her eyes round in anguish, observed her sister as if she were debating whether to disclose some wretched secret.

At last she covered her face with her hands, and her shoulders shook.

"I think — I'm scared — oh, Sonsee, promise me you won't breathe a word. Promise me!" Alana gripped Sonsee's forearm with both hands.

Stunned by this turn of events, Sonsee silently stared at Alana, afraid to promise silence lest that would ensure the killer's freedom and guarantee Taylor's doom.

"I've been having the most horrible doubts about Hermann and Natalie and Rafael. For some reason, I just —" She gulped. "Hermann and I have always been close. He would be devastated if he knew I was doubting him —"

"But if he's the one who did it . . ."

"Exactly. Even though I always thought he really loved Father, there's just this nagging suspicion that won't go away."

"And what about Rafael and Natalie?" Sonsee asked, leaning forward.

"I don't know Rafael that well," Alana said.

"Neither do I."

"But I'm not sure Natalie would be able to pull off something like that by herself."

"So you think that if Natalie is involved, then Rafael is in it with her?"

Alana nodded. "Yes. Or all three together," she murmured. "And I feel like Benedict Arnold."

"Well, I suspected them from the start," Sonsee declared. "And I don't feel the least bit guilty. If one of them *is* responsible, I look forward to the day . . ." She trailed off as a snug band of tension tightened around her soul — tension she recognized as the convicting power of the Holy Spirit. *Vengeance is mine, says the Lord, I will repay.* The verse from Matthew reverberated through her mind, and Sonsee had never wanted to reject a biblical truth as fiercely as she wished to renounce this one. With every passing hour, her need to see the criminal captured was escalating into a burning desire for personal retaliation. At this moment, if she were given the chance to avenge her father's death, Sonsee would be hard-pressed to deny the opportunity.

"God help us, Sonsee," Alana breathed.

Sonsee scrutinized Alana more intently than ever before and was shocked to see so much of herself. All these years she had presumed that her half-siblings and she were poles apart. Even though she and Alana resembled each other in their hair and skin tone, Sonsee fervently denied that the two shared any personality traits. With Alana forever offering accusatory digs that reflected resentment over Jacques' favoritism, Sonsee had viewed her older sister as less valuable. But sitting across from Alana, Sonsee recognized that she had allowed her father's misplaced doting to color her own attitudes. And what she saw today was an older version of herself. The expression in Alana's eyes suggested she had read Sonsee's every thought. As Alana had mentioned beside the car, the two sisters were trapped in the vortex of the same dark emotions. Both loved their father. Both wanted justice. Both were ready to execute that justice.

"God help us is right," Sonsee repeated.

"What are we going to do?" Alana studied a drop of water as it trickled down the side of her glass.

"We can't do what we're thinking. They'll put *us* in prison."

"Yes. And we would displease God in the most atrocious way."

Sonsee eyes widened.

"Don't look so surprised. I'm not quite the heathen you think I am." A sad smile played across Alana's features.

Sonsee's regrets increased. She had no idea that Alana professed a relationship with the Lord.

Perhaps I've been too hard on her.

Through the years, Sonsee had reveled in the love of her six friends. She had often thought that Marilyn, Kim Lan, Jac, Melissa, Sammie, and Victoria were way better to her than her own sisters. But possibly that was because Sonsee had been way better to them than she had ever tried to be to Alana or Natalie.

"Alana, I feel like I have so much to apologize to you for . . . a lifetime of stuff." Sonsee reached for her sister's hand. "Honestly, looking back I feel like I've been a spoiled rotten brat. All these years, I couldn't figure out why you were always so . . . why our relationship was so difficult. But recently I've begun to see some things, or I guess the Lord has been showing me some things. And frankly, I don't know what to do or what to say to make —"

"I just always felt like I could never measure up to you," Alana said, shaking her head. "I always felt like Father compared the two of us and you always came out on top. No matter what I did . . ." Alana placed unsteady fingers against her lips.

"I'm *so* sorry," Sonsee said, repeating the sentiment she had voiced when finding Alana crying in their father's den.

"Me, too," Alana whispered. "I think we

were both caught in the middle. Frankly, I feel like Mother tried so hard to mend the hurts, but —"

"Mother was an angel."

"Yes. She treated me just like her own, and I still resented her." Alana tugged on a wisp of hair, arranging it over the bruise near her eye. "There's so much I'd like to say to her now, and she's not here. I just barely remember my biological mother, and . . ."

"Then I came along." Sonsee laid a consoling hand over Alana's.

"It's so ironic that everyone seemed to think we were lucky because we lived in that mansion and Father was wealthy."

"I don't think wealth changes a thing when it comes to relationships. I really don't. As a matter of fact, I'm not sure exactly what I'm going to do about what I've inherited. Seems to me that lots of money only complicates things. Recently my friend Kim Lan has been giving to organizations who help the needy. I see a new happiness radiating all over her, and I might just do what she's done. Frankly, I'm perfectly content to stay in this townhouse and drive my Honda and earn my own living. I'm seriously considering even selling LeBlanc Manor. Do you think

Natalie would hold it against me for the rest of my life? She wanted that old mansion so badly."

"If you're really thinking about selling, I might be interested in buying. Nick and I . . ." Alana touched the bruise. "I'm going to need a different house, it looks like."

"Has he been hitting you?" Sonsee asked, concern softening her voice.

"Yes. For years." Alana pressed her lips together. "We've separated several times — even right before Father died I kicked him out. But he came back yesterday, and this time he had his girlfriend." She twisted her fingers into a tight knot. "Really, I've never thought I was worth all that much." Her gaze faltered. "And I let him get away with a lot because he convinced me I deserved it." She waved her hand. "It didn't take much to convince me." Alana grabbed her soda and gulped the liquid.

"It's because of Father," Sonsee said, shaking her head. "He made you feel —"

"I don't blame him completely, Sonsee. I can't." Alana set her glass back on the table. "I added to the problem with my own resentment. I think part of the problem with my relationship with Father was that I was always so prickly and at

279

times, I guess I was downright paranoid. There were many times he did try to connect with me, but it always ended with my storming away." She sighed and stood. "I've gotten back into church lately, and I have been talking to my pastor a lot. She's helping me a lot. That's part of the reason I came today. I felt that I owed you an apology for the way I acted at the will reading. I acted more like a fifteen-year-old than a thirty-six-year-old woman."

"Yeah, well, I wasn't exactly the picture of maturity myself." Sonsee glanced around the cluttered room, trying to remember if she had experienced even one mature moment since she'd heard of her father's death and of Taylor's being blamed. The upheaval of the whole week descended upon her anew. Sonsee placed her elbows on the table and covered her face with her hands.

"You look like you could use some sleep," Alana observed.

"I've got to go into the clinic." Sonsee checked her sporty gold watch, a gift from her father, to see that only an hour and a half had lapsed since she'd discovered her apartment had been trashed. "I've had a substitute vet filling in all week, but I need to make an appearance anyway."

"Would you like me to stay and start cleaning up some of this mess?" Alana asked.

"You'd do that?" Sonsee looked up as a warm rush bathed her in awe.

Alana tilted her head to one side and placed hands on her plump hips. "Like I already told you, I'm not quite the heathen you think I am."

"Well, I'm probably not either." Sonsee smiled impishly. She slowly stood and took a long drink of her soda, then gradually rolled the glass in her hands as the winds of new concern swept across her spirit, stirring it like grains of sand in a dune. "So, where are you going now? It sounds like Nick kicked *you* out this time."

"I know it all sounds so horrible, but really, I've gone through every stage of grief known to mankind over this marriage. Now that I know for sure that it's over, I'm relieved and strangely at peace about the whole thing. My pastor and I have been praying that the Lord would somehow show me the right direction. Anyway, I was thinking of just getting a hotel for right now." Alana fidgeted with the back of the straight-back chair in front of her.

"Want to go to LeBlanc Manor?" Sonsee asked. "You're welcome to stay as long as you want. Move in, if you need to. I'm certainly not going to live there any time soon — if at all — and that old house needs somebody there."

"That would mean more to me than you'd ever know," Alana whispered.

Another thought struck Sonsee, and she stopped herself before voicing it. Alana had mentioned buying LeBlanc Manor. Sonsee wondered if she ought to just give her the old mansion. Such a gift would undoubtedly continue to heal the rift between them and answer Sonsee's dilemma about what to do with the place. At least this way she would be free of the burden and the homestead would stay in the family. But Sonsee remembered the key; she remembered the map; she remembered the secret door. She decided to hang onto LeBlanc Manor for awhile longer.

"What are you going to do about Carla?" Alana asked.

"Good question." Sonsee peered toward the kitchen counter, laden with the strewn cabinet contents.

"I think we both agree that she's lying about Taylor," Alana claimed.

Her convinced tone riveted Sonsee's attention, and she posed the first question that entered her mind. "How do you know? Do you have proof?"

"Nothing concrete." Alana shook her head. "Just my gut instinct. She's been really nervous ever since this whole thing happened. She acts like she's trying to avoid all of us. That's just not like her."

The phone's ring grated against Sonsee's taut nerves. She knew who the caller would be. "Excuse me, Alana," she said. For the second time, Sonsee raced up the stairs and into her bedroom. With thoughts of Carla dogging her, she silently closed the door, picked her way through the clutter, and retrieved the receiver. Sonsee had reestablished the downstairs phone to its rightful spot on the end table. Nevertheless, she wanted to answer this call upstairs, safely out of Alana's earshot.

"Are you okay?" Taylor asked, anxiety spilling from his voice.

"Yes, I'm fine. Everything is fine," Sonsee said. The first time Taylor called — only forty-five minutes ago — she had been a bit perturbed by his lack of trust in her judgment. But this time a genuine warmth spread through her soul. Taylor's protective instincts were certainly in overdrive, and Sonsee enjoyed the sensation of his wanting to guarantee her safety.

"Is she still there?"

"Yes. I think she's going to stay at LeBlanc Manor for awhile. We've been talking and are making some peace that should have been made years ago. I guess that if nothing else good comes out of Father's death, at least it has opened our eyes to some mending that needed to happen. Taylor, I really don't think Alana was involved in the murder at all. She's as ready to see the killer nabbed as I am. She also told me she doesn't think you were involved."

Taylor's answer came in the form of thoughtful silence.

"She even offered to help me clean up this mess."

"Are you going to let her?"

"I *do* need help, and she's available."

"Did you find a broken window?"

"We looked. We can't find any signs of breaking and entering — not even on the front door. And . . . and my car was moved and . . . and the interior has been shredded." Sonsee rubbed her forehead as her faint headache increased.

"Whoever did this somehow got your keys," Taylor said.

"All I can figure is they must have gotten copies made."

"Sonsee, are you sure Alana isn't involved? Don't you think it's a little strange that after all these years of being obnoxious, she's suddenly turned over a new leaf?"

The doubt in Taylor's voice doused Sonsee in a new onslaught of speculation. She toyed with one of the tassels on the lamp shade, and it swayed back and forth as an extension of her vacillating emotions. Whoever entered her home had been close enough to get her keys, have copies made, and place the originals back in her purse. Anyone staying at LeBlanc Manor this week could have been responsible. That included Alana. Yet Sonsee recalled the weeks before her father's death. Even then the Lord had been prompting Sonsee to begin trying to mend their relationship. And Alana's confessions had confirmed everything Sonsee had sensed from God.

"I really think Alana is clean, Taylor. *I really do.*"

Taylor let out a defeated sigh. "Okay, okay, if you're that convinced, I'll stop chewing my fingernails to the bone. Right now, I only have three fingertips left anyway."

Sonsee chuckled.

"I'll be sending you the doctor bill for finger reconstruction." The smile in his voice represented the wit that had colored Sonsee's life for as long as she could remember. "Melissa isn't really happy with me right now anyway. I called her earlier, threatening to return to Baton Rouge, and I think she's ready to skin me alive if I set one foot out of her house."

"Good for her."

"Meanwhile, you need to replace the lock on your front door," Taylor responded, skillfully ignoring the jibe. "Do you have any idea how to do that?"

She snorted. "Oh ye of little faith!"

"I know you well enough — that's your way around telling me you're clueless."

"Well, it can't be all *that* hard, can it? You're talking to a woman who could perform a tonsillectomy on a lizard, let alone —"

"Yeah, right," Taylor jeered. "Don't waste time. Go get the new lock. I'll be waiting for you to call me. I'll talk you through it."

"Not on your life, buddy. I'll take care of it myself."

"In your dreams. I know you. When it comes to mechanics, you're as clumsy as a twelve-toed ballerina."

Sonsee spewed forth an abundance of spontaneous laughter. As the chortles died, she recognized the first true joy she had known in days. And Taylor was responsible. But he had always been responsible for much of her laughter. The breathtaking longing to unite her life with his surged through her like a seductive breeze off an azure summer ocean, tantalizing and sweet. Sweet and promising. Promising and potent. Sonsee imagined their wedding day. She savored the resulting intimacy of mind, body, and spirit. She almost tasted the kisses that would bring fulfillment to the void in her heart.

"Well, I'll let you go, then," Taylor said, an undeniable hunger lacing through the sensual rise and fall of his voice.

"Okay," Sonsee answered, her voice husky. "I'll — I'll call later."

"Yes, when you buy the lock." His gentle words sent a shiver down her spine, and Sonsee tugged on the lamp tassels until they quivered.

"Yes. The lock. I'll let you know when I get it," she whispered, not certain they were talking about the lock at all. As she hung up the telephone, Sonsee felt as if Taylor swept into the room, wrapped his arms around her, and held her in a forever kind of embrace.

He's falling in love with me. The thought

sent an arrow of ecstasy straight through Sonsee's heart. On the heels of elation came an icy dagger of reality and a recollection of her own traitorous thoughts from only seconds before. She had felt as if she could taste the kisses that would *fill the void* in her heart.

Once again, Sonsee recalled the spiritual victory she thought she had won on the mission trip to Vietnam. She had sensed the Holy Spirit's definite urging to be satisfied *without* Taylor — to look to God as her fulfillment, and to never buy into the notion that another human being should be her reason for living. Sonsee staggered under the reality that in Vietnam she had only scraped the surface of the spiritual stability the Lord planned for her. In Vietnam, releasing Taylor had been easier because she believed he was not and never would be available for her. But now that seemed to be changing. Sonsee doubted she had the strength to walk away from a relationship with him, even if the Lord required it.

"Oh, Jesus," she whispered, closing her eyes against the havoc in her room, the chaos that reflected the turbulence in her soul. "I've wanted Taylor for so long, please let this follow its natural course. I don't want to have to choose between You and him. Everything is so hard for me right now. In one minute, I want to retaliate against Father's murderer. In the next minute, I know that's wrong. I'm struggling in all sorts of areas. This is the hardest time of my life. Please, if I could just have Taylor, I think I could make it through. Remember, I'm a human being. *I need companionship.*"

Downstairs, Alana gently replaced the telephone's receiver, then busied herself with restoring the torn couch cushions to their rightful places. When Sonsee entered the room, Alana wanted to present the image of a woman intent upon helping her younger sister. Yet the eavesdropping had confirmed her suspicions. Just as Hermann declared, Sonsee knew where Taylor was. The present conversation suggested he was staying with one of Sonsee's friends who had attended the funeral.

Alana remembered Melissa Moore. At the funeral, she had stood beside Sonsee along with five other friends. Dr. Moore had remained in Alana's mind because she was the only one who bothered to ask Alana about her life. The rest of the sisters had maintained a distant politeness, as if they were afraid to interact too much. Melissa, on the other hand, had almost asked one too many questions, stopping just short of what Alana would call nosy. Alana had learned the doctor practiced medicine and lived in Oklahoma City. All Hermann's suspicions now materialized into reality. Sonsee was helping Taylor hide by enlisting the aid of one of her closest friends.

Sixteen

Thanks to Alana's help, Sonsee's home was soon improved — not completely clean, but definitely less chaotic. Alana had volunteered to go to the hardware store for a lock. After struggling for an hour over the task, the two had managed to ensure Sonsee's safety. While Alana cleaned, she had insisted that Sonsee take a much-needed nap. After the nap, Alana headed to LeBlanc Manor, and Sonsee worked at her animal clinic all afternoon.

By seven o'clock that evening Sonsee's nap had worn off; her eyelids sagged and her shoulders ached. Nevertheless, she forced herself to sit down at her personal computer in the guest bedroom. An hour ago, Mel had called to tell Sonsee the "sisters" were planning an internet chat session. Sonsee booted up the machine and sat back in the chair to await the appearance of an array of icons on the screen. She glanced around the room and admired the work Alana had performed. The surviving perfume bottles now rested back in the curio. The CDs and computer disks were neatly filed. Sonsee had helped Alana repair the mattress with duct tape and make the bed. As much as Sonsee wanted to chat with her friends, she would have preferred flopping into the bed. But she suspected her six sisters had arranged the session specifically for her benefit, and she wouldn't let them down.

Within minutes, Sonsee had logged on the internet and entered the chat room, where a roster indicated all the friends were waiting. Sonsee envisioned every one of them: Marilyn Langham — glowing in the aftermath of her recent wedding to Joshua. Certainly, the Lord had given her a second chance at happiness after a gut-wrenching divorce. Kim Lan Lowery — supermodel extraordinaire, exquisite as always, yet the new light in her dark, exotic eyes indicated a deeper commitment to the Lord. Melissa Moore — pensive and observant. However, when Sonsee left Mel in Oklahoma City, she had noticed new shadows in her friend's eyes — shadows that appeared to belong to Kinkaide Franklin. Jac Lightfoot — the pint-sized private eye with a face that defied ethnic definition with its bronzed skin and finely chiseled features. Jac was always filled with the usual high-energy of a woman who spends her life solving mysteries. Victoria Roberts — petite and ladylike. Victoria — the consummate domestic engineer, who would probably fuss around the room trying to help straighten the remaining mess. And Sammie Jones would no doubt flip her fiery-red hair over one shoulder and begin taking notes about the latest developments in Sonsee's life in order to fuel a plot for her next novel.

After a brief delay, the group began a lively exchange, and the tension of Sonsee's day slipped away in the face of the warmth and love expressed on the screen. At last, the conversation turned to more serious matters.

Melissa: Sonsee, I told the gang about your house. Is there any more news?

Sonsee: I'm assuming you got the scoop from the individual who called me today?

Melissa: Yes.

Sonsee: Well, there's one small detail I decided not to share with him. He was already hitting the ceiling, and I didn't want to add to his worries. When I first came home to find my house in shambles, somebody left through the front door.

Jac: Did you get a look at him?

Sonsee: No. I think the person tripped in the living room, and that's when I knew I had a visitor. The front door was closing by the time I arrived at the top of the stairs. I also think that whoever trashed my house had a key to the front door. We couldn't find any evidence of breaking and entering.

Marilyn: We?

Sonsee: Yes. My sister Alana came and spent several hours. She helped me at least get a start on cleaning up. You guys pray for her and me. We worked through some issues today that we've needed to talk about for a long time. For the first time in my life, I think I really like my sister. We've had such a crummy relationship. That's awful to admit, but it's the truth. By the way, Alana and I replaced the lock.

Sammie: Did you report the break-in to the police?

Sonsee: No way. I don't want to draw any attention to me right now. Alana mentioned that they had been questioning her about the location of a certain someone. Now I'm scared I'll be next. The last thing I want right now is to see a blue uniform.

Jac: It's inevitable, Sonsee. Just get ready.

Sonsee: Thanks for the words of encouragement.

Jac: I know that's not what you wanted to hear, but this whole situation is a time bomb.

Melissa: "You know who" just stepped into the room and wants to know what we're up to.

Sonsee: Oh, tell "you know who" for me that I'm much less clumsy than a twelve-toed ballerina. But don't dare tell him it took an hour to replace the lock. It took three tries, and we got it in backward once.

Melissa: Chuckles. I'll let you tell him. He just said to tell you he's calling you after we get off-line.

Sonsee: Great. Tell him I'll call him. That way it'll be on my dime. And mum's the word on the intruder being in my house.

Melissa: Got it.

Jac: My flight is scheduled to leave Saturday morning at six. I should be to your place by noon, at the latest, Sonsee. Don't panic. Hang tight. We're going to get to the bottom of this!

Melissa: We should be there early Saturday morning. Pray for a safe flight.

Sonsee: Will do. Here's something else to pray for. While I was at work, a friend's mom left a message on my machine. She was concerned because she's having no luck reaching her son. She's touring Egypt right now and won't be home until next week.

Jac: Egypt?

Sonsee: Yes. A group at church got together a tour, and she's wanted to travel for years. Anyway, she's really concerned about missing her son and left her hotel room number on my machine. But my friend does not want her to know what's going on right now because it will devastate her. But she needs to know. So when you pray, remember to pray for her.

Sammie: I'm praying like crazy.

Victoria: Me, too.

Marilyn: So am I. Sonsee, please don't think I'm being unfeeling, but we haven't set the place and time of our next sister reunion. Would you mind if we discuss it?

Sonsee: Not in the least. That will give me something different to think about.

Melissa: Sorry to interrupt, but "you know who" is back. Sonsee, he says uhh . . . to tell you he misses you. Okay, he's gone now. Whew, Sonsee! What have you done to him? He's pouting around here like a love-sick puppy.

Kim Lan: Honey, y'all got it bad.

Sammie: Wolf whistle!

Marilyn: Wolf, wolf, whistle, whistle. I'm not passing up one opportunity to pay back all the teasing you put me through when I met Josh.

Jac: What gives, Sonsee? The last I heard, he wasn't an option.

Victoria: Hey guys, let's back off. She's been through a lot right now. The last thing she needs is teasing.

Sonsee: I knew I loved you, Tori.

Kim Lan: Sonsee, I hope you don't mind my changing the subject? (Ha ha!)

Sonsee: Bless you, Kim! :-)

Kim Lan: Anyway, just in case any of you are wondering, Mick and I set our wedding date for November 15, so that's not a good month for me for the sister reunion. Start planning now to fly to Boston for the wedding. I'll arrange for your plane tickets. Mom and Dad want to put you up at their house. It's nice and big and comfortable. Oh, and we're keeping the wedding really simple.

Marilyn: Sure . . . that's what Josh and I said.

Kim Lan: Seriously, we're only inviting you guys, our families, and a few of Mick's friends. It's going to be at the church where Mom and Dad attend, just north of Boston. We're not even going to have attendants, just me and Mick and the preacher.

Marilyn: I'm impressed. :-D

Victoria: What about December for our sister reunion? We could plan a Christmas bash.

Marilyn: Groaning. Do you know how busy a parsonage is at Christmas time?

Melissa: What about New Year's then? We could all crash here. I've got plenty of room, if you don't mind bunking together.

Sonsee: Works for me.

Jac: I hope nobody faints, but I'm planning to take off work then anyway.

Victoria: Oops! Just fell out of my computer chair.

Sammie: Pausing to swoon.

Jac: I'm not half the workaholic you guys think I am.

Kim Lan: Probably more like twice the workaholic we think you are.

Jac: Yeah, yeah, yeah! With friends like you, who needs enemies? ;-)

Sonsee: That's right. We've got all the bases covered. You won't find a more versatile bunch of women in America.

Melissa: He's here again, Sonsee! This time he wants to know if you're still planning to sleep at your clinic tonight. He's worried since I told him you were on your computer at home.

Marilyn: From all my experience, worry is the first sign of love.

Sonsee: Yes, MELISSA (Marilyn, if you feel ignored, then it's on purpose), please tell him I just came home long enough to try to straighten up the house a little more and to chat with you guys, check my messages, and grab an overnight bag. I'm going to spend the night at the clinic, then work all day tomorrow.

Kim Lan: Honey, y'all got it bad.

Sonsee: Give it a break, will ya?

Taylor left Melissa's home office and walked into his room, determined not to interrupt her internet chat again. He slumped into the wing back chair sitting near a small round table. On the table lay Taylor's Bible. All day his thoughts had centered around that book, around matters of the soul. He had stumbled upon a section of Scripture, Isaiah 54:10,11, that had vividly stroked his heart's canvas. As he had already done a dozen times before, Taylor leaned forward and reread the verse: " 'Though the mountains may be removed and the hills may shake, but My lovingkindness will not be removed from you, and My covenant of peace will not be shaken,' says the LORD who has compassion on you. 'O afflicted one, storm-tossed, and not comforted, behold, I will set your stones in antimony, and your foundations I will lay in sapphires.' " From the Scripture, his attention trailed to the painting over the bed. The title once again thrust itself upon him: "A Shelter from the Storm," and beneath the title, "Be still, and know that I am God."

For once in Taylor's life, God had the rancher still. He was trapped in Melissa's house with nothing but a television for entertainment. And for some reason TV left him flat today. He couldn't even find interest in the sports channel. So as the hours had stretched on, Taylor alternated sessions in the Word of God with reflective prayer time.

The day had been a long one. A revealing one. A day of spiritual confrontation from a God who loved him. As the hours marched on and the Lord continued whispering in his soul, Taylor realized he had been living a shallow spiritual existence — one far from what the Lord wanted for him. Looking back on his acknowledgment of Christ as his Savior, Taylor began to realize that he had not grown much past his initial mental steps toward the Lord. He had asked Jesus

Christ to be his Savior, then shrank away from allowing Him to be Lord of his heart, of his life, of his past, present, and future. He shied from making a commitment to Jesus that would forever change his life focus from self to God and cause him to eat, drink, and sleep the presence of the Lord.

Taylor rested his head against the back of the wing back chair, folded his arms, and extended his long legs in front of him. Broodingly, he observed the painting over the bed. Unquestionably, his faith had not even begun to touch the image that picture portrayed — an image of a man assaulted by the storm, an image of a man completely certain of his shelter in the Lord, an image of a man who had thoroughly grasped the message of Isaiah 54. Looking back, Taylor never remembered feeling as if the Lord sheltered him.

I guess I've been so busy sheltering my heart myself that I've kept God from doing His job. Once again his mother's advice posed itself: "The Lord would heal you if you would only be still long enough to let Him. Be still . . . be still . . . be still and know that I am God."

Taylor leaned forward, propped his elbows on his knees, then placed his head in his hands. He curled tense fingers into springy hair and strained against a supernatural urgency to destroy the walls around his heart — a destruction that would allow the Lord to reach deeply into his soul and begin the healing of a little boy who still wept for his father and scoffed at true love.

Let Me heal you. Let Me be your shelter. Let Me fill your life with the joy you try so hard to feign. The words caused a chill along Taylor's spine as they circled around his mind like a holy chant from the corridors of heaven. And for the first time in his life, Taylor knew God had him right where He wanted him. Taylor was still. Completely still. And he caught a glimpse of what really knowing God was all about. Like the shaft of light in the picture, Taylor felt as if a holy beam surrounded him, filling his heart and mind with a warm assurance he had never known.

At last Taylor acquiesced to the voice of the Lord — a voice he had once been too frantically busy to hear, a voice that called him to taste the waters of emotional healing. "Okay, Lord," he whispered, his throat tight, "I'll let go of these walls. I'll let you in — completely in — to do as You will. I'll — I'll stop holding everyone at arm's length, and I'll start being still and learning who You are."

Taylor recalled a childhood Sunday school story about the walls of Jericho. In his mind, he replayed what he had envisioned as a child: gigantic stone walls crumbling outward, creating a boom that echoed like continual thunder, the dust forming a mushroom cloud boiling toward the sky. He had seen people running in all directions, terrified that their protection had been removed. Except this time, only one person remained where the walls had once stood. One person who huddled near the earth, cringing for fear of more torment. One person — Taylor Delaney. And a giant, gentle hand reached from heaven to surround him in steadfast love, tender forgiveness, and the beginning of healing a past that had emotionally crippled him.

As Taylor's quivering increased, he could hold the tears no longer. Like the man in the painting, he stood, opened his arms, and extended them heavenward. His life lay broken at his feet, like a ship crashed against unforgiving stone. The ocean waves rushed upon him, growling like a sea beast intent upon swallowing him alive. The lightning, like forked tongues of fire, whipped at him from dark, rolling clouds.

But Taylor never once wavered in his stance. No longer was he storm-tossed and uncomforted. He fully embraced his shelter in the storm . . . the shelter of God's unrelenting love.

After fifteen more minutes of lively chatting, the "seven sisters" disbanded with promises to pray diligently for Sonsee and "you know who." No one once mentioned Taylor's name on the internet, despite the claims to privacy such cyberspace chat rooms boasted. Sonsee, thankful for her friends' sensitivity, threw the necessary toiletry items into her overnight bag and headed for the front door. With one last glimpse over her shoulder, she paused to scan the room that showed signs of her and Alana's cleaning efforts. The apartment still needed many more hours before it was back to normal.

"Just like my life," Sonsee mused aloud, eyeing the couch, whose shredded cushions looked as tattered as her aching heart. With the final rays of sunshine spreading summer warmth from the horizon, she stepped onto her small porch and darted a wary glance across the courtyard. The numerous cypresses and oaks rustled in the warm breeze heavy with humidity. They seemed to whisper that all was well. Sonsee's fingers, tight around the doorknob, relaxed a fraction as she prepared to shut the door. The phone's shrill ring halted her.

Sonsee swiveled to go back into the house, yet stopped, debating whether to answer or allow the machine to get it. Thoughts of Taylor ended her debating. She had sent the message through Mel that she would call him from the clinic, but he might have decided to call here anyway. Sonsee stepped back into the apartment, locked the door, and rushed to the cordless phone resting on the end table.

"Hi," she quipped into the receiver, certain the caller must be Taylor. Yet as soon as the greeting left her mouth, she scolded herself for taking his call on the cordless phone. Sonsee opened her mouth ready to tell him she was moving to the upstairs phone when a somewhat familiar male voice floated over the line.

"Hello."

She struggled to identify the caller. After a lengthy pause, the man supplied his name.

"This is Rafael — Rafael Houk — your brother-in-law, remember?" he teased.

"Oh, hi," Sonsee said, her hackles rising

as she slowly sat on the couch's arm. "I was expecting someone else. You threw me off guard."

"That's fine," Rafael said, a smile in his voice.

The hair on the back of Sonsee's neck prickled. The last time she saw Rafael at the will reading, the tall blond had broodingly hovered near Natalie as if he were prepared to take up all offenses for his "fragile" wife. *Why are you being so nice now?* she wanted to demand but held her tongue.

"Listen, the reason I'm calling," he soothed, "Natalie and I were wondering if we might be able to stop by for a visit tonight."

"Tonight?" Sonsee's toes curled inside her sandals, and she ran her damp palm along the crease in her red linen shorts.

"Yes, Natalie and I have an . . . offer we'd like to pass by you before we leave town."

"Oh?"

"We decided to postpone our return home to take care of some business. We're here in Baton Rouge tonight and thought this might be a good chance to talk together."

"I see," Sonsee said, recalling Natalie's

pouting when she didn't inherit LeBlanc Manor. "Actually, I'm sorry, but this isn't a good night for me." Despite attempts to keep her voice pleasant, Sonsee still sounded like a disinterested tour guide, coldly reciting a preprinted program.

Rafael's silence stretched into an ominous minute, and Sonsee fought the urge to hang up. "I see," he finally intoned. Ironically, his chilled words brought a sense of comfort. Sonsee knew how to deal with Rafael Houk in his usually rude mode; the pleasant Rafael left her grappling for equilibrium.

"Is this, um, offer something you could tell me over the phone?" Sonsee asked, curious if her hunch were correct. Rafael and Natalie most likely wanted to buy LeBlanc Manor. But Alana expressed an interest in the mansion as well. She should be settled in at the family homestead by now, and Sonsee was glad that at least one family member occupied the premises. Once again, she considered deeding the property to Alana. *That would send Natalie into a rage,* she thought. *So what else is new?* The caustic remark only added to her growing discomfort with the phone call.

"Well, I guess if you aren't available to talk in person, then perhaps I should go

ahead and just mention what we are interested in." The cordial subtlety was back in
his words, and Sonsee ground her teeth together.

"Yes, please do." Standing, she paced toward the corner rocker that dated from her
infancy and perched on the edge of the
cherished heirloom to await Rafael's explanation.

"Natalie and I were wondering if you
would consider selling LeBlanc Manor.
Natalie seems to think that you probably
won't keep it."

Images of that rusting key tucked in her
purse flashed through Sonsee's mind.
Speculations about what lay behind that
third floor vault increased her uneasiness.
*If Natalie and Rafael were involved in Fa-
ther's murder, then they might be after whatever is in that hidden vault. If they owned
LeBlanc Manor, they would rightfully possess
the vault. But so would Alana.* For the first
time since Alana left, a cascade of doubts
descended upon Sonsee. So far, Alana and
Natalie had both offered to buy the family
mansion. Alana had even managed to get
an unlimited invitation to stay at the
homestead. *Have I been duped?* Sonsee
stood and walked back to the end table.
With every step, she recalled Alana's sin-

cerity, her spirit of restitution, her own certainty that Taylor was not the murderer. Finally Sonsee dashed aside the doubts concerning Alana. Yet Sonsee's speculations about Rafael, Natalie, and Hermann escalated. Alana had mentioned that all three might have been involved. The idea gained plausibility with every passing hour.

"So . . ." Rafael prompted.

"Uh . . ." Sonsee searched for the right words. "Presently, I'm not ready to sell." She painstakingly chose her every word. She didn't want to alert Rafael to even the slightest hint that she suspected him or Natalie of her father's demise.

"But if you *do* decide . . ."

"If I decide to sell, I'll try to make sure the mansion stays in the family."

"Great!" The single word held the triumph of a knight, victorious in his latest joust. "Natalie will be relieved to hear that. The mansion means so much to her."

"It means a lot to all of us," Sonsee said, then ended the call.

Seventeen

"Stop right here," Louis ordered as the lights of an oncoming car illuminated the dark taxi. He reached into his back pocket for his wallet and prepared to pay the driver.

The cabby pulled to the side of the road and asked no questions. "That's fifteen dolla'," he said with a Cajun accent.

Louis paid the fare and stepped out of the taxi, all the while gripping the canvas bag heavy with ancient keys. His mission pushed him forward, and the grating of tires against gravel accompanied his swift journey toward the brick arch marking LeBlanc Manor's driveway.

Louis walked down the winding lane, through the star-studded night laden with the smells of heavy foliage and the sounds of screeching crickets. Like a panther stalking through the shadows, he crept around the sparsely lit mansion and strained to view the parking area at the end of the driveway. Only one sporty Cadillac claimed a spot under a tree. The vehicle confirmed the presence of another and underscored the need to be alert. But, more importantly, Carla's aging Ford was missing. Louis determined that he could slip past the Cadillac's owner, but he had lived through his share of doubts about getting past Carla. A great cloud of tension lifted from Louis' hunched shoulders. Without Carla to worry about, tonight's endeavor would prove nothing short of a huge success.

Using the house key Cerberus had demanded Carla give them, Louis unlocked the back door and crept through the midnight gloom spreading its wiry fingers along the narrow corridor. As he neared Carla's room, Louis slowed and nudged the slightly ajar door. It swung inward with a gasp and soft squeak of hinges. In the faint glow of moon rays squeezing through half-opened blinds, Louis noted that Carla's bed remained unruffled. He stepped farther into the room, into the clinging hint of perfume. Louis reached into his bag and retrieved a penlight. He clicked it on and directed the narrow beam across her room. No personal items remained. Louis stepped toward the narrow closet door and tugged on the aging doorknob. Only a few hangers claimed the closet rail. One pair of worn sneakers sat in the bottom.

Louis paused briefly and pondered Carla's disappearance. Cerberus had threatened to do away with her. Louis hoped he had not followed through. Nonetheless, she was no longer present at LeBlanc Manor. He hoped the maid had simply disappeared to go into hiding. Certainly, if he were her, that is exactly what he would have done. He detested the thought of Cerberus ending her life. One death on Louis' conscience was enough for a lifetime. The fact that Carla's car no longer claimed its usual spot and her room was void of personal belongings suggested she had departed under her own power. Cerberus had thoroughly intimidated her, enough to ensure her lying to the authorities, enough for her to remove Sonsee's keys from her purse, enough to provide keys to the back door of LeBlanc Manor. Keys that proved handy tonight.

Shoving aside concerns of Carla, Louis turned off the penlight, departed the room, and stole up the stairs to the third floor. At last he arrived at the room that held the secret treasure. Feeling as if the ghosts of years past tugged him toward the ancient fireplace, Louis stepped into the room's musty embrace. A satisfied smile tugged at the corners of his mouth as he contemplated Cerberus' shock upon discovering the vault had been relieved of its contents.

Wasting little time, Louis stepped toward the fireplace, grasped the lion's cold nose, twisted it, and the panel swooshed upward. Once again, Louis retrieved the penlight from his bag. He clicked on the beam and examined the rust-touched vault. The time for action had arrived. *If I have to dig through the steel with my bare hands, I will penetrate the safe tonight.* He reached into the bag again and pulled out three of the keys. One other time in his life, Louis had managed to jiggle a key in an unmatched lock until the key had worked. The older the lock, the more likely an alternative key would work. The night was young; he still had six hours before dawn. By then, the treasure would hopefully be gone. So would he.

The fact of Cerberus' fury sent a chill along Louis' spine. He seriously doubted his partner would hesitate to kill him when his deceit was discovered. In answer to this worry, Louis determined to outrun Cerberus. He had no other option. He had to take what he came to New Orleans for and leave. If he spent much more time under the pressure this town evoked, Louis feared a mental breakdown. The mere touch of the vault produced the sensation of evil on his palms. He scrubbed his hands against his shirt, then eyed his sore, scabbed fingers. His impulse to race for the lavatory seized him. He forced the first key into the lock and gripped the protruding end as if it could grant him the power to stay the impulse. Instead of bolting, Louis clamped his teeth, and embarked upon the plan he hoped would seal his financial security.

Sonsee awoke with a start and groggily gazed around the small room. She blinked hard, rubbed her eyes, and tried to remember where she was. Glancing at a nearby digital clock, she was greeted with blue numbers that boldly proclaimed 5:06. Sonsee propped herself up on one elbow and swung her legs off the narrow cot. Finally, the events of last night fell into place. After the computer chat with her friends, she had packed a bag. The call from Rafael had slightly postponed her arrival at the clinic. She had called Taylor shortly after eight, and by 8:30 she landed in bed.

Sonsee gazed around the diminutive room, which was located next to her office. The narrow cot where she now sat brought back memories from early in her career, when she had worked enough for two veterinarians, despite her father's pleas to assist her financially. Sonsee firmly rejected his help. Jacques paid her way through college and even placed the down payment on the office building on Perkins Road that Sonsee turned into an animal clinic. After that, she needed — desperately needed — to prove to herself that she could make it on her own. Her whole life she had survived on "Father's money." The time had come to be her own woman.

The room, sparsely furnished, contained all the original items Sonsee had purchased at a used furniture store: a worn couch, an old cot, a small refrigerator, a hot plate, and several kitchen utensils. The utilitarian bathroom facilities further attested to her frugal beginnings. Sonsee and her employees now used this room for their lunch hour, but it had been a Godsend early in her career. The first two years, she wound up living in this room. She spent many nights working into the wee hours on paperwork or remodeling the office, only to collapse on the cot until the next morning when her duties as a veterinarian began. Two years ago she finally agreed to her father's urging to use part of her trust fund for a down payment on the townhouse, but only because she assured herself that she could survive on her own. Sonsee hadn't spent the night at the office since then. Until last night.

Yawning, she stood and stretched her fingers toward the ceiling. After a quick trip to the bathroom, she considered snuggling back under the sheets for a prolonged snooze. However, her mind was already whirling with the problems the day presented. So she flipped on the fluorescent lights and searched out the coffeepot, stained from wear.

Everything at the clinic had run smoothly without her. The visiting vet, a young man whom Sonsee was considering inviting into her growing practice, had handled each patient with precision and care. She had decided that, if everything continued smoothly this morning, she would leave the clinic in Mark's care for the afternoon. She had waited long enough to explore that mysterious fireplace. Even though Taylor would be back with her tomorrow morning, Sonsee didn't want to wait until he arrived. Furthermore, she needed to have a serious conversation with Carla. Hopefully, Sonsee would be on the move enough in the next couple of days that the police wouldn't catch up with her. She had no idea what she would say if they did question her. She detested lying, but the truth would expose Taylor.

After filling the coffeepot with water and grounds, she left it brewing and showered and dressed. Not bothering to dry her hair, Sonsee ran a comb through it, then she prepared a cup of coffee. By 5:30, she settled onto the sofa that reminded her of the color of her father's worn fishing boots.

Several weeks ago, Jacques had paid his daughter a surprise visit and waited in this room until Sonsee could leave for lunch. Over lunch, he had offered to help her dispose of all the old furniture and spruce up the room with something new.

"If you'll get rid of your yucky old fishing boots, I'll refurnish the room," she challenged with a smile.

"Not on your life," he playfully growled, his lips twitching.

"The room helps me remember the years I struggled to make it on my own. I love what it stands for, and I just can't change it right now," she explained. "Just like your old boots. Didn't you tell me Grandpa gave them to you right before he died?"

Jacques nodded, and with an understanding glimmer in his eyes he said, "Sometimes I wonder what I did that was so right with you, Sonsee. When I offer to assist Alana, Natalie, or Hermann, they don't hesitate to take me up on it. But you . . . I had to *make* you take part of your trust fund to make the down payment on your house. I'd say you are a hardworking LeBlanc through and through, but I suspect your mother had more to do with your attitudes than I did." With those words, a sweet reminiscent smile touched Jacques' lips. A smile tinged with sorrow.

Pressing her fingers against her eyes, Sonsee held the tears at bay. An icy vengeance, tinged with an unforgiving frost, demanded the death of the murderer. An echo from the past suggested a journey toward forgiveness, yet she chose to ride the winds of revenge. Winds that swept her ever higher into the sphere of rage.

She doubled her fists, closed her eyes, and imagined the murderer at her mercy. Would that person be Hermann or Rafael or Natalie? Sonsee envisioned Alana beside her, assisting in the retribution. Yet no peace arrived after the deed — only increased agony. Agony and anxiety. Anxiety and accusation. Accusation and acrimony. Catching her breath, Sonsee opened her eyes and reeled with the power of her dark desires that starkly contrasted with the woman of God she had come to be.

Wrinkling her brow, she coerced herself into a new track of thought. Instead of mentally dealing with the murderer, Sonsee imagined her father and mother, now both in heaven. That ethereal vision brought a hint of peace deep into her soul. She wasn't sure she could ever understand why the Lord had allowed her father's murder — a death that was proving harder to deal with than even her mother's demise from cancer. But having the assurance of knowing he was in the arms of Jesus brought immeasurable comfort.

Thoughts of her father's passing ushered in images of Taylor and his concern during their phone call last night. Even though the conversation had been brief, Taylor's endearing voice had promised more than Sonsee ever dreamed possible.

"There are some things I really want to tell you, Sonsee," he'd said before ending the call. "I've been doing a lot of thinking and praying. But the phone isn't the place to say what I need to say."

When Sonsee hung up, she had shivered.

Now, reflecting upon Taylor's unspoken promises, she shuddered with expectation. She gripped the coffee cup with both hands and sipped the hot liquid. If Taylor proposed, her life would be complete, the void in her heart would be occupied, and she would be a woman fulfilled. Sonsee felt as if she were teetering on a precipice of spiritual decline as a gentle voice, deep in her spirit, whispered, *Let Me be your complete fulfillment.*

Frowning, Sonsee leaned forward. She had never claimed to have the gift of observance with which God had blessed Melissa. That woman could walk into a room of six people and, with a few well-placed questions, determine the emotional state of each person. However, Sonsee had enough powers of observation to see, without any doubt, that Taylor Delaney was warming up to at least giving a deeper relationship with her a try. If nothing else, their electrifying kiss should have posed ample reasons to reconsider his claims of not being able to fall in love. The sparks that ignited between them suggested *both* their hearts were involved. Looking back, Sonsee wondered if Taylor's heart had been inclined toward her longer than he had the courage to admit. After all, as they grew into mature adults he depended on her as much as she depended on him. Hardly a week went by that they weren't on the phone or e-mailing one another. Looking back, Sonsee couldn't say she blamed her father for contriving that romantic trip to Hawaii.

But is a deeper relationship with Taylor God's perfect will for me, or am I so in love that I can't even see what the Lord wants? On the tailwinds of this disturbing question came other queries: *Am I looking to marriage to spiritually fulfill me instead of God? Does Taylor mean more to me than the Lord?*

The tiny refrigerator across the room blurred while the questions tormented her. A pop tune wove its way through the disturbing reverberations. After that tune, another one, then another one, until Sonsee felt as if she were choking on the themes so honored by the culture. Themes that suggested another human being should be a woman's reason for living. Themes that applauded total dependence on a sweetheart. Themes that proclaimed true fulfillment could be found only after romantic fulfillment was achieved. The various snatches from lyrics slammed into her soul like one revealing breaker after another. Sonsee jumped from her seat. The hot coffee sloshed on her hand as she deposited the cup on the tiny table beside the cot.

She paced the room. With every step, Sonsee became more deeply convinced that she had been culturally conditioned since childhood to look for spiritual completion through marriage. During the mission trip, she had stood on the hotel room's balcony with Kim Lan and Melissa and told them she thought the Lord was asking her to let Him be enough for her. She had attained a measure of spiritual victory during that trip — or so she thought. As long as she knew Taylor was unattainable, Sonsee had been able to keep the Lord at the center of her life. But the closer she and Taylor came to a relationship, the more she was tempted to replace God with Taylor, to search for fulfillment through human romance rather than the true Lover of her soul. The plan God revealed to Sonsee in Vietnam had not changed. The Lord wanted to be her ultimate source of contentment; and only from the abundance of that holy relationship would her human relationships flourish.

As the predawn light stroked the windows with fingers of gray, Sonsee was faced with the toughest question of her life. A question instigated by a holy God that left her quaking in spiritual battle: *Who is my reason for living — God or Taylor?*

After a sleepless night, Taylor lay in bed and listened to the morning sounds of Melissa getting ready for the day. At seven o'clock, the faint purr of a car engine attested to Mel's departure. Yesterday morning she had left at eight, so Taylor figured her duties must be starting early this morning.

Resolutely Taylor crawled from bed and hit the shower. As if he were determined to scrub all skin cells from his body, he furiously lathered then washed. While toweling himself dry, Taylor gazed into the bathroom mirror to see a man whose dark-blue eyes sparked with conviction. A man whose shoulders, erect and sure, suggested a person with a mission. Although not restful, the night had proven fruitful, and a new realm of decisions were ushered in upon the wings of the dawn. Decisions from a man who had spent the midnight hours in prayer.

Wasting little time, Taylor found some bandages in the medicine cabinet and redressed his dog bite. He downed a dose and a half of ibuprofen. Taylor dressed, packed his backpack, and slung it over his shoulder. He limped toward the kitchen, gritting his teeth against the dull ache in his thigh. Hopefully the wound would give him less discomfort as he used his muscles and the painkillers took effect.

In the kitchen, Taylor reached for the phone book tucked in a wall rack beside the phone. He flipped to the yellow pages and jabbed his finger at the first cab service he saw. He phoned and ordered a taxi to take him to the airport, then replaced the receiver.

Taylor glanced toward the saucer of bran muffins near the microwave. Melissa had left him a note near the muffins, and he briefly scrutinized it.

Taylor,
Didn't want to wake you. Bacon in microwave. Help yourself to the coffee. I made a pot just for you, extra strong, this time. Thought you might like bran muffins better than the blueberry. See you tonight.

Mel

"The woman doesn't miss a beat," he muttered to himself. Taylor grabbed two muffins, popped open the microwave, and scooped up the five pieces of bacon from the plate. He deposited the bacon on the muffin saucer and searched until he found some disposable cups, all the while devouring the bran muffins. Taylor filled a large Styrofoam cup with inky coffee and savored the smell before dousing his tongue with the hot liquid. The bitter bite left him satisfied. He polished off the bacon and scribbled a brief note to Melissa on the back of her note.

Mel,
Gone to Baton Rouge. Thanks for everything. I owe you big.

Taylor

Adjusting the backpack, he limped toward the front door to await his taxi. Once he arrived at the airport, he would stop in the first gift shop he saw and purchase some dark glasses and a hat. While he didn't believe a hat and glasses would disguise him forever, he hoped they would at least allow him to get to Baton Rouge without being recognized. Once in Baton Rouge, he had a few things to say to Sonsee. After that, he was heading to LeBlanc Manor to find out exactly what lay in that old fireplace. He also planned to confront Carla Jenson. If she called the police, so be it.

Eighteen

Melissa pulled her Toyota down Windsor Drive, a street in Nichol's Hills. A suburb of Oklahoma City, Nichol's Hills featured a classic, aging neighborhood lined by majestic oaks with drooping arms laden in lavish leaves. Upon spotting the two-story frame home, she applied the brakes and prepared to turn into the circular driveway. Her hands produced a thin film of sweat as her fingers reflexively tightened on the steering wheel. Fluid renditions of contemporary prayer choruses poured over the car's stereo system. Choruses expressed from the heart of a pianist . . . a pianist named Kinkaide Franklin. Yesterday evening Melissa had taken home all his CDs. One by one, she unwrapped them and forced herself to listen to parts of each of them. The time had come to stop preserving the past and accept what could never be.

"It's been six years," she muttered. "Might as well face the music." Mel grimaced over the literal truths of that cliché.

She pulled into the driveway that led to the "Leave It to Beaver" home where Kinkaide grew up. According to her mother, he was visiting his parents. Darla Moore had called Melissa last night. Toward the end of the mother-daughter conversation, Darla mildly mentioned Kinkaide. Melissa, knowing her mother well, asked her if she had given Kincaide her addresses.

"Well, of course I gave them to him," Darla admitted, her voice holding no hint of conspiracy. "I assumed the two of you would enjoy talking after all this time."

"When did he call you?" Melissa had asked.

"Oh, he didn't call me."

"Did *you* call him?" She envisioned her mother learning of Kinkaide's visit and phoning him with a well-placed hint. The longer she contemplated the possibilities, the more intensely she frowned.

"Of course not, Mel. I would never do that!"

Mel's facial muscles relaxed a fraction.

"I saw him at church. I probably wouldn't have noticed him in the crowd — you know, our church has gotten so big and has such a great singles program now . . ."

"Yes, I know," Mel replied with more patience than she felt.

"Anyway, during the last year, his parents have started worshiping again with our congregation. When the pastor learned that Kinkaide was present, he asked him to play the offertory. It was divine! He has a touch that you'll never forget."

How well I know. Mel's mental retort was reflective of the last time Kinkaide kissed her — the night before their wedding — a deceptive kiss that had filled her with longing and promises of things to come . . .

"Anyway, I just had to tell Kinkaide how much I enjoyed his playing. And, well, one thing led to another and I gave him your addresses."

"Did he *request* my addresses?" Mel asked.

"He asked about you," Darla rushed on. "And I told him you were doing great, that you were now a successful pediatrician and that you were still single."

"So you just *offered* my addresses?" Mel had pushed, her hand gripping the phone tighter with every conversational curve.

"Of course," Darla said in a matter-of-fact tone. "But he was a very willing recipient."

With a groan, Mel curled her toes and tried to stop herself from feeling manipulated.

Now, as she steered the car around the curve in the driveway, her toes curled anew. All her life she had lived under the cloud of her mother's manipulation. Darla's motto for parenting centered upon control, not guidance.

Even when Mel began considering a career choice, Darla had made her opinion known. Early in her exploration of the medical profession, Melissa had expressed a vague interest in pediatric medicine. Darla suggested that Mel would make a better nurse. That only fueled Melissa's determination to answer God's call to become a children's doctor. Now that she had succeeded, Darla oozed to anyone who would listen about her daughter, the doctor. Only last year did Melissa learn from her younger sister that their mother had really wanted her to be a pediatrician all along. She tried to steer Mel toward nursing because she knew her daughter would be all the more determined to enter med school. Even now, Mel's nostrils flared with the memory, and she wondered if her mother would ever learn to take her hands off situations and allow God to do

His work. Melissa would have become a pediatrician without her mother's stratagem, but she didn't know if Darla ever saw that truth.

She slowed the car to a halt and put it in park as Kinkaide's fingers spilled forth the final notes of "Open Our Eyes, Lord." Automatically, Mel breathed a prayer, beseeching the Lord to open her spiritual eyes to His strength — a strength she desperately needed at this moment in time. Gripping the floor shift, she observed the home's front door, the color of evergreens, and nervously glanced at her wristwatch. Paying an unexpected visit at seven-thirty wasn't on Mel's list of favorite activities. She hoped Kinkaide's mother, the queen of social graces, wouldn't consider her unforgivably rude.

Kinkaide hadn't let propriety stop his unexpected calls upon Mel. But then, he never let propriety stop him from doing anything he chose. His mother, a stickler for societal rules, had inadvertently bred a rebel. That was part of what was so endearing about Kinkaide. He possessed a certain boyish charm that had snared Mel's heart. On their first date, Kinkaide hopped into a park fountain and dragged her in after him. Soon the two of them were kicking up water like preschoolers. Never had Mel laughed so hard. Never had she felt so carefree, so alive.

She removed her seat belt and pondered the irony that a first date that left her breathless led her to this spot at this moment. Kinkaide's stealing her heart turned into brutal rejection. Today, she would return the favor. She had thought about calling Kinkaide; she would have *rather* called. But that would have been the coward's way out. Besides, if she rang him up, Melissa would miss the look on his face when she told him she wasn't even remotely interested in renewing their acquaintance on any level. Apparently, the great Kinkaide Franklin thought he could step back into her life, and she would melt into his arms.

"Well, you've got another think coming," Mel whispered, then popped open the car door. Kinkaide would soon learn that where he was concerned she was far from melting. Or, rather, she was far from letting him know she was melting.

As she got out of the car and closed the door, Melissa admired the well-kept lawn. Everywhere she looked, she encountered memories. Near a group of towering oaks resided the varnished park bench where she and Kinkaide sat that summer after Kinkaide arrived at the University of Texas. Ironically, they had grown up in the same church, but the congregation was so large they hadn't really gotten to know each other until they signed up for the same English class at U.T. After a semester of getting to know each other, Kinkaide had dared kiss Mel on the park bench in front of his parent's home. The tender grass surrounding the bench seemed just as tender as their love, once budding and fresh. The flower beds full of ferns represented their relationship as it flourished. And the pungent scent of the geraniums, sitting on a decorative plant stand, reminded Mel of the bitterness of her disillusionment. Only the sounds of sparse traffic suggested that Melissa hadn't stepped into an exclusive, horticulturist's haven — a haven that rendered heartache. Kinkaide's father possessed a knack for turning a desert into a garden; his son had accomplished the opposite effect upon Mel's heart.

Squaring her shoulders, Melissa turned toward the house and schooled her features into a disinterested mask. Kinkaide need never know that she was far from unaffected.

"Melissa?"

She stiffened as the melodic male voice floated along the morning breeze like a wisp of yesterday. Melissa observed Kinkaide walking around the side of the house, pulled along by a curious poodle. When the dog noticed her, his puff-ball tail went rigid, and he produced a battery of high-pitched barks.

Smiling indulgently, Kinkaide walked toward his former fiancée. "Mom's only had this little guy about six months. He's a pitbull in the body of a poodle."

With a nod, Melissa acknowledged Kinkaide's remark, and an awkward silence settled between them, a silence that screamed the question so evident in Kinkaide's silken-brown eyes. Without a flinch, Mel held his inquiring gaze and noticed his hair, in damp curls along his neck. Her hands balled as she recalled the feel of his thick hair as if she had touched it only yesterday.

"Would you care to join us for breakfast?" As Kincaide swiveled to motion toward the house, Melissa glanced over his lean physique. Clad in shorts, T-shirt, and jogging shoes, he looked as if he hadn't gained a pound since she last saw him. Melissa, on the other hand, had put on about fifteen pounds. Thankfully, the business jacket hid the bulges the years had bestowed.

"N-no," Mel stuttered then cleared her throat. "No, thank you. Actually, I —"

"Mel, I —"

The two started simultaneously then each tried to concede to the other. Finally, Melissa began her preplanned speech she hoped would put a swift end to any chance of his future visits.

"Kinkaide, my mother told me she gave you my addresses." Melissa shoved her hands into the pockets of her twill slacks and gazed downward at the carpet of plush grass between them.

"Yes, she did," he said, an intrigued edge to his voice.

"Well, I came to first apologize on her behalf. I'm sorry that she was so pushy. I know you probably received all sorts of mixed messages from her. I love her dearly, but she can be so manipulative."

"Some things never change, right?" he said through a chuckle as the poodle tugged on its leash. Kinkaide took a few steps. "Care to join me?" he asked, arching one dark brow in a fashion that once attracted Mel. It still did.

She fell in place beside him and maintained a stoic demeanor, despite her mind's whirling with suppositions of what might have been. "I would also like to apologize for being rude yesterday morning in my office," Melissa continued, congratulating herself on her ability to naturally voice the memorized speech.

"That's quite all right." He shrugged. "You looked as if you were under a lot of pressure."

"Part of what was going on was funny, I guess," Melissa continued, realizing midsentence that she was deviating from the memorized speech. "Just last week I lectured one of my nurses about the new office rules — no male callers, in person or on the phone. Then —"

"I showed up," he supplied.

"Exactly." Mel paused beside him as the poodle took his time sniffing the base of a tree trunk. The sounds of the birds celebrating the morning did precious little to ease the knot in the pit of Mel's stomach. The puddles of shadow and light, dancing along the lawn, didn't catch her fancy in the least. A heightened awareness of the man nearby engulfed her in a struggle to survive the strained encounter. His faint scent of Ivory soap only added to her sensory experience and threatened to hurl her into the throes of illogical babbling.

"So, how's life treating you?" Kinkaide leaned against the tree and crossed his arms. He stroked his trimmed beard and observed Mel in a way that left her scrambling to remember where she had detoured from the memorized speech. The last thing she needed was a heartfelt conversation, a catch-up on old times, a let's-pick-up-where-we-left-off. Desperately she searched for an answer that would bump the conversation back into the vein of her original plan.

At last she decided to use the direct approach. Mel thought of her six best friends and knew every one of them would probably be able to steer the conversation more gracefully than she ever could. But this was not the time to worry about being graceful. She needed to communicate, and communicate clearly. Never again did she plan to open her office door and see Kinkaide Franklin awaiting her as if he thought he were her Christmas morning surprise. Furthermore, when Melissa drove away, she wanted him irrevocably convinced of her stance.

"Life's been good. Really good," she said, then crossed her arms.

"Your mother told me you're doing quite well in your practice."

"Yes, really well. God has blessed me."

"Your mother also said —"

"What . . . impression did you get from her, Kinkaide?"

He cut a glimpse toward the poodle, now tugging on his leash.

"Honestly, I wouldn't put anything past her." Melissa grabbed the line of thought that would lead right back to her pre-planned comments.

"Oh?" Shooting a glance toward Mel, he relented to the dog's desires and followed in its wake.

"Well, yes." Melissa walked beside him. "And I'd like to say that I appreciate seeing you, and thanks for coming by, but . . ." Suddenly overtaken with a bout of vacillation, Mel searched for a way to make herself express her "get lost" message.

"But you aren't interested?" His spontaneous laugh rankled.

"Exactly." Her voice successfully covered her heart's traitorous yearnings.

"I'm okay with that. Thanks for being honest. I guess that's one of the things I always admired in you. You never let anything stand in the way of the truth," he said with a hint of irony. Kinkaide stopped and swiveled to face her, despite the poodle's yelp of displeasure.

Melissa caught her breath with the intensity of his appraisal. Involuntarily, she stepped backward, only to bump into a tree. Feeling like Eve in the Garden of Eden, she feared that Kinkaide sensed exactly what she didn't want him to know: She still loved him — desperately loved him. She had never gotten over him. She never would. Mel stiffened her legs and prohibited herself from bolting.

"So I guess it's my turn to be honest," he said in a deceptively soft voice. "I don't believe you."

"Your belief or lack of it doesn't change reality," Mel replied, certain she would win the Oscar if this performance were filmed. Yet a band of conviction tightened around her heart, suggesting she was pushing the boundaries of God's approval.

A spark of aggravation stirred Kinkaide's eyes, and a wry smile lifted one corner of his mouth. "I've already said it once, but you know, you haven't changed a bit."

Melissa adjusted her glasses, cleared her throat, and inched toward her car.

"I'm tempted to ask why you came by instead of calling considering your . . ." Kinkaide's grimace was discernible, and Mel fought a smirk. "Considering your message. But I think I can pinpoint your reason."

"Oh?" Mel tightened her crossed arms, as if to guard herself from a potential barb.

"Of course. You most likely thought phoning would make you look like a coward. Besides . . ." He hesitated as if he were savoring the bouquet of every word. "I'm sure it's much more rewarding to deliver your rejection in real life. Phoning would undoubtedly rob you of the pleasure of repaying tit for tat."

She compressed her lips as a shock wave of heat spiraled from the base of her soul. Yet Melissa, accomplished in the art of remaining poised under pressure, mustered every scrap of leftover composure and began self-talking. *You will behave in a calm manner. You will behave like a mature adult. Calm and mature. Calm and mature.*

"You know," Mel said through a smile she knew couldn't have neared her eyes. "The last time I saw you, you had just jilted me. Really, I think you've gotten off rather lightly, don't you?" Yet Mel's visit had backfired. She had gotten off far from lightly. The longer she stood in Kinkaide's presence, the more she felt the old wounds reopening. Reopening and bleeding. Bleeding and begging for bandages. Pivoting, Melissa marched toward her car, hungering to fling herself back into the quest for success. That quest had served as the emotional bandage covering her wounds, which had enabled them to fester and spread their infection throughout her spirit.

"You haven't forgiven me," Kinkaide said, his words laced with incredulity.

Mel halted, her fingers closing around the car handle as if it were her anchor to sanity. She peered over the car and shot a final arrow at her victim. "Did you honestly think I'd be glad to see you?"

The flash of pain in his eyes didn't bring the satisfaction Mel had presumed. Instead, her heart thudded with regret. Regret and longing. Longing and love. A love that would never be requited.

She opened the door, plopped into the driver's seat, and cranked the engine. Within minutes, Melissa was pulling out of the driveway, and the final chords of "Open Our Eyes, Lord" floated from Kinkaide's CD through her soul. She had prayed for the Lord to open her eyes to His strength. Instead, He had made her aware of a hideous cancer eating a hole through her soul. The cancer of unforgiveness.

Nineteen

Louis squinted, his eyes gritty and heavy with the all-night vigil. A mound of ancient keys rested against the fireplace hearth. Already, he had laboriously tried each key in the lock at least six times. Early in his attempts, he had been fueled by certainty of success. Then the flames of conviction had decreased to the coals of hope. Finally, the coals of hope had diminished into cold desperation. Desperation that drove him frantically toward his goal. At last, he allowed himself to suspect that he might not be able to open the vault, that his plan could be a failure.

Pressing his lips together, Louis glanced toward the window where morning's light forced itself around the boxes precariously leaning toward the pane. Already he had tarried far longer than his original intent. Yet knowing what lay inside the vault drove him to the limit. *Perhaps one more round,* he mused, fighting the hopelessness threatening to pervade his mind. "One more round," he whispered, then grasped a key lying atop the pile.

Louis placed a flattened hand against the cool, metal door, inserted the key into the elongated slot, and jiggled it with the furor of a man fighting for his life. One key followed another and another until he once again held the final key. With the musty smell of long-agos seeming to smother him, Louis crammed the ancient key into the lock and cruelly manipulated it until the instrument bent in his brutal grasp. Growling, he stood back and slammed his tennis shoe against the lion's brass beard, forcing himself not to bark out an accusation. In response, the lion's mouth fell open, and an iron key tumbled out, clinking against the stone hearth.

Blinking, Louis gazed at the key as if it were a foreign object the likes of which he had never encountered. Then he recalled the servant's note to Idella Marie, claiming that she had hidden another key. He slowly bent to retrieve the key. He closed his eyes to savor the feel of cool iron against a palm damp with sweat. In reverence of the moment, he held his breath. Tugging the bent key from the slot and dropping it on the hearth, he inserted the new key into the lock and gently turned. A series of faint clicks preceded the door's swinging open with the sigh and rasp of unoiled hinges. Louis fell to his knees and gazed into the vault, his heart palpitating with an intensity that left him breathless. Breathless and elated. Elated and giddy.

He thrust both hands into the riches and pulled out a mound of priceless antiques: two gold goblets, each garnished with rubies; a strand of pearls interspersed with garnets; a wide gold bracelet encrusted in diamonds; a tarnished silver dagger, the handle lined with rubies. Rubies that reminded Louis of blood . . . the blood of Jacques LeBlanc.

His fingers quavered. His stomach churned. His ears roared with a new cycle of staccato accusations. *If only I had kicked the lion's beard last week, Jacques LeBlanc would still be alive!* As the thought ricocheted through the corridors of his soul, the gold, the silver, the jewels seemed to heat his perspiring palms until the very touch of the treasure burned like lava. As if the valuables were a viper inserting venomous fangs into tender flesh, Louis cast the pieces onto the hearth, stood, and stumbled backward.

"The evil . . . the evil . . ." he muttered.

Wringing his hands, Louis gazed down at his scabby cuticles and bolted toward the door. "A sink. I-I must f-find a sink," he whispered, feeling as if burning blood were coating his hands and creeping up his arms. But at the room's doorway, the drive to scrub his fingers was superseded by the clamor of greed.

Louis stopped. He gripped the door-frame. He inspected his hands . . . the hands that had killed an innocent man. His spine stiffened. "There is no blood on my hands," he whispered. "That's crazy. It's crazy. Get a grip on yourself." Yet the tell-tale huffing attested to a man in torment. His words did little to stop the feel of warmth slithering from his hands to his elbows.

"Stop it!" he growled, raking his finger-nails against his heavy cotton shirt. Thin streaks of blood and torn cuticles attested to his frenzied need to purge himself. When every scab was peeled away, every wound opened anew, Louis clawed his forearms until they stung as severely as his hands. Then, and only then, did his labored breathing decrease.

He turned and peered toward the fire-place until the lion's golden face, dulled by time, grew bleary, distorted, and eventually took on the features of Jacques LeBlanc. Louis stumbled forward like a zombie. He fell to his knees beneath the lion and gripped the chilled snout. "I'm sorry," he muttered. "I'm so, so sorry." A chant from childhood began a slow cadence from the pit of his soul. *Thou shalt not kill. Thou shalt not steal. Thou shalt not bear false witness against thy neighbor. Thou shalt not covet.*

Louis arrived at a crossroads. One road led deeper into the cavity of death. The other road wound upward, toward the lush hills of life. Hills through which his mother had once tried to guide him. As the tug-of-war raged in his soul, Louis pondered leaving the treasure, going back home, selling everything he owned, and exiting the country. He and his wife could start over again — perhaps in Switzerland — far away from this insanity. His sons, now grown and married, would understand. They would have to. Then he considered turning himself into the authorities, admitting his guilt, and facing the punishment.

A thin shaft of sunlight penetrated the window to highlight a dust-laden diamond nestled in a golden bracelet. Even dulled with the mist of yesteryear, the diamond weakly winked as if the stone were begging Louis to snatch it to his chest. He grabbed the bracelet, yanked open the oversized canvas tote, and dropped the jewel-encrusted masterpiece into the bag's soft folds. Like a man possessed, Louis scooped up the remaining pieces from the hearth and slung them into the bag. The clink of gold on gold . . . silver on silver . . . jewels on jewels fueled his voracity. In a matter of minutes, the large tote bulged with the contents of the chest. Louis pushed the useless keys inside the vault and locked it.

Despite the essence of evil forming a new layer upon his palms, Louis purposefully chose his path. A depraved path, now familiar and worn. The holy hills of life, verdant and virginal, would have to wait.

Sonsee collapsed onto the worn recliner in the room where she had spent the night. A bag emitting the smells of a burger and fries lay in her lap, and she drew heavily on a cold soda. The morning had proven frantic, replete with a dog-in-a-wreck case and a traumatized preschooler who bewailed the passing of her parrot, Petey. If nothing else validated Sonsee's need of a partner, today did. By eleven o'clock she had made her decision to invite Mark Allen to join her practice. Sonsee had been tied to this clinic for five years and had only taken two vacations — one to Hawaii with her father and Taylor and then the trip to Vietnam. Ironically, both of those trips had occurred in the last seven months, specifically because Mark had agreed to work in her place each time. The possibility of Mark's continued presence ushered in all sorts of new options for Sonsee — options that included the beach and mountains and perhaps another mission trip or two.

She glanced at her wristwatch. The fourteen-carat timepiece forever reminded Sonsee of her father's steadfast love. "One o'clock already?" She had planned to be on her way to LeBlanc Manor by now.

Her stomach growled as the inviting smells floated from the bag. She rummaged through the sack until she pulled out her lunch. She hadn't eaten since last night. This morning, she had been too uptight over her spiritual struggles to even consider food. Presently, thoughts of her tendencies toward vengeance and issues of her relationship with Taylor created a tight knot in her stomach. Pursing her lips, she shoved aside these concerns and began devouring the burger.

"Whatcha up to, Red?" Taylor's Texas

drawl, laced with humor, sent a shiver up her spine. She dropped the hamburger, and twisted toward the door, her eyes widening. He wore a chocolate-colored golfer's hat that looked ridiculously out of place on a man who usually clung to a Stetson. After closing the door, he turned the lock and removed his dark shades.

Holding her breath, Sonsee stared at Taylor as if he were an apparition. "H-How did you get here?" she stammered. "Is Melissa here?"

"Nope. I came on my own. Actually, I flew down."

"You flew!" Sonsee plopped the half-eaten burger and leftover fries into the fast food bag, dropped the sack onto the floor, and stood. "Have you lost your mind? Aren't you afraid somebody's going to recognize you?"

Taylor dumped his backpack, hat, and glasses on the floor near the recliner. The dark circles under his eyes suggested the man needed large doses of sleep. "I've been doing a lot of praying and thinking, Sonsee." Taylor shoved his hands into his jeans pockets. "I guess the time alone at Mel's gave me some time with God that was long overdue. He has really shown me some things that I guess I've been running from for years." Taylor placed hands on hips and paced toward the small sink across the room. "First, I need to apologize to you." He swiveled to face Sonsee and paused.

"Really?" Attempting to absorb this sudden turn of events, Sonsee gulped. Furthermore, the warmth pouring from his sapphire-blue eyes increased her discomfort. A warmth that left her knees weak. A warmth she had once prayed to find.

"Really." He crammed his hands back into his pockets. "I'm sorry for having involved you in all this business of my running from the law. I should have never asked you to take such a risk for me. It was nothing short of cowardice."

"But —"

Taylor held up one hand and began pacing again, this time toward the recliner. "That's part of the reason I decided to fly down here on my own. I left Melissa a note. Unless she's found it, she doesn't know I'm gone yet. I was equally selfish to involve her. What in the name of common sense was I thinking?" Taylor stopped, his back to Sonsee. He rubbed the nape of his neck.

"Didn't you tell me someone shot at you? That's reason enough to —"

"Reason enough to get you and Mel involved and possibly get you shot at, too!" he scoffed, raising his arms as he traipsed toward the sink.

"So what are you going to do now?" Sonsee, barely able to form a coherent thought, attempted to absorb the full implications of Taylor's openly boarding a plane and flying to Louisiana. Too many escapades like the present one, and Taylor would either land behind bars or come face to face with the person who was trying to frame him. The outcome of both scenarios clawed at Sonsee's soul.

Taylor walked back to Sonsee, grasped her upper arms, and peered deeply into her eyes. "I'm going to LeBlanc Manor to face Carla. I'm going to demand that she tell the truth."

"But what if she calls the police?" Sonsee rasped, feeling as if her mouth were full of sawdust.

"Then so be it," he growled, his lips tight. "God delivered me from false accusations twenty years ago. He can do it again." The flame in his eyes increased in fervor and attested to more than Taylor's simply exercising his natural spunk. Never did Sonsee remember his speaking of the Lord with such conviction.

"I've been doing a lot of praying, Sonsee," he continued, his grip diminishing to a caress. Gently, Taylor slipped his callused thumbs under her elbow-length sleeves and massaged her arms with tiny, circular strokes. The gesture resulted in Sonsee's fighting the urge to lean closer. She would have loved to accept his unspoken invitation, step into his arms, and drown in the drowsy rush of pleasure that his mere touch promised. Yet an annoying remembrance, an echo from the morning, stopped her as if she had slammed into a steel wall. *Who is my reason for living — God or Taylor?* Sonsee teetered between bolting from Taylor and flinging her arms around him.

"All my praying culminated into a deeper commitment to the Lord — I guess while you and your friends were chatting on the internet. Then after that, I prayed most of the night. I don't think I've ever prayed so much in one day in my life. But it was something that had to be. During the night I realized that I had used you and Mel and that I had to make some changes in the current situation. On the plane trip, I even began to wonder if the Lord allowed me to be accused of the crime in order to get me still long enough to talk to me."

"Oh, really?" Sonsee said, not certain she possessed the mental capabilities to produce logical commentary.

"Anyway," Taylor continued, as if she hadn't spoken, "last spring you and I had an . . . interesting discussion, if I recall."

Sonsee's face grew hot, and her teetering ended. She looked down, stepped out of his reach, and crossed her arms. Yes, she recalled the whole conversation, word for word. Even now the memory of Taylor's admitting that he knew she loved him immersed her in a heated sea of mortification.

"You said that perhaps my not being able to fall in love was linked to my father's d-deserting me and my mom." The pained stammer demanded that Sonsee look up. She dismissed her own chagrin in the face of the raw heartache stirring Taylor's eyes. The laugh lines around his mouth, the lines that usually attested to a great sense of humor, now bore signs of sorrow. A sorrow he finally gave full rein.

For the first time in their twenty-four year acquaintance, Sonsee saw the real Taylor. The Taylor who had covered his devastation with humor. The Taylor who loved her. A gasp, spontaneous and awestruck, sprang from her inner being.

"I guess we were both wrong last spring." Taylor knitted his brows as if he were struggling for his next words. "It wasn't a case of my not being able to love you, Sonsee, or that I was too stubborn." One corner of his mouth lifted in synchrony with his rising brow. "I think I've been in love with you for awhile, actually, it's just that I was so devastated that I built walls around myself and everybody else — including God. The only person I really let in was my mother." He shrugged. "And, I guess, in some ways, I even kept her out. Anytime she tried to bring up my father, I would pounce on another subject like a duck on a June bug."

"Now, that's a new one," Sonsee quipped, her palms damp with her desire to shift the subject. "Where'd you pick up that turn of words?" The way this conversation was progressing, she expected Taylor to propose at any given moment. Ironically, the one situation Sonsee had prayed for was swiftly becoming her bane.

"It's a Texas cliché," Taylor said through a chuckle. "You should visit me more often. You'd probably learn a lot." Yet his limpid eyes, sparkling like sapphires under a mellow light, belied his teasing tone. "Or perhaps we could get married and you could just move to Texas, Red. Would you like that?" His gaze devoured her features, as if he were seeing her for the first time. The vulnerability of Taylor's request, the purity of his heart, drove Sonsee to voice a ready yes.

But one pivotal issue erected itself to prohibit what her heart longed to voice. *Who is my reason for living — God or Taylor?* Once again a barrage of pop tunes played through her mind, tunes which suggested that a man could be her everything, that she would find ultimate fulfillment through romantic love. Then Sonsee recalled the trip to Vietnam, the peace she found in Christ — a peace for which her troubled soul now panted.

"Sonsee?" Taylor questioned as he neared. Gently he tucked his fingers under her ear lobes and stroked her cheeks with his thumbs. The feel of his hands against tender flesh engulfed Sonsee in an ardent rush of pleasure. "If I don't survive all this . . . I want you to know I love you. I think I was on the verge of falling hard in Hawaii, but I wouldn't let myself." As Taylor spoke, his words slowed and his attention settled on her mouth.

Sonsee caught her bottom lip between her teeth and felt as if she were being tugged under by an irresistible current, balmy and inviting. Slowly Taylor cupped her face in both hands and gradually leaned toward her.

Yes, this is what I've wanted for months! Yes, I love you, Taylor. Yes, I want to marry you. Oh, dear God, please let me have this moment . . . just this moment. If any man could bring me contentment, it's Taylor Delaney.

Only intimacy with Jesus Christ can bring you true contentment. The heavenly missive, sharp as a sword, sent a rush of cold tingles down Sonsee's spine — tingles that dashed all romantic passion and left conviction in their wake. As if she were jolted from a hypnotic spell, Sonsee stumbled backward, away from human romance, toward the Lover of her soul.

"Sonsee?" Taylor queried, his brows raised.

"Taylor, I — I . . . I can't."

"What?" He shook his head as if trying to comprehend her motive.

"I — I can't agree to marry you." The words tumbled out of their own volition.

"What?" he blasted again as if she had just posed an outrageous hypothesis.

The room felt as if it were spinning, and Sonsee inched her way backward until she leaned against the wall at the foot of her cot. Deliberately, she determined not to collapse on the makeshift bed. "I said I can't —"

"But I thought you loved me!" The heightened emotion in Taylor's voice accompanied a slight flush rising up his cheeks.

"I do, but —"

"Good grief! What's the matter with you? I've never in all my life been so confused by a woman." He grabbed the back of his neck. "For the last seven months, you've looked at me like you were some kind of love-sick puppy and practically hornswaggled me to fall in love with you. Now I have, and —"

"I beg your pardon." Sonsee's spine stiffened against the wall as her face grew cold. "I never *hornswaggled* you into anything, Taylor. What in the world does that mean anyway?"

"You really *do* need to get to Texas more often, don't you?"

"I'm doing just fine in Baton Rouge!"

"Lord, help me," he muttered under his breath, as if he were the only person in the room. "Just about the time I think I know a woman, she turns on me. And, frankly, I think this one is losing it!"

"I am *not* losing a thing!" Sonsee stormed.

"Oh, pardon me!" He raised his arms. "I forgot — you have to have it before you lose it." He gestured like a choir director demanding staccato performance, then swiveled, retrieved his backpack, hat, and glasses, and stomped toward the door.

"Where are you going?"

"I'm going to New Orleans."

"You're not going without me."

"Watch me." Without a backward glance, he unlocked the door, whipped it open, stepped through, and slammed it as he exited.

"Taylor!" Sonsee ran after him and flung open the door. "Taylor Delaney, don't you *dare* leave without me!" She caught but a glimpse of his striped shirt as he stepped through her office doorway, toward the waiting room. The telephone's piercing ring added a new level of irritation to the atmosphere, taut with tension.

Sonsee raced to her desk, yanked open the bottom drawer, and grabbed her purse. Within seconds, she rounded the receptionist's cubicle near the front door. "Tell Mark I'm out of here as planned. I should be back Monday. Tell him I'll call." She flung open the door to run smack into Taylor's back.

"Okay, okay! I give up!" Fighting to

maintain his balance, Taylor pivoted to face her. "You'd think this was the Super Bowl, and I was running the winning touchdown or something. What are you going to do next, for Pete's sake? Drop kick me through the goal posts?"

"Dr. LeBlanc, wait!" Peg's urgent request cut off Sonsee's retort. Still gripping the doorknob, Sonsee leaned back into the office. "This is your friend, Melissa Moore. She says it's imperative that you talk with her." Peg's dark eyes reflected Mel's bent toward commands.

"Just tell her he's here and fine and not to worry," Sonsee said.

As soon as Peg repeated the message into the receiver, she produced a series of nods and affirmative remarks. "She said to tell you that Jac is there now."

"What? She wasn't due until tomorrow morning." Sonsee stepped toward the brunette. On second thought, she grabbed Taylor's arm and dragged him back into the clinic. "I'll take the call in my office, Peg. Thanks!"

"Everyone else is at lunch," Peg called. "I'm going, too."

"Okay," Sonsee said before entering her office. "Lock the door on your way out."

Twenty

Taylor feigned a relaxed aura and deposited himself in an office chair. Nonchalantly, he propped his booted feet on the edge of Sonsee's desk and scrutinized her through the guise of half-interested appraisal. As Sonsee picked up the receiver and spoke a clipped greeting into the mouthpiece, she frowned and nudged at his boots. With a resigned sigh, Taylor made a monumental job of placing his feet on the floor.

Even though the woman might as well have turned him upside down and rattled his brain, Taylor purposed to hide any signs of emotional disturbance. Nonetheless, he reeled with confusion. Confusion and doubts. Doubts and disillusionment. Before his proposal, Taylor had planned for what he predicted to be the worse case scenario — that Sonsee would ask for a few weeks to consider his offer. Never had he suspected a cold no. Sonsee's saying she loved him but rejecting his proposal fit perfectly with the rest of his life — absolute, illogical chaos.

Deciding that *not* watching Sonsee proved easier on him, Taylor idly gazed around the room, noting the dying corn plant by the window that looked out onto the alley. The crisp brown leaves attested to the poor thing's imminent demise. Sonsee always said that for every animal's life she saved, she killed a dozen plants. This sad-looking victim was on the way to the graveyard, to join a host of predecessors. The sun, seeping past the open blinds, created lines of light and shadow on the plant and along the floor — shadows that reflected the dark forces hovering over Taylor's life.

"Yes, Jac, I understand. I'll try to stop him from going." Sonsee's comments broke into Taylor's musing, and he returned her pointed glance with lazy-eyed assessment. "But he seems to have his mind made up, and once he sets his heels about something . . ."

Taylor leaned forward, placed elbows on knees, and made a tent of his fingers. "I'm not a basset hound, Sonsee," he groused. "I understand every word you're saying."

"Yes, okay. I'll let him talk with you." Sonsee extended the receiver toward him.

"It's Jac. She changed her plans and flew in a day early in order to talk with you before you drove down together. She's with Mel at her office now."

As Taylor reached for the receiver, the hair on the back of his neck prickled, his spine stiffened, and a sudden horror flashed over him like a fountain of flames. *The blinds. The blinds are open. Close them now!* Ignoring the phone, Taylor lunged forward only seconds before the window exploded, and a whizzing bullet rocketed above him to pelt the far wall. He and Sonsee shared a stunned stare. Then Taylor flung himself at her, knocking her to the floor as the receiver flew from her hands. Amid a collection of grunts, the two landed beside the desk. Another bullet crashed into the wall and into a sizable framed photo of Sonsee, her mother, and her father. The photo collapsed to the accompaniment of crackling glass.

"Get under the desk," Taylor demanded, pushing Sonsee forward.

"It's not me they're after. You go first."

With a frustrated growl, Taylor hurled aside the rolling chair and shoved Sonsee under the desk. He huddled close to her as another bullet erupted against the wall.

"This is the reason why Jac and Mel and

I think you should have stayed put."
Sonsee stared at him, nose to nose. The "I
told you so" glimmer in her eyes couldn't
be mistaken, even under the shadows of
the desk.

Taylor reached around the desk and
grabbed for the phone's receiver, still
resting on the floor. He pulled the telephone from the desk, and it crashed downward with the complaint of plastic against
carpet.

Sonsee nabbed the receiver. "Jac . . . yes,
it was gunfire . . . yes, we're okay . . . we're
getting out of here. I have no idea where
we'll be."

Taylor grabbed the receiver. "Jac, we're
going to LeBlanc Manor as planned."

"Are you crazy?" Jac demanded, her
cold-as-rocks Midwest voice attesting to a
woman with grit.

"Not in the least. I've got to find Carla.
She's the key to this whole mess."

"You're going to get yourself killed —
and what about Sonsee?"

Taylor glanced toward the woman he
loved. The mixture of adoration and stress
and uncertainty streaming from her eyes
reflected his own emotions. "I've already
tried to leave her here once, and she
wouldn't cooperate."

"I'm heading to Baton Rouge now. Stay where you are until I get there. Got it?" Jac demanded.

"Come on down if you like, but you'll be meeting us at LeBlanc Manor," Taylor snapped, then dropped the receiver into the cradle. "Let's go, Sonsee."

The plan worked. Cerberus smirked and lost little time pulling into traffic, three cars behind Sonsee and Taylor. The criminal had watched Sonsee for two days now, waiting for signs of Taylor. The patience paid off. Never once did Cerberus aim the snub nose .357 to wound Taylor — only to scare him out into the open. Cerberus had gambled on Sonsee or Taylor possessing the key. Hopefully they were at last heading toward the treasure. If Cerberus' calculations were correct, the two of them were as greedy as the rest of the family. With the .357 stuffed under the driver's seat, Cerberus focused on the task at hand. Most likely the pair would step right into the trap that was awaiting them. As soon as they ascended the third floor and opened the vault, the police would receive an anonymous phone call. After Taylor was arrested, Cerberus would deal with Sonsee, relieve the secret safe of its burden, and exit the country a multimillionaire.

Louis, that imbecile pawn, would probably never learn the whole truth . . . that Cerberus had actually pushed him into the ocean . . . that plans to murder Jacques for his wealth had preceded Louis' presence by months . . . that he had been nothing more than a tool to orchestrate the mastermind's plans.

As Sonsee wove her way out of Baton Rouge and headed south on I10, Cerberus chuckled. *All is well. Within two hours, I'll be escaping with a priceless treasure, Taylor will be in jail, and Sonsee . . .* Cerberus frowned. Sonsee certainly posed a problem.

⁓

"Taylor, I guess I owe you an explanation about . . . about . . ." Sonsee gripped the steering wheel and glanced into the rearview mirror at the line of cars behind them. Sonsee spotted no one who appeared threatening, but every car that passed potentially contained a passenger ready to shoot at them. For the last ten minutes, neither Sonsee nor Taylor had spoken.

Initially, Taylor had tried his hand at humor by making a sarcastic remark about Sonsee's car and its interior.

"Looks like you're having a bad uphol-stery day," he'd quipped, motioning toward the seats.

Sonsee had just rolled her eyes and started the engine. And that interaction had ushered in a dense cloud of interper-sonal uneasiness sprinkled with wariness and expectation.

Taylor glanced over his shoulder and scooted down in the seat. Regardless of his nonchalant demeanor, Sonsee sensed his fear of being followed. She also perceived his confusion about her, his disenchant-ment concerning her rejection, and his em-barrassment over the whole interaction.

"I'm sorry about what . . . um . . ." She cleared her throat and toyed with the gear shift. "I'm sorry about how things turned out back at the clinic."

"Yep, getting shot at isn't exactly my idea of a good day. I'm startin' to miss my cattle in a big time way, li'l lady," he drawled in his John Wayne voice.

Sonsee, recalling those moments when Taylor had revealed so much of himself, saw through his ploy. "You know that's not what I'm talking about," she whispered. "And it's time you stopped hiding behind John Wayne, don't you think?"

"I think you've got me so confused I

don't know which end is up." All traces of John Wayne vanished in the path of Taylor's sincerity.

Sonsee dashed a glance toward him and wished she hadn't. Even though he wore the golfer's hat and dark glasses, the set of his features suggested a knight beseeching his maiden to reconsider her refusal. Sonsee stopped herself from pulling the car over to the side of the road, falling into his arms, and begging his forgiveness.

"T-Taylor, this might sound crazy to you, but . . ." She grappled with voicing her spiritual struggles.

"Try me. I've been known to have a crazy moment or two here lately. As a matter of fact, looks like this whole thing between me and you fits right in with everything else that's happened this last week."

"Okay." Sonsee reached to flip on the "oldies but goodies" station she enjoyed, only to be greeted by a tenor proclaiming "You're my everything." Immediately, she turned off the radio and curled her toes against the soles of her loafers. "Here's the deal," Sonsee began, then she decided to turn the music back on. "Listen to this." As the tune expressed the heartfelt longings of a love-struck male, she discerned Taylor's blank stare but didn't take her attention from the cars in front of her.

"Are you trying to tell me something?" he said through a cautious chuckle.

"Yes," she ground out. "I'm trying to tell you that I've been guilty of doing what that song says." She pointed to the radio. "It all started in Hawaii. I fell hard — or better yet, I fell big. I'm not really sure how long I-I've —" She stuttered to a halt as her chest tightened in the face of speaking her love.

"How long you've been in love with me?" The question floated around the car like a caress on the ears that penetrated the heart and reverberated with expectancy.

"Yes." Sonsee gripped the gear shift and noticed a pine tree standing alone near the road. In the distance, a clump of trees huddled together. Sonsee wondered if she would forever be like that lonely tree, always seeing others happily married, but never finding divine release to pursue matrimony. Dread galloped through her spirit like a dark steed bent upon trampling her every hope.

"I guess in a way we're in the same boat," Taylor said as if he were fishing for her exact meaning. "If the truth were known, I had a few . . . thoughts . . . in Hawaii myself."

"Yes, except that I — I — oh good grief, how do I explain all this?" Sonsee waved her hand then pinched her bottom lip. "It's just that, somewhere along the line, I've put my desires for romantic love and — and I guess for — for . . . um . . . you . . ." she cleared her throat, ". . . above my desire for God."

"Hey, don't knock romance. God invented it, you know."

Sonsee darted him a sidelong glance. "That's a profound statement, coming from a man who's run from romance most of his life."

"Well, you live and learn. I can change and grow too, you know," Taylor said, pointing to his chest.

"I think I see a lot of growth in you, Taylor. It's all quite breathtaking, if you want the truth. But, seriously, God is constraining me from committing to you. All I can think of are the love songs our culture produces and how we have this misconception that another human being will bring ultimate fulfillment. I'm not saying God didn't create us with a need for human companionship. I guess I'm just beginning to see — or struggling to see — that true happiness will not come until we truly experience God's fulfillment." As the words left her mouth, Sonsee blinked with their potency.

Taylor whistled. "That was a mouthful."

"And I don't know where it came from, but I think it's what the Lord has been trying to show me for months now. In Vietnam I honestly thought I had gotten a grip on the whole thing. I prayed like crazy after I accidentally called you that night —"

"Come on, was that *really* an accident?"

"Excuse me!" Gaping, Sonsee stared at him.

"Don't forget you're driving," Taylor growled.

Sonsee looked back at the road. "Yes, that was an accident," she insisted, amazed at how Taylor could make her want to melt one minute and thoroughly exasperate her the next. "I was going to call Father, and I wound up dialing your number. Don't be so quick to compliment yourself."

"Yeow! You just scored two points."

Sonsee snorted. "Yeah, and you just lost about ten."

"Sounds like I'm already in the negative, so what's ten more points?"

"Oh, Taylor," Sonsee sighed, "this is such a mess. It would be a mess if the only thing I'm struggling with involved you and me. But, besides that, I really think that given the opportunity I would . . ." Sonsee swallowed against the bile of vengeance. "I think it would be really easy for me to push Father's murderer off the nearest cliff," she uttered through gritted teeth.

"I can understand why you'd feel that way," Taylor said in a pious voice. "Of course, I, being the spiritual giant that I am, would never contemplate such a hideous thing. Right now, I would just love to invite the murderer over for dinner and serve the jerk my best T-bone, rounded off with cheese cake laced with hemlock," he finished in the most pleasant of tones.

Sonsee dashed a glimpse toward Taylor to see traces of her own troubling emotions nibbling at the corners of his mouth. "Well, I could probably live with that scenario, too," Sonsee said, speeding up to pass a line of slow cars. The sporty Honda's engine revved to the task, creating a purring vibration as she accelerated. "But all those thoughts of retaliation fly in the face of forgiveness."

"I know. But the kind of forgiveness we need is not for wimps, Sonsee. It's tough as nails to pull off, and it might take some time, especially when you consider the person might be a family member."

"Speaking of which, Rafael called me last night."

"Oh?" Taylor asked, as if he weren't surprised.

"He and Natalie are interested in buying LeBlanc Manor."

"Now that's smooth. They buy the house; they get the vault."

"That's exactly what I was thinking. But Alana mentioned perhaps buying the place as well."

"I still don't trust her," he said with conviction.

"She seems to think the same of Hermann, Natalie, and Rafael."

"All four of them could be in on it. I just wish you hadn't let Alana in your house."

"But —"

"I know, I know." Taylor held up his hand. "But I think it's a little suspicious that she was so eager to help you clean the place after someone trashed it. How do you know she wasn't just continuing the search she had already started?"

Once again Sonsee vacillated between trust and suspicion. Then she pondered the bruise on Alana's temple, the sincerity of her apology, her cries for a father she felt she never knew. "I really don't think Alana was involved, especially not after our talk yesterday. We made a lot of headway toward reconciling our relationship. Besides, the person who fell in my apartment was male. He sounded too big to be female, and he let out a roar when he landed that was definitely masculine. I'd come closer to thinking the intruder was Rafael or Hermann than Alana."

"What *are* you talking about?" Taylor interjected. "Someone was in your house while you were there?"

"Oh, no," Sonsee groaned, rubbing one temple.

"So you're keeping secrets from me, is that it?" Taylor shifted in his seat.

"No — I mean yes. Yes, I am — or I was. I just didn't want you to worry, that's all."

"Is there anything else you've conveniently forgotten to tell me?" he growled impatiently. "Has anyone held you at gunpoint or —"

"No, that's it. And the reason I didn't tell you about the intruder is because you were already worried. I figured if you knew I'd been home when that man was there, you'd probably do something rash like fly to Baton Rouge so you could protect me or something."

"Makes sense to me." Taylor propped his head on the headrest. "I just wish you'd told me. I don't like you hiding stuff from me."

"Now that's refreshing," Sonsee quipped. "You've tried to hide yourself from me and everybody else the whole time I've known you." She maneuvered the Honda into the right lane as the undercurrents of their relationship threatened to tug her into waters she dared not tread.

"Well, those days are over. I promise." Taylor's voice, vulnerable and pleading, stroked Sonsee's soul as his callused fingers caressed the back of her hand. She clenched the gear shift while an onslaught of longing, fresh and potent, raced through her.

"If I get out of this alive —"

"I just hope I'm not going to have to forgive *two* murders." Sonsee skillfully and swiftly maneuvered the conversation, sweeping aside traces of romance, yet dropping them into a dark sphere of impending doom. A fist full of dread settled in the pit of her stomach as another upbeat "oldie but goodie" floated over the radio. Sonsee moved her hand from beneath Taylor's to press the tiny black button that ended the music. She gripped the steering wheel with both hands as silence descended upon the car. A silence interrupted only by the sounds of traffic. A silence screaming in terror.

"It's not too late to turn back," Sonsee rushed, as the memory of those whizzing bullets sent a prickle of panic, like fingers of ice, along the base of her neck. Shivering, Sonsee redirected the air conditioner's cold blast. "You don't have to go to LeBlanc Manor. Why don't you wait until Jac gets to Baton Rouge? If she can't get the truth out of Carla, nobody can. She'll have so much more insight into what to do at that point —"

"Meanwhile, whoever shot at me waits for another opportunity." He turned to peer out the back window. "Right now I feel like a sitting duck."

"Well, it's your own fault," Sonsee snapped. "You should have stayed at Mel's until —"

"I'm through with hiding behind you and your friends. It's not fair for you to take the risk of hiding me."

"Well, what's worse? Getting shot at or taking the risk?"

"If you hadn't dragged me back into your office, you wouldn't have been shot at, remember? I was trying to get out of there."

"Oh, sure! And what would have happened if I hadn't pulled you back inside?

That idiot might have just shot you on the street and left you."

"Look, you don't have to take me to New Orleans," he challenged. "I tried to get you to stay in the first place. I could have easily hired a taxi. As a matter of fact, I'd rather you *didn't* take me. If you're having second thoughts, you can just pull over to the side of the road and I'll —"

"Oh, great! Now you're *really* using your brain." Sonsee darted a glance in the rear-view mirror; she relaxed but a fraction with the seeming innocence of those in her wake.

Taylor expelled a hissing breath. "And I guess you're just the reincarnation of Einstein at this point?"

"You know," Sonsee mused, "you can be really exasperating when you want to be."

"Please allow me to return the compliment," Taylor said, his words laced with a taunting smile. "It always annoys me when you purposefully change the conversation. If I remember correctly, we were talking about you and me, not about whether or not we should be going to New Orleans."

"I thought we settled the you–me thing for right now."

"It's a long way from settled, Sonsee, and you know it."

Twenty-One

Louis stood at the base of the stairway, gripping the banister with fingers tender from scouring. The shadows from the darkened third floor drooped downward like shrouds, cloaking the steps in dense dusk. The canvas bag, laden with treasure, felt as if it weighed a thousand pounds. For every hour that crawled past, the bag grew heavier. Louis tightened his grip on the banister, his eyes tired from the stress of the sleepless night and the recent hours of torment.

After removing the treasure from the vault, Louis had intended to leave LeBlanc Manor, never to return. He had envisioned himself arriving at the heirloom collector's office by nine, making his sale, transferring the funds, and taking the first flight home to North Carolina. But he had never left the aging mansion. Instead, he had hidden in the room where he'd rested after the boating accident. The room where Cerberus had approached him with the offer.

The room where the dark deed had taken root. Every time he started to order a taxi to leave the mansion, he felt as if he were choking. The mere feel of a telephone under his fingers ushered in new waves of incrimination.

Louis, strained with distress, dared glance down the spacious hallway toward the particular room, now closed, that had tugged his soul into the torments of a fiery abyss. A faint sob resonated from behind the door. Louis gripped the banister until his tender fingers protested in pain. Throughout the morning, he knew he was not alone. Frequent checks out the window validated the white Cadillac had never moved. However, he had managed to avoid the owner. The sound of her crying from her father's bedroom produced the same effect on Louis as did thoughts of exiting the premises. His throat constricted. His gut churned. His common sense urged him to replace the treasure, cut his losses, and leave the country.

The crossroad from this morning posed itself again. Louis, impelled by a force that defied explanation, turned from the paths of darkness and hurried up the stairway. His footfalls, light on the aging staircase, produced but a few faint squeaks as he panted under the pressure of the moment. The closer he grew to that hidden vault, the heavier the canvas bag became, the more intense his urgency.

Swathed in the musty smells of years gone by, Louis stepped over the room's threshold and lowered the oppressive bag to the floor. His fingers throbbed with the release. He snatched the tote's handle and dragged his burden the remaining distance. The afternoon sunshine, beaming through the smudged window, highlighted the blanket of dust swirling as he neared the vault. His arm aching with the treasure's growing weight, he halted in front of the lion. A sneeze clawed its way upward from deep within his sinus passages. Louis pinched his nose, covered his mouth, and managed to suppress all but a muffled release of the explosion.

The brass lion's sunken eyes seemed to stare in challenging accusation. Mesmerized by the inanimate beast, Louis gazed back at the feline as though held by some ancient power locked deep in the lion's eyes. As if the cat spoke some silent incantation, the canvas bag shifted, and the sounds of precious metal against stone tore Louis from his hypnotic stance. He fumbled in his shirt pocket, wrapping his fingers around the iron object that could have saved Jacques' life — the second vault key. Louis removed it, grasped the lion's chilled, metallic nose, and twisted. The wooden panel in the back of the fireplace struggled upward, revealing the vault. With the clink of metal against metal, Louis inserted the key, turned the lock, and the door swung outward. The slight squeak of hinges sounded like the distant call of a blood-thirsty panther. A call that sent a shiver down Louis' spine.

He turned to the bag and hovered over its contents like a dragon looming over a village full of children he intended to devour. The silver. The gold. The diamonds, rubies, sapphires, opals, and emeralds. All beckoned Louis to cruelly assess Jacques' murder as a necessary step to the ultimate goal: financial freedom, more money than Louis had ever possessed.

Ten million dollars. Ten million! Am I crazy? I could have been well on the way to North Carolina by now. By tomorrow, Brenda and I could follow the money to Switzerland and never look back.

However, the previous hours of invisible bondage had chained Louis to LeBlanc Manor and prohibited his freedom. Those laborious hours, filled with torment and grief, trudged through his mind like soiled mummies from a putrid tomb. His hands, pulsating with the panic of a filthy heart, dug into the bag, pulling out a wad of multifaceted, golden beads interspersed with garnets. The very treasure that had driven him to murder now insisted he leave empty-handed. As if he were possessed by a power stronger than he, Louis gritted his teeth and dumped the treasure back into its wooden cask, hearing the thuds of precious metal against wood.

The muffled sound of footsteps neared from down the hallway, and Louis' face grew as cold as a corpse's. He grabbed the empty bag, locked the safe, and twisted the lion's nose. The panel fell back into place with a telltale bump that sent a cringe through his gut. The footsteps grew closer, and Louis' exhausted mind imagined Cerberus ready to orchestrate revenge. Wildly, his gaze darted from one corner of the room to another in search of refuge. At last he spotted a narrow closet door.

Louis gripped his bag and scurried toward the only haven available him. As the footsteps halted outside the room, he stepped into the tiny closet, silently shut the door, and cringed as the knob produced a barely discernible snap. His legs threatened to buckle, and he wasted little time lowering himself to the floor. The only light in the inky darkness seeped from under the door. He pulled his knees close to his chest and rested his head against the wall. For the first time in more than thirty hours, Louis' tormented mind resigned its perpetual plotting, and his eyes drooped in sleepy stupor. As the footsteps entered the room, he forced his lids open with tender fingers and admonished himself not to acquiesce to the summons of fatigue. If the visitor were Cerberus, Louis needed every mental facility at the peak of vigilance.

⁓

"It's been a long time since I've seen him, but that guy looks like Kinkaide Franklin, doesn't he?" Jac Lightfoot jerked her head toward an Oldsmobile pulling up beside Mel's Toyota. With dread, Mel opened her trunk and peered into the Olds to see the unmistakable profile of her ex-fiancé. When he looked up, straight into Melissa's eyes, she wanted to groan.

"Yes, that's him," she mumbled. "Just ignore him. Maybe he'll go away."

"Sounds like a good plan to me," Jac said, the practical line of her mouth witnessing the pint-sized private eye's usual focus on her task. Her black, bobbed hair swung in sync with her movements. Jac plopped her one piece of check-in luggage on the curb. As she shouldered her carry-on bag, she scanned the airport portico and parking lot beyond. "I feel like someone is watching us," she said under her breath.

"Probably *him*," Melissa hissed back, barely jerking her head toward Kinkaide.

"No. That's not it," Jac replied, her ebony eyes as cautious as a hunted doe's. "I just wish Taylor had waited until I got to Baton Rouge to head to New Orleans. I've got a gut feeling something really nasty is going to go down. Taylor should have listened to me and *waited*." Creasing her dark brows, Jac scanned the area once more.

Melissa rolled her eyes and slipped damp palms into her twill slack's pockets, feigning a relaxation she was far from feeling. "That man was in my home for two nights, and I can guarantee that once he makes up his mind there's no changing it. If Sonsee winds up marrying him, she's got her work cut out for her."

Jac, adjusting her carry-on bag, showed her itinerary to the curbside clerk and attended to the necessary details of arranging her luggage check in.

"Hi, Mel." Kinkaide's melodious voice

sent an undeniable warmth through Mel.

She fought the urge to hunch her shoulders while swiveling to face the man she had seen that very morning. "What brings you here?" she asked, her voice stiff with the memory of their recent conversation.

"I'm following you," Kinkaide supplied, his dark eyes solemn. This morning, Kinkaide had been dressed in jogging gear; now, he wore pleated khaki shorts and a white golfing shirt. Either way, he addled Mel. Kinkaide jerked his head toward a Chrysler parked nearby. "The man in the gray sedan is following you, too."

"I knew it," Jac said. Her ebony eyes alert, she pushed up the sleeves of her oversized oxford shirt as if she were preparing for battle.

"I was actually pulling into your clinic when you pulled out, and I noticed the gray car behind you. At first I thought it was a coincidence, but he followed you all the way here. Then he parked there. The best I can tell, he's just sitting in the car reading, as if he's waiting on someone." Kinkaide glanced over his shoulder.

"Maybe he's waiting on someone else." Melissa, ready to rid herself of Kinkaide at any cost, barely acknowledged the man's profile.

"Does he look familiar?" Jac asked.

Mel peered toward the car, straining to see the man. "I really can't tell at this distance." She turned to Kinkaide. "What were you doing at the clinic?"

"I came to see you." He arched one dark brow over eyes that held a daredevil gleam.

"I thought you understood that I don't need any male visitors at the clinic right now."

"I did." He shrugged. "I decided to come anyway."

The bustle of airport activity continued, but Mel felt as if she had been dropped into a time warp, back to an era when Kinkaide kept her alert with unexpected twists and turns. She schooled her features into a bland mask and stifled the telltale expectancy that tried to bubble forth. "What did you need?"

He glanced around the airport. "This isn't exactly the place to talk. Besides, I'm more concerned about that guy in the Chrysler right now than what I wanted to say."

"I agree," Jac said, accepting her luggage tag from the curbside clerk.

"Have we met?" Kinkaide, glancing toward Jac, smiled in polite query.

"I'm Jac Lightfoot. We met a couple of

times several years ago." She extended her hand, and Kinkaide shook it.

"Yes, I remember you. You're one of Mel's six close friends. The 'seven sisters,' right?"

"Exactly. And I guess you could say I'm the renegade among them." She paused for a slight grin. "While Mel, here, is in a more traditional career, I live a little closer to the edge."

"Jac's a private eye," Melissa supplied.

"Oh, yes," he said with respect. "Didn't you bust that drug ring about two years ago? It landed you on national television, if I'm not mistaken."

"Yes. That was me, and the whole thing was an accident. Or should I say divine intervention? I didn't have that much to do with it — unless you count being at the right place at the right time, and that was just a God thing within itself." Jac glanced at her silver-toned wristwatch, then peered past Kinkaide. "My plane departs in thirty minutes. Mel arranged the last available seat on this flight through her travel agent, and I don't want to miss it. Would you keep an eye on her for me? That guy bothers me. He might be waiting on someone else, or he might be up to no good. In case you don't know, we're in the middle of something that could be dangerous. I'm not really comfortable leaving Mel here with that cat on her trail, but I've got something more urgent calling me south."

"Sure, I'll be delighted to watch Melissa," Kinkaide said, as if he were a satisfied tomcat.

"I don't want to be looked after. I'm due to make hospital calls, and I don't need a companion. I'll be okay," Melissa snapped, wondering if the man had completely forgotten their conversation from the morning. *But how much more blatant could I have been? I stopped just short of telling him to get lost.*

"Thanks," Jac said, as if Melissa had never spoken. "It might not hurt to use the direct approach and just ask that man what he's up to. As a matter of fact . . ." Jac glimpsed her watch once more, then cast another gaze toward the car. "I think I'll take care of that right now. Won't take but a minute."

Before Melissa or Kinkaide could utter another word, Jac marched toward the suspicious vehicle.

"She's going to get herself killed one day," Melissa said, balling her hands into fists. "She's too brazen for her own good."

"I guess that, unlike you, she probably won't ever need a man to look after her," Kinkaide said with a smirk.

"With all due respect to Jac and her notions, I would prefer if you —"

"Just disappeared?"

Melissa narrowed her eyes and let the silence speak for her.

"Well, I don't believe you," Kinkaide said with an assurance that rankled.

Crossing her arms, Mel focused on Jac, and Kinkaide followed suit. As the private eye neared the Chrysler, the engine came to life and the car eased from the parking lot to join the stream of cars, heading toward the highway. "I guess that's that," Melissa said. "Looks like fearless Jac just scared him off."

"It's going to take a lot more to scare me off, Mel. A lot more," Kinkaide said under his breath.

Remain calm, Melissa instructed herself. *Do not react. Stay cool.* "And it's going to take an act of God to get me to change my decision," she said in a disinterested voice.

"Okay, then, I'll start praying for God to act." Kinkaide placed a hand on his hip with apathy that repudiated the warm undercurrents of his voice. "He does that, you know."

Jac's rapid approach accented her precise words. "I don't know who he was, but I might have seen him before somewhere. Not sure. I didn't get that close a look but . . . Anyway, at least he's on the move now. He might have been hired to keep an eye on you." Mel and Jac exchanged a wealth of silent communication.

"So what's going on?" Kinkaide rapped out.

"I've really got to run," Jac said, glancing at her watch again. "They're going to start the boarding call soon."

"Okay." Melissa grabbed her friend in a brief, potent hug.

"Like I said, Kinkaide, keep an eye on her, will ya? I'm a little nervous about leaving like this." Jac squeezed Kinkaide's arm as if to incite him to heed her request.

"Yes, of course." A shadow scurried across Kinkaide's features as he watched Jac rush through one of the numerous glass doors.

"Looks like we're blocking traffic," Melissa said, inching toward her car.

"What's going on?" Kinkaide laid a restraining hand on Mel's shoulder.

She tensed and fought a flurry of varying responses. Kinkaide's very touch dropped her into another flashback of the last time she saw him. Simultaneously, his desire for more information about Taylor and Sonsee's predicament heightened Mel's need for discretion.

"When I was at your house earlier this week, you acted as if you were hiding something . . . or someone," he mused. "Then, in your office, you received that odd phone call. Is everything all right with you, Mel? Do you need —"

"It's nothing that really involves me." Melissa removed the car keys from her pocket and impatiently jingled them as a horn sounded from behind. "I can't tell anyone anything right now." She glanced toward the line of cars in back of them. "We need to get out of here or someone's going to tow you away. You're smack in the middle and nobody can get around you."

"Okay, okay." Kinkaide raised his hands. "I'll follow you to the hospital, and tag along while you make your calls."

"No! *Do not do that!*"

Yet Kinkaide rounded the Oldsmobile and plopped into the driver's seat as if she had never spoken.

Twenty-Two

Sonsee pulled her Honda along the winding driveway, toward the pillared mansion surrounded by weeping willows. Never had the trees seemed so forlorn. The park benches and flower gardens that once welcomed now repelled with a barrage of dark memories. Even the rose vines, clinging to twin trellises, appeared more thorns than blooms.

"Okay, we're here," Sonsee said over her shoulder as she steered the vehicle toward the parking area behind the house. As the car halted, Sonsee peered over the driver's seat toward Taylor, lying in the back. After some planning, the two had decided that the wisest move involved Taylor's initially keeping a low profile.

The white Cadillac, several feet away, proclaimed Alana's presence. The only other vehicle was the yardman's worn truck. "Carla's car isn't here," Sonsee said through a frustrated sigh.

"Oh, great," Taylor growled.

"I'm going in to check it out — just to make sure she isn't here." Sonsee put the Honda into park and turned off the ignition switch.

Peeking over the seat, Taylor scanned the grounds. "Isn't that Alana's Caddy?"

"Yeah."

"Then I'm going in with you. I don't trust her."

"No, you're not."

"Yes, I am." Taylor sat straight up and fixed his jaw in the determined line that broached no argument.

"Okay, fine!" Sonsee snapped. "Just waltz right in and get yourself reported to the police, then."

"It looks like nobody but Alana and the yardman are here, anyway," Taylor said as he pointed toward a man whose stomach pushed sullenly against the lawn tractor's steering wheel as he fought the perspiration streaming into his eyes. "If Alana is as trustworthy as you seem to think she is, why worry about her turning me in?"

His challenge released arrows of doubt that pierced Sonsee's newfound faith in her sister. Speechless, she gazed into the depths of Taylor's eyes. Eyes as blue as a winter's sky just after sunset. Eyes that reflected a conviction that she was wrong about Alana. Without a word, Sonsee whipped open the door and got out. Taylor put on the sunglasses, pulled the golfer's hat low, then followed her to the backdoor that opened into the servant's quarters. Sonsee unlocked the door. They stepped into the shadowed corridor and neared Carla's room.

Sonsee shoved against the half-opened door and blinked in dismay at the stark vacancy before her. None of Carla's possessions remained. The tidy bed spoke of the maid's insistence on order. The simple dresser was topped with a vase of wilting flowers that seemed a melancholic reminder of the employee's deception. As a child, Sonsee sat on the braided rug at the base of the corner rocker. The maid had often taken the time to read a favorite book to Sonsee. But the bitter facts of adulthood now tainted the childhood memory.

"Looks like she's outta here," Taylor said.

"Doesn't really surprise me." The barely discernible smell of Carla's perfume created a sour recollection of their last encounter. Carla had been in the kitchen and refused to look Sonsee in the eye. "She's probably running for her life. Whoever convinced her to lie —"

"Do you think they're after her?" Taylor asked, the question falling like jagged rocks amid a tumultuous river.

"Don't know. But there's no reason why we can't at least try to catch up with her at her daughter's."

"You know where she lives?"

"Yes. I've never been there, but F-Father kept a record of emergency addresses and numbers on anyone who worked here." Sonsee cleared her throat and attempted to gain control over her wavering voice. The very mention of her dad heightened her urgency to trail Carla. "The information is in his desk in the library."

"Good. Let's go." Taylor whisked up the hallway as if he expected Sonsee to immediately follow.

"Taylor, wait!" Sonsee whispered.

He swiveled to face her, and she caught her own reflection in the dark glasses. A distorted reflection. A reflection that mirrored the warped images that filled her dreams.

"Why don't we go check out that third-floor fireplace first? I've got the key and we're here. We could take the back stairs." She pointed toward a door that connected the utility room to the servant's hall. In the utility room, a narrow stairwell offered access to the upper floors — a perfect convenience for any housekeeper.

"Good thinkin'." Taylor walked toward the utility room and removed the sunglasses as they approached the stairs.

With a mixture of dread and anticipation, Sonsee trudged past the washer and dryer, toward the dark corridor leading upward. At the base of the stairs, she paused long enough to switch on the light. An eery glow illuminated the passage. As Sonsee entered the tight enclosure, a rare onslaught of claustrophobia demanded she halt on the fourth stair.

With a faint grunt, Taylor ran into her. "Hey, little lady," he drawled. "What's got you so skittish?"

"You go first." Restraining herself from dashing back to the laundry room, Sonsee stepped aside. She tugged Taylor's arm until he squeezed past her and stood on the next stair up. "I'm not handling this all that well. I feel like the walls are pressing in on me."

"Probably because they are." Taylor's grim words implied that much more was pressing than the walls. Certainly life's circumstances were crowding them both into a corner. A tight corner. A corner with no room for escape.

"All of a sudden, I'm really scared." Sonsee gripped the narrow handrail and coughed. The corridor's yesteryear odor mixed with the laundry room's clean scents like a combination of dark precognition and hopeful promises. "It's not that I haven't — haven't been scared before now, but this — this is different. It's almost like we're finally going to get to the bottom of part of th-this nightmare, and that's good. But at the same time, I'm terrified of what's in that strange fireplace."

Instinctively, Sonsee wrapped unsteady fingers around Taylor's forearm. He covered her hand with his callused palm and gently stroked the backs of her fingers. Overwhelmed by the intensity of their lives, Sonsee felt as if her last scrap of strength were vanishing. Although she had spent many hours in prayer and sensed God's presence, the tragic events rushed upon her, demanding the warmth of human consolation. The invitation, so blatant in Taylor's beseeching eyes, wrapped invisible arms around Sonsee and coaxed her to draw near to the man who loved her.

"Sonsee?" Taylor breathed.

The mere mention of her name instigated her movement toward him, and all obstacles that lay between them were momentarily swept away in the fervor of the moment. Taylor tugged her onto his step and into the haven of his waiting arms. Sonsee, desperate for his touch, leaned into the warmth he offered. A warmth full of security, trust, and love.

"I'm scared, too, Sonsee," Taylor murmured as he stroked her hair. The soft tattoo of his heart beneath her cheek stirred the fires of yearning that had been smoldering in desperation. Taylor pulled on the band that held her ponytail in place, and her hair fell to her shoulders. "Your hair is so soft," he marveled.

Squeezing her eyes tight, Sonsee clung to him. She clung to her dreams. She clung to the memories of who they had been together and to the promises of what they might be from this day forth. The gentle kiss on her temple proved a predecessor to the fiery meeting of lips that plunged two frantic souls into a whirlpool of longing — a whirlpool that swept Sonsee to a hidden world below churning waters. The dangerous waves, chopping above, blurred in the presence of the ardent haven enveloping her spirit.

At last, Taylor's lips moved to rain a slow trail of kisses along her cheek. "Sonsee, I never knew it could be like this between you and me." His whispered plea only increased her need of him.

An apprehension deep within suggested Sonsee might never have another moment like this. The greater the apprehension, the tighter Sonsee clung. The tighter she clung, the more tempted she was to vow she would never let go — not for God or anyone. Taylor's proposal from that very day sprang upon her, as if it were a banner of holy forbidding. In the path of that banner came Sonsee's own words, confronting her with the reality of where she stood: *It's just that, somewhere along the line, I've put my desires for romantic love and — and I guess for — for . . . um . . . you . . . above my desires for God.*

As if those words released a revealing force within, a hidden door deep in the recesses of her soul sprang open. Behind that door cringed a part of Sonsee she had refused to release to Jesus: the control of her future, the undaunted desire to map her own destiny. In a flash, Sonsee saw herself pulling away from the support of her earthly father when she carved out her own business. *And I'm trying to do the same thing in my relationship with Taylor — make the relationship happen regardless of my heavenly Father's desires.* Looking back on all her prayers, she realized she had almost demanded that God make Taylor fall in love with her instead of waiting before a Holy Creator and saying, *Your will be done.* In Vietnam, Sonsee sensed that she had come very close to capitulating her will to the Lord's. However, the test had come when Taylor became available. Sonsee was failing that test.

When Taylor's lips neared hers for yet another kiss, she stiffened. As if he read her thoughts, he stilled. A cloak of awkward silence, chilling and final, dashed aside the ardor that had ensnared them in rhapsody.

"Nothing has changed," he stated with regret.

"No, n-nothing," Sonsee desperately whispered. She pulled back and leaned against the wall, wondering if she would dream of that stolen moment for the rest of her life.

Tightening his jaw muscles, Taylor turned from Sonsee and grabbed the handrail, smooth with wear. Her kiss had promised so much. Sonsee had clung to him as if she were ready to ride the tide of romance. Her heart beat in synchrony with his, affirming their love. Yet her rejection afflicted like a knife in the abdomen.

This has got to be some cruel twist of divine justice. Taylor placed one boot on the next step up and leaned forward, all the while restraining a disappointed roar. With painful clarity, he relived the moments of spiritual splendor when he allowed God to walk the corridors of his soul and begin the long overdue spiritual and emotional healing. The hope of the Lord's protection and presence had given Taylor the courage to fly to Baton Rouge and brazenly face the consequences at LeBlanc Manor. The Lord's nearness had further empowered Taylor to admit his growing love for Sonsee — a love hidden and denied. *I even proposed,* he thought, amazed at the irony of their predicament. His spiritual growth meant he could embrace his love for Sonsee. Her spiritual growth meant she must release her love. His hand clenching the rail, Taylor trudged up the stairway, his dog-bit thigh occasionally protesting. He didn't dare look back at Sonsee, and that act, intended to preserve his last scrap of pride, only succeeded in leaving him alone once more. Taylor had spent so many years internally isolated from humanity that the loneliness beckoned as only the familiar can. When the second-floor landing came into sight, Taylor struggled with the temptation to resurrect the walls that had protected him all his life — protected him against suffering more agony such as that now ravaging his heart.

Yet a radiance, steady and comforting, spread from the inner recesses of Taylor's soul, a holy radiance he had never perceived when the walls were securely standing. Then, that verse from Isaiah wove its way to his mind and reassured him of his place in the shelter of God's hand:

> "For the mountains may be removed and the hills may shake, but My lovingkindness will not be removed from you, and My covenant of peace will not be shaken," says the LORD who has compassion on you. "O afflicted one, storm-tossed, and not comforted, behold, I will set your stones in antimony, and your foundations I will lay in sapphires."

Taylor scraped together every ounce of bravado at his disposal and decided he must never resurrect the walls. *Never.* They might have protected him from pain, but they had also stopped him from experiencing abundant life spiritually, emotionally, and even mentally.

As if he were entering a new realm,

Taylor cautiously approached the second-floor landing. Warily, he paused on the last step, leaned forward, and snatched a glance up and down the hallway. The main stairway, massive and forbidding, lay in the distance. That stairway proved the only access to the third floor.

A movement from close behind alerted him to Sonsee's proximity. With an inexplicable strength coursing through his veins, Taylor turned and extended his hand. Hesitantly, she placed her fingers against his, and he squeezed them in assurance. Her gaze, troubled and questioning, never wavered.

"It's okay," Taylor whispered. "Whatever happens in this whole mess . . . it's going to be okay."

Cerberus stepped into the laundry room and silently approached the stairway. The servants' access to the second floor would undoubtedly prove the wisest move in enabling the fiend to keep a low profile. Yet one glimpse up the stairs sent a shock along a rigid spine. Cerberus shied away from the stairwell doorway. The image of Sonsee and Taylor clasping hands at the top of the stairs created a dollop of satisfaction amid the shock.

"All is well," the criminal muttered with a wicked grin. "The plan is flawless." The cellphone, removed from a loose pants pocket, rested against a hand steady as steel. The numbers 9-1-1 had never proved so delightful to dial. When the urgent female voice floated over the line, Cerberus answered a round of pertinent questions, then supplied the reason for his call, "You can find Taylor Delaney on the third floor of LeBlanc Manor. The front door is unlocked." Cerberus disconnected the call and prepared to ascend the stairs. A treasure awaited; beyond the treasure, a plane to France.

Twenty-Three

Melissa pulled onto the hospital grounds and parked in the usual spot designated by a "Reserved for Dr. Melissa Moore" sign. She glanced into her rearview mirror to see a shiny black Oldsmobile cruising behind her then claiming a place about forty feet away. Groaning, Mel rested her head against the steering wheel. Kinkaide was as good as his word. Nothing Mel said curbed his tagging along.

At the moment, the man who might or might not be following Melissa seemed far less threatening than having her ex-fiancé present during hospital rounds. She imagined Kinkaide lurking at a distance and the interested expressions of the hospital staff. News traveled fast along the Medical Center grapevine. By sundown, the whole medical community in Oklahoma City would probably have Dr. Moore heading for a Cancun honeymoon by the end of the week. Nothing was further from the truth.

I will not allow him to sway me into another relationship, Melissa asserted while she climbed out of her taupe Toyota. *I will not,* she repeated as he approached, his rhythmical gait reflecting the music forever spilling from his soul.

"Hi-ya again." Kinkaide's too familiar greeting heightened Melissa's determination to detour him before entering the building.

Head bent, she strode toward the massive medical complex, only pausing to dash Kinkaide a glance while she spoke. "Look, why don't you just wait downstairs by the hospital entrance. That ought to be sufficient, don't you think?" she asked, finally accepting the fact that he would never agree to leave. At least this compromise would guarantee Mel some space and avoid plunging her into the rumor eddy.

"Excuse me! Dr. Moore!" A man's distant call, urgent and insistent, halted Mel in her tracks. As if Kinkaide sensed the impending threat as keenly as Melissa, he loosely gripped her upper arm in proprietal protection. Images of the man from the airport stomped through Melissa's mind, and she searched the busy parking lot like a harassed hare trying to escape a fox's field.

"It's him," Kinkaide bit out just as Mel spotted a masculine figure running straight toward her from a parked, gray sedan. As if on cue, Mel and Kinkaide simultaneously turned and bolted toward the safety of the hospital.

"Wait!" the man yelled. "I'm Sonsee LeBlanc's brother! I need to talk with you!"

Mel stopped short and whirled toward the nearing man. The closer he grew, the more familiar Hermann's features became. She remembered him from the funeral, only days before. All Mel could imagine was perhaps a tragedy with Sonsee and Taylor.

"Sonsee! Is she okay?" Melissa demanded as Kinkaide urged, "Let's get inside. He was following you. I don't trust him."

"She's fine, as far as I know," Hermann acknowledged as he stopped only inches away. "But from everything I can gather, you aren't!" His flashing eyes, the color of steel, underscored the challenge in his words. Furthermore, the drawn brows, flushed face, and tight lips reminded Mel of Sonsee when she was angry.

"Look," Kinkaide ground out. "I don't know what you want —"

"Dr. Moore, I know you're hiding Taylor Delaney in your home," Hermann accused. Placing hands on hips, he spaced loafer-clad feet apart, as if preparing for a duel.

Mel sensed Kinkaide's confusion and stopped herself from pausing long enough to explain the whole twisted situation. Instead, she calmly eyed Hermann. "Why are you so sure?" she asked, refusing to allow the churning from her midsection to affect the timbre of her voice or her expression.

"I have my sources," Hermann unbuttoned the cuffs of his oxford shirt and hastily rolled up the sleeves. Mel debated whether his actions were a defense against the summer heat or a further readying for battle.

"I've come to ask you to turn Taylor over to the authorities." An oppressive, summer breeze whipped sweltering air from the concrete and swirled it around them like the winds from a fiery abyss. A drop of sweat, trickling from the recesses of Hermann's mousy brown hair, slid down his temple while perspiration slithered along the back of Mel's neck. Nonetheless, Hermann's gaze held the chill of Antarctica. "You can either cooperate or I'll call the police and have them arrest *you* and Taylor."

Kinkaide placed his arm along Melissa's back and tugged her closer to him. For the first time that afternoon, she didn't resist her former fiancé. While her six friends often referred to Mel as "the independent one among us," she had a long way to go before matching Jac Lightfoot's bravado.

"Look, I don't know what you're talking about," Kinkaide snarled, "but you've worn out your welcome, buddy —"

"Your whole reputation will go down the tubes overnight and that will be the end of your career," Hermann sneered, never taking his attention from Mel.

"If you're so certain he's at my house, then feel free to take a tour." Melissa narrowed her eyes as if she were a female version of Clint Eastwood. Some perverse little voice even added a snide, *Go ahead. Make my day.* An inappropriate giggle teetered around her mind, a giggle that represented a woman whose nerves had stretched beyond the realms of logic. Meanwhile, Hermann's shocked blink sent a warm path of satisfaction flowing through the pit of her stomach.

"We could go now," she offered, stepping toward the parking lot. Yet her assured stance covered the uncertainties raging through her. Mel frantically hoped Taylor had left no identifying traces of his presence. She hadn't noticed any sign of him during her trip home at lunch; but then she had not thoroughly examined the guest room or hall bathroom.

"Fine," Hermann said evenly, his satisfied smile suggesting he didn't believe her. "And I'll arrange to have a couple of officers meet us there. How's that?"

"Suit yourself," Mel said with a nonchalant shrug while formulating a host of mental prayers.

"Furthermore, you're going to ride with me," Hermann continued as if he were a card shark dealing one winning trump after the other. "That way you can't use your cellphone to call and warn him that we're coming."

"She's not going anywhere with you," Kinkaide bit out. He stepped between Melissa and her foe, towering over Sonsee's brother in a way that demanded Hermann no longer ignore him. "I have no idea what the two of you are talking about, but I *refuse* to allow Mel to ride with you."

"Who are you, anyway?" Hermann interrogated.

"I'm her future husband," Kinkaide claimed, and Mel prohibited an aghast gape.

"But Alana said Dr. Moore is unattached," Hermann insisted as if he sensed Kinkaide's stretching the truth. "I made certain of that fact." His eyes shifted as if he were a wolf resorting to any deviltry to snare his prey.

"Oh, so it's easier to harass a single woman than one who has a man to back her up. Is that it?" Kinkaide took a threatening step toward the opponent.

"Did Alana tell you I was hiding Taylor?" Mel demanded. She stepped beside Kinkaide as Hermann inched backward, his eyes twitching at the corners.

"That's immaterial," Hermann ground out. "Now, you've got a choice. You can either turn my father's murderer over to the authorities yourself or you will force me to alert the police to your part in this whole cover-up."

"Taylor Delaney is not at my house."

"Fine," Hermann said with a bland smile. "Then you won't mind my calling the police and asking them to meet us there, will you?" He removed a phone from the waistband of his slacks, turned it on, and calmly pushed three buttons. The accompanying beeps sent miniature shocks of apprehension along Mel's spine. When Kinkaide wrapped his hand around hers, she clung to the strength he offered.

While Hermann placed the small phone against his ear and waited, a host of people hurried past, all of them seemingly oblivious to the intrigue playing out in front of the hospital.

"Hello," Hermann finally purred into the phone like a panther satisfied with his catch. After answering several brief questions, he stated his mission. "From what I understand, all police departments across the U.S. have been notified concerning a criminal named Taylor Delaney. He murdered Jacques LeBlanc in New Orleans earlier this week and hasn't been seen since. There's supposed to be a nationwide warrant out for his arrest. I believe I know where he's located. A *respected doctor* in Oklahoma City, Melissa Moore . . ." Hermann scrutinized Mel as if she were scum, ". . . seems to be up to her pretty little neck in the whole ordeal. You can find Mr. Delaney in her home in the 'Eagle Lakes' division." Hermann's lips twisted as if savoring the nuance of every word. "Yes, I'm certain. I have a taped statement from someone who overheard Mr. Delaney identify his locale in a phone conversation. Of course I'll be glad to bring my information to the police station now."

Louis strained to hear the movements coming from beyond the closet door. At first, footsteps echoed on bare floors, eventually halting across the room. The best he could tell, the individual walked straight toward the fireplace. Horrified, Louis recalled dragging the treasure-laden bag across the floor. Subsequently, the tote stirred up a trail of dust in its wake — a trail that undoubtedly was visible.

The unmistakable swish of the panel alerted Louis that the lion's nose had indeed been twisted and increased his certainty that Cerberus had arrived. A thousand conflicting thoughts raced through his head. He held himself rigid, terrified to so much as twitch. He anxiously wracked his memory, hoping he hadn't left any incriminating signs near the fireplace or any evidence that would point to the closet.

"Ready?" Taylor asked as Sonsee cautiously glanced up and down the hallway.

"Yes," she rasped. "Let's go." She followed Taylor into the wide passage, toward the third-floor stairway. Thoughts of Alana discovering Taylor's presence added flight to her feet, and the two of them safely ascended the final stairs.

Still gripping Taylor's hand, Sonsee stepped into the ominous embrace of the third-floor shadows . . . shadows that had engulfed her only days ago, before meeting Taylor in the hidden room. Now another secretive chamber beckoned, promising the unknown, presenting one more piece of evidence to this complicated conspiracy. The typical creaking of aging wooden floors accompanied their approach to the designated room.

As the two stepped toward the doorway, Sonsee relaxed a fraction as her mind spun in anticipation of what they might find.

"You've got the key?" Taylor asked.

"Yes. It's here in my purse." She reached deeply into her leather handbag and held up the ancient key.

With a nod of acknowledgment, Taylor reached forth to shove open the half-closed door, and Sonsee stared into Alana's widened, fear-filled eyes. She stood near the far wall, in front of the fireplace, twisting her fingers as if she were a child, caught in the throes of some horrid transgression.

Sonsee's face went cold, and Taylor's sharp intake of air accompanied her gasp. She grappled over a dozen or more things to say, only to dismiss each one. Simultaneously, Taylor's constant distrust of Alana replayed in her mind like a recurring chant.

"I — I was in Father's room and I . . . I . . . last night I thought I heard someone up here," Alana claimed, her alarmed gaze trailing to Taylor. "I was — was afraid to come up here last night, so I waited until now. I just got here and — and saw all the footprints in the dust and the drag marks all the way to the f-fireplace. There's been a prowler here."

As if on cue, Sonsee and Taylor stepped forward and peered at the floor.

"Then — then — um, Sonsee, did you know that if you turn this lion's nose that a panel swishes up and there's a safe of some sort behind it?" Alana babbled. She swiveled to touch the tarnished brass lion's snout. "When I got here, I noticed the nose was a little crooked, as if someone had been turning it, so I completely turned the thing and then there's this safe." As Alana spoke, she nervously arranged a strand of brassy red hair around her eyes, and Sonsee recalled the bruise she so desperately wished to hide.

With a silent communication of *What do we do now?* flashing between them, Sonsee followed Taylor as he crept into the room. All the while Taylor watched Alana, and

Sonsee despised the vacillating opinions raging through her. On one hand she longed to continue trusting her elder sister. On the other hand, Alana's interest in staying at LeBlanc House, coupled with her presence near the fireplace, left her appearing less than innocent.

"Alana?" The question, purling through her mind, forced itself from Sonsee's lips. "Everything you told me yesterday . . ." The suspicion, dripping from Sonsee's voice, heightened the color of Alana's flushed cheeks.

"I meant every word I said," she pled. "Every word. Oh, Sonsee, you can't imagine that I'd be involved in . . . in . . ." A sob broke from her and she covered her face. "The only thing I've done . . . I didn't intend any harm. I guess it was more out of curiosity than anything else. And I wanted to call and tell you after — after I talked with Hermann. He was here last night, you know. He came looking for Carla."

"Carla?" Taylor interrupted. "Do you know where she is?"

"When I arrived yesterday, she was leaving for her daughter's, but Hermann called and they refused to let him speak with her. They told him they'd call the po-

414

lice if he went to their house."

"What did Hermann want with her?" Sonsee, her shoulders stiff with the resentment of years past, neared Alana.

"He wanted to question her about whether or not she had seen — seen Taylor since he was accused . . . then somehow I clued him in on your knowing where Taylor was, Sonsee."

"How did you know I knew where Taylor was?" A knot as cold as iron formed in Sonsee's throat.

"When I was in your apartment helping you clean up, I picked up the phone and . . . and . . ."

"Oh, great!" Taylor exploded.

The shame, oozing from Alana, seemed to weight her lids, and she peered downward at her strappy sandals. For the first time, Sonsee realized Alana was nothing more than a child in the body of an adult. The issues relating to their father must have somehow stunted her emotional growth. At once all Alana's negative behavior made perfect sense — even her disdain at the will reading. All these years Sonsee had been dealing with a six-year-old, not a grown woman. The insight increased her ease. Somehow Alana had managed to hide her vulnerability behind disdain, a pathetic, naive vulnerability that would never permit her to be involved in a murder.

"Oh, Sonsee," Alana continued, covering her face with both hands. "I knew you knew where Taylor was. I just knew it. And when the phone rang twice, and you went upstairs both times to answer, as if you *knew* who the caller was, I couldn't resist listening for just a few minutes."

"Why in the name of common sense did you tell Hermann?" Taylor erupted.

"I — I don't know how it all slipped out. I didn't *mean* to tell him." She gulped. "But, Sonsee, you know how Hermann is. He's always b-been able to get-to get me to tell him what I know. He used to do the same thing to you when we were growing up. Once I gave him a clue, he continued pushing until he had everything." The last words tumbled out like an orchestra's rushed crescendo.

"Exactly what did you know?" Taylor quietly demanded as he closed in on Alana.

She pressed herself against the fireplace and stared at him like a wide-eyed rodent about to be devoured by a swooping eagle. "I-I knew that you-you were staying with Dr.-Dr. Moore in Oklahoma C-City. You mentioned something about her in your conversation, and I figured it out."

Groaning, Sonsee rubbed her eyes.

"Then . . . then . . . I didn't know he was taping the whole thing!" she wailed. "I guess he was prepared to interrogate Carla and tape everything she said, but instead, he wound up taping me!"

"This is *not* good," Taylor blurted. "Not good at all."

"Oh, but I think it *is* good," a cunning voice said from behind. "Very good indeed."

Twenty-Four

"What is going on?" Kinkaide asked as he propelled Melissa toward the Oldsmobile.

Not bothering to argue about riding with him, Melissa whipped open the door as soon as he unlocked it. She plopped into the passenger seat, buckled her seat belt, and looked up at Kinkaide. "I'll tell you on the way," she said. "Just get me to my house!"

Barely a minute elapsed before they pulled into traffic. Kinkaide began taking a series of quick turns down back roads.

"Do you remember my friend Sonsee LeBlanc?" Melissa asked.

"I think. Isn't she one of your group of six friends?"

"Yes." Mel gripped the door handle and sucked in a lungful of new-car smell as Kinkaide took a turn at breakneck speed.

"Want me to slow down?"

"No!"

"So this involves Sonsee?"

"Yes. Her father was murdered earlier this week."

"Murdered?" Kinkaide's incredulous tones matched Mel's initial reaction to the news.

"Yes. And a close family member, Taylor Delaney, has been framed. From what I can gather, the police are combing New Orleans for him."

"And you've been hiding him?" Gaping, Kinkaide glanced toward Mel. The stupefied cloud in his eyes spoke what his silence left unsaid: *Are you crazy? How do you know he really isn't the murderer?*

"He needed a place to stay for a few days!" Melissa raised a hand in defense. "What was I supposed to do? Sonsee is one of my best friends. If she believes he's innocent —"

"But does Sonsee represent a rational view? Good grief, Mel! Is he at your house now?"

"No! I wasn't lying back there. He left this morning. At lunch I found a note from him saying he was going to Sonsee's in Baton Rouge. The crazy man flew down there. He says he's tired of hiding and is going to New Orleans to try to flush out the killer himself." She checked her wristwatch. "He's probably there right now. Jac tried to get him to stay in Baton Rouge, but he refused. When you followed us to the airport, Jac was catching a last minute flight to New Orleans to try to catch him before he does something stupid."

"Ay, ay, ay. This is a huge mess! And all I wanted to do was play the piano when I grew up."

"Well, I didn't exactly vote to be sucked into this, either. Now I've got a whole herd of police descending on my house, and I'm wondering if Taylor left any evidence of his presence."

"Wait a minute," Kinkaide said, slowing the vehicle. "Don't they have to get a search warrant before they can go into someone's house? I'm not an expert in the law or anything, but I've watched a few police shows in my life. If they're anything to go by, it might take a few hours before they arrive. And who's to say Hermann's character evidence is enough to assure a search warrant anyway?"

"Good point," Mel said. The tension in her neck uncoiled a fraction.

"Meanwhile, let's just get to your house and make certain he didn't leave any evidence," Kinkaide said. "Whether Taylor Delaney is guilty or not, you certainly don't need to be dragged any farther into this situation. I'd hate to know your helping a friend wound up harming your reputation."

"Thanks," Mel said, grateful for Kinkaide's assistance.

"Anytime." His flirtatious wink went right along with his claims of being her future husband.

But you aren't, she insisted with renewed resolve. *I appreciate your help but that doesn't mean I'm marrying you — ever. You ripped my heart out once, and I'm not going to give you another chance to destroy me again. Forget it!*

"Mind if I use your phone?" she asked, reaching for the small device resting in a receptacle under the air conditioner.

"Not in the least."

"Great. I need to notify the hospital that my visits this afternoon will be later than usual. I don't like to leave the parents of my patients hanging."

"Just like I figured, Mel, you're probably the best pediatrician in the whole state of Oklahoma."

As she dialed the number, Melissa couldn't deter the rush of pleasure Kinkaide's praise evoked. *All the more reason to run in the opposite direction the next time I see you,* she thought as the shadows in her heart affirmed the bitter remnants of a grudge still tainting her spirit — a grudge six years old.

"Rafael!" Alana exclaimed.

Sonsee gaped at her brother-in-law and his menacing revolver.

He stepped into the room, a satisfied smile creating surly lines on either side of his mouth. "So, Taylor, you and Sonsee finally made it up here, I see. I counted on your being just as greedy as the rest of us." He deposited a sizable leather case on the floor.

"What are you talking about?" Sonsee gasped.

"You're the one who murdered Uncle Jacques, aren't you?" Taylor asked. Sonsee, sensing Taylor's increasing aversion, took in his countenance. Never had she seen the twist of revulsion so mar a kind man's features — a revulsion that equally matched her own.

"Of course not," Rafael said. "I would never kill another human being," he mocked, his mouth twitching in cruelty. "All I'm after is that key you're holding." He pointed to the key in Sonsee's hand. "It happens to fit the safe in the fireplace, or did you already know that?"

"Yes, we know," Taylor said in an emotionless voice. "That's why we're here."

"So you came for the treasure, did you?" Rafael slowly approached Sonsee and plucked the key from her icy fingers.

"Treasure?" Sonsee asked, trying to make sense of his words.

"Take this, Alana." Rafael extended the key toward his sister-in-law. "Unlock the safe."

"The two of you are in this together, aren't you?" Taylor ground out.

"No!" Alana cried. "I had nothing to do with —"

"Just take the key and do what I told you!" Rafael yelled.

Alana jumped and obeyed. The sound of the key grinding in the aging lock grated along Sonsee's nerves. The vault door's squawking seemed to be that of the doorway of avarice opening in Rafael's eyes. Sonsee glanced behind her, into the recesses of the safe, to the gold goblets, ruby-studded daggers, and tarnished silver beads . . . the sapphire-studded pearl necklace, the emerald crusted bracelets, the antique brooch with an opal center. The priceless baubles mingled together, slinking over the top of a wooden cask like tangled yarn meshed a hundred different directions. Sonsee sucked in a swift, sharp breath as Taylor uttered a disbelieving exclamation.

"Now do you know why we trashed your house, Sonsee?" Rafael taunted. "You're looking at ten million dollars. All we wanted was the key to this little safe." Taylor placed hands on hips as if he were determined to fight. "So, you and Alana —"

"No, you idiot," Rafael bit out, his finger quivering on the gleaming revolver's trigger. "Alana had nothing to do with this." The criminal's hand snaked out to snatch the key from Alana as she stood from her task.

"I'm innocent," Alana insisted, clinging to Sonsee. "You've got to believe me, Sonsee. I would never —"

"I believe you," Sonsee said. Nodding her head in confirmation, she covered Alana's chilled fingers with her own. The witness of an increasing sisterly bond flashed between them. "I believe you."

"Then which of our sorry relatives is in on it with you? Hermann or Natalie?" Taylor demanded.

Rafael's harsh laugh denied the plausibility of either option. "Hermann is too much of a daddy's boy, and Natalie is a weakling." He stepped back and hooked his canvass shoe alongside the black case. Rafael compressed thin lips and kicked the case toward Alana. It slid forward with the rush of leather on grit, creating a whirl of dust in the shafts of sunlight filtering through dingy windows. "Alana, put the treasure in the case and close it. When you're through, push it back to me," he demanded. The dust inched into Sonsee's nose, creating a musty sting.

Alana scooped up a handful of the cache. The clink of precious metal on rare stones accompanied the distant sound of tires grinding against concrete. The slamming of a car door punctuated the silence heavy with expectation. "That would be the police," Rafael sneered. "They're coming for you, Taylor. I called and told them they could find you here."

Sonsee, her stomach rolling with nausea, tried to steady herself in a room spinning like a tornado filled with debris.

"You followed us from Baton Rouge!" Taylor accused.

"Yes . . . after flushing you out. Where have you been the last few days, anyway? Hiding behind mama's skirts?"

Taylor took two steps toward Rafael, only to halt when the criminal extended the double-action revolver.

"How can you do this?" Sonsee choked out as Alana shoved the filled case back toward the criminal then stood. "Taylor is an innocent man. You're destroying his life."

"No, I'm not." Rafael's mild manner only intensified Sonsee's awareness of his heart of darkness. "Taylor destroyed his own life when he decided to kill your father for the inheritance." Rafael licked his lips with the tip of a tongue that seemed forked. "At least that's what you need to go downstairs and tell the police."

"No!" Taylor's face, void of color, set in stubborn lines that broached no argument.

"Okay, then." Rafael grabbed Sonsee's arm, yanked her forward, and crammed the gun into her ribs. "She dies."

Wincing, Sonsee whimpered against the pain of the blunt barrel buried in her side. Simultaneously she fantasized the cruelest retaliation while wishing she could think clearly enough to pray.

"All right, all right. I'll do it," Taylor said, his stubborn expression melting into horror.

"Good," Rafael purred, "because that's the only way she'll live."

A sharp ache shot through Sonsee's ribs as the gun chewed deeper into tender flesh. Alana released a series of sniffles and

Rafael snarled a wicked, "Shut up!" Both Sonsee and her sister jumped. Alana clamped her hand over her quivering mouth as tears spilled from eyes, desperate and appalled.

Rafael jerked his head toward the door and glared at Taylor. "Now, I want you to go on downstairs like a good little boy and turn yourself over to the police. I've been planning this for months, and I don't want you to mess it up now."

"You've known about the safe that long?" Alana blurted.

"No, you idiot. That's a more recent development." He smiled. "I was going to kill Jacques to get my hands on the money I married Natalie for in the first place. But this is even better. The other way, I had to hang around and put up with Natalie. This way I can take the treasure, sell it, and leave the country a wealthy man."

"What about Sonsee and Alana?" Taylor asked, his shoulders pathetically drooping with the hint of defeat.

"They'll be fine. As soon as I know you and the nice police officers are gone, I'll tie them up so they can't break free until I'm long gone. But if you make a false move, they're both dead."

You're lying, Sonsee inwardly raged, a

thin film of perspiration forming on her upper lip. *You can't let us live — period! You'd have two witnesses that you framed Taylor.*

"I'm going to count to three, Taylor," Rafael threatened like an overbearing parent. "If you don't head downstairs, Sonsee dies." He jabbed the gun barrel against her side. Flinching, Sonsee leaned into the gun, desperate for any relief from the stabbing pressure.

Taylor edged toward the doorway, his boots ominously thumping against wood as he eased away from Rafael. "What's going to stop you from killing her once the police and I are gone?"

"Trust me," Rafael drawled.

Carla Jenson, shoulders hunched, slowly approached LeBlanc Manor. She paused near the doorway to the servant's quarters and looked up to observe Sonsee's bedroom balcony. The last time she saw Taylor, he had landed near the dining room windows — most likely from that balcony. Rafael had once again threatened her life that night, yet she had not told him about Taylor. Looking back, Carla recognized those moments as the turning point for her, a turn that brought her to this place at this very moment.

Until Alana arrived yesterday afternoon, Carla had stayed at LeBlanc Manor as Rafael demanded. But the farther Carla progressed into this dark cave of deceit, the less she could bear the presence of any LeBlanc family member. Therefore, she had packed her meager possessions and retreated to her daughter's home in the New Orleans Garden District. So ashamed was she of her dastardly deeds, she hadn't mentioned a word of the scheme to her daughter and son-in-law. When Hermann called, she had gone into hysterics, begging her son-in-law to prohibit Hermann's visit. The young man's threat to call the police had taken Carla by surprise, but, thankfully, Hermann had not arrived.

This morning, Carla had arisen with a new clarity of mind that put the events of the last week into a pragmatic light. Unfortunately, she had stumbled upon the scene of a murder. In the heat of the moment, she had been scared for her life and agreed to lie to the police, copy Sonsee's house keys, and produce an extra key to the back door. In the aftermath of the 10,000-dollar agreement, Carla had assumed more money would ease her conscience and make her lie worth the agony of guilt. But she had been wrong. No amount of money could erase the blight putrefying her soul. Furthermore, the image of Sonsee's incriminating expression as she stood at the base of those stairs wouldn't leave Carla be. The maid could never fool Sonsee with her ill-planned lies — perhaps everyone else, but never Sonsee. Now she intended to rectify her mistakes.

In her purse, Carla carried the 20,0000-dollars from Rafael and Louis. The money that once appealed now plagued. Every time she examined the stack of hundred-dollar bills, the green ink looked more and more like mold, as if it were the decay of her morals.

With a shiver of repugnance, Carla inserted the key into the backdoor. She glanced over her shoulder and once again noted the cars in the parking lot. With misgivings, she recognized not only Alana's vehicle, but also Sonsee's. A green sedan, foreign to Carla, claimed the spot beside Sonsee's Honda. Originally Carla planned to deliver the money and the signed statement to Alana. This morning, she arranged with her sister to stay at her beach house in Galveston until the police caught up with Rafael and Louis. The scheme seemed solid — until Carla arrived and noted the extra cars.

She placed a clammy palm against the doorknob and twisted. As the door produced its customary sigh, an impulse to flee bolted through her. Yet she stiffened her resolve and stepped over the threshold. Though the presence of the others introduced new complications, she must forge forward. The weight of duplicity had proven more exhausting than she ever imagined. The path to relief now beckoned, and she shrank from altering her course.

I can't take any more of this! The frenzied thought hurled her forward, up the hallway, into the anteroom, toward the main stairway, and straight into the path of Taylor Delaney.

"Carla!" Taylor rushed down the remaining stairs and towered over Carla, an odd mixture of relief and antagonism stirring his eyes.

A rush of hot tingles left her cheeks cold, and the maid staggered backward. Her tongue, as stiff as drying paste, forbade her to utter a word.

"How could you have lied about me?" Taylor demanded, his eyes ablaze.

"I . . . I . . ." Carla plunged her sweating hand into her bag and dragged out the manila envelope she had intended for Alana. Panting, she crammed the missive into Taylor's hands. "I-I'm sorry," she pleaded. "I'm so sorry! They made me. I-I was scared for my life." A sob, broken and contrite, burst forth, sending hot rivulets of tears down the sides of her nose. "Oh, God, help me! This will clear you. I-I promise!" she coughed out.

While Taylor examined the bulging envelope as if it were a message from Mars, Carla whirled around to race from the room, away from bondage, toward freedom. For the first time in almost a week, the claws of deceit no longer needled her spirit, and her shoulders stopped sagging with the burden of blame.

Twenty-Five

Sonsee, staring wide-eyed at Rafael, held her breath and imagined Taylor's being hauled away by a band of powerful officers. Hovering nearby, Alana sniffled while Sonsee tensed her legs against collapsing. With a snarl, Rafael cruelly shoved Sonsee against an unforgiving wall, then he reached for Alana. She lurched away from his touch and collided with her sister.

"You're — you're going to kill us an-anyway, aren't you?" Sonsee stammered as a fresh flood of abhorrence surged upon her. For the last week, Sonsee had imagined facing her father's murderer and wreaking an unholy revenge. Even now the bitter bile of vengeance swelled through her wailing spirit, a spirit that demanded this man pay in full for the death of her dad.

"What do you think?" Rafael sneered.

Alana clasped her sister's hand. Their quivering fingers entwined. And Sonsee sensed that if they survived their relationship would be irrevocably healed.

"If I let you live, then there are two eyewitnesses," Rafael taunted. "We can't have that, now can we?"

A muffled holler erupted from the closet and the door banged open as if a violent bear were bursting from a dark cavern. Sonsee, her legs almost failing her, shrank into the wall as a burly Viking-like man hurled himself toward Rafael. With a shocked cry, Rafael raised his arms while Sonsee scrambled toward Alana and the two tumbled into a heap on the bruising floor. Like a linebacker, the Viking slammed into Rafael. The two sprawled into a stack of boxes, sending them toppling as if they were children's toys. Rafael's revolver spun across the floor, stopping within inches of Sonsee. While she and Alana struggled to untangle themselves, the cold metal seemed to hiss "Sonsee! Sonsee! I'm here for you!" begging her to act out her malicious fantasies.

"You set me up!" the attacker bellowed, the smack of flying fists accompanying his words. "You were going to kill Jacques all along! You just used me to do your dirty work!"

The revealing words sent a cold blade of

rancor through Sonsee's heart. Her face hardened. She scrutinized the Viking. *He's Father's murderer!*

"Let's get out of here," Alana said, dragging herself to her feet.

"And I'll — I'll go to prison myself before I let you kill anyone else," the maniacal man screamed as Rafael shoved him aside and managed to land on top.

"Just remember," Rafael growled, grabbing for Louis' neck, "you're the one who pulled that trigger — not me. And guess what? I'm the one who shoved you into the ocean — not Jacques!" Rafael, straddling his prey, tightened his hold around the villain's neck as the dust whirled around them like swirling fog in shafts of sunlight. "I could have done you in then, and I will now," Rafael snarled through gritted teeth.

As if Rafael's words ignited fresh fury within the Viking, another primeval roar erupted from him. He broke Rafael's hold and slung the younger man into a decrepit hat rack. The wooden stand smashed into a storage box that spilled forth an array of figurines from Sonsee's childhood. A marble lamb thudded against Rafael's temple. His floundering to regain the advantage ceased, and he collapsed into an unconscious heap. The lamb, as white as snow, tumbled near the gun.

"Let's get out of here!" Alana insisted, tugging on her sister's arm as the Viking struggled to right himself.

Yet the double action revolver continued whispering Sonsee's name. She recalled her father's love . . . his faithfulness . . . his friendship. She envisioned the last time she saw him . . . their hugs . . . their laughter . . . their reminiscing. She endured the agony of losing him . . . the sobbing herself to sleep . . . the injustice of Taylor's setup.

At last the lamb blurred as the gun's summons became too strong to deny. Sonsee extended fingers, taut and eager, and wrapped her hand around the weapon.

"Sonsee?" Alana questioned.

Feeling as if she were spurred by a force more powerful than she, Sonsee aimed the gun at the Viking, placed her flattened hand on the floor and balanced herself as she stood.

"No, Sonsee, no!" Alana yanked on her sister's arm.

The Viking, recovering from battle, slowly swiveled to face Sonsee, his eyes glazed, his lips convulsive.

"Shoot me!" he demanded.

The adrenaline pumped through Sonsee, and her self control brinked the precipice of bedlam. The trigger, firm and ready, rested beneath her finger. A voice within urged her to give the man his wish.

"Shoot me and put me out of my misery!" Crumpling onto the floor, the murderer massaged his palms as if trying to rid them of an invisible film. "I should have never killed your father." He lifted unsteady fingers heavenward, revealing a host of bloody scabs. "Look at them! Look at them! They're covered in burning blood and I can't — I can't get it to stop," his voice grew thick as he rubbed his hands against the front of his white cotton shirt.

"Sonsee . . . Sonsee . . . Sonsee . . ." Alana's voice echoed from another land miles away, a land where sanity ruled.

As the man raked his fingers along his shirt, Sonsee gripped the gun tighter and followed his movements, as if she were hypnotized by his actions. New streaks of blood blended with dark-brown streaks already present, and Sonsee wondered how long the man had been sitting in the closet scraping his fingers along his shirt.

"Oh, please, shoot me . . . shoot me. Oh, help me! I never wanted to kill anyone . . . never . . . never. This blood. I can't get it off."

Suddenly another voice within Sonsee

combatted the dark forces — a voice of wisdom, a voice of love. *Vengeance is mine. I will repay.* Her abdomen, tight as stone, relaxed a fraction as the deranged man grabbed the sheep figurine and scrubbed fingers against marble, as if the lamb were hyssop. Choked denial sprang from Sonsee's soul, and her finger twitched away from the trigger.

"Sonsee, don't! Please don't!" Alana's voice came through louder, and Sonsee glanced toward her sister, whose horrified eyes rained buckets full of tears. "They'll only send you to prison!" she lamented.

"Prison. Oh, Brenda . . . she'll never understand. Oh, Brenda! And what about my sons? I killed a man! God, forgive me!" The weeping man, still gripping the lamb, collapsed forward, extended his hands in front of him, and pressed his face against the dust-laden floor.

Sonsee, gradually lowering the gun, gulped for air as Alana burst forth with a new round of relieved sobs. *Vengeance is mine. I will repay. I will repay. I will repay.* The words rotated around Sonsee's mind like a sacred mantra, filling her with the peace of a sovereign God. For the first time since the outbreak of this hideous storm, Sonsee understood that the natural consequences of sin punished far more than any form of human retaliation.

With an abhorrence of her own weakness, Sonsee looked down at her hands . . . hands that had spent hours clasped in prayer . . . that had lovingly held a worn Bible . . . that had stopped just short of taking a human life.

"God forgive me," she whispered, echoing the cries of the man on the floor. "Forgive me."

"Sonsee?" Taylor's voice, soft and beseeching, floated from the doorway.

"Taylor!" Alana flung herself at Taylor, and the two shared a relieved embrace as three police officers rushed upon the criminals.

Sonsee watched Taylor as he patted Alana's back yet peered at her. Silently Sonsee shook her head. A flash of unspoken communication flickered between them as Taylor's gaze wandered to the gun in her hand, and settled back on Sonsee. He pulled away from Alana, she stepped aside, and Taylor clasped Sonsee's free hand.

"Everything's okay," he whispered in a voice so assuring it almost convinced her. Without protest, Sonsee extended the gun to one of the officers and allowed Taylor to guide her into the hallway, wrap his arms around her, and cradle her head against his shoulder.

⁓

By nine o'clock that night, Sonsee collapsed onto her dilapidated sofa with Taylor following suit. Within minutes, Jac Lightfoot walked in from the kitchen and extended two sodas toward the expended pair.

"I might not have gotten to LeBlanc Manor in time to help with the major problems, but I can handle minor problems, too," she said with a smile.

"Thanks, Jac." Sonsee gripped the icy can and greedily gulped the effervescent liquid.

"You guys have no idea how good it feels to be free again," Taylor said between sips.

Jac settled onto one of the disheveled armchairs, her cropped hair swinging with every move. "I haven't personally lived through anything like you just did," she said, "but I've seen your expression plastered on a few other faces in my time. In my line of work you get that occasionally."

"I really appreciate all your help while we filed the charges at the police station," Taylor said. "I must say that I'm intrigued by Sonsee's friends — all six of ya. It's been years since I've seen some of you, and we haven't ever had the chance to get to know one another."

"Why don't you come to our sister reunion New Year's?" Jac offered. "It's going to be at Mel's this year."

"Hey, you traitor!" Sonsee quipped. "That's supposed to be a sisters-only event."

"Well, Kim Lan arranged for Josh to be at the reunion last November and nobody protested, remember?" Jac said.

"Yeah, but —" Sonsee stopped herself from blurting that Josh had proposed. After Marilyn Langham's heartbreaking first marriage, the Lord had given her a second chance at happiness with a man of honor. The sisters had all cheered when Josh surprised Marilyn at the reunion with an engagement ring and a kiss to seal the promise.

"Maybe we could change the format on this reunion and let everyone bring their guys. It will probably be easier on everyone anyway, since New Year's is a holiday."

"If this involves all Sonsee's friends, sounds like the place I need to be." Taylor's eyes danced. "I like people of the female persuasion, especially when they're the quality of ladies you are. It looks to me like the whole bunch of you are as loyal as coonhounds to one another."

"That's just what I enjoy — being compared to a coonhound," Sonsee chided, observing the poster-sized picture of all seven of the friends hanging above Jac's chair.

Taylor tossed a loose pillow at her face, and Sonsee knocked it aside. "Stop it. You're going to mess up my hair or something."

"Oh, yeah, right," Taylor laughed. "Your hair's a mess anyway." Like a bothersome brother, he rubbed the top of her head.

"Stop it!" Sonsee hit at his hand.

"How long have you two known each other, anyway?" Jac asked, snickering.

"Too long," Sonsee teased, tossing the pillow back toward Taylor.

"Well, long enough to fall in —" Taylor abruptly ended his remark, and his unsaid words echoed around the room louder than any spoken communication. *Long enough to fall in love . . . to fall in love. We've known each other long enough to fall in love. We're in love. I love you, Sonsee!*

Sonsee's toes curled inside her loafers, and she frantically groped for something to say. She glanced toward Jac, who was doing her best to look politely nonplused, although she'd undoubtedly caught the full force of Taylor's unstated message. Unlike Mel, whose curiosity often raged beyond the boundaries, Jac tried not to pry into personal matters and expected the same from others.

"Jac, you have no idea how much I appreciate your flying down," Sonsee rushed, nervously propping her feet onto the walnut coffee table. She snuggled deeper into the corner of the couch, as if she were reveling in the feel of cushions against her aching shoulders. In reality, she needed as much space between her and Taylor as possible. Sonsee maintained a firm focus on Jac while her mind raced with memories of the kiss in the stairwell earlier that day.

"I just wish I could have been more help." Jac leaned forward, placing elbows on the tops of her knees. "Honestly, it was a little anticlimactic when the taxi pulled into LeBlanc Manor and the police were already there with Rafael and Louis in handcuffs."

"Sorry," Taylor said. "Next time we'll hold off calling the police until you get there. So what if one of us gets killed in the meantime? We're replaceable." He waved his hand.

"You're a *nut!*" Jac said, shaking her head.

"Yes," Sonsee agreed. "He won that status fair and square a long time ago."

"Hey! Have some respect, will ya?" Taylor, raising his right brow, gave Sonsee a lopsided grin — a grin that teased in childhood, offered friendship in adulthood, and charmed her heart in Hawaii. Despite the flirtatious smile, Taylor's deep-blue eyes stirred with the unspoken questions that created an electric undercurrent between them. Jac's presence diminished in the glow of Taylor's appraisal, and they were alone in the room. Alone and in love. In love and groping for answers. Answers Sonsee could not provide.

The phone's shrill ring prompted Jac's relieved, "I'll get it, if that's okay."

"Uh, sure," Sonsee said, fidgeting with a throw pillow as the pint-sized private eye stood and picked up the receiver.

"Oh, hi, Mel," Jac said after the initial greeting. "Yes. She's here. Everything's fine here." She covered the mouthpiece. "It's Mel. She wants to know what's going on."

"Okay." Sonsee stood, glad to distance herself from Taylor.

"She says Hermann has been there throwing around some threats." Jac pulled the phone away from her face and didn't bother covering the mouthpiece. "He tried to get the police to search her house for Taylor, but they didn't have sufficient evidence for a warrant. She's afraid he might be back tonight. Kinkaide won't leave until Hermann is out of town, and she really needs to talk to you. The woman sounds desperate."

"I *am* desperate," Mel's claim, faint yet firm, erupted from over the phone line.

"Tell her I'll take the call upstairs. That way we can all three chat. I've got Hermann's cellphone number in my organizer. I'll call him ASAP and tell him what happened in New Orleans."

"If Alana hadn't told him where I was hiding, there wouldn't be a problem," Taylor groused.

"Don't be too hard on her." Sonsee headed for the stairway and heard Taylor following. "She's been just as mixed up as the rest of us by this tragedy."

"Wait a minute, Sonsee," Taylor said from close behind.

Sonsee, her every nerve on end with his close proximity, turned to face him.

"Yes?"

"Would you mind if I borrowed your car for the night? I think I'm going to just head for a hotel room. I'll return the car in the morning." A sad smile nibbled at the corners of his mouth. "And if you don't mind, I'll hang out here until my ranch manager comes to pick me up. I shouldn't be in your hair long."

Sonsee, feeling as if her heart were about to walk out the door with him, silently nodded and went for her purse on the kitchen table. She removed the keys from their ring and placed them in his hand. Taylor eyed the keys as if he were debating what to say.

"I was really proud of you at LeBlanc Manor," he said at last. "I haven't mentioned what happened because I didn't want to make you feel uncomfortable, but —"

"I can't believe I was that tempted to kill Louis," Sonsee said, the abhorrence of her emotions rushing upon her anew.

"I think it's called being human and loving your father. It's part of the grieving process, I'd say."

"I'm just so thankful I had the sense — or I guess that I listened to the voice of God." Sonsee rubbed her temples and recognized the beginnings of a stress headache. "I think I still have a ways to go in forgiving Rafael and Louis, but today helped me at least get through those feelings of needing to retaliate."

"Me, too," Taylor agreed. "And I think Alana is in the same boat with us."

"I'm seriously thinking about deeding LeBlanc Manor to her."

"Oh?" His brows rose. "That's mighty kind of you," Taylor admired.

"Well, she needs a home, and I think owning Father's estate might help her bring some closure to the rifts in their relationship. I don't need that big ol' house, anyway. I've got this." She waved her hands with a flourish. "Isn't it just a beauty right now?"

"Oh, well, lil' lady, I probably won't be back on the trail a week before you'll have the place all gussied up as good as new," Taylor drawled. A smile, endearing and melancholic, tilted the corners of his mouth, and Sonsee had to resist the urge to snuggle into the embrace she sensed he was longing to bestow.

"So . . ." he said at last, his gaze faltering to somewhere across the room, "should I call you or is this a 'Don't call me; I'll call you'?"

Feeling as if her heart were tearing, Sonsee blinked against her stinging eyes and forced herself to contain her emotions. "I-I'm sorry, Taylor. It's just that I need some time. Right now, I'm so confused . . .

so much has happened . . . I really think that it's going to take a few months for me to get my wits again." Sonsee placed her hand on the back of a nearby chair and hung on as if she were drowning. "Frankly, right now I feel like a borderline spiritual failure. I thought I had grown so much after mother's death — and I guess I did. My friends even started calling me the group prayer warrior. But I still have so far to go. Today . . . today was scary, to say the least. And I'm still struggling with what to do with our relationship. Right now, I want to hang on to you and never let go. There's this struggle deep within between my will and God's. And to put it bluntly, I'm miserable. I don't think I've ever loved anyone, even God, as much as I love you — and that's the whole problem."

Taylor stroked her cheek with the backs of his fingers, his gaze helplessly roaming her features.

Swallowing, Sonsee closed her eyes and gave in to the need to lean into his embrace, into the promise of what might be. Taylor inched his arms around her, and Sonsee's heart beat in rhythm with his. His lips brushed hers in a light kiss that asked nothing in return. Sonsee, enveloped in sweet agony, clung to Taylor, clung to their years of friendship, clung to the love he was extending without reserve.

Yet in the midst of all her clinging, a gateway opened before her. A gateway that ended the search for spiritual fulfillment through human relationships. A gateway that led to a point of peace where Sonsee had yet to tread. The serene meadows beckoned, inviting her to make God, not Taylor, her reason for living.

She gently disentangled herself from Taylor and took a courageous step backward. "I'll keep in touch," she mumbled.

"Well, there's a big ranch in Texas that could sure use an in-house vet." Taylor lifted her fingers to his mouth, bent like a chivalrous knight, and pressed his lips against the tops of her fingers, never once breaking eye contact. "I'll wait forever if I have to."

I'll wait forever if I have to. Taylor's promise haunted Sonsee during the following hours. While talking with Melissa and explaining the facts to Hermann, all Sonsee could envision was Taylor's willingness to wait as long as she needed. As bedtime approached, she decided that Taylor had been through enough without having to endure her indecision. But even more importantly, Sonsee had kept the Lord at arm's length long enough.

By eleven o'clock, Sonsee settled Jac in the guest room then crawled between her own clean-smelling sheets, feeling safe for the first time in a week. Although her room still needed some cleaning, Sonsee enjoyed feeling as if her life were going to be stable again. Yet her struggles were certainly not over. As she reached to click off the lamp, her hand brushed a worn Bible lying on the bedside table. Her parents had given it to her for her high school graduation present. Never had she needed the Bible's comfort as she did tonight. She picked up the holy book and cradled it to her chest. Closing her eyes, she hugged the Bible closer, as if its physical touch could somehow erase all her confusion.

There was a time when Sonsee would have called her father and discussed her troubles with him. Those days were now over. The ache of having lost both parents struck Sonsee anew and fresh tears sprang upon her. With a sniffle, she dashed at her cheeks as a prayer chorus, gentle and serene, entered her mind and posed itself on her lips. "There is a place of quiet rest, near to the heart of God," Sonsee sang. "A place where sin cannot molest, near to the heart of God. Oh, Jesus, blest redeemer, sent from the heart of God, hold us who wait before Thee, near to the heart of God."*

Softly, Sonsee crooned the second and third verses, allowing the words to transcend her mind and enter her heart. "I'll wait forever if I have to." Taylor's claim mingled with the melody, and Sonsee decided that tonight would dictate her answer to Taylor.

"I won't make you wait forever," she whispered, then turned her thoughts heavenward. "Oh, Father, give me the courage to release him to you and not look back. Take me to that place of rest," she prayed, recalling the gateway she had envisioned when clasped in Taylor's embrace. A gateway that led to the meadows of spiritual intimacy with a holy Creator. On the other side of that gate, the Lord waited, nail-scarred hands spread, calling Sonsee to a more powerful spiritual existence. At last, Sonsee extended her hands, palms up, and every human tie slipped through her fingers, each relationship paling in comparison to the love shining before her. She stepped through the gate and locked it behind her, forever securing her decision before a righteous God.

*Lyrics by Cleland B. McAfee, 1903.

Twenty-Six

New Year's Eve night, Sonsee stood on the edge of the group of close friends gathered around Melissa's dining room table. As Jac had suggested, the four sisters with families brought their husbands and, if applicable, their children for the New Year's bash. As more of the sisters got married, their semi-annual reunions were metamorphosing to meet their needs. What was once a ladies-only slumber party, shopping spree, two-days-to-play event had been altered to a down-home, New Year's get-together. With the smells of homemade Mexican food still hanging in the air and a CD spilling forth a pianist's version of "Sleigh Ride," the women huddled in the breakfast nook, taking in the special photos Kim Lan brought.

The husbands, who had spent the evening getting better acquainted, sprawled in the living room to enjoy a prerecorded football game. Only one man had yet to make an appearance — Taylor Delaney, Sonsee's husband of six weeks. Occasionally, the men's cheers erupted from Mel's elegant living room, and Sonsee strained to hear the doorbell over the male voices, her friends' chatter, and the laughter of three children in the hallway.

"Look, Sonsee!" Kim Lan, her exotic eyes sparkling, held up a photo from the Vietnam orphanage where she, Sonsee, and Melissa traveled last spring. "This is Khanh Ahn in the center, but look in the background. That's the little boy you really liked. He still doesn't have a family assigned to him."

Sonsee took the picture and examined the child in the center of the photo — Khanh Ahn. During their journey to Vietnam, Kim had fallen in love with the special-needs child speculated to have Down Syndrome. Mick, likewise, shared a love for the toddler. Now that the two were married, they had already started adoption procedures. Standing behind Khanh Ahn, a toddler with inky eyes and a head full of dark hair held a set of plastic keys and looked straight at the camera as if he were dazzled by the light. Sonsee's heart stirred with the memory of how soft his cheeks had been, how tight his arms hugged her, and how she whispered a prayer that one day she might go back to get him. However, this morning's unexpected news had altered her plans for adoption, and Sonsee hoped that some deserving couple would claim the child as their own.

"Mick and Kim are going to get Khanh Ahn in June." Marilyn beamed while tucking a strand of blonde hair behind one ear.

"Didn't you finally decide to donate your share of the treasure money to some orphanages around the world, Sonsee?" Mel asked.

"Well, yes, my portion. The police decided to use photos of the treasure for the trial since they didn't want to be responsible for such valuable evidence. As soon as they released it, I decided to go ahead and divide the treasure evenly between my sisters and brother. Then, other than the few special pieces that Taylor and I kept, the rest of the money went to Kim and Mick's mission outreach."

"We're focusing the treasure money on several orphanages. A lot of babies and kids are going to be helped," Kim Lan explained.

Sonsee imagined the faintest scent of baby powder, and she instinctively touched her abdomen.

"Well, we were all talking and figured that since you were already involved in helping orphans, you and Taylor might be open to adopting the little boy you liked," Melissa said. "You guys could travel with Kim and Mick in June. Kim Lan says there's still enough time to synchronize the trips if you start proceedings now."

"Mel!" Jac hissed, punching her friend as if she had just revealed a grand conspiracy the six friends had cooked up on Sonsee's behalf.

All six of them silently observed Sonsee: the redheaded Sammie, her eyes narrowed in the calculating angle of a newsreporter; Victoria, the gracious homemaker, curious but tactful; Melissa, avid for any and all details; Jac, interested more than she would ever admit; Marilyn, her doe-brown eyes filled with the longing of a woman who wished she were adopting; and Kim Lan, ready to urge everyone to adopt a child from her mother's homeland. Each of them continued to scrutinize Sonsee, as if they were prepared to put her on the next plane to Asia.

"Um . . ." Sonsee hedged, squirming under the steady appraisal. "When I was in Vietnam, I *did* say that I wanted to adopt one day, but that was before Taylor and I got married. We've hardly had time to talk about kids! We . . ." As her voice trailed off, her friends looked at her, then at each other. And once again, Sonsee's senses summoned a smell . . . the smell of baby lotion. She rubbed her thumb against her fingers, as if she were stroking creamy moisturizer along an angel-soft tummy.

The doorbell rang, and Sonsee jumped. Glad to escape her sisters' well-meant interrogation, she started toward the living room. "That's probably Taylor, now," she said over her shoulder. Sonsee rushed for the front door, past the sounds of the football game, leaving her sisters to continue talking about the photos.

When Sonsee opened the front door, no one was there. Curious, she crept onto the half-moon porch into winter's early night. She tugged the door behind her and scanned the manicured neighborhood, looking for signs of a young prankster. A shadowed movement from the bushes snared her attention, and she squeaked out a tiny scream as a hand snaked out to clamp over her mouth.

"Okay, I've got ya now, lil' lady," Taylor said in the voice of an outlaw as he hauled her close. "Either hand over the deed to the ranch, or I'll be forced to carry you off on my trusted steed — otherwise known as a Ford truck." While the words tumbled forth, Taylor loosened his hold and Sonsee turned to face him.

Reveling in their growing love, she slipped her arms around his neck. "Okay, cowboy, you can have the ranch and the cattle as long as you promise to hang around awhile. I've got something I'm bursting to share with the whole world, but I've waited because you should be the first to know!"

Taylor inched back to study her, the porch light illuminating his probing eyes.

"I'm pregnant," Sonsee whispered as a wintry breeze penetrated her angora sweater. Her heart fluttered. Her eyes misted over. And she searched Taylor's face for the same exuberance bubbling up within her.

He sucked in a long breath, his eyes widening. With a whoop, he picked up Sonsee and twirled her around. Amid joint laughter, Taylor deposited her back on her feet.

"Oh, no, what am I thinking!" He reached to cover her abdomen with gentle hands. "I shouldn't be picking you up like that. You need to be lying down with your feet up, eating pickles and ice cream or something!"

Fresh laughter gurgled from Sonsee. "I'm okay. Really! And pickles and ice cream are the *last* thing I want right now!"

"Sonsee!" Taylor hauled her close and spoke against her ear. "This is the best New Year's present I could ever imagine!"

"It's God's gift to both of us," Sonsee sighed. "If it's a boy, I hope he looks just like father and you."

"I was hoping for a girl who looks like you!"

"Maybe there'll be two!" Sonsee shook her head. "What am I thinking?"

They shared another round of giggles.

Pulling away, Taylor rested his forehead against hers. "Well, I've got a surprise for you, too. Now it's even more special! I had originally planned this for Christmas, but they couldn't get it finished because of the Christmas rush."

Taylor inserted his hand into his jacket pocket and pulled out a box covered in blue velvet. "I hope you like it," he said as he opened the box to reveal an emerald surrounded by a row of glistening diamonds. "I had this made from one of the brooches in the vault. It's the color of your eyes. I've always loved your eyes, Sonsee, even when we were kids."

"Oh, Taylor!" Sonsee murmured. "I love it." He removed the ring from the box and slipped it onto her finger.

"Every time you look at this ring, I want you to remember that you hold my heart — all of it. I'd be lying if I said that there aren't moments when I'm still a little scared by the intensity of our love. I feel like I'm on a roller coaster at times, but it's sure exciting!" Taylor covered Sonsee's lips with his, and she drank in the sweetness of a love that had fully blossomed from the tender blooms of youth.

The sound of an engine purring up the street accompanied the lights of an approaching vehicle. The two reluctantly eased apart as a sleek black car pulled to a halt near the curb.

"Is Melissa expecting someone else?" Taylor asked.

"Not that I know of."

Eventually an oversized bouquet of roses emerged from the vehicle, followed by a tall man with dark hair and a beard. He approached and the porch light revealed his identity. Sonsee recognized Kinkaide Franklin more from the covers of his CDs than the memory of his courting Mel. "Hi," he said, halting near the porch. "I'm a friend of Mel's —"

"Aren't you Kinkaide Franklin?" Sonsee asked.

"Yes."

"She's mentioned you."

"Oh?" He grinned, and Sonsee didn't have the heart to add that Mel's words hadn't been enthusiastic. Despite Kinkaide's ardent overtures the last few months, Melissa often told her sisters that she wished he would back off. Apparently the man didn't stop until he got what he wanted.

"Well, I would like to leave these roses for Melissa. Is she home?"

"Yes," Sonsee said. "I can go get her, if you like." With a gleeful grin, she imagined the sisterly teasing this visit would evoke.

"No . . . no, don't do that," Kinkaide insisted.

"Oh, well, okay, then —"

"Just give her the flowers and-and this." He extended a white envelope to Sonsee and offered the massive bouquet to Taylor.

"We can handle that, I think," Taylor said.

"Thanks. And tell her I said happy New Year."

"Consider it done," Taylor responded.

Kinkaide turned, walked to his car, got in, and pulled away from the curb.

"Hello," Mel said, opening the front

door. "Everything okay out here?"

"Couldn't be better," Taylor answered.

"Sonsee walked out and didn't bother to come back in," Kim Lan said, appearing in the doorway behind Mel. "We were just making sure she didn't get kidnapped."

"Oh, she didn't get kidnapped," Taylor answered, "but . . ." He hesitated and darted Sonsee a silent question. She nodded and Taylor exclaimed, "We're going to have a baby!"

A chorus of congratulations erupted as all six friends poured onto the porch, and everyone hugged the newlyweds.

"Have you guys been spying on us?" Sonsee's eyes narrowed.

"Who us?" Marilyn gasped and placed her hand over her chest.

"Well, there were just those few moments at the front window," Jac admitted. "But that was Mel's idea. We were wondering what was taking you so long."

"Then Mel saw Kinkaide leave the flowers," Kim Lan chimed in. "And she decided we'd better check on you guys — despite the fact that she isn't the least bit interested in those roses or that mysterious white envelope or Kinkaide himself, and even though she *is* playing his Christmas CD as we speak."

"Give the woman a break!" Taylor chided.

"Give *her* a break?" Sonsee held up the envelope as if she were going to open it. "Are you kidding? She's the mouth of the South. She needs to give *us* a break!"

"Let me have that," Melissa said through gritted teeth while the rest of the sisters produced a round of wolf whistles.

"You guys are tough on each other," Taylor said, shaking his head. "I had no idea."

"Yeah, but we love one another." Sonsee extended the envelope to Mel, who playfully frowned at Sonsee then followed the rest of the friends inside.

"And I love you," Sonsee whispered as Taylor placed an arm around her waist.

"I love you, too," he said. "And this is going to be the best year of our lives. In some ways, I feel like I'm starting life all over again."

"So do I," Sonsee whispered. "So do I."

Author's Note

Dear Reader:

Has there ever been a time when you felt as if the storms of life would destroy you? I have been there. When I was 15, my mother became a mental patient and I was sexually abused. When I was 24, I obtained protective custody of my mother. At the printing of this book, I am 37 and have had custody of my mother for almost 13 years. She lives in a foster home for adults, and I am the family member who bears responsibility for her. These few words have just described a 22-year horror story.

In order to survive emotionally, I spent many years hunkered down behind the emotional walls such as the ones Taylor Delaney constructed in his life. I purposefully insulated myself from others in order to protect my heart. People do this in numerous ways, humor being only one of them. Most people who knew me during my years of emotional torment never guessed that I was fighting to hide my shredded, bleeding heart, that I was terrified to let anyone too close. I've always been the outgoing sort, the fun one, the life of the party, much like Taylor. But in reality, all the time I was laughing on the outside, on the inside I was sobbing uncontrollably and afraid that I would be hurt even more deeply.

But eventually, when I started seeking God with my whole heart, His healing embraced me and the walls came crashing down, much like the walls of Jericho. I have a theory about these walls. I think that when emotional walls hold a long-term place within our lives they are reflective of walls between us and God. But He wants to tear down the walls and wrap His arms around us.

The treasure in this novel serves as a metaphor for Taylor's heart, for your heart, and for mine. Indeed, we are God's treasured possessions — treasures He wants to free from bondage. But, as with Taylor, there's a huge difference in making mental assent to Jesus Christ as the Son of God versus allowing Him to permeate every corridor of our hearts. Only when we give Christ the keys to our hearts and full permission to fill every inch of our beings can we stop cringing behind walls of fear. Jesus becomes our shelter in the storm. He gives us the courage to embrace others.

Are you free to embrace others? Or are you bound by the fears caused by past pain? Jesus Christ never held anyone at arm's length. He impacted His world by melting love over everyone He encountered. Only when we allow Him to truly heal our hearts and melt love within our souls are we free to stop holding people at arm's length and extend the unconditional love that starts with Him.

In His Service,
Debra White Smith

In four years nearly 500,000 copies of **Debra White Smith**'s nonfiction and fiction books have been sold! Her award-winning writing, entertaining humor, and solid biblical knowledge have made her a reader favorite and a much-sought-after conference speaker. Debra holds an M.A. and B.A. in English with a minor in communications. She lives with her family in East Texas.

You may contact Debra at:

P.O. Box 1482
Jacksonville, TX 75766

or visit her website:
www.debrawhitesmith.com